Annick suddenly open... heart started to pound like... She grabbed the two charts, laid them out on Jay's desk and quickly opened them side by side. She turned to the emergency room record and read each entry carefully. She was right. Justin Silva had been admitted through the emergency room on the same day Michael Flannery had his laceration sewn up . . . but neither of them had become ill until the next day.

"This can't be possible," she whispered. Annick flipped to the emergency room nurse's notes and again reviewed both charts. "My God," she said in a hush.

How could two unsuspecting children being treated at a major children's hospital ingest botulism toxin from a tray of food provided by that hospital?

PLAGUE

GARY BIRKEN, M.D.

BERKLEY BOOKS, NEW YORK

PLAGUE

A Berkley Book / published by arrangement with
the author

PRINTING HISTORY
Berkley edition / December 2002

Copyright © 2002 by Gary Birken, M.D.
Cover design by Marc Cohen.

All rights reserved.
This book, or parts thereof, may not be reproduced in any form
without permission.
For information address: The Berkley Publishing Group,
a division of Penguin Putnam Inc.,
375 Hudson Street, New York, New York 10014.

Visit our website at
www.penguinputnam.com

ISBN: 0-425-18707-1

BERKLEY®
Berkley Books are published by The Berkley Publishing Group,
a division of Penguin Putnam Inc.,
375 Hudson Street, New York, New York 10014.
BERKLEY and the "B" design
are trademarks belonging to Penguin Putnam Inc.

PRINTED IN THE UNITED STATES OF AMERICA

10 9 8 7 6 5 4 3 2 1

For
Carrie, Matt, Alison and Katie

Acknowledgments

When an author finally holds a completed manuscript in his or her hands, more frequently than not, it is the product of a group effort. My heartfelt thanks goes out to my very talented editor and friend, Joan Sanger. My agent, Loretta Barrett, has once again provided essential assistance and perceptive advice. At Berkley, I want to extend a special thanks to Natalee Rosenstein and Esther Strauss. I would also like to recognize all of my friends, family and colleagues who offered their unique input during the development of this novel.

Finally, a special acknowledgment to the "Boys of Sunday" who continue to tolerate my marginal skills, help me maintain my sanity and provide a colorful group of characters to draw upon.

a dozen times over the last three months. It was exactly sixty paces past the print shop to the kitchen. Stopping for a moment, he leaned against the wall to check his watch. Two stout ladies wearing fine hairnets and dressed in pink hospital uniforms opened the kitchen doors and pushed three large stainless-steel carts filled with thirty-six dinner trays each into the hall.

He had observed the same ritual numerous times before and knew he had between five and ten minutes before two kitchen assistants arrived to deliver the trays to the patients. He cast a final glance down the hall and then approached the carts. Trying to ease the throbbing of one of his predictable afternoon headaches, he slowly massaged the bridge of his angular nose, but the repugnant aroma of the hospital food left him nauseated and made the pain worse.

Each tray was sealed by a sheet of clear plastic wrap pulled tightly over the corners. His breathing remained calm and his pulse never quickened as he slipped the bottle from his pocket. The only sound was the dull hum of a large commercial refrigerator standing in a dimly lit alcove just beyond the entrance to the kitchen.

He peeled back the corner of the plastic of two trays, uncovering a bowl of clear chicken broth on each. Slowly unscrewing the cap, he whispered a sarcastic prayer for the children he was about to poison and then, using a thin pipette, delivered a micro-drop of the lethal botulism toxin into each of the two plastic bowls. With rock-steady hands, he slowly screwed the top of the bottle back on.

He paused for a moment to study the patient labels on each of the trays. Michael Flannery and Justin Silva were both patients in the emergency room. Two boys brought to Franklin Children's Hospital by trusting parents for very different medical problems, but destined to share a disease with catastrophic symptoms . . . a disease feared by generations of physicians because of its unpredictable and lethal nature. But to merely poison these two boys without having the pleasure of watching them suffer would fall well short of the mark. By tomorrow, when the toxin was coursing through their bloodstreams and ravaging their tissues, he would set into motion the second part of his plan—to bear witness to their agony. This was, of course, a calculated risk, but one he was nevertheless prepared to take, because to successfully poison someone and then be deprived of reveling in their suffering would be akin to acquiring a masterpiece of art and never removing it from its crate.

It took him only a few seconds to reseal the plastic covers on the trays just the way he'd found them. After a quick look around, the man returned to the stairwell and easily disappeared into the bustling activity of the hospital.

PART
One

Chapter One

After examining seven-year-old Michael Flannery for more than twenty minutes, Dr. Annick Clement, a third-year resident in pediatrics, was decidedly perplexed by his illness. She had seen Michael twenty-four hours earlier in the exact same examination bay when his mother had brought him to the emergency room with a jagged laceration on his leg. Michael had been a real trooper, remaining brave and stoic while Annick placed five stitches to close the wound. But tonight, he was hardly the same child. The bright and animated eyes she remembered so clearly were now sunken and hollow. He was cotton-mouthed and breathing rapidly, his arms and legs flailing sluggishly without purpose or tone like a Raggedy Andy doll.

"I just want to go home," he whined to his mother in a raspy voice, barely able to lift his head off the pillow. Annick studied him carefully, keenly aware of his apparent difficulty in swallowing and focusing his eyes.

Annick Clement was a talented resident with clinical skills and medical acumen far beyond that of most of her fellow residents. Completely European in appearance, she was slender, with long auburn hair and large seductive sapphire eyes. Born and raised in France, she had attended medical school and begun her pediatrics training in Paris. Her father was American, an international venture capitalist and single parent who preferred living in France. Because he had insisted upon it from the day she uttered her first word, Annick's English was perfect.

When she was approached by her program director to be the first resident to participate in a Franco-American exchange program, she jumped at the chance. The first twelve months of her residency at Franklin Children's Hospital had been an unqualified success. Not only was she thrilled with her training, but she loved living in the United States.

"What's wrong with him, Dr. Clement?" Caryn Flannery asked. "When we left yesterday you said he'd be fine."

"It's difficult to say," Annick answered. "We'll have to run some tests and—"

"But he seems to be getting worse," she interrupted with an added degree of desperation in her voice. Turning away from Michael, she stared out into the hall for a few moments before turning back around. "Is it possible that all this is related to the cut?" she asked abruptly.

Annick shook her head and then placed her stethoscope, a gift from her father the day she was accepted to medical school, in her large waist pocket. "I assume you're referring to tetanus."

"I'm not a doctor, but it crossed my mind."

Caryn Flannery approached her son with watchful eyes. Her features were plain but she was made attractive by her trim, athletic figure. A single parent and a professor in the economics department at Hofstra University, she was a bright, self-assured woman.

"I don't think the problem is tetanus," Annick explained. "He's been fully immunized and the laceration looks like it's healing normally. Is anybody else in the house sick?"

Caryn answered immediately. "Besides Michael, it's just me and my daughter, and she's fine."

"Are you sure he hasn't vomited or had a fever?" Annick asked for the third time, making every attempt not to appear exasperated.

"No, as I told you, he was fine until this morning. I had trouble getting him out of bed, and when I finally did, he barely touched his breakfast and then went straight back to his room. Maybe he's just getting the flu."

"I'm afraid it's more than just the flu," Annick said, placing Michael's clipboard on the white countertop behind her.

The examination room was one of fifteen identical units. This particular one was large and painted a bright shade of green. Several small cartoon images had been expertly painted on the far wall, making the room quite child-friendly.

Annick noticed Michael's breathing had changed and was now more rapid and shallow. Almost instinctively, she opened the curtain and signaled for a nurse. Megan Darcy had worked in the emergency room for fifteen years and could take one look at a resident's face and measure their level of urgency. She responded immediately and entered the examination bay.

"What's up?" Megan asked.

"We need to put this little guy on a monitor," Annick said, trying to maintain an even tone to avoid exciting Caryn Flannery. "I'd also like to get an IV started."

"You're starting to scare me, Dr. Clement. Do you really think all this is necessary?" Caryn asked.

"If it's not we can always remove the IV later," Annick said. "It's always better to play things on the safe side."

Megan had already attached the heart-monitor leads to Michael's chest and arms and was just finishing up calibrating the machine. A moment later, she placed a tourniquet around his forearm, selected a suitably engorged vein on the back of his hand and without a hint of hesitation deftly threaded an IV into place. As she began taping the IV, she looked up, fixing Annick with her eyes. Michael had barely reacted to the pain when she started the IV. The ominous implication was obvious to both of them.

"What's his pressure?" Annick asked.

Megan reset the blood-pressure apparatus for an immediate display. "It's eighty over forty."

"Is that okay?" Caryn asked, looking directly at Annick. "I don't like what's going on," she said in a fearful voice. "Is my son going to be okay?"

"I'm afraid he needs a spinal tap," Annick said.

"Why?" Caryn demanded.

"We may be dealing with meningitis," Annick explained to her calmly.

"Meningitis? My God, are you sure?" she asked, taking a step backward and then falling into a small wooden chair in the corner.

Approaching the stretcher, Annick placed her hands softly on Michael's neck and felt for muscle tightness. "I won't know for sure until I have the results of the spinal tap but we have to rule out the possibility." Before Caryn could respond, Annick added, "I'd like you to step outside for a few minutes. We're a little short on space in here and we have a lot of tests to do."

Under normal circumstances Annick wouldn't have asked but she was completely unsure what the next few minutes held for Michael Flannery, and if they did have to start moving fast, his mother was the last person they needed in the room.

More overwrought and scared than anything else, Caryn said, "I . . . I'm not sure I'm comfortable stepping out right now. Maybe if—"

"It would really help me if you could," Annick insisted with a cordial smile. "I'll come and get you if there are any changes. I promise."

Annick replaced her stethoscope in her ears, knowing full well she was being studied by her patient's mother. In the next moment, Caryn stood up, hoisted her purse high on her shoulder, took a few short steps and stood next to her son. She stared at him for several seconds before kissing him lightly on the forehead. "I'll be right outside, Mikey," she whispered, and then looked up at Annick, who had just finished listening to his heart and lungs. "Please do everything you can for him," she whispered, betraying the fear and anxiety she struggled not to express outwardly, and then, without another word, she walked quickly from the room.

"Stay with me," Annick instructed Megan.

"What the hell's going on? This kid looks terrible."

"I think it's something infectious," Annick answered with a guarded conviction. "I'm just not sure what yet. Let's get some blood cultures and do a spinal tap."

"I'll get the supplies."

Over the next few minutes, Michael's efforts to breathe continued to deteriorate. Annick checked the monitor. His pressure had dropped to seventy. Reaching over, she opened up the IV to its maximal rate. His skin was now cool and moist, and his face was rapidly becoming the color of chalk. Annick took a few quick steps toward the central corridor, poked her head out into the hall and yelled, "I need you back here now, Megan." Without waiting for an answer, she raced back to the bedside and gently shook Michael's shoulder. "Can you hear me, buddy?" When there was no response, she knew it was only a matter of seconds before he'd stop breathing.

An instant later, Megan came running into the bay pushing a red crash cart stocked with every medication and device necessary for a full-scale cardiopulmonary resuscitation. Two other physicians and a respiratory therapist were a few steps behind.

"I need a laryngoscope and a number-six ET tube right now," Annick instructed Megan with a controlled but heightened intensity. Megan had already ripped the seal off the cart and had the top drawer open. She reached in and pulled out the laryngoscope Annick had requested. Snapping it open, the light on the end of the instrument came on. Annick moved quickly to the top of the bed and gently tilted Michael's head back. Ignoring the fine tremor in her hands, she carefully inserted the scope into the back of his mouth. His neck muscles were flaccid. As she attempted to see his vocal cords, which mark the beginning of the windpipe, she could feel the carotid arteries in her own neck pounding.

With her free hand, she reached out and snatched the plastic breathing tube from Megan. Without moving her eyes from the back of Michael's throat, she gently slid the tube between his vocal cords and down into his windpipe.

"Let's tape this tube in place," she told the respiratory therapist, who immediately attached a bag to the end of the tube and began gently squeezing oxygen into Michael's lungs. After only a few breaths, his ashen color was replaced by a pink complexion and his blood pressure climbed to over a hundred. "I want a chest X-ray, blood cultures and routine labs," Annick announced. "And bag him for a urinalysis. Let X-ray know we may need a stat CT scan of the head." After checking the monitors again, she looked back at Megan. "Have the antibiotics been started yet?"

"They're hanging now," came the response.

"Good. And set me up to do a spinal ASAP," she added. Annick could feel the rate of her own pulse slowing now that Michael was, at least for the moment, out of the trap.

Thom Brunswick, the attending physician and Annick's immediate supervisor, finished a cursory examination of the boy. Always the consummate diplomat, Dr. Brunswick was a superb clinician with an encyclopedic fund of knowledge.

"You've done a nice job, Annick. He seems to be stable now. What do you think about getting the intensive care physician on call down here? They may want to continue his treatment and diagnostic tests upstairs in the unit."

Annick looked up and nodded. She would have preferred to stay on the case but she knew Brunswick's suggestion was appropriate. Michael belonged in an intensive care unit, not the emergency room.

"I agree," she said.

"Why don't I give them a call while you go out and speak to Mom?"

Annick glanced over at Megan, who continued to work on Michael. As she always did when she was deep in thought, Annick shoved her hands in her pockets and then returned to Michael's bedside. A few minutes later, when she was quite sure his condition was stable, Annick left the emergency room to discuss Michael's condition with the physicians on call in the ICU.

As she approached the large double doors that accessed the ICU, Annick slowed her pace to give herself time to ponder Michael's condition. In spite of her efforts, his illness remained a diagnostic enigma, leaving her filled with anxiety and the uneasy feeling that she might have missed something.

It was just after nine P.M. when Annick pushed the doors to the ICU open and reflected for a final time on the list of possible illnesses that might have stricken Caryn Flannery's only son; unfortunately, botulism never crossed her mind.

Chapter Two

The remainder of Annick's emergency room shift passed uneventfully. Fortunately, none of the patients she treated were nearly as ill as Michael Flannery. After giving her report to the ICU physicians, Annick had spoken with Michael's mother at length about her son's condition. Under the circumstances, Caryn took the news fairly well, thanked Annick for being so attentive and began a long night's vigil in the ICU waiting room.

It was midnight when Annick was finally able to return to the intensive care unit. She was dressed in baggy green surgical scrubs covered by a long white coat. Her hair was pulled straight back, and as was her custom, she wore hardly any makeup. At great expense, the entire unit had recently been renovated and transformed into a state-of-the-art facility. Annick tapped the metal plate, triggering the large wooden double doors to automatically swing open. Going directly to the nursing station, she checked the board to see which room Michael had been admitted to.

The senior infectious disease fellow, Dr. Mac Eastwick, stood at the foot of Michael's bed reviewing his chart. Just over six feet tall, he looked younger than his thirty years. Rawboned with sharp facial features, Mac was a talented physician who was clearly focused on his future. He was six months away from finishing his training and finding a job in the real world. As a result of his exemplary work ethic, political finesse and skill as a clinician, he had distinguished himself as one of the finest doctors the hospital had ever trained.

Franklin Children's had a particularly busy infectious disease service that had captured national attention for its expert handling of a lightning outbreak of bacterial meningitis during the summer of 1998. Under the direction of Dr. David Howe, a nationally recognized expert on viral illnesses, who also served as the hospital's chief of staff, the division continued to attract the most difficult diagnostic enigmas from all over New York.

Annick had been introduced to Mac when she started her residency. He had been particularly nice to her during those first few difficult months. His reputation as an excellent diagnostician preceded him, and she had frequently called upon him when faced with a challenging case.

The gossip network at Franklin was as efficient and sophisticated as most hospitals' and Annick was well aware that Mac was high on the nurses' eligible bachelor list. He handled the adulation with grace, moving from one relationship to the next without tarnishing his reputation as a physician. In spite of his active interest in women and obvious attraction to Annick, he had never hinted at crossing the line with her.

"I was hoping I'd find you here," Annick told Mac as she slid the glass door closed behind her. "I took care of this little guy in the E.R. earlier this evening."

Michael was still on the ventilator and heavily sedated. The cubicle was brightly lit with a large bank of monitors beeping rhythmically above his bed.

"What was your admitting diagnosis?" Mac asked.

She shrugged. "I'm not sure . . . something infectious was my first guess. What did the spinal tap show?"

"I didn't do one."

Annick's mouth dropped open.

"Aren't you worried that he might have meningitis?"

Mac turned, drumming the chart with his fingers. "I don't think that's his problem."

Impatient since the day she was born, Annick crossed her arms in much the same way she did when she was pouting. Mac loved her Cupid's-bow mouth and agreed with most of his male colleagues that Annick was an exceptionally attractive young lady.

"C'mon, Mac. You're playing with me. You have two more years of training than I do. I concede that you're a more experienced diagnostician. Okay?"

"I think he may have botulism," Mac said easily.

"Botulism? That's impossible." Annick jumped in without stopping to consider the possibility that Mac might be right. "I went over everything he's eaten in the last three days in detail with his mother."

Mac set the chart on a small wooden table next to the bed and began thumbing through a stack of lab reports. "When I was a fourth-year medical student in Boston we took care of several kids with botulism. One kid looked just like him," he said, pointing to Michael.

"A lot of illnesses resemble each other," Annick offered, trying hard to recall in more detail the clinical picture of botulism.

"Well, it's an easy enough diagnosis to prove. We've already gotten blood and stool samples. We'll do the EMG tomorrow."

"An EMG?"

"An electromyelogram," he clarified, enunciating each syllable individually.

She placed her hands on her hips. "I know what it stands for," she said, trying not to get up on that same high horse that her father had told her to stay off of so many times while she was growing up. "I was just wondering why you ordered one."

"The test measures nerve conduction and muscle response. It's very specific and almost always abnormal if a patient has botulism."

"What about the blood test?"

"It's also a very accurate test. If there's any botulism toxin in Michael's bloodstream, we should know in the next couple of days. I've already contacted California."

"Why California?"

"That's the only state that supplies human botulism antitoxin." Mac replaced the lab slips on the table, cast a glance in her direction and asked, "How about a soda? I was just going to grab one from the nurses' lounge."

She looked down at her watch. It was late and she was anxious to get home, but at the moment she was more interested in picking Mac's brain about Michael. "Okay, I have some time. Let's go." Mac nodded and pointed to the door.

"You should be almost done with your emergency room rotation," he said to her as he opened a small white refrigerator and reached for a Diet Coke. "What are you having?"

"Orange juice. As a matter of fact, tomorrow's my last day."

"You don't sound very disappointed," he commented, handing her the small carton of juice.

"It was okay. I got a lot of experience, but I didn't come to the United States to study emergency medicine."

"Really. Why did you then?"

She took a sip of the drink and wondered if he was teasing her a little. In spite of his courtly behavior, her instinct told her he had more than a professional interest in her. Annick was still recuperating from a nightmarish relationship with a Dutch graduate student she had met in Paris. Since arriving in the United States, she had confined her social life to a handful of fix-ups, none of which had gone anywhere.

At the moment she was more interested in discussing Michael's illness but it seemed as if Mac was more inclined to talk about her professional interests. As he was the chief fellow on the service, offending him was not the way she wanted to begin the rotation.

"Actually," she began slowly, "I'm interested in studying infectious diseases. In fact, I was hoping to get your job in two years."

He smiled and tapped her juice carton with his soda can in a mock toast. "Well, since I'll be long gone, it's all yours."

"I hope after we work together you'll be able to make that recommendation to Dr. Howe."

"Our fearless department chief? I'm not sure my opinion would count for very much."

She gazed across the table at him, wondering if he was purposely playing it coy. He was considerably more mature and polished than most of the other male residents she had worked with.

"I assume you know I'm starting on your service tomorrow," she said. "I'll be with you for the next twelve weeks." She raised the juice to her lips, watchful of his expression.

"That's right. I had almost forgotten. You're our next resident."

Annick exchanged a polite glance with him and then became lost in thought. It was absolutely incredible the way his personality and behavior resembled her father's. They both possessed that same aloof but self-assured manner, a trait she loved about her father, which he used to cleverly camouflage his true sensitive and indulgent nature.

A few moments passed before she went on. "I'm very excited about being on your service."

"I hope you'll enjoy the experience."

She stood up and straightened the stethoscope that hung around her neck.

Annick still had several questions regarding Michael but she could see the fatigue in Mac's face. She was sure he'd be polite and discuss the case further with her, but her better judgment told her to hold off. "What time are we making rounds in the morning?" she asked.

"Seven. I'll meet you right here in the ICU and we'll go over the patients together."

"Sounds good," she said. "I'll read up on botulism tonight and see you at seven."

Mac smiled and walked toward the door. "Just go home and get some sleep. There will be plenty of time for reading after your rotation starts."

She tossed her empty juice carton in the trash and wondered about Mac and her upcoming rotation on the infectious disease service. In spite of his comment to the contrary, she suspected Dr. Howe would value his opinion with respect to her qualifications for the fellowship. The fact that she found Mac attractive was not something she wanted to think about. Getting romantically involved at this particular time of her life was not part of her master plan and would only complicate things.

Before leaving the hospital, Annick stopped in the ICU waiting room. It was a small room, painted beige, with two couches and a wall-mounted television. Besides Caryn, who was sitting in the corner with a leg tucked underneath her, there was no one else present. She was sipping a cup of coffee slowly, and Annick immediately noticed the vacant look in her eyes.

"Mrs. Flannery."

"Yes," she said in a startled voice, almost spilling the coffee as she stood up.

"Michael's doing fine," Annick reported. "We've finished up most of the tests and hopefully should have a better handle on things when the results start to come back."

"Do you have any idea yet what's going on?" she asked, placing the Styrofoam cup on a small end table.

"I just discussed Michael's illness with Dr. Eastwick of the infectious diseases service. He thinks he may have botulism. We're going to send off—"

"Oh my God," Caryn murmured, covering her mouth. In the next instant, her eyes swelled with tears and the color drained from her face. "Is . . . is Michael going to die?"

"Of course not," Annick said without considering that she might be wrong. "We've already ordered the antitoxin from California, just in case."

"I'm not sure I understand," Caryn said. "You said just in case. Are you sure that's what it is?"

"Absolutely not. It's just one of several possible diagnoses we're considering."

Caryn slowly sat back on the couch. Her breathing was far too rapid. Annick noted the potential problem and reminded Caryn to try to stay calm. They spoke for another few minutes before Annick was comfortable leaving. Before she did so, she promised Caryn she'd be back around six-thirty to give an update. As she expected, Annick's suggestion to Caryn that she go home and get some sleep fell on deaf ears.

Chapter Three

The man responsible for poisoning the two children in the emergency room of Franklin Children's Hospital had lost his moral compass more years ago than even he could remember. Charming and accommodating when the situation called for it, he managed to innocuously blend in to society. Masterful at concealing his dark side, he was, in fact, a coldhearted monster who drew his inspiration from the suffering of others.

His fascination with poisons began as a child growing up in rural Virginia. He ordered every book on the subject and kept his ever-expanding library secured in a footlocker that slid neatly under his bed. By the time he reached high school he had created his own recipe book of death, complete with specific methods of administering each of the poisons and toxins that he had become so familiar with.

Naive and trusting, his doting mother and absentee father never gave it a second thought that the baby mice he kept as pets died at such an alarming rate. As he grew in years, so did his misdirected ambition. At the age of seventeen, he was arrested and stood trial for cruelty to animals. The charge stemmed from his practice of obtaining dogs from various charitable adoption programs and seeing how they'd react to toxic doses of pesticides. He cleverly defended himself at the trial, and the judge found him to be a pathetic burden on society rather than a menace and sentenced him to counseling and two hundred hours of community service, and prohibited him from owning a pet for five years.

Stopping in front of the doors to the pediatric intensive care unit to fasten the middle button of his white coat, he tapped the metal plate that triggered the automatic doors. The unit was large, brightly lit and composed of sixteen patient bays arranged in a circle with the nursing station at the center. A large chalkboard listing the patients and their room numbers hung over the chart rack.

It took him only a second to spot Michael Flannery's name and to locate his room. Each bay had a large glass door but it was very rare for the nurses ever to close them, at least during the day shift. Holding a large manila envelope with the most recent lab results in his hand, the man walked right toward Michael's room. Slowing his pace, he could see the boy clearly.

A large plastic tube extended from his mouth and connected to a ventilator that delivered exactly twenty breaths a minute of life-sustaining oxygen. With each breath, Michael's chest heaved. His eyes fixed on the boy's complexion, which was pallid and pasty. His fingertips were the color of chalk and lightly quivering. Confident in his ability to make such assessments, the man who had caused the tragedy gave him no more than twenty-four hours to live.

He approached the nursing station and placed the manila envelope atop a large stack of mail filling the in box. He understood the importance of control and was able to fend off the smirk of self-satisfaction that was attempting to cover his face. Without a particle of remorse, he turned and again walked past Michael's room before leaving the intensive care unit and heading for the parking lot.

It was just after four P.M. when he drove his Lexus SUV slowly down his quiet street, smiling and waving at his neighbors. Port Washington was a typical town on the North Shore of Long Island. Most of the homes were pre–World War II, had reasonable-size lots, slate roofs and were adorned with large oaks and high hedges. Just as he approached his house, he spotted a FedEx truck pulling into the driveway. He caught up to the driver in front of his house, where he signed for a small package. It was a cool, clear fall day, exactly the type of weather he preferred.

The house he rented was a plush four-bedroom Tudor with a high chimney and several tall leaded-glass casement windows. The owners, who had moved to Europe, had furnished it impeccably. He unlocked the front door, climbed two flights of stairs and opened a small wooden door leading to a very small attic. A half dozen cardboard boxes secured with duct tape were stacked along the side walls, leaving barely enough room for anything else. He took a few steps forward and felt around the side of the far wall until his fingertips found the edges of the false wall he had spent many hours laboring to build when he first moved in. With one quick tug, the plasterboard wall turned on a central post, allowing him access to the much larger portion of the attic. This part of the attic was of ample size with a steep-pitched ceiling and unpainted wooden walls.

Along one wall there were two three-foot-high bookcases filled with pamphlets, notebooks and texts. Directly across from the bookcases, an old rolltop desk sat under the only window. A wooden bench, covered with laboratory equipment as fine as any hospital's, sat against the far wall. Two twelve-gauge shotguns, an assault rifle and three semiautomatic handguns were in a steel case next to the window. If he was ever threatened and was able to reach this room, he'd never be taken alive.

He placed the FedEx box on the workbench and sat down. Using a penknife, he opened the package with great care and removed a small inhaler that was wrapped in plastic bubble wrap. Its appearance was identical to the type used by asthmatics for opening blocked air passages during a breathing attack. He grinned and then turned the box upside down. A business-size white envelope fell to the desktop. He gently slit the envelope open and read the short note:

THE SHIPMENT IS READY.
NO FURTHER PREPARATION IS REQUIRED.

In the past he had confined his interest to poisons that were administered by mouth. Pleased with himself that his expertise and level of sophistication were expanding, he carefully rewrapped the inhaler in the bubble plastic, set it squarely in the middle of his desk and left the attic.

He had done his homework and would be ready for Monday. He had no special compassion for children, and in fact viewed them no differently than any other obstacle that stood between him and a perfectly executed plan. His own parents never seemed to care for children and were both unaffectionate and without a great deal of patience.

By eleven he was in bed. Falling asleep quickly, he never gave a second thought to the little girl who was also sound asleep not ten miles away—a little girl he intended to infect with one of the most devastating diseases to have ever plagued mankind.

Chapter Four

Linda Vitale loved her only child, Dana, more than life itself. Energetic and bright, Dana was a shining star at Great Neck South Junior High, excelling not only in academics but also as a defensive specialist on the field hockey team.

It was seven A.M. and Dana had just finished packing her weighty book bag. If it weren't for her mother's insistence, she wouldn't have even touched the bowl of cereal she had found on the kitchen table.

"Hurry up, Dana. I'll drop you at school. I'm late for the hospital."

Dana looked around and shook her head. "Mom, I think I'm the one who's ready to go. You're still putting your makeup on."

"Nobody likes a wise guy, honey," came Linda's sarcastic but affectionate voice from the bathroom. A moment later she emerged in a quick walk and nudged her daughter out the front door, down the driveway and quickly over to their Chevy Blazer.

"Put your seat belt on, Dana."

"I'm tired," she said, buckling her belt and throwing her book bag on the floor in front of her.

"Maybe if your flight wasn't four hours late last night, we both might have gotten some more sleep." Linda lowered her window a crack and then looked over at her daughter. "We didn't get a chance to talk very much last night. How was your visit with Dad?"

Dana's eyes lit up as she became more animated. "We had a great time. His new house is right on the ocean. It's awesome. There are movie stars all over the place in Malibu." Dana leaned forward and flipped the radio on to a station her mother couldn't stand.

"Really, that sounds wonderful," Linda said, trying to hide the envy she felt for the millions her ex-husband had mysteriously acquired right after their divorce. "What else did you do?"

"We saw a couple of plays and went out to dinner a bunch."

"Just the two of you?" Linda asked as nonchalantly as she could.

Dana frowned. "C'mon, Mom, you know the rules. Dad doesn't ask me any questions about your social life."

"What social life?" she mumbled under her breath.

"What?"

"I said sorry, but I really couldn't care less," she informed her daughter while turning the volume down. "I was just trying to make conversation."

Dana laughed and then leaned over and kissed Linda on the cheek. "Sure, Mom."

The ride to school took a predictable ten minutes. They confined the remainder of their gab to innocuous topics. Linda handed her daughter five dollars for lunch, kissed her good-bye and shooed her out of the car.

Linda Vitale had been employed by the laboratory services at Franklin Children's for ten years. It was the only job she'd had since coming to New York from Pittsburgh, where she had worked at Allegheny General. Hard-working and innovative, Linda had recently been promoted to a supervisory position and had become a valued part of Franklin Children's team.

Preoccupied and in a hurry, Linda sped off without ever noticing the van that had been parked across the street. The man in the driver's seat grasped the wheel loosely with both hands and then leaned forward on his forearms. He was dressed in gray slacks, a striped tie and navy-blue blazer.

He watched carefully as Dana made her way along a chain-link fence that ended at a large parking lot. Just on the other side of the lot, an expansive area consisting of several athletic fields with neatly cropped grass wrapped around the west side of the school. Gazing in both directions, the man slowly exited the van, crossed the street and began retracing Dana's path to the school.

Picking out a bench near one of the soccer fields, Dana sat down and unzipped her book bag. She purposely picked this spot, having staked it out in the past and knowing it would remain relatively quiet until it was time to go in. There was no wind and it was still warm enough to sit outside before school began, but Dana knew that within a month or so she'd have to give up her little retreat until spring.

She figured she had about twenty minutes before the doors opened, leaving her just enough time to do some last-minute cramming for a large vocabulary test that dangled over her head like a sword of Damocles. Looking toward the street, she saw the elderly crossing guard donning his bright orange vest. She watched as the portly man motioned a group of students across the street.

She opened her notebook and turned to her most recent vocabulary list and began reviewing the words. Engrossed in trying to recall the definition of "persnickety," she didn't notice when the man from the van approached and stopped in front of her.

"Hi," he said. "My name is Mr. Turcott. I'm a substitute teacher. Do you know what time the doors open?"

Dana smiled. "I think the teachers can get in any time they want through the faculty entrance. It's around the side," she told the skinny man, pointing toward the side of the main building.

"Thanks a lot. This is the first time I've substituted here. It seems like a nice school from the outside." Before she could answer, the man began to cough. He reached into his right pocket, pulled out a small inhaler, put it in his mouth and gave it a few quick puffs as he breathed in deeply. Dana had several friends who were asthmatic and she knew exactly what the inhaler was. She had remembered the school nurse telling her that kids almost always outgrow asthma and that very few adults have the disease.

"That's better," he said, replacing the inhaler back in the same pocket. He looked around. "Maybe I'll see you in school."

"What class are you teaching?" she asked, wondering why he didn't have a briefcase with him.

He raised his shoulders and then smiled. "I don't know. They haven't told me yet. But I can handle whatever they throw at me." He chuckled for a moment and then began coughing again. This time, he reached into his left pocket, quickly pulled out an identical inhaler and began fumbling with it. He was no more than three feet from her when the inhaler slipped from his hand. As it did so, he grabbed it in midair by the pump, which sent an immediate spray into Dana's face. She quickly rubbed her eyes and nose and then looked up to see the man had backed up a few paces and was now standing several feet back.

"I'm really sorry," he said, no longer coughing. "If I drop this thing and it breaks, I'm in big trouble."

"I'm okay," she assured him with a smile. "It's only medicine."

He looked at his watch and then took another two steps back. "I better get going. You did say the faculty entrance was around to the side. Right?"

"Yeah, it's right over there."

"Thanks," he said. "You're sure you're okay?"

"I'm fine."

"Maybe I'll see you later."

Dana waved as he walked away and then buried her face back in her spiral notebook.

The man who called himself Mr. Turcott made the long walk back across the field but never went in the faculty entrance. Instead, he came around the side of the school and went directly to his Lexus SUV.

The intense rush he felt was all-consuming. Nothing compared to the triumph of selectively deciding who lives and who dies. Seated behind the wheel, he thought about how much he enjoyed working at Franklin Children's Hospital and wondered when the chain of events he had just set in motion would spell the end of Dana Vitale's tender life.

Chapter Five

Mac and Annick stood in front of Michael Flannery's bed. Although the lab still hadn't reported the results of all the tests, it was fairly clear from his symptoms, the EMG report and hospital course that the young man was surely a victim of botulism. Although he remained on a ventilator, Michael was demonstrating very subtle signs of improvement.

"I only see a small improvement from yesterday," Annick told Mac as she looked over Michael's vital signs and other key clinical information laid out on his chart. He remained heavily sedated with a feeding tube in his stomach. Three separate IVs emerged from his arms. His hands and feet were well padded to avoid the formation of bedsores. He was motionless, the only change coming when the ventilator triggered, inflating his lungs with oxygen. "He must have gotten a whopping dose of the toxin," she added.

"It's still relatively early," Mac offered with a sigh as they exchanged an optimistic glance. "This game's not over yet."

"At least the human antitoxin we received from California seems to be helping," she said. "I don't think he would have done very well without it. I spoke with his mother last night," she said, handing the chart to Mac. "She's numb. It's like talking to someone who's one step away from catatonia." She shook her head. "I still don't understand."

"Understand what?" he asked.

"We went over everything he had to eat. Nothing could have contained botulism toxin."

"Well, he got it somewhere. It's just a matter of—"

"Maybe we're wrong," Annick suggested in a more animated voice. "Maybe he doesn't have botulism and we're spending a lot of time treating the wrong disease."

Mac raised his eyebrows. "He's got it, Annick. You can take it to the bank. The EMG was positive and the blood test will be back in a few days, and I'll bet you anything it will show that young Michael over there has traces of botulism toxin in his blood."

Annick closed her eyes and took a deep breath. "I'm going to speak with Michael's mother and then to the E.R.," she said.

"Why the E.R.?"

"Don't you think it's a little unusual that we haven't seen more cases? I mean, what's the chance of only one person getting poisoned?"

"It's been reported," he answered. "But if you really want to know, you'll have to call every E.R. in the city." He paused for a moment, quickly read her expression and said, "But you've already done that . . . and . . ."

"There haven't been any other cases," she said. "It just doesn't make sense."

"I don't mean to change the topic but Dr. Howe moved rounds to this afternoon. He wants to go over every detail of Michael's case. You're presenting, so take some time to prepare."

"How come he moved rounds to this afternoon?" she inquired.

"I'm not sure but I think there's some hush-hush meeting with all the hospital bigwigs this morning. There must be something cooking, but it hasn't made its way to the hospital's gossip Internet yet. I have a feeling it's about Michael."

Annick checked her watch. "I have to get going. Call me if you need me," she said as she went through the door.

•   •   •

Caryn Flannery stood in silence next to her son. Since his hospitalization, she hadn't slept for more than a few hours a day. The puffiness below her bloodshot eyes testified to her exhaustion. It was nearly ten P.M. and the intensive care nurse caring for Michael was seated at the foot of the bed. Annick stood outside the cubicle looking at Caryn, trying to think of something encouraging to say. Before she could, Caryn sensed her presence and turned around.

"How's my son doing, Dr. Clement?"

"He's holding his own," she said, stepping forward.

"That's not exactly the same as getting better," Caryn said in a monotone.

"I think he is getting better, but more importantly, he's not getting worse."

"Should I be encouraged?" Caryn asked with a very faint hint of hope in her voice.

Annick took another couple of steps forward. "Yes, I think you should."

The two women stood shoulder to shoulder without saying anything. They had spoken at least twice a day since Michael's admission. Annick admired her strength and patience.

"Do they have any idea where Michael might have gotten the botulism in his system?"

"Not to my knowledge," Annick answered honestly. "They've checked every can in your house and they've been out to his school at least a half dozen times."

Caryn stroked her son's straight blond hair as it angled across his forehead. "There haven't been any other cases reported?" she asked.

Annick shook her head. "Not a single one. We've been in touch with every hospital on Long Island."

Annick watched as Caryn shook her head and then heaved a breath of frustration. Annick had called the state lab daily for confirmation of the diagnosis, but as of six hours earlier the results were still not available.

"If he survives," Caryn began in a whisper, "do you think there'll be much brain damage?"

Annick placed her hand on Caryn's shoulder. "In the first

place, he's going to survive. And in the second, the CT scan we did yesterday was normal, which is a very good sign."

"And his kidneys?"

"They're better."

"So he won't need to go on dialysis?" Caryn asked.

"No. It doesn't look that way."

Caryn sighed. "That's good news."

"He's a strong guy, Caryn. He's going to make it."

"I'll hold you to that," Caryn said with the first real smile Annick had seen in days. "I promised him a bowling party for his birthday next month. I'm sure he'll want you there."

"I wouldn't miss it for anything."

The room was brightly lit and a little warm. Annick watched the digital display as the ventilator delivered one synchronized breath after another. The color had improved in Michael's cheeks and he was requiring a little less oxygen, which were both good signs.

"Dr. Clement?" a woman's voice called from the nursing station.

"Yes."

"They need you in the emergency room ASAP. The charge nurse said it was urgent."

Annick turned back to Caryn. "I'll keep an eye on him tonight. Why don't you go home and get some rest?"

"I think I'll be more comfortable in the waiting room."

"I'll speak with you later," Annick said, and then left the cubicle.

As she walked quickly across the ICU, she wondered what problem awaited her in the emergency room. Totally preoccupied, she never noticed the rawboned man with a Franklin Children's Hospital white coat and identification tag milling around the nursing station pretending to be checking something on the computer. From his vantage point he had an excellent view of Michael and took every opportunity he could to study his prey. Hardly an expert on medical affairs, but more knowledgeable than most, he was fairly convinced the boy was knocking on heaven's door. From the technical standpoint, he had attained the unattainable. He had successfully poisoned a random victim, made them gravely ill but still hanging on for dear life. It was surely a masterful stroke on his part.

Having accomplished his mission and not wanting to arouse any suspicion, the man stood up, straightened his tie and walked toward the exit. He would return in twenty-four hours—assuming, that is, the boy was still alive.

Chapter Six

The emergency room was relatively quiet, which surprised Annick when she thought about all the crazy nights she had spent there over the past two months. As soon as she approached the nursing station, Maxine Sotherby flagged her down. Maxine had been an E.R. physician for twenty years. She was the only black woman in her medical school class and from the day she matriculated was determined to be number one in the class. After four years of grueling work, she had missed by only one student. Maxine, a petite and beautiful Jamaican, was an excellent teacher.

"Hi, Dr. Sotherby," Annick said.

Sotherby smiled. "Are you our I.D. expert this month?" she asked, peering through the smallest glasses Annick had ever seen.

"I'm on the infectious diseases service if that's what you mean, but that hardly qualifies me as an expert."

Sotherby glanced up at a large clock on the wall. "Well, it's after ten P.M. . . . so that makes you the expert."

Annick half smiled and then chuckled. "I'll give it my best."

Sotherby picked up a chart and handed it to her. "Have a look at the little girl in eight. She came in with a twelve-hour history of swollen lymph nodes in her neck, fever, chills and a cough."

Annick opened the chart. "It sounds like the flu . . . or maybe mono."

Dr. Sotherby removed the stethoscope from around her neck and tucked it into the enormous pocket of her white coat.

"I don't think I would have asked you down here for a case of the kiddie crud, Annick. Give me a little credit."

"Sorry."

"She's a little too sick for that. And her mono test came back negative. She's in room eight. Go have a look. Her chest X-ray's up on the view box and the rest of her lab's on the chart. I've got a floundering intern to go check on. Give me a holler before you leave. Oh . . . and Mom's a lab supervisor here."

"Will do," Annick said as she began looking through the lab slips on her way to the examination room. Apart from an elevated white count, which can occur in almost any infection, the child's lab was all normal.

As she approached Dana Vitale's bed, Annick recognized Linda immediately.

"Dr. Sotherby told me you worked here but I didn't make the connection." She stopped for a moment and glanced down at Dana. "What's going on with Dana?"

"I'm not sure," Linda began after taking a deep breath. "She started acting like she was getting the flu this morning. I kept her home from school and stayed with her hoping it was just a twenty-four-hour bug, but she's getting worse."

Annick walked over to Dana. Her color was pasty and her skin moist. Her shallow breathing made Annick immediately concerned. "What's going on, honey? Aren't you feeling so hot?"

"I feel awful," Dana answered. "Am I going to miss school again tomorrow?"

Annick smiled at the child. "Well, that's hard to say right now. Let's have a little look around and see if we can figure out what's making you so sick." Dana put on a smile, clutched the small remnant of the pink blanket she'd had since infancy and let her head fall back on the pillow. Linda stopped pacing and positioned herself at the end of the bed.

"Has she vomited?" Annick asked.

"Not really, but she hasn't eaten a thing all day."

"How high has her fever gotten?"

Linda thought for a moment. "It was a hundred and two around dinnertime."

Annick gently slid a hospital sheet above Dana's waist. "Have you had a headache today, Dana?"

"Yes." Annick quickly noted the enlarged lymph nodes in Dana's neck and gently began to palpate them. "Ouch," she yelled and pulled herself back.

"I'm sorry," Annick said with a smile to reassure the little girl and to conceal her concern from Linda that the nodes were so tender to the touch. When she reached under her arms and found a similar group of abnormal nodes, she was met with the same painful objection from Dana.

Annick completed her examination over the next thirty minutes and remained baffled. Dana's symptom complex didn't seem to fit any particular disease that she was familiar with. Linda had started pacing again.

"Has she been out of the area recently?" Annick asked.

"She just got back from California. Why? Do you think she has Lyme's disease?"

"I don't think so," Annick said, hardly surprised by Linda's question. It seemed to be the first diagnosis that all moms made when their child developed a fever. "I'd like to give Dr. Eastwick a call. He's the senior fellow on the service and I'd like to have him come in and take a look."

Linda's jaw dropped. There was a clear sense of terror visible in her eyes.

"What do you think's going on?" Linda asked. "You must have some idea."

"Actually, there are a number of possibilities, but I think we need more tests."

Dana suddenly leaned forward and began coughing violently. Her lips became cyanotic and she gasped for breath. Annick walked quickly to the head of the bed, unwrapped an oxygen mask from a plastic cover, turned on the flow and placed the mask over Dana's face.

In a few moments, the coughing stopped and Dana caught her breath. Annick slowly removed the mask and observed

Dana breathing comfortably. Just as she was about to place the mask back on the child's face, she noted two spots of bloodstained mucus on Dana's gown that she had obviously coughed up. She stole a glance at Linda, whose eyes were fixed on the blood.

"Please go call Dr. Eastwick," was all Linda could manage as she made her way to her daughter's side and took her hand gently in her own. "Everything's going to be okay, honey."

Annick stopped on her way to the main desk to ask one of the nurses to place a monitor on Dana and start an IV. Her phone call with Mac was short. He listened to her description of the patient, told Annick to quarantine the child and that he would be right in.

Mac spent forty-five minutes examining Dana and speaking to her mother. He asked her a number of questions regarding exposure to animals such as squirrels and mice—questions that hadn't crossed Annick's mind. He ordered Dana admitted to the isolation unit, started on antibiotics and the institution of droplet precautions, which essentially meant to use masks at all times in the event her illness was contagious by airborne particles. Mac was excellent with parents and Annick watched carefully as he calmed Linda down with clear assurances that appropriate treatment had been initiated and that within a few days they should have an answer.

"What's going on, Mac?" Annick asked as soon as she could get him alone outside the examination room.

"I'm not exactly sure."

"What were all those weird questions about?" she asked.

He shook his head. "Just casting my line into the water and hoping to pull something out, I guess. Listen, I'm going to give my friend in New Mexico a call."

"Now?" she asked with an incredulous look on her face.

"Relax, Annick. It's not a personal call. He's in the pediatric I.D. department at the University of New Mexico. I've known him since med school."

Mac disappeared into a small office used by the senior residents to dictate charts. He left the door open and Annick studied him as he spoke to his friend. Every few seconds he'd rub the back of his neck and extend his head all the way back. The call lasted about ten minutes.

"We have to give Dr. Howe a call," he told Annick as soon as he joined her at the nursing station.

"What's going on, Mac? Dr. Howe's not on call tonight. Johnson is. Why don't we call him?"

Mac crossed his arms in front of him. "Because Dr. Howe hauled me into his office yesterday and told me that if any bizarre cases were admitted, I needed to call him at once."

Annick swallowed hard. "What do you think she has? You're acting like she's got the black death, for God's sake."

Mac's expression was as serious as she'd ever seen it. "That's exactly what they used to call it in Europe."

Annick felt her breath catch before her lungs were filled with air. "You think this child has the plague?"

"It's a little hard to—"

"Are you saying she has *pneumonic plague*?" she repeated, grabbing his arm.

Mac looked around. "Keep your voice down, Annick. The last thing we need's a panic. We have to get this child isolated as soon as possible."

"I can't believe that—"

"I have to call Dr. Howe and then the CDC in Atlanta. And before the night's over, everyone who's been within two meters of this kid needs to be started on antibiotics . . . especially her mother."

"Mac, the only place in the United States where plague is still reported is in the west."

"I'm well aware of that," he answered evenly.

"I want to talk with you when you get off the phone."

"No problem," he said. "As soon as Dana's tucked away, I'll meet you in the gym."

Her shoulders sagged. "The gym? Do you have any idea what time it is?"

"We're doctors. A hospital's like a casino: no clocks," he explained. "I'll get into some scrubs and meet you there in about half an hour."

Annick caught herself thinking in French as Mac walked down the hall. It was a habit she'd been trying to break since coming to the United States. Arrangements were already in motion to move Dana to the isolation unit.

Annick grabbed a gown and mask from the isolation cart, put them on quickly, and with as much composure as she could muster went straight back to Dana's side.

Chapter Seven

Mac Eastwick's daily workout was inviolate. Irrespective of what time he finished seeing patients, he'd stop at the hospital's fitness center before heading home. The hospital had spared no expense in equipping the center with the most modern exercise equipment.

Positioning himself squarely on his back and straddling the bench, Mac placed his feet firmly on the floor. He preferred free weights but found the machines a very acceptable substitute. Mac filled his lungs with air and then slowly let about half of it out. He then easily pressed two hundred pounds and slowly returned the weights to their resting position.

"What do you know about bioterrorism?" Annick asked the moment she walked through the door.

"I don't know," he answered with a grunt. "What do you know about it?"

"I spent three months with Dr. Jacques Aaron at the Pasteur Institute in Paris. Most people interested in bioweapons and tactics consider him an authority on the subject."

"I'm familiar with his work."

She had never been in the hospital workout facility before. It was actually bigger than she expected, and nothing at her medical faculty in Paris could compare with its modern decor.

The carpet was navy blue and clearly of an expensive commercial grade and the entire back wall was mirrored.

"So, how much do you know about bioweapons and terrorist tactics?" she asked again.

Mac swung his feet over, sat up and then picked up a towel and wiped his face. "Well, I've never been to the Pasteur Institute, if that's what you mean." He stopped for a moment and dabbed some perspiration from his face. "Now that I think about it, I've never even been out of the United States."

"C'mon, Mac. I'm serious." She crossed her arms as an impatient schoolteacher might, waiting for an answer.

"I've attended a few conferences on the subject. It's become a very hot topic in infectious diseases over the last several years." Mac tossed the towel down beside him and then pointed at Annick. "This sudden interest in biological weapons wouldn't have anything to do with Michael Flannery and Dana Vitale, would it?"

Annick had no intention of being coy about the matter and was not put off in the slightest by his question.

"Of course it does," she admitted. "Botulism and now pneumonic plague? You'd have to be an intellectual wasteland to totally dismiss the possibility."

"A what?" he asked with a chuckle.

She fixed her sights on him and grinned, a little relieved he hadn't taken her comment too personally. "You have to admit, it's at the least an intriguing thought."

Mac stood up and walked over to one of the two pull-down machines, adjusted his grip and then took a deep breath. He was actually more receptive to the conversation than she anticipated. When he had done about twenty bench presses, his cheeks had become bright red and the veins on his forehead, engorged with blood, popped out. He suddenly stopped, letting the heavy weights crash back to their resting place.

"Cholera, glanders, smallpox, Venezuelan equine encephalitis, Ebola. The list goes on and on. There's nothing new about biological weapons," he said with a grunt as he leaned against the machine. "The only thing that's changed over the years is our increasing fund of knowledge and sophistication in using deadly bacteria, viruses and toxins as weapons." He paused for a few seconds to catch his breath, then started another set of exercises, which he completed in about two minutes. "Warring countries have been using bacterial weapons since the sixth century B.C. I'll give you a perfect example. In the mid thirteen hundreds the Tartar army rounded up corpses of plague victims and hurled them over the city walls of their enemies. Within days, an epidemic broke out, forcing the city defenders to surrender."

"That's an interesting bit of history. But my question is how can you so easily dismiss the possibility that Dana and Michael are the victims of biological weapons?"

Mac shook his head. "Biologic agents directed against children. What would be the political gain?"

"I don't know," she answered in a hesitant tone. "Maybe it has nothing to do with politics. Maybe it's just some lunatic with the knowledge to do it."

Mac finished his third set of exercises, walked over to the wall and slid down in exhaustion. He dropped his chin to his chest, which heaved with each breath.

"What's the bottom line here, Annick?"

"Simple, and this is the main thing I took away from my rotation at the Pasteur Institute. The average person out there hasn't the foggiest notion how simple and inexpensive it is to make biological weapons of mass destruction."

Mac nodded. "That's probably true."

"Then why is my concern about our two patients upstairs so off-the-wall?" she demanded.

Mac stopped for a moment to take his pulse. "I never said it was off-the-wall. But there's a lot of room between off-the-wall and improbable." He stood up, walked over and sat down next to her. "Look, there's no question that plague and botulism are two of the most commonly cited biologic agents that have been researched as potential weapons. There are—"

"That's exactly what I'm saying. If you just—"

Mac raised his hand. "Slow down and listen to me for a second. We know Dana was in California right before she became ill. Right?"

"Of course, Mac. What's your point?"

"I guess I feel that the likelihood of us eventually figuring out where Michael legitimately got botulism is a lot greater than discovering that one or both of these kids were the victims of bioterrorism."

"I see your point, but will you at least concede that it's possible that there may be more here that meets the eye?"

"Purely as an academic exercise or for an idea that makes for good theater, anything's possible."

Annick's expression was earnest, her lips pressed tightly together. "I don't know. It's just awfully difficult to dismiss consecutive cases of botulism and plague without even considering the possibility." She looked past him for the moment and toward the mirrored wall. The tone of her voice changed. "I just have a bad feeling about all this."

"You don't strike me as the type with an overactive imagination. Especially when it comes to being a physician. That's not what medicine's about."

"I understand that and I'm not—"

"I think you'll feel better when we eventually figure out where Michael got botulism from."

"And Dana?" she asked.

"If it turns out that she has plague, we have a perfectly rational explanation in view of her recent trip to California, where they report plague cases every year."

Annick's expression didn't change. She was well aware of Mac's expert skills as a diagnostician, and it was true that medicine was a science based on logic and proven fact. But that didn't mean there wasn't a place for a well-founded hunch.

"It may be all a coincidence," Annick admitted. "But I'm going to, as you say in America, keep my eyes and ears open."

Mac laughed out loud. "As we say in America? Your English is better than mine for God's sake."

Mac stood up and extended his hand to her. When she took it, he covered it with his other and helped her up. The romantic tingle she felt was more than pleasant and not totally unexpected. She watched Mac finish his workout on the treadmill. Mac was physically attractive, self-assured and mature, and the chemistry was there for her. It was more than instinct that told her he found her attractive as well. Romance in the workplace was not a practice she endorsed but the more she looked at Mac, the more she was drawn to him.

Chapter Eight

In view of the strange cases recently admitted to the I.D. service, Mac was hardly surprised when Dr. Howe called a meeting to include him and the other residents on the service. As the most senior, Mac was charged with making sure that the junior resident, Annick, and the intern, Kevin Killpatrick, were there. Kevin was a mediocre intern who Mac found unreliable, defensive and difficult to work with. Mac was a little surprised when Dr. Howe mentioned that John Scanlon, the CEO of the hospital, would be attending.

Mac, Annick and Kevin sat around an oval conference table in a library that adjoined Dr. Howe's office. It was small, tasteful in its decor and in no way as lavish as the hospital's main administrative conference room. Per Dr. Howe's very specific request, Mac and Kevin were dressed in a shirt and tie. Having been seated for about ten minutes, Mac had dodged most of Annick's and Kevin's questions, urging them to be patient and wait and see what Dr. Howe had to say.

At exactly ten minutes after nine he walked into the room. Dressed in a dark pin-striped suit with the knot of his solid blue tie just slightly off center, he took a seat and set his leather attache on the table. His fingers were firmly interlocked in what Annick interpreted as a solemn gesture.

"I'm sure it's no mystery to any of you that we have a problem. I've already spoken to the other attending faculty members on the service and they've been brought up to speed." Annick studied Howe's eyes as he gazed up at a large wall-mounted clock with bold black roman numerals. His hands had a slight tremor, something she had not noticed in the past. "Mr. Scanlon should be joining us momentarily to give you the hospital's position." Dr. Howe reached forward, picked up a silver pitcher of ice water and poured himself half a glass.

"Is there anything we should do differently from a patient care standpoint?" Mac asked.

Dr. Howe put his glass down. "Absolutely not. It's business as usual. We're dealing with children afflicted by infectious diseases. We're the experts and quality of care remains our principal objective. Michael Flannery and Dana Vitale have unusual problems. We're all aware of that. But they are eminently treatable and regardless of how they were contracted, it's our job to treat and hopefully cure them."

"Are we still meeting today at two to discuss their care?" Annick asked.

"Of course," he answered directly. "As I said, it's business as usual."

Before Dr. Howe could continue, John Scanlon entered the room and immediately took the seat next to Howe. Annick had only met Scanlon twice since beginning at Franklin. He was fifth-generation English, but with his blond hair and piercing blue eyes he looked more like a Nordic seaman. An effective administrator, he ran the hospital strictly by the book. Scanlon had always made it his business to meet and stay acquainted with all the residents. In return, they regarded him as a fair and cooperative administrator who, for the most part, had their best educational interests at heart.

He smiled courteously, stood up for a moment and slipped off his black sport coat and hung it on the back of his chair.

"I just want to begin by telling all of you that the administration is well aware of the sensitive nature of the present situation and wants to commend you all on your professional behavior." Scanlon reached into the top pocket of his blue pin-striped shirt and pulled out a three-by-five card. "There are a few things I want to go over with you. With Dana Vitale's tests coming back positive for plague, we have notified the plague office of the CDC out in Fort Collins, Colorado. In view of her recent travel history to California they don't see the need to send a survey team in."

"Supposing she hadn't been to California?" Kevin asked.

Scanlon looked to Dr. Howe for an answer. He was quick to accommodate. "If an individual contracts plague and cannot demonstrate a travel history that would have taken him or her into an area where the disease still exists, well . . . the plague center's level of concern would approach urgent and they would unquestionably send a full team in to investigate."

Scanlon nodded and then took a deep breath. "Now, this brings us to the very touchy issue of the media. We've already had several calls about the two unusual cases we are presently treating. Fortunately we have rational explanations for them and at least for the time being the media seems to be content with that." Scanlon paused to study each of the residents' faces. "I think it would be better if all of you avoided any comments or discussions with the media."

"I can't imagine that will be a problem," Howe jumped in to assure him.

Annick watched as Scanlon continued to study the group, taking a moment to lock eyes with each of them. It was almost as if he were trying to read their minds.

"What about state medical authorities or the CDC?" Annick asked.

Howe furrowed his brow at the question, which she assumed was a tacit disapproval of her inquiry.

"I'm not sure I understand your question, Annick," Scanlon said. Annick immediately regretted broaching the topic. The double foot tap she received from Mac under the table had come too late.

"I was more concerned about what to do if we were approached by an official agency," Annick tried to explain.

"We don't want to play into the hands of the media," Scanlon explained. "We're a prestigious institution with a national reputation. We don't want to behave in a way that will make us look like a three-ring circus."

"I know we're all in agreement about that," Dr. Howe said, forcing a smile to his face.

Scanlon went on. "On the other hand, if anyone in an official capacity should request information from you, those requests should be referred to either Dr. Howe or the hospital administration." Scanlon fiddled with the three-by-five card for a moment and then cleared his throat. "Without beating around the bush, it's the position of the hospital that BT is not an issue in this case."

"BT? What the hell's BT?" Kevin Killpatrick asked Annick in a whisper.

Without turning her head she answered, "Bioterrorism."

"Oh shit," he murmured.

"You better believe it," Mac said, overhearing the short exchange between the two of them.

Scanlon answered a few more questions from the residents before thanking them for coming. Dr. Howe restated the importance of professional behavior and the need to avoid the media. Mac, Annick and Kevin were then dismissed. As they were leaving, they were encouraged to keep the lines of communication with the administration wide open.

"What do you think?" Scanlon asked Howe.

"They're a good group," he answered. "Mac Eastwick's one of the best fellows we've ever trained. I'm afraid he's a little infatuated with Annick Clement at the moment," he added with a smile, "but that shouldn't be a problem."

"And the intern?"

"Kevin's a bit argumentative but he'll be off the service soon. He's not exactly a team player but I'm certain we can persuade him to cooperate. After he finishes his residency he wants to do a fellowship in cardiology here. Unfortunately, his performance has been only average and probably not of the caliber we'd accept into the program. Is there something else?" Howe asked.

"No, nothing at all," Scanlon said and then patted Howe on the shoulder. "It's just that these things can have a funny way of getting out of hand."

"You're dealing with professionals, John. They may be young and still in training, but they know the rules."

"I'm sure you're right," Scanlon said. "Actually, I'm much more comfortable after our meeting." He looked up at the clock. "I have to get going. I'll see you tomorrow at the executive committee meeting."

Scanlon scooped up a manila file he had brought with him and left the room immediately. Howe waited for a minute, deep in thought about John Scanlon's uncharacteristic nervousness. The two men had a close working relationship and a casual personal one. Howe whipped his memory trying to remember a time when Scanlon had been so uneasy regarding a hospital problem. After a few more minutes of thought, Howe could only conclude that there must be much more going on than administration felt comfortable divulging to him.

Chapter Nine

"Have you eaten yet?" Mac asked Annick in his signature blasé tone, pretending to scan the last patient's chart before returning it to the rack. It was just past nine P.M. and they had finally finished making evening rounds.

Annick peered in disbelief over the top of her half-moon reading glasses. "Mac, we've been working straight through since three this afternoon. I've been practically attached to your hip. When did you think I took a break for dinner?"

"I guess I forgot," he said with a shrug. "I was thinking about going over to Friday's. Why don't you join me?" Annick stared at him for a few seconds and then continued to ponder the proposition until Mac finally smiled and said, "The United States Supreme Court doesn't take this long, Annick."

"Just give me a second," she said, still studying his face. "Okay, let's go."

"On one condition," Mac insisted.

"On one condition? A second ago all you wanted was a yes or no."

"That was then and this is now," he said.

"Okay, what's the condition?"

"No shop talk."

She resumed the same intense stare. "What do you mean? I have a million questions about—"

"I'm sorry," he insisted. "No medical talk. My terms are nonnegotiable and unconditional."

"So my choice is either to accept your terms or eat alone."

"Your grasp of the obvious is extraordinary," he said.

"Okay. I accept. Friday's it is."

They were just about to leave when Kevin approached, appearing somewhat bedraggled. His white coat looked like it hadn't been cleaned in a week and he needed a shave. "Are we finally done?" he asked.

"I think so," Mac said. "Did you remember to draw the blood cultures on that kid in the E.R.?"

Kevin crossed his arms, scoffing at the question. "Of course, but I don't know why I'm working so hard."

"What do you mean?" Annick asked.

Kevin sat down and put his feet up on the opposite chair. "C'mon, Annick. It's no secret they don't think very much of me around here. I busted my chops for these guys when I first started but they still gave me shitty to mediocre evaluations."

"What about the cardiology fellowship?" Mac asked. "If you really want it, you have to try and change their minds."

Kevin laughed. "Fat chance of that. The people running this residency, especially Dr. Howe, are the biggest bunch of pompous buffoons I've ever met. Pseudo-intellectuals . . . that's all they are."

Mac and Annick exchanged a dubious glance, tried for another minute or two to cheer Kevin up and then told him they'd see him in the morning.

The restaurant was less than a mile from the hospital. The typical weeknight college crowd filled the bar area to capacity. Fortunately, there were several empty tables in the main restaurant. A young hostess with curly blond hair who reminded Annick of Shirley Temple showed them to a booth. They hadn't been seated for more than a minute or so when a young man with a red striped shirt appeared, handed them each a menu and quickly took their drink order.

"What's it like living in France?" Mac asked. The music coming from the bar was a little loud so he leaned forward over the table to better hear her.

"Living in Paris is different," she answered.

He motioned her forward with his fingers as if he were coaxing a nervous child into the doctor's office and whispered, "How's it different?"

"Well, it's a beautiful city but the bureaucracy is enough to drive you mad. Parisians are generally misunderstood by foreign visitors, it rains too much and the pastries are out of this world." She stopped for a moment and waited as the server placed their drinks down.

"Are you going to go back?" he asked.

"I haven't decided yet," she said, taking the first sip of her light beer. "Where are you from? You never talk about it."

"I grew up in Gainesville, Florida. My parents were both professors of psychology at UF. As soon as I finished high school, I was out of there."

"Where did you go?" she asked.

"Boston University undergrad and then Tufts medical. As soon as I finished in Boston I moved to Long Island and started my residency at Franklin."

"Brothers and sisters?"

"Nope. I was an only child. I think my parents purposely arranged it that way because that was their field of research. I remember growing up participating in all of these research studies with other 'kids without sibs,' as they called us."

Annick listened as Mac continued to talk about his childhood. It was already obvious he was a different person outside the hospital. Easy-going, gentle and insightful, he had learned much from his parents and continued to have a close relationship with them. The server returned, flipped out his pad and jotted down their order for a couple of hamburgers.

"You had an interesting childhood," she said.

"Part of it, anyway. What about you?" he asked as he took the first sip of his cold beer. "What was your life like before coming to New York?"

"My father's very wealthy. We have a beautiful apartment in Paris." She smiled. "I was what my parents' friends called a trust-fund baby. I've always thought it was a funny label."

"You once said your dad was American."

"He is, and he spent a lot of time in New York while he was

growing up because my grandparents were both in the U.S. diplomatic service."

"What about your mom?"

Annick looked down. "She was born in the States but was raised in France. She never gave up her American citizenship but never had any desire to live anywhere else except Paris."

"Has she been over to the States since you started your residency?"

Annick looked past Mac for a moment to gather herself. "She was killed in an automobile accident when I was five."

"I'm . . . I'm sorry. I didn't know. Does your father still live in Paris?"

"Absolutely," she said with her animated expression returning. "He would never leave Paris." Annick was distracted for a moment when a rowdy table of kids watching a football game in the bar howled in unison. "All of his memories are there."

"What does he do?" Mac asked.

"What doesn't he do would be a better question," she answered, preening as she did. "The best way I can put it is that he's an incredibly successful entrepreneur, corporate mogul and venture capitalist all rolled into one. I gave up a long time ago trying to figure out which company he was acquiring, breaking up or restructuring."

"Sounds exciting."

"We had so much fun when I was a kid. I remember the corporate jet was always fueled and ready to go. When I was out of school, he took me everywhere with him on business, and always made sure to spend as much time with me as he was able. We have a great house in Nice. The south of France is one of the most beautiful places in the world. I still love going there with him."

"He sounds great."

"He's the most wonderful, attentive father anyone could hope for. I consider myself very lucky. I still talk to him three or four times a week."

"I'm a little envious," Mac confessed.

"Of what?"

"I'd love to see Europe, especially Paris." Mac lifted his hands off the table as the server approached with their hamburgers and set them down. He took the last swallow of his beer and ordered another. Annick reached into her purse and pulled out a small leather planner that had been given to her by an overzealous pharmaceutical salesman.

"My father will be here in about ten days. I'm going back to Paris with him. There's always plenty of room on the jet if you're interested."

It wasn't often that Mac found himself speechless. Her offer seemed so spontaneous and casual that he wasn't quite sure if she were serious. He prayed his dumbfounded expression wasn't too obvious.

"The jet? Uh . . . that's very kind of you to offer," he finally managed. "But I'm not sure we're at a stage to consider—"

She lowered the frosted mug from her mouth just before she was about to take a sip. Five seconds sooner she would have choked from laughing at his silly comment. "For goodness sakes, Mac. Are all you American guys the same?" She shook her head, picked up her burger and took the first bite. "I'm not offering you a half interest in my bed, just a ride back and forth to Paris."

The subtle blush that came to his face was clearly out of character. But even a guy with Mac's confidence with the opposite sex could be caught off guard. He knew he was blushing. His only hope was his face would return to its normal color quickly.

"God. You are serious," he said.

"Yeah."

He leaned forward, scratching the back of his head. "I . . . I don't know. Would you be able to show me some of the city?" he asked in an uncertain tone.

"Of course. What did you think? I was going to dump you at the airport? I'll even take you on a tour of the Pasteur Institute. We think it's every bit as advanced as the CDC in Atlanta."

"Are you kidding? I'd love to see the Pasteur Institute," he said, as if it were a fait accompli that he was going. Mac rubbed his head again, still shell-shocked from her offer. "I don't think I could afford to—"

"You can stay at our apartment. My dad's chef is great. You won't even have to pay for food."

His eyes widened with each of Annick's offers. Nobody was more aware of the fact than Mac that he was a man of limited means. Opportunities like this for financial bottom feeders didn't come along every day. Still unable to make eye contact, and totally lost in thought about the prospect of seeing Paris, he really wasn't thinking about what he was doing and found himself looking straight ahead at her chest.

"I'm up here, Mac," she said, pointing to her face.

Mac's eyes snapped upward as if they were propelled by a rubber band. "I wasn't really—"

"Sure, Mac. Listen, our apartment's four thousand square feet with six bedrooms. I think we can find you a suitable room."

Mac picked up his hamburger for the second time, but before taking a bite set it down again. "I really don't know what to say."

"You don't have to say anything. If you want to go, well . . . you're invited. If not, it's no big deal."

Still unable to get a handle on the situation, Mac sat there with a dazed expression. For the next hour they talked about everything under the sun except anything even remotely related to the hospital, especially Michael Flannery or Dana Vitale.

After finishing their hamburgers, they each ordered another draft, which they sipped slowly as they talked. After about two hours, Annick yawned, made no attempt to conceal her exhaustion and told Mac she was ready to head home. They had taken separate cars, which obviated the need for any touchy conversations regarding who would be dropping who where and for how long they'd be staying.

When Mac went to pay the bill, Annick insisted they split it. He resisted but she eventually prevailed. As she stepped into the aisle, she caught the silhouette of a man in a beige topcoat leaving the bar and heading for the front door. She stopped and squinted, trying to improve her focus, but an instant later the man was out the front door, leaving her with a bewildered expression.

"What's up?" Mac asked.

"Uh . . . nothing. I thought I might have seen somebody I know."

"It's a popular restaurant. It wouldn't surprise me."

"Well, this guy's from Paris," she said.

"Some people say that every one of us has an exact double somewhere. Maybe you just saw your friend's."

"It's not possible," she said, more to herself than Mac.

When they stepped outside of the restaurant, Annick took a quick look around. It was getting late, and apart from one couple holding hands outside of their car, Annick didn't see anyone else. Mac walked her to her car.

"I enjoyed having dinner with you," he said, keeping the distance between them more than respectable.

She looked over at him, giggled and then opened the door to her red BMW convertible. "You're an interesting guy, Mac. I'll see you at seven for rounds."

As he drove home, Mac thought about Annick and had to concede he had just shared dinner with someone who was very arresting and unique with none of the usual first-date uneasiness and tension. Mac tried again to think of other women he had known who were like Annick but was unable to come up with a single one. He had been in and out of several relationships over the last few years but he had never been romantically consumed by anyone and wasn't quite sure he was comfortable with the vulnerability that accompanied the feeling.

He remembered a conversation a few months ago with Russ Leahy, a fellow resident and good friend, in which he admitted that he couldn't even recall most of the women's names that he had dated. Russ responded by informing him that it was probably because most of them weren't worth remembering. An innocuous comment, perhaps, but one that had left a lasting impression on Mac.

Mac was within minutes of his house when the hospital paged to let him know that Dana Vitale wasn't doing well and they needed him right away. He asked them to page Annick as soon as possible and ask her to meet him at the hospital.

Shifting gears as quickly as his vintage 280-Z would tolerate, all thoughts of romance left his mind, being replaced by the frustration of what to do for a child who was dying of the same disease that wiped out two-thirds of Europe over seven hundred years ago.

Chapter Ten

By the time Mac reached the ICU, Dana Vitale was within hours of dying. In spite of the highest concentration of oxygen the ventilator could deliver, her lips were pale blue and her failing lungs continued to fill with frothy, blood-tinged fluid. The mottling of her skin had progressed dramatically since Mac had seen her just a few hours ago. Two nurses and a respiratory therapist had positioned themselves around Dana's bed responding to the alarming monitors that all seemed to be going off at the same time.

"What's her blood pressure?" Mac asked Bev Connors, the charge nurse.

"Ninety over fifty," she answered.

"Is she still making urine?"

"Not for the past three hours," Bev responded.

"What about a recent chest X-ray?"

Bev pointed to a view box about ten feet away. "We got that one about thirty minutes ago."

Mac walked over, crossed his arms and studied the film. There was no question that it was worse than the one he had seen earlier. The patchy areas of infection were rapidly spreading in spite of the intensive antibiotic therapy.

When Mac returned to the bedside, Fred Smith, the fellow

in intensive care medicine, was waiting for him at the bed-side. Fred had been completely bald since his early twenties, at times persnickety but never far away when help was needed.

"This isn't looking good," he told Mac.

"She looks septic," Mac said, reaching for her chart.

"There's no question about it. The blood cultures we sent off yesterday are growing out plague." Mac had become an expert on the treatment of plague since diagnosing Dana's illness and was well aware that once the bacteria was in a patient's lungs and growing in their bloodstream, there was little hope of recovery.

"Have you spoken to her mom?" Mac asked.

"Less than an hour ago. Her family doc prescribed some Valium for her but so far she's refused to take any. Linda's a pretty bright woman. I'm afraid she knows exactly what's going on." Fred rubbed the top of his head. "Do you want to make any changes in the antibiotics?"

Mac shook his head. "I don't think that will help. She's already on the best drugs we have for plague."

"I thought I should ask," Fred answered.

Mac spent another twenty minutes poring over Dana's chart in the hopes he could find something to try that Fred hadn't thought of. He was just about to give up when he felt the presence of someone behind him. He turned to see Annick standing at the end of the bed staring at Dana.

"What's going on?" she asked.

"She's not doing well," he said and then handed her the chart. He could tell from the tone of her voice that she was shaken by Dana's spiraling course. Mac and Annick had discussed the emotional shock of a child's death one day after rounds. While no physician who has dedicated their career to caring for children ever really accepts the fact that death is sometimes inevitable, most develop some mental strategy for dealing with it. From their conversation, Mac was far from convinced that Annick had accomplished that as yet.

She pulled up a small wooden chair and sat down beside Mac. She studied the chart for a few seconds and then looked at one of the monitors.

"Maybe it's not as bad as it looks," she finally said as she placed the chart down on a small table.

"Yes, it is, Annick. She's dying."

"We haven't tried changing the pressors yet. Did you speak to Fred about—"

"He's aware of the situation. If her pressure drops any lower he'll try something different." Mac watched as the look of desperation on Annick's face only intensified. She looked away from Dana and then gazed across the ICU with a hollow stare.

"How about trying—"

"Why don't we get out of here?" he suggested. "Fred's as good as they come. He promised to call me if anything changes."

"Okay," she said, barely above a hush. "I have to make a stop before we leave. I'll meet you in the lobby."

"I'll be there."

Walking slowly toward the residents' sleep room, Annick barely noticed when a man in a short white coat approached the nursing station. He picked up one of the charts off the counter, flipped it open and began reading it. Becoming more aware, Annick slowed her pace as she got closer and noticed it was Michael's chart the man was studying. His face was familiar but she couldn't quite place what department he was from. She knew he wasn't a doctor because all of the residents wore white coats that were cut to mid-thigh.

He looked up and smiled at Annick, who had now stopped a few feet away.

"Hi, Dr. Clement. You're here kind of late tonight."

"It's been a long day, Mr. . . ."

"Simione, Grady Simione. We've met a couple of times. I work in the lab. I guess I'm kind of a forgettable character. I was just putting some culture slips on the charts."

"I thought the secretaries usually do that."

He nodded in agreement. "I always bring the slips down. If they're busy, I just go ahead and put them on. Hey, we all gotta pitch in and work together."

"That's very thoughtful of you. We can use some more of that spirit around here," she said.

"To tell you the truth, it gets kind of boring in the lab sometimes. I like to get down here from time to time and watch some of the action. I was pre-med myself in college. My grades were pretty high but I didn't have the money to go to med school."

Annick smiled politely. She had heard the same story dozens of times before from wannabe physicians who, for one reason or another, had bailed out on their dream. With the amount of loan and scholarship money out there, lack of funds never prevented anyone from going to med school. She wished Grady luck, left the ICU and went straight to the residents' on-call room to pick up some things before heading to the lobby to meet Mac.

Just as they were about to leave the hospital, Mac and Annick decided to double back to the ICU waiting room to offer some comfort to Linda Vitale. There were no other parents present. The TV was on but the volume had been turned all the way down. The overhead lights were fully dimmed, leaving the room illuminated by whatever light streamed in from the hallway. Linda sat in a small club chair with her legs fully flexed at the knees and tucked up alongside her. She was dressed in jeans and a white sweatshirt.

Annick took the initiative by trying to offer Linda a small amount of hope, but at the same time being honest about the gravity of the situation. The conversation was short; Linda listened calmly and asked no questions. She acted like someone who knew what was going to happen and had resigned herself to the fact that it was only a function of time. In spite of her apparent efforts to avoid it, Mac noticed Annick's eyes swell with tears toward the end of the conversation.

They walked in silence to the parking lot. Mac tried once or twice to say something, but it was an exercise in futility. Just before they reached their cars, Mac offered to drive Annick home and pick her up in the morning.

"That's okay," she said.

"Are you sure?"

She looked at Mac for a moment and then said, "Actually, I wouldn't mind having some company for a little while. Why don't you follow me home?"

Driving home alone, Annick used the time to compose herself. They met in the parking lot and once in her apartment, they talked until one A.M. They started to watch a romantic old movie on TV but Mac fell asleep on the couch, and instead of disturbing him, Annick threw a blanket across his shoulders and then went to bed.

Chapter Eleven

The intense vibration of his pager awakened Mac instantly. He sat up, illuminated the beeper and read the display. A small amount of light from Annick's kitchen was all he needed to find the phone.

The call was from Fred. Dana Vitale had died a few minutes earlier. Linda was with her priest and ex-husband, and according to Fred, holding up okay under the circumstances. Mac thanked him for all he had done, hung up the phone and considered waking Annick to tell her.

"I heard you on the phone. What happened?" came a voice from the doorway of the bedroom. Annick was dressed in pajama bottoms and a dark sweatshirt.

"That was Fred," he said with a sigh. "Dana Vitale just died. I'm sorry, Annick."

Annick withdrew into her room and slowly closed the door. Mac rubbed his neck for a few moments and then located his keys. He stared across the room for several minutes thinking about Dana Vitale. Just as he was about to leave, Annick emerged from her room.

"Where are you going?" he asked.

"To the hospital," she said in a cracked voice as she crossed the room.

"Do you really think that's—"

Annick stopped and turned. "Yes, I do. I'll see you at seven for rounds." Almost before she finished the thought, she was out the door. Mac interlocked his fingers behind his neck, gazing out into the hallway. After a few minutes, he left her apartment and headed home. It was not that the thought hadn't crossed his mind to join her at the hospital, but after some reflection, he realized she needed to be alone.

Chapter Twelve

When Mac reached the hospital at a few minutes before seven, he found Annick sitting in the residents' lounge. It was a relatively large room located on the top floor of the hospital. The walls had been painted a hideous shade of green, but fortunately dozens of photographs of past residents covered up much of the paint. There were two black leather couches, a large-screen TV and a very old refrigerator.

Annick sat off to one corner of the larger couch with her knees pulled in.

"There's something funny going on around here," she said without looking up.

For the moment, Mac didn't say anything. He picked up a mug and filled it from a hot coffeemaker provided by the hospital that was kept brewing twenty-four hours a day.

"Annick, I know you're upset about Dana but you have to maintain your objectivity." He took a few steps toward her. "A child makes a trip to California and almost immediately upon her return she becomes ill with symptoms consistent with plague. A sample of her blood is submitted to the lab, which confirms our diagnosis. Now, granted, it's a very unusual case, but there are others just like it reported every year. I know what you're thinking but this is not about bioterrorism."

"What makes you so sure?"

Mac moved across the room and sat down on the couch next to her. "I've been thinking about something for a few days," he said, setting his cup down on a glass corner table that sat between the two couches. "Maybe Michael was exposed to botulism from the cut you sewed up. The disease has been reported to gain entrance to the body via open wounds. Not every case comes from ingesting contaminated food."

Annick frowned. "Cut it out, Mac. You're talking to me like I don't own a textbook of infectious diseases. And since I know you could probably write one, don't insult my intelligence."

Mac put on a surprised expression. "What are you talking about?"

"His wound? You think he got botulism from his wound?"

"It's possible."

"Really? What's the incubation period for botulism acquired through a contaminated wound?"

"I'm not sure I remember," he lied.

"Well then I'll remind you. It takes about five days for someone whose wound has been infected with botulism to develop the symptoms. As you will recall, I saw Michael in the emergency room less than twenty-four hours after he cut himself."

Mac listened carefully until Annick had finished her explanation. "There could have been another cut on his body that he acquired earlier. A much smaller one that wouldn't have required stitches."

She tilted her head to the side. Her pessimism filled the room. "I see," she said sarcastically, as if it were a revelation. "A small cut or bruise, perhaps."

"Maybe."

She waved him off in a dismissive manner. "For goodness sakes, Mac. I'm not an idiot. I watched you examine every square inch of his body in the ICU."

"I'm human. I could have missed it," he offered.

"Did you see the report from the state health lab on his botulism test?" she asked, barely hearing his last comment.

"Dr. Howe's secretary told me the state lab found evidence of botulism toxin in his blood but the actual report wouldn't reach his chart until either late today or tomorrow."

Annick stood up and walked over to a small trash receptacle in the corner, flipped up the top and tossed what was left of a corn muffin in the bin.

"I was in Dr. Howe's office when the lab called. He was at a meeting so I spoke with them."

Mac leaned back, extended his legs and crossed his ankles. "And?"

"They couldn't identify the exact serotype of the toxin."

Mac looked perplexed. "They only test for six different types of botulism toxin," he said, as if he were again talking to a med student. "A through F. The blood tests available should be able to identify which one affected Michael."

"No kidding," she said. "But unfortunately they couldn't. It's not any of the usual six. They're going to send the sample down to Atlanta to see if the CDC might be able to make heads or tails of it."

"That's a bit strange," Mac admitted. Off guard for the moment, his mind started to ponder the unusual information Annick had just given him.

"My feelings exactly," she said, and then noticed the distant look in his eyes. "What are you thinking?"

His expression suddenly snapped back from an absorbed one to a half smile. "Nothing. It's nothing."

"I'd like to hear anyway."

"Well, the only serotypes that differ from the standard botulism toxins that I'm aware of are . . . are those derived in experimental protocols."

"What kind of experimental protocols?" she asked.

"Ever since World War Two, various governments have been conducting research on botulism as a potential weapon. It was rumored that the Russians had developed a super-strain and had actually perfected a delivery system."

"When was that?"

"In the mid-seventies." Mac plucked a pen out of his top pocket and began rolling it between his fingers in a trick that he had learned in high school. "Let's wait and see what the CDC has to say. Maybe the state lab had a technical problem running the test. It's not exactly like they do it every day."

"I called the CDC," Annick said.

Mac rolled his eyes. "I should have guessed that. What did they say?"

"They've seen this problem before and can usually sort it out in a day or two. I have a name up there to call. And I still think it's strange that we only saw one case of botulism."

"We already discussed that," Mac reminded her. "Anyway, I'm not sure how important all this is. Michael's really turned the corner the last twenty-four hours. He's breathing on his own, he's alert and answering questions. He'll probably be home within a week."

"Maybe he was just lucky," Annick said.

"I'm only interested in results," Mac stated. "I'm not going to dwell on how much luck or good fortune contributed to a successful outcome. The kid had botulism, we recognized it, treated it and now he's almost ready to go home. That's all I'm interested in."

"So if he had died, you would be more interested in analyzing the circumstances surrounding the case?"

"Maybe . . . I don't know," was his answer.

"So then how do you explain Dana Vitale's death . . . or maybe that's not something we should discuss."

"I was hoping you wouldn't want to talk about it."

She reached over and put her hand on the back of his wrist and then leaned to within a few inches of his face. "Try to keep an open mind, Mac. I'm really worried about what's going on around here."

"Uh . . . of course. I am too. We're both scientists. Right?" he asked, trying to appear undistracted by the presence of her hand on his.

"I spoke to my father after our dinner last night. Have you made a decision about Paris?"

"Actually, I'll have to speak with Dr. Howe to make sure he has no problem with me taking a few days off." It looked to Annick as if he were trying to remain as aloof as possible. "I'd love to go," he went on, "but I'm just not sure the time is right."

"It's just a city, Mac. I'm not sure timing is so important."

"It really sounds great. Can I let you know tomorrow?"

"The plane will be here a week from Monday. We're leaving from Newark Airport at around eight P.M. Don't beat yourself up too much over this thing. If you want to go, just give me a call. I'll give you the specifics of which area we leave from. You can even park your car there. My father and I would be delighted to have you. Okay?"

"Okay," he said, still feeling a little strange about the prospect of hobnobbing with the jet set.

"It's about time to start rounds," she reminded him.

As they left the lounge, Annick thought about the night before when she first invited Mac to visit Paris. It wasn't that her offer was insincere, but she certainly wouldn't have been crestfallen if he'd refused. So why was it that now she was truly hoping that he'd decide to make the trip?

Chapter Thirteen

The traffic on the northbound Cross Island Parkway was unusually light for a Friday morning. The man responsible for infecting Dana Vitale with plague peered from behind his aviator-style sunglasses at the large signs indicating the way to LaGuardia Airport. It was a gray, overcast day with the temperature barely reaching forty degrees. The usually clear view of Little Neck Bay was obscured by the low-hanging fog. In spite of the weather, a number of die-hard boaters, mostly high school kids, tried to squeeze every last day out of the season.

The scene reminded him of his own youth. Especially his high school years, when he spent many a lazy fall afternoon adrift in his family's weather-beaten rowboat in a small lake just north of town. Following graduation, he enlisted in the army. His three years in the artillery were basically uneventful. His request to join the Special Forces unit was never given serious consideration by his superiors. Embittered by the rejection and with a growing disdain for authority figures, he spent every bit of his free time studying and perfecting his hand-to-hand combat techniques.

Soon after his general discharge, he enrolled in a small college in Virginia, and after four and a half years successfully earned a degree. A series of dead-end jobs then ensued, which prompted him to consider moving. When he became aware of an opportunity at Franklin Children's Hospital, he finalized his plans and moved to Long Island. Pathologically jealous of those who had attained financial success, he became obsessed with the accumulation of wealth and material possessions. With this trait subtly woven into the fabric of an already diseased personality, he was becoming more dangerous with each passing day.

Reaching the airport at ten minutes before nine, he found his way to the short-term-parking lot and then proceeded directly to the US Airways terminal. He was dressed in a belted beige topcoat with large front pockets and a black mock turtleneck sweater. For as long as he could remember, airports had always intrigued him; he viewed them as the perfect choice for a clever mass-poisoning scheme disguised as the insane act of some fanatic or terrorist.

Entering the terminal through the tall glass doors, he strode past the long check-in counter until reaching a large gift shop. He checked his watch, took a quick glance around and guessed he was a few minutes early.

A frazzled woman with an expensive-looking carry-on bag chased frantically after her obstreperous twins. The boys, who couldn't have been more than three, were dressed in matching denim overalls and laughing uncontrollably. He shook his head in disgust. If people were foolish enough to have children, then why in hell couldn't they keep them under control? The only thing he felt more lucky about than being an only child was never having had any children himself. He never quite understood the unnecessary and maudlin value society placed on kids.

The entire scene reminded him of his teenage days as a baby-sitter. How he loved to kiss up to the parents and then, as soon as they were gone, torture their kids with promises he had no intention of keeping. One chubby six-year-old, whom he particularly disliked because he whined so, was his first victim. After making him beg for his dessert until nearly nine P.M., he finally gave him the vanilla ice cream he was crying for, but only after adding just enough ipecac to give him terrible stomach cramps and vomiting.

He turned for a moment to study the group of eclectic travelers lined up at the cashier. He was just about to take a closer look when he was suddenly bumped from behind.

"I'm so sorry," the woman with the twins said. "Ever since they started walking, it's been impossible."

He stared over at the boys, who were now a few feet away trying to pull each other's hats off. "It's a difficult age. My kid brother was a handful. In fact, I'm just on my way to visit him. He's a Ph.D. in biochemistry. He teaches at the University of Michigan in Ann Arbor."

The woman smiled, wished him luck and took off after her unmanageable sons. He watched with a self-satisfied smirk as she struggled to corral them. Distracted only for a few moments by the woman, he quickly turned his attention to the magazine rack, where he was supposed to meet a middle-aged man in a black sport coat carrying a tan leather attache. A large clock over the rack indicated the man was five minutes late. Tardiness was not something he appreciated.

Spending the next fifteen minutes impatiently browsing through the magazines, his blood started to boil. He checked out each businessman in a dark sport coat who approached. Finally, he reached into his pocket for his cell phone. A broad smile came to his face when he felt the package, which was no bigger than an aspirin bottle. Slowly pulling it from his pocket, he held it in his left hand while rubbing his chin with his right, trying to figure out which one of the men at the magazine rack had made the drop. He had assumed the individual would identify himself, but the more he thought about it, he realized that none of the men got within two feet of him. Taking a second look at the package and knowing exactly what was in it, he carefully returned it to his pocket.

None of it made any sense until he suddenly thought about the woman with the twins who had bumped into him. He quickly looked around the store and then gazed down the concourse, but as he expected, she was long gone. He grinned as if he had just discovered that he'd been the victim of a very clever practical joke. Under normal circumstances, the thought of being duped by a woman, even if only for a few minutes, would have been intolerable. But she had delivered what he wanted and for today he would make an exception, marveling at her skill and giving her all the credit in the world for a well-executed plan. When you stopped for a moment and considered the type of business his supplier was in, you really couldn't blame him for taking every precaution possible to ensure a smooth transfer of a very delicate and illegal item. He covered a short burst of laughter with his hand. At an appropriate time, he would have to personally commend the individual who came up with the idea of the frenzied woman traveler with twins.

With no other business to conduct, the man left the terminal and went directly to the parking garage. When he was safely behind the wheel of his Lexus he turned on the CD player to a Bach symphony, removed the tiny vial from his pocket and held it up to eye level. A highly purified strain of cholera, he could almost feel its devastating potency as he rolled its smooth glass surface lightly between his fingers, fantasizing the entire time about the incredible amount of human suffering he held in his hand. A disease that could destroy a person in twenty-four hours, it remained a grave health problem that continued to cause worldwide suffering and death.

His plan to poison children using cholera was an extraordinary one. Born from genius, he was unconditionally committed to its success. After all, what better place to poison children than in a hospital where the powers that be were a bunch of jellyfish and dolts. As long as there was any plausible reason for the strange illnesses, the hospital would accept it with open arms, shun the media and avoid getting the authorities involved at all costs. They didn't realize it, but he knew it was just a matter of time until their house of toothpicks would tumble around them.

He descended the spiral parking ramp, paid the cashier and was soon on his way back to eastern Long Island. The melodious symphony was soothing. Things were going so well, he couldn't help but wonder if there was anybody at all at Franklin Children's who even approached his intellectual level.

Chapter Fourteen

It was seven P.M. when Annick finally finished her checkout rounds. She loathed night call, which all of the residents were required to endure every fourth night, but it was a necessary evil and she resigned herself to grin and bear it. By the time she reached the cafeteria, the dinner rush was over and most of the tables were vacant. She went through the line quickly, selecting a small Caesar salad and a hot turkey sandwich. After paying for the meal she decided to sit at a more secluded table against the far wall. She had just set her tray down and pulled out her latest pediatrics journal when a thin, middle-aged woman with short chestnut hair approached.

"Are you Dr. Clement?" she asked.

Annick looked up, closed the journal and tried to smile. "Yes, I'm Dr. Clement." In general, Annick was very generous with her time, but it had been a long day and she was hoping for a quiet half hour to eat her dinner.

"May I?" the woman inquired, pointing to the chair.

Annick looked across the table. "I'm sorry. Have we met?"

"No, my name is Joelle Parsons. My nephew was recently a patient here."

Annick assumed the mystified look on her face must have given the woman a clue that she preferred not to be disturbed.

"I'm sorry. I . . . I don't understand. Is there something I can—"

"He died a few days ago, Dr. Clement. One of the nurses taking care of him suggested I talk to you."

Annick sensed the heightened urgency in the woman's voice, capitulated and invited her to have a seat. She was wearing light wool slacks with a matching cardigan.

"I'm not sure I understand, Ms. Parsons."

"Please call me Joelle."

"You have a French name," Annick said.

"As do you. I bet most people can't even detect your accent."

Annick reached for her Diet Coke and took a sip. "Are you from France?" she asked.

"Actually, I'm French Canadian. I grew up in Montreal. My husband owns a business in Garden City. I've lived in the United States for the past twenty years."

"I see. You mentioned your nephew was . . . a patient—"

"Justin was a diabetic. He was twelve years old. He developed an infection in his leg last week and came to the emergency room. He was seen by the chief resident, who decided to admit him." Annick studied the woman carefully as she spoke. Joelle lost eye contact and looked down at Annick's tray. "My cousin's a surgery resident in Toronto. I know you guys don't get much time to eat, so please go ahead."

Annick grinned. "What happened after your nephew was admitted?"

Joelle pulled her chair in closer and then placed her large leather purse on the table. She waited for a few moments as an elderly woman from the custodial service cleaned some trays off a nearby table.

"He did fine for the first night, but by the next evening he was really getting sick."

Annick was hungry, and in view of what Joelle had just suggested, she picked up her fork and took the first bite of her salad.

"Listen, I'm not really sure there's anything I can do to—"

Joelle took a deep breath. "I beg you. Just hear me out, Doctor."

Annick looked directly across the table and nodded. "I'm sorry, go on."

"Justin developed the strangest symptoms. He became very weak. It was almost as if it started from his neck and shoulders and worked its way down. After a while he started having trouble breathing and they transferred him to the ICU."

"Do you remember if he had a fever?" Annick asked, still a little intrigued by Joelle's accent, which seemed more French to her than French Canadian.

Joelle closed her eyes and let her head fall back a little as she thought. "I'm not a hundred percent sure but I'm almost positive he didn't."

"Then what happened?" Annick asked.

"He just kept getting sicker and sicker. He couldn't even move after a while. They had to intubate him and put him on a ventilator. He died that night."

Annick tilted her head to one side. "You said intubate. That's an unusual word for a layperson to use. Most people would have said put a breathing tube in or something." The two women exchanged a cautious glance. Joelle opened her purse and pulled out a small packet of tissues.

"I'm a nurse, but I haven't practiced in the last five years."

"Why did you decide to speak with me?"

"There have been a few stories on TV and in the paper about the boy with botulism. One of the local channels even did a health spot on the subject. They talked about the symptoms and even a little bit about the use of botulism toxin in plastic surgery to remove wrinkles and for certain muscular diseases."

"You mean Boaxin," Annick said.

"Yes. After Justin died, I became suspicious that he might have had botulism."

"Excuse me. But where were his parents in all this?"

"His dad died several years ago and his mother is in denial and won't listen to a word I have to say. We don't have the greatest relationship. Anyway, she's not interested in pursuing any of this."

"I see," Annick said. "And the reason you're coming to me?"

"I spoke to Justin's attending endocrinologist, Dr. Neuman, who politely told me my theory was preposterous and since I wasn't Justin's mother, he really couldn't discuss the matter with me." Joelle placed her hands palm-down on the table next to her purse and looked across the room for a few seconds before continuing. "I tried to speak with one of the administrators about it, but that was a waste of time. She told me the cause of death was overwhelming infection and there was no reason to look elsewhere for a cause."

Annick renewed her question. "What they're saying is quite possible. I'm still not sure why you've come to me."

"I spoke with Ali Roth, the charge nurse in the ICU. She told me you were taking care of the little boy with botulism and that you might be able to help. She was very nice."

"I'm not sure that was a good suggestion."

There was desperation in Joelle's eyes. "Nobody else has been willing to help us," she said in a voice just above a whisper.

"What else did Ali say?"

"She mentioned you had expressed an interest in seeing if there were any other cases of botulism. That's why I've come to see you this evening."

Annick found herself at a loss for words. She moved her tray a couple of inches over. Her dinner looked cold. The woman sitting across from her was both well informed and quite sincere, hardly some eccentric oddball. Of more interest was the account of her nephew's strange death. Intriguing to say the least, especially when one considered how closely his symptoms resembled those seen in botulism.

"Where are you going with all this, Joelle?"

"If my nephew died of botulism, I want to know about it. To my knowledge, nobody even considered the diagnosis. I'm pretty sure that no blood tests were sent. I think that's why I've hit a roadblock trying to find out what happened." Joelle picked up the packet of tissues and cracked the plastic seal. "I was hoping you'd help me."

Annick didn't have to think very long before answering. "You have to listen to me. This is way out of the normal chain of command. I could get into all kinds of trouble. It could end my career."

Joelle plucked one of the tissues from the packet, reached

for her purse and stood up. "I understand, Dr. Clement. Thank you for speaking with me."

Annick stood up as well. "I'm sorry. I wish there were something I could do . . . uh, what was your nephew's last name?"

"Silva," she said.

Annick felt the muscles in her neck tighten as she watched Joelle slowly walk away. There was something disturbing—something she just couldn't put her finger on. Perhaps it was a missing fact . . . or something that didn't make sense, or maybe even a question she should have asked.

"Joelle," she called across the cafeteria. The woman turned around immediately. Annick walked down the aisle until she reached her. "You said Justin came in through the emergency room."

"That's right. Is that important?"

"Not really. I was just thinking . . . uh, it's not important. Would you mind leaving me your phone number?"

"Of course not. I'll write it down for you." Opening her purse, she located a small notebook, wrote the number down, tore off the piece of paper and handed it to Annick. "You can call me anytime."

Annick watched as Joelle walked away. She felt comfortable with her split-second decision not to share her anxiety about Joelle's nephew's death. More than uncomfortable about the account of Justin Silva's hospitalization she had just listened to, Annick decided immediately to review the boy's chart in detail the first opportunity she got.

Chapter Fifteen

"You looked pretty slick doing that spinal tap, Doctor," Mac told Annick as she finished putting a Band-Aid on the three-month-old who she suspected of having meningitis. The nurse who had assisted Annick wrapped the baby in his blanket, picked up the chart and left the treatment room.

"Thank God you were here. I never could have gotten through it without you peering over my shoulder like a mother hen," she complained. "I've only done about fifty of these since graduating medical school."

Mac explained, "It's part of my responsibility as the senior fellow on the service to supervise the residents when they do procedures. A responsibility," he added with all the seriousness he could gather, "that I take extremely seriously."

"Really," she said. "Then why don't you spend some time monitoring Kevin? He's only an intern."

"Kevin's a little too weird for me. I wish I knew what made that guy tick." Mac couldn't help but notice her fragrance. It was more subtle than most and unquestionably the most provocative he had ever experienced. "That perfume you're wearing," he mentioned.

"What about it?"

"I wouldn't wear it around the asthmatics. It could bring on an attack."

Annick shook her head. She was getting used to his corny sense of humor, and it took every drop of self-restraint she could muster not to laugh at his hackneyed jokes for fear of encouraging him.

"There's something seriously wrong with you, Mac," she said. "I guess it would be pretty easy for a female terrorist to knock off a horny, unsuspecting male resident by putting anthrax spores in her perfume."

Mac frowned. "Are we back to bioterrorism again?"

"I never left it. Did you ever hear of the Biological Weapons Convention?"

"Refresh my memory," he groaned. "If you must."

"In the early seventies, the Russians, the Americans and about a hundred and forty other nations signed a document in which they agreed not to develop, manufacture or stockpile biological agents that could be used offensively in a war."

"Yes, now that you mention it, I recall reading about it."

"But the Russians didn't abide by the terms and their research and development continued to boom for the next twenty years until they had developed the busiest and most sophisticated bioweapons program in the world."

Mac rotated his head from side to side trying to loosen the annoying spasms in his neck.

"But as I recall," he noted, "by the early 1990s they finally did suspend experimentation and destroy all of their weapons."

"But the technology and personnel are still out there. Hundreds of starving, unemployed Russian scientists with nowhere to peddle their deadly expertise. Some of them very eager to assist smaller nations and terrorist groups in developing and deploying bioweapons."

Before Mac could respond, Annick's pager went off. She checked the digital display, which indicated she had a call holding from outside the hospital.

"I hope that's an urgent call," he said and then watched as she walked past him on her way to the phone. Unable to resist the temptation, and using as much finesse as possible, he stole a look at her butt as she walked by.

"I saw that," she let him know, and then picked up the phone and waited a few seconds for the operator to connect the call. "Hi, Daddy," she said with a broad smile on her face. "I didn't think you were going to call until tonight. Where are you? Prague? What are you doing there?"

Mac glanced over, noticed a small stool and took a seat. "I'll just grab a seat over here," he said, more to himself than Annick.

"Are we still on for Paris?" When she heard that his plans were unchanged and that they would be flying back to Paris together, she smiled even more broadly. She had been working very hard since starting her rotation on the I.D. service and she couldn't wait for the few days off to spend some time with her father in Paris. "I don't know," she answered after her father asked if Mac was coming. "He's right here. I'll ask him." Annick turned to Mac. "My dad wants to know if you're coming." She extended her arm and pointed to the phone. "He wants to talk to you."

Mac almost fell off of his stool. "I can't talk to him," he whispered.

"Why the hell not?" she asked with her hand over the mouthpiece. "C'mon, he's calling from his plane," Annick urged, waving the phone at him.

"I can't. I've never spoken to anyone with that kind of money."

"This is no time for any of your stupid jokes," she insisted and again waved the phone at him.

"Okay," he said, getting off the stool and taking the phone from her. "How are you, Mr. Clement? I can't thank you enough for your kind invitation." Mac nodded his head as he listened to Annick's father for at least a minute. Each time Annick tried to get her ear close enough to the receiver to hear what her father was saying, Mac swiveled away. "Well, if you're sure it wouldn't be an imposition, I'd love to come along." Mac listened for a few more seconds before saying good-bye and handing the phone back to Annick.

"No, he's not always that nervous," she assured her father. "After a couple of drinks on the plane, he'll loosen up." She talked for another few minutes before promising to call him later.

"Well, that's that," he said in a self-satisfied tone. "I guess I'm now officially one of the rich and famous."

"I asked my dad how he convinced you to come along. Do you know what he told me?" Mac just shook his head. His complexion was still red. "He said he made you an offer you couldn't refuse. But he wouldn't tell me what it was."

Mac grabbed his white coat from a hook on the door. "I guess that will just have to be something between me and Luc."

"Luc is it now?" she asked.

"That's what he told me to call him," was Mac's final comment as he left Annick giggling in the examination room.

Jay read the list of patients and then said, "If you want to have a look at the charts, they're sitting on my desk."

"Great," she said. "That will save me a trip to Medical Records."

Annick thanked him and tucked the three-by-five card in the top pocket of her white coat. Her suspicions about Justin Silva, the patient who died unexpectedly on the endocrine service, had been gnawing away at her since her conversation with Joelle, and in spite of what Mac said, she still found it perplexing that there were no other cases of botulism reported. Perhaps it was a long shot, but she was going to find out if there were other ones that had slipped past the attention of the medical staff.

It was four-thirty and the secretarial staff was just leaving when Annick entered the Pathology Department. After years of steady pressure from the physicians, the offices had been recently refurbished and were now among the nicest in the hospital. Annick easily found Jay's desk and, just as he had promised, the charts were stacked on top in alphabetical order.

The first patient was a four-year-old girl who had end-stage leukemia; she had arrived at the hospital in a coma and died shortly thereafter. Annick took a brief look at the chart but dismissed it as a possibility. The next three patients were long-term hospitalized patients who expired in the intensive care unit. None of them had anything to eat for several days prior to their demise, making Annick conclude they could not have been the victims of botulism.

Reaching for Justin Silva's chart, she opened it and turned immediately to the physician's progress notes, hoping to get a clear understanding of the child's illness, with special attention to the flow of the events. Surprisingly, Joelle's account was remarkably accurate. Hardly an expert in diabetes but having a reasonable fund of knowledge about the disease, Annick was baffled by Justin's symptoms.

"There's nothing about this that even looks like diabetes," she mumbled. But what was remarkable was how consistent Justin's symptoms were with botulism. But, in view of his admitting diagnosis, it wasn't hard for Annick to understand why

nobody entertained the possibility that he might have ingested botulism toxin.

Annick rocked back in Jay's soft manager's chair and closed her eyes. She wasn't a forensic pathologist and had no idea what political and medical hoops she'd have to jump through to test Justin for botulism. It would be impossible to predict his mother's response to such a request. The more Annick thought about the prospect, the less sense it made. Justin did not come to the hospital with symptoms suggestive of botulism . . . but Michael Flannery did. As she was drumming the chart with her fingers, it suddenly dawned on her. The first night she had seen Michael was the night she sutured his laceration, and he didn't have any signs of botulism then.

Annick suddenly opened her eyes and sat forward. Her heart started to pound like a jackhammer. She grabbed the two charts, laid them out on Jay's desk and quickly opened them up side by side. She turned to the emergency room record and read each entry carefully. She was right. Justin Silva had been admitted through the emergency room on October fifth, the same day Michael Flannery had his laceration sewn up. Both of them were seen between three and seven P.M. Michael was subsequently discharged but returned the next day and was admitted. Both of the boys were seen in the E.R. on October fifth, but neither of them became ill until the next day.

"This can't be possible," she whispered. "Where is it?" Annick flipped to the emergency room nurse's notes and again reviewed both charts. Both Michael and Justin had been served a clear liquid tray in the emergency room. "My God," she said in a hush.

Annick closed the charts and thought about the night she had first seen Michael Flannery. He had been in the department a long time before she had finally gotten to examine his laceration. Her recollection was strikingly clear. When she had first entered the cubicle to sew up his wound, he was just starting on a hospital dinner tray. He wanted to finish it but his mother, impatient from the long wait, slid it away from him with the promise she'd take him to McDonald's as soon as his cut was sewn up. But on the other hand, and for all she knew, Justin could have consumed his entire tray.

Annick tossed the charts back on top of the pile, stood up

and paced nervously in front of Jay's desk. She kept shaking her head in total disbelief. Stopping for a moment, she gazed at a porcelain statue of an elderly physician seated over a microscope that sat on the corner of the desk.

If she were correct about her theory, where would she find the answer to the obvious question?

How could two unsuspecting children being treated at a major children's hospital ingest botulism toxin from a tray of food provided by that hospital?

Chapter Seventeen

Bobbie Whitman had been the director of the microbiology lab at Franklin Children's for the past ten years. Unflappable by nature, she was a consummate diplomat who never put on airs. A former academic scholar at Brown University, Bobbie was an attractive, goal-oriented woman.

It was just after two P.M. when Annick arrived at her office. Pausing in the doorway, she saw Bobbie with her head buried in a large manual. Her office was barely large enough to fit a small desk, a metal bookcase and a workstation for her computer. Sharing a genuine mutual respect, the two women had become well acquainted since Annick began her residency and had never had a bad word between them.

"Bobbie?" she called at the same time she rapped on the large glass window.

Dressed in a dark green business suit under a full-length white lab coat, Bobbie looked up, smiled and waved Annick into her office. She may have been five feet tall, but if Annick had to guess she'd put her closer to four feet ten and weighing less than a hundred pounds. Her strawberry-blond hair, oval blue eyes and lightly freckled nose combined nicely to provide her with an air of affability.

"How's everything?" she asked in a distinctive resonant voice as she pointed to a chair in front of her desk.

"Great. How have you been?" Annick asked.

"Never better. So, what can I do for you? You sounded a little stressed on the phone this morning."

"Uh . . . I guess I was." Annick turned and looked out into the hall. "Should I close the door?"

Bobbie wrinkled her brow in a look of mild bewilderment and then leaned to one side to take a quick peek out into the hall. "I haven't closed it in ten years, but if you feel the need, go ahead."

Annick nodded slowly. "How many cases of botulism have you seen over the years?"

"Besides Michael Flannery, we had a small outbreak about seven years ago from contaminated vegetable soup out on eastern Long Island. A couple of the victims were kids."

"How did they do?" Annick asked.

"As I recall, fine. They both recovered in a couple of days."

"Have you ever had to do studies on an expired patient to see if botulism was the cause of death?"

Bobbie thought for a moment. "No. But I can't imagine it would be a problem. The toxin shows up fairly easily in both blood and stool. It wouldn't be a major task to draw blood before the patient was transferred to the funeral home."

Annick raised her index finger and tapped her forehead a couple of times. "Actually, I was thinking more in terms of the situation when . . . well, if the patient had already been transferred to the funeral home."

"Are you kidding?" she asked in a disbelieving voice.

"I'm afraid not," Annick answered.

"I'm not sure. I don't know if the embalming process would render the toxin undetectable."

"I know you're an expert in toxicology as well as microbiology," Annick said. "Would it be a real chore to find out?"

"I don't think so. There are a few people I can call who'd probably know. When do you need an answer?"

"As soon as possible?"

Bobbie closed the manual. "Why the big rush?"

"Well . . . I'm trying to—"

"C'mon, Annick. What's this all about?"

Annick stood up and smiled. "Would you be real offended if I didn't go into that right now?" She only asked the question because she felt she knew Bobbie well enough to predict she'd comply with her request.

Bobbie filled her lungs with a deep breath and then nodded. "I'll get right on it."

"Thanks."

"I'll try to call you in a few days. How's that?"

Annick stood up, reached across the desk and shook Bobbie's hand. "That's great. You can get me on my pager."

Annick had already started for the door when Bobbie asked, "Have you spoken to Dr. Kincaid?"

"Bart Kincaid, the plastic surgeon?"

"Yeah. He's got a major research project going on the safety of botulism toxin when used for clinically indicated reasons."

"I assume you mean Boaxin."

"Uh-huh," Bobbie said. "The drug companies always come up with such great names."

"I didn't know anyone was doing botulism research at this hospital."

"Major research," she emphasized. "He's got a big lab on the third floor right across the street in the research center. He might be able to help you. He's a bit strange but don't let that scare you off."

"What do you mean, strange?"

"Ever since his son died a couple of years ago, he's never been quite normal."

"How old was his son?" Annick asked.

"Eleven. He came in with a ruptured spleen from a bike accident. His blood count dropped but Kincaid didn't want him to have a blood transfusion. The poor surgical resident on the case wasn't aware of his wishes and ordered a unit of blood hoping to spare the kid a trip to the operating room."

"Are you saying his son bled to death?" Annick asked.

"No, he did fine. There was no further bleeding and he went home."

"So what was the problem?"

"He got hepatitis from the blood transfusion and needed an emergency liver transplant. He died three days after the oper-

ation from acute rejection. For some reason Kincaid never for-
gave himself. The resident who ordered the transfusion transferred to another hospital because he thought Kincaid was
going to kill him."

"My God," Annick whispered. "That's horrible."

"Kincaid's still screwed up over it."

"Well, hopefully when I speak to him, it won't come up,"
Annick told her. "Thanks for the help."

Annick checked the time and realized she was late for
rounds. Without paying much attention, she hurried out of
Bobbie's office, turned the corner quickly and banged shoulders with one of the laboratory techs, Grady Simione, who was
heading in the opposite direction.

"I'm so sorry, Doctor," he said in a genuinely apologetic
tone. "I guess I was distracted. Things have really been hectic
around here the last week or so. I should have been more careful. Are you okay?"

"It's my fault," she said, recognizing his face but stealing a
peek at his ID to refresh her memory as to his name. She
reached up and rubbed her shoulder. "I guess I wasn't looking
where I was going either. I'm sorry. Have a nice day."

Grady apologized again and then studied her carefully as
she walked out of the lab. Walking by Bobbie's office, he exchanged a pleasant smile with his boss even though he knew
she didn't have much respect for him. It wasn't his practice to
eavesdrop on conversations, but when he'd seen Dr. Clement
go into Bobbie's office, he just couldn't resist the temptation.
He knew he wasn't the only one in the lab who did it, and as
long as Bobbie chose to keep her door open . . . well, she
couldn't really blame anyone for being a little curious.

Grady returned to his work area and set aside the microscope slides he'd been working on. He didn't hold Bobbie in
very high esteem, but there weren't too many people in positions of authority that he did. He didn't like Dr. Clement very
much, either. She was attractive enough, bright and everybody's pick for resident of the year, but to him, she was little
more than an overeducated trust-fund baby with an attitude.
She was polite enough to him, but he'd been looked down the
nose enough to recognize it when he saw it.

Grady stacked the half dozen or so slides in front of him

and began wondering why Dr. Clement, a spoiled and insignificant second-year resident, was suddenly so interested in young children in funeral parlors that might have died from botulism.

Chapter Eighteen

Mac and Annick sat in matching leather chairs in front of Dr. Howe's desk. It was five minutes to four and Annick was quite sure that Howe would stroll through the door within the next five minutes for their daily meeting to discuss the patients on the service. She watched as Mac checked over his shoulder to make sure Howe's very loyal and very nosy secretary was out of earshot.

"I'm not saying you're wrong, Annick. I'm only saying that it appears quite clear that the hospital's not looking for any negative publicity, especially if it concerned some mad bio-terrorist stalking its hallways."

"A child has died, Mac, and we almost lost another. Negative publicity would seem to pale when compared with those facts."

"You haven't listened to a word I've said," Mac insisted in an exaggerated whisper. "Michael's ready to go home and there was nothing we could do to save Dana."

"What's your point?"

Mac turned his chair toward her. "My point is that it's a done deal, and for the moment, there are no other cases involving bizarre diseases."

Just as Annick was about to answer she heard Howe enter

the outer office and stop to talk with Sue. She exchanged a frustrated look with Mac, crossed her arms in front of her and waited for Dr. Howe to join them.

"Where's Kevin?" he asked the moment he entered his office.

"He's stuck in X-ray," Mac explained. "I asked him to join us as soon as he's free."

Howe frowned. "Afternoon card rounds"—as he called their daily meeting—"is important. It's one of the best teaching opportunities we have. In the future, unless it's a real emergency, I want Kevin here with us." Howe took a deep breath, mumbled something under his breath and sat down behind his desk. "Let's begin with Michael Flannery," he suggested.

"He's just about ready for discharge," Annick said.

"What about outpatient rehabilitation?"

"We have it scheduled for twice a week," she said.

"He certainly made a remarkable recovery," Howe stated and then began shuffling through a stack of three-by-five cards listing the patients on the service that he kept religiously up-to-date.

"I thought it was strange that there were no other cases of botulism," Annick mentioned. Mac moved forward in his chair, immediately cleared his throat and then fixed her with a glare.

"It's not that uncommon," Howe said. "There have been a number of isolated cases of botulism reported in the scientific literature."

Annick leaned forward to even her shoulders with Mac's. "That's true, but most of those were from home canning mishaps. Michael's mother said he's never even been near any food product that wasn't from a supermarket."

Howe removed his reading glasses, tucked them into the top pocket of his white coat and said, "We've all seen cases where the actual cause is never found—"

"But isn't it true that—"

Howe raised his hand, silencing Annick. "I know it's very uncommon, but it happens. Do we have any more information on the specific type of botulism toxin that affected Michael?" he asked.

Mac shook his head. "Not yet."

"That seems unusual," Annick commented.

Howe answered, "It's the reality of modern medicine. Not everything moves as quickly as we'd like. I'm sure as soon as the CDC has anything, they'll call us."

"Sir, were you aware that there may have been another case of botulism in the hospital at the same time?" Annick asked, ignoring the pained look on Mac's face.

Howe's thick eyebrows suddenly lifted. "I beg your pardon?"

"There was an unexplained death on the endocrinology service. The child's symptoms were consistent with botulism."

"How come I wasn't aware of this patient?" he asked Mac.

"We were never officially consulted on the case," he responded.

"Then how did you learn about it?" Howe asked.

"One of the residents mentioned it to Annick," Mac explained.

"Were the appropriate studies sent to confirm?" Howe inquired.

"Unfortunately, no."

Howe looked at each of them briefly. "We can only act upon the cases we're asked to see. Now, perhaps if the child were still alive, I could place a call to one of my colleagues in the Endocrinology Department, but even that's stretching professional ethics a little."

Annick jumped in. "I was thinking perhaps—"

"Why don't we go on to the next patient?" he suggested, ignoring Annick and looking intently at Mac.

It was more than obvious to her that Howe had no interest in pursuing the possibility that there might have been another case of botulism. She half listened as Mac presented the next patient, but her mind was still fixed on Michael Flannery.

When it came to dealing with the hospital administration, Howe was a master politician. She was sure they had a firm armlock on him about the touchy nature of the recent cases. If she had any hopes of Howe having a sympathetic ear, he had quickly dispelled them.

Card rounds lasted another thirty minutes. Kevin never showed up and the conversation did not return to either Michael or Dana. Just as they were about to adjourn, Dr. Howe requested a word in private with Mac. Only slightly offended she was excluded, Annick waited for Mac in the outer office. Five minutes later, he exited Dr. Howe's office, raised his finger to his lips and escorted Annick out into the hall.

"What was that all about?" Annick asked as they walked toward the emergency room to see a new patient.

"Relax, it wasn't anything about you specifically. Just routine stuff."

"What kind of routine stuff?"

Mac slowed his pace. "He wanted to make sure all the residents were reminded of the hospital's position on any adverse publicity . . . and that the Michael Flannery case was closed."

"I see," she said in one breath and then pressed her lips together in the next.

"Listen, Annick," Mac finally said. "I really don't believe these cases are about some radical political group or madman armed with bioweapons who is targeting innocent children."

"Mac, all you have to do is read the papers. You don't have to have an advanced degree in microbiology to learn enough about bioweapons to make one. Open up any *Soldier of Fortune* magazine if you don't believe me. Any basement with a home microbrewery could become a makeshift lab for the production of bioweapons."

Mac released his hand from her arm, sighed and then ran his fingers through his hair. "A home brewery?"

She stopped for a moment and waited for Mac to do the same. When he turned to face her she said, "I'm theorizing that an emotionally disturbed individual, maybe a disgruntled parent . . . or even some psychopath who's fixated on children, might be capable of such a thing."

"I guess if you put it like that, anything's possible," he confessed.

"It might even be someone who works here."

"C'mon, Annick. You're starting to get a little dramatic now."

"We all know that stranger things have happened," she cautioned him. "It wouldn't surprise me if some other kid gets admitted with some unexplained disease."

"You're not taking into account the sensitive—"

Her eyes widened. "If you're going to bring up concerns about making waves with the administration . . . well, maybe their attitude will change when some kid comes in with small-pox or some other deadly disease."

"Take it easy, Annick."

"I guess my conscience won't allow that. I'll see you in the emergency room."

Annick jammed her hands deep into the waist pockets of her white coat and jogged ahead, leaving Mac speechless, baffled and walking alone to the E.R.

She did decide one thing from their brief conversation. Even though Mac Eastwick had a great butt and was probably the nicest guy she'd met since coming to the United States, he wasn't about to make any waves with just a few months left before he finished his training.

Chapter Nineteen

Annick arrived at the Three South nursing station before Mac, Kevin and the medical students. After stealing a quick look at her watch, she realized she had about fifteen minutes before afternoon rounds started. She was just about to make a phone call when her beeper went off. The number displayed on the pager was one of the extensions on the hematology unit. Before he picked up on the second ring, she had a feeling it was Mac.

"How's it going?" he asked.

"I'm waiting for you guys," she said.

"Anything I should know about before we start rounds?"

She forced herself not to grin. If his tone were any sweeter she might have gotten sick. "Everything's fine, Mac." They hadn't spoken since yesterday. Annick assumed he hadn't called her last night for fear she'd start badgering him about bioterrorism again.

"Are you sure there's nothing I should know before we start rounds?"

"Like what?"

"I thought maybe you were still annoyed at me," he said flatly.

"That was yesterday, Mac. I'm fine now."

"Are you sure?"

"I'm positive. I've seen all the patients and new consults. Everything's under control. We can talk about them when we make rounds."

"Before you abandoned me in the hall yesterday, there was some talk about going out for a drink tonight. I was just wondering if . . . well, if we're still going?"

"Of course we're still going. I've been looking forward to it . . . assuming, that is, that you still want to go."

"I still want to go," he stated with a sudden note of confidence in his voice. "We'll make plans after rounds, okay?"

"Sounds divine, Mac."

"Divine is it? I'll see you in a few minutes."

As soon as she finished her call with Mac, she dialed the main number of the CDC. She suspected her patience would be tested waiting for the appropriate person in just the right lab to come to the phone but she remained undaunted. To her surprise, a pleasant enough operator answered and connected her call immediately.

"This is Dr. Rachel Warren. May I help you?"

"My name is Dr. Annick Clement. I'm calling from Franklin Children's Hospital in New York. We submitted a blood sample for botulism evaluation. I was just told the matter was forwarded to your lab."

"You're referring to Michael Flannery, I assume," came an immediate answer. Rachel's voice was soft but melodious.

Annick sighed with relief. "I am."

"Your specimen is quite . . . interesting."

"Interesting?" Annick asked.

"Actually, I'm ready to pull my hair out over it. How's young Mr. Flannery doing?"

"We weren't quite sure he was going to make it but he turned the corner and is recovering slowly."

"That's wonderful news," Dr. Warren said. "Perhaps that means a lot of what I'm doing is nothing more than an academic exercise."

"How close are you to identifying the serotype?"

"Not as close as I'd like. What's interesting about this toxin is its remarkable resemblance to type F."

"But you're implying it's not," Annick said.

"I'm afraid not. What bothers me is that, biologically, it appears to be more potent than the usual botulism toxins we see. You should congratulate yourself on your patient's recovery."

"Do you think this is a new serotype?" Annick inquired as a number of questions popped into her head.

"That's difficult to say. But it's a distinct possibility."

Annick took caution with her tone when she asked, "Is it conceivable that the toxin is one that has been genetically altered?"

"That's an interesting question. As I recall, a pretty complete clinical history was provided to us when the specimen was sent."

"I know," Annick said. "I prepared it."

"Well then, I have to assume you understand the implications of your question."

"I do."

Annick moved the phone to her opposite ear and then opened the buttons of her white coat. She looked up hoping to see a thermostat in the area. It certainly seemed warmer than usual.

"We have a division of bioterrorism at the CDC, Dr. Clement, but the circumstances surrounding Michael Flannery's case didn't raise any red flags."

"You mean apart from the fact that you can't identify the serotype," Annick said.

There was a pause. "How much do you know about BT?"

"Enough to know that a major portion of the research conducted by countries actively involved in bioterrorism investigation was dedicated to genetically altering toxins such as botulism to make them more virulent."

"We believe most of that research was done in the USSR." Dr. Warren's tone was a bit defensive.

"I agree, but I believe the U.S. was also conducting similar experiments," Annick said. "It's quite conceivable that existing vaccines and antibiotics against these new super-bacteria, viruses and toxins would be rendered useless and ineffective." Annick looked up when she realized her voice had become a little too loud. A couple of nurses were standing across from her but were preoccupied enough with their own work not to have taken an interest in Annick's conversation.

"I'm quite familiar with those theories," Dr. Warren admitted. "If it will make you feel more comfortable, I did forward some of my work to BT for an opinion."

"Even though there were no red flags?"

"I . . . I guess I had the same hunch you did," Dr. Warren confessed.

Annick leaned forward. "What was their opinion?"

"Actually, they're still looking at it. But for the moment, I'm sure it's low probability."

"Low probability doesn't mean no probability," Annick said.

"I couldn't agree more."

The two women spoke for a few more minutes. Annick found her to be quite open and helpful. When Annick asked if she could call again in a few days, Dr. Warren more than encouraged her to do so.

Deep in thought and completely oblivious to what was going on around her, Annick slowly replaced the receiver. When she finally looked up, she noticed Mac getting off the elevator and walking toward the nursing station. As she began to gather up the patient charts for rounds, Annick felt quite certain that the CDC would not be able to prove the botulism toxin found in Michael's bloodstream belonged to any of the commonly known six types.

In fact, if she were a betting woman, she'd risk a month's salary that the toxin that nearly killed Michael Flannery didn't even originate in this country.

Chapter Twenty

At the time he decided to give up his private practice, Bart Kincaid was one of the busiest plastic surgeons on the North Shore of Long Island. On the heels of his son's tragic death, Bart became fed up with the posh world of cosmetic surgery. At age fifty-two, he was financially secure and looking for a change. When the opportunity presented itself to do full-time scientific investigation at the research center of Franklin Children's Hospital, he jumped at the chance. Eccentric in his appearance and at times fussy, Bart Kincaid was a decent man struggling to get his life back together.

"Dr. Kincaid?" Annick asked as she rapped a couple of times on the open door to his lab.

Kincaid, almost entirely bald except for two shortly cropped gray crescents of hair that appeared pasted over his ears, looked up from studying a lively white mouse running up and down in its cage.

"Yes, can I help you?"

"Thank you. My name is Annick Clement. I'm one of the pediatrics residents. I was hoping you'd have a moment to talk with me."

"Of course," he said, waving her in and then replacing the

cage in a large steel rack against the wall. "Come in and have a seat."

Annick sat down in a small wooden chair with no armrests. There was a distinct absence of the usual medicinal odor that seemed to permeate most research labs she had been in. She glanced around for a moment. The lab was immaculate and amply equipped with modern scientific instruments.

"I'm interested in the clinical uses of botulism toxin. I spoke with Bobbie Whitman in the microbiology lab the other day and she mentioned that botulism was your field of interest."

"That's true but my research is still in its infancy," he mentioned as he took a seat behind his desk. "It's an intriguing area. Are you looking to spend some time in the lab?"

"I wish I could," she exaggerated. "But the clinical demands placed on us are quite time-consuming."

"What service are you on?"

"Infectious diseases."

He nodded and then barely smiled. "Hence the interest in botulism toxin. I heard about the case you recently had. In fact, Dr. Howe called me about it."

"Really?"

Kincaid leaned forward, clasped his hands and rested them on his desk. His eyes were slightly red, with just a hint of puffiness.

"We may be a little isolated over here but we don't exist in a vacuum. We attend most of the clinical conferences. Michael Flannery's case has been presented several times. So how can I help you?"

"I'm interested in Boaxin," Annick said.

"I'm impressed."

"I don't understand," she said with a slight hesitation.

"That you know the drug company name for the specific type of botulism toxin I'm working with."

"Bobbie mentioned the name to me," she lied.

"It's a fascinating drug. Most people view it as a deadly toxin and don't realize how many people have benefitted from it. We're presently using it for severe muscular spastic diseases, eye muscle problems, and of course for cosmetic indications. What area are you specifically interested in?" he asked.

"All aspects," she said. "But I'm especially curious about its preparation and even more so in the risks involved in its use."

Kincaid moved a pile of computer printouts to the opposite side of his desk. Annick couldn't help but notice his large muscular hands.

"Well, it's simply a purified form of botulism toxin."

"Which serotype?" she asked.

"We use type A. It's a little tricky to prepare but the pharmaceutical companies seem to have it pretty well figured out. The lethal dose in a mouse is about one unit."

"What about inadvertent botulism?" she asked, fairly certain he'd be familiar with the term. It had been widely adopted over the past few years to describe those patients who had been treated with very low doses of botulism toxin for any number of reasons, but who had developed mild to severe symptoms of botulism—a result that was obviously far from what was desired.

"Inadvertent botulism," he began slowly, "is definitely a real entity. It's uncommon but it can be devastating."

"Are you working to modify the toxin?" she asked.

"That's part of what we do."

"Is that to eliminate the side effects of an overdose?"

"Yes, it is," he answered.

"Do you ever worry about the toxin falling into the wrong hands?"

Kincaid looked at her for a second. His eyes were weary, not distrusting.

"I'm not quite sure I understand your question," he finally said.

"I guess I was interested in the measures taken to safeguard the toxin."

"Why? Are you interested in stealing some?"

"Hardly," she answered with a faint smile.

"Then you must have an interest in bioterrorism. As I mentioned," he began, "a major portion of our research is directed toward modifying the known strains of botulism toxin . . . but certainly not for illegal or some other fanatic purpose." Kincaid drummed his desktop and then pointed in her direction. "I remember Dr. Howe mentioning that you never figured out how Michael Flannery got botulism."

Her face was serious when she said, "So far, that's true."

"So far? Is that what this is all about? You think my toxin was the cause of his illness?"

Annick sidestepped Kincaid's inquiry. "My question was a general one."

"I'm going to assume your inquiries are of a completely professional nature." His tone was cautious but fell short of suspect.

"I assure you they are."

"Okay. Every dram of Boaxin is meticulously accounted for. We have a very sophisticated system for doing that and an equally foolproof one for making sure it all remains in our lab."

Annick listened politely. She desperately wanted a sample of Kincaid's toxin to send to the CDC so it could be compared to the one found in Michael's system. If the two samples were identical, she would have irrefutable evidence that the toxin that poisoned Michael originated from Franklin Children's Hospital.

Annick leaned forward and then scooted her chair toward Kincaid. Proceeding without offending Dr. Kincaid was paramount on her mind.

"The CDC is having a hell of a time trying to isolate the specific type of botulism toxin that poisoned Michael. I know it's a long shot but I was hoping to acquire a sample of your toxin, submit it to the CDC and see if the two matched."

Kincaid removed his thick black glasses. "Does Dr. Howe know about your request? The reason I ask is because it's of such an unusual nature that I would expect it to come from him."

Annick stood up, walked over to the door and closed it. When she turned around, she could feel Kincaid studying her.

"Nobody knows about this request. I'm kind of exploring an idea on my own. I was hoping you wouldn't mention our conversation to him. Will you help me?"

"It sounds like you're on a fishing expedition." He stopped for a few seconds and then let out a slow breath. "Okay, I'll give you a sample. But under a couple of conditions."

"Anything you say."

"Number one, I send the sample to the CDC myself, and number two, this stays completely between you and me. When the test comes back that the two toxins are different, and I assure you it will, I can use the information as I see fit."

Annick began nodding when Kincaid began his list of conditions and continued until he finished. Speechless for the moment, she didn't quite understand what he meant by using the information as he saw fit, but she was hardly in a position to look a gift horse in the mouth.

"You seem surprised," he finally said.

"In all honesty, I am," she said plainly.

"Why?"

"I . . . I'm not sure."

"I'm not going to rain on your investigative spirit," he promised. "I'm a good listener. Maybe when you have some time, you'll stop back in and share your theories with me."

Annick's expression was hardly coy. "How do you know I have a theory?"

"Because I was your age once." He closed his eyes for a moment. "My son was a little like you," he said in a voice just above a whisper.

Annick heard his last comment but pretended she didn't. "You never know. I may take you up on your offer," she said.

He extended his hand. His eyes were a little weepy. "If you'll provide me with the name of the appropriate person at the CDC, I'll overnight a specimen to them."

"I'll have the information for you tomorrow. You've been very helpful. I can't thank you enough."

Annick reached out and shook his hand. A few minutes later, she was crossing the street heading back to the hospital. Thinking about her brief meeting with Kincaid, it occurred to her that he was perhaps too cooperative about providing a sample of his work for the CDC to look at. Her pace slowed as she wondered just how many types of botulism toxin he was working with . . . and if there were more than one, how would she know which one he'd send to Atlanta?

Once on the opposite sidewalk, Annick stopped for a moment and then turned around to look at the three-story research building. Lost in thought, she suddenly jumped back when she felt a couple of taps on her shoulder.

"Take it easy," Mac said with a laugh. "What are you so jumpy about?"

"Are you stalking me?" she asked sarcastically with the hope that Mac wouldn't start asking her a lot of questions.

"Actually, I was on my way over to the virology lab . . . but to answer your question, and I'm hardly an expert on the subject, I don't think a lot of stalkers walk up to their prey and tap them on their shoulders."

Annick took a couple of steps closer. "I'll agree with some of what you said."

"Really? What part would that be?"

"When you mentioned you weren't an expert on the topic."

Mac chuckled. "I had a nice time last night," he said, like a thirteen-year-old gloating after his first real kiss.

"I had a nice time too," she said. "We'll have to do that again soon."

Mac grinned like a conquering hero and said, "I'll look forward to that."

"I forgot to ask you something last night. Did you arrange coverage for us while we're in Paris?"

"I spoke with Lori Dunn and C. C. Henry. They're both on light rotations this month and offered to cover us. They've both already been on I.D. so there shouldn't be a problem."

"Was Howe okay with them?"

"He likes them both. He said fine."

"Are you getting excited about going?" she asked.

"Are you kidding? I'm checking the days off on my calendar. As far as I know when they compiled the list of the rich and famous, I wasn't on it. This is a big deal for me."

"I'm glad to hear that," she said. "I think you'll have a great time."

Mac put his hand on her shoulder. "I know I'm going to have a great time. Listen, I'm going over to check on some cultures. How about going with me?"

"Will I learn anything?"

"If you spend enough time with me, I guarantee it," he said with a wink.

Annick's chin fell to her chest. "Another man with a one-track mind," she muttered as they started across the street.

Chapter Twenty-one

Grady Simione sipped his coffee slowly in the employees' lounge, lamenting about working the night shift for the fourth time in two weeks. It was ten-thirty and he only had about five minutes left on his break. The lounge was empty at the moment, the way he preferred it. As soon as he finished his coffee, he washed his mug and returned it to the same hook in the cupboard he always used.

Grady returned to the laboratory and had been working for about an hour on a routine urinalysis when one of the other techs asked him to take a call from a resident who was inquiring about the results of a spinal tap.

"May I help you?" Grady asked. He pinned the phone between his shoulder and ear so that he could continue to look through the microscope.

"This is Dr. Clement. I'm calling about a spinal tap done on a six-month-old this morning. Her name is Mandy Coe. Do you have the results yet?"

"How are you, Dr. Clement? It's Grady Simione." He was tempted to mention something about her interest in botulism but decided against it.

"I'm well." The response came in a controlled voice.

He placed the phone on hold. He crossed the lab, entered the incubator and quickly found Mandy Coe's culture plates. Grady took a careful look at the plastic dishes filled almost to the top with the special nutrient material that bacteria thrive on. After he studied the plates for a minute or so he left the incubator, walked directly back to his lab area and picked up the phone.

"Dr. Clement?"

"Yes."

"I just checked the plates. There's absolutely no growth."

"I beg your pardon?" she said.

"No growth," he repeated.

"But I was sure she had meningitis. Are you positive?"

"Her spinal fluid is normal. There are no bacterial colonies visible."

"I'm a little surprised," Annick said with caution in her tone. "When will the official report be on the chart?"

Grady paused for a moment, tapped a few commands into his computer and said, "Looks like tomorrow morning."

"Thank you," she said.

"You're certainly welcome, Doctor."

Grady hung up the phone and gazed across the lab. He thought about college and his missed opportunity to apply to medical school. If he had received an MD degree, he would have had the sense and professionalism never to have gotten a swelled head just because he was a doctor. Grady's eyes were half closed when the phone rang. A little startled, he picked it up, listened carefully and then told the nurse from the quick care clinic that he'd check the latest throat culture results and get right back to her.

Annick continued to stare at the telephone. Tempted to go to the lab and check the plates herself, she decided against it when she looked down at her to-do list, which was long enough to keep her hopping for the next two days. She took a deep breath and shook her head. If she did get a spare moment, the first thing she'd do was go to the lab to have a look at those culture plates.

Chapter Twenty-two

It had been several days since Annick had spoken with Joelle Parsons about the death of her nephew, but her description of Justin's mysterious hospital course was still vivid in her mind. After considerable deliberation and knowing full well it was a long shot, she decided to go to the main laboratory to make some inquiries.

Annick walked down two flights of stairs and exited the stairwell at the main laboratory. Occupying almost the entire second floor, the laboratory service was an enormous operation consisting of seven different labs. Stopping at the information desk, Annick was informed that the evening supervisor was Rick Van Owen and he could be found in the hematology lab.

Scanning the large lab, Annick spotted Rick at the far end hunched over the back of one of the techs. She walked past a long line of black Formica benches. Against the wall, stacked side by side, the latest state-of-the-art diagnostic equipment was rapidly cranking out blood test results. About a dozen technicians, all in waist-length powder-blue coats, scurried around the lab checking the machines and then entering data into their computers.

"Rick."

"Hi, Annick," he said, stealing a quick peek over his shoulder. "What brings you to our little shop at this time of night?" Rick was a decent enough man but suffered from a lackluster personality and a forgettable appearance. He was, however, a knowledgeable lab supervisor and an experienced manager.

"Do you think I could have a word with you when you're done?" she asked.

"You bet."

Annick took a couple of steps back and waited for Rick to finish up explaining one of the protocols to the tech. He turned to Annick, pointed to a small office immediately adjacent to the entrance and followed her over. Rick sat on the side of a short steel desk, while Annick took a seat across from him.

"About a week ago, there was a young man admitted with diabetes. His name was Justin Silva. He died within twenty-four hours of admission. I'm not quite sure we know why."

"I'm sorry to hear that," Rick said.

"There's a blood test that I don't think was run that might have helped us answer the question." Annick took a breath, noticing Rick's puzzled expression. "I know this is a long shot but I was hoping you might have frozen a tube of his blood that hadn't been discarded as yet."

"Didn't you say this kid died about a week ago?"

"That's right."

"Sometimes we hold on to an extra tube of blood for a day or so in case added tests are needed so the child doesn't have to be stuck again, but a week . . . and the child expired. I . . . I don't think there's any chance we still have a sample of his blood. I'm sorry, Annick."

She sighed. "As I said, it was a long shot."

"Sorry I couldn't help."

"How's everything else going?" she asked with a smile, heading for the door.

"Just fine. Was the kid on a research protocol?"

Annick stopped dead in her tracks. "I'm not sure. Why do you ask?"

"Because you mentioned he was a diabetic," Rick answered. "Franklin's a major research center for diabetes. We're on about every national experimental protocol there is."

Annick interlocked her fingers and let her hands fall in front of her. "I hate to sound obtuse, but I guess I'm still not getting it."

"The diabetes research lab keeps their specimens for a long time. There's a good chance that your patient was part of a study group. If that's the case, they may still have a tube of his blood on ice."

Annick's eyes widened. "Are you sure?"

"Well, I'm sure there's a diabetes lab and I'm sure they keep their blood samples frozen for a long time . . . what I'm not sure about is whether your patient has a specimen over there or not."

"I love you, Rick," she said, wasting no time in planting a big kiss flush on his cheek. Rick immediately raised his hand to the exact spot on his face.

"What test did you want done, anyway?" he asked as she bolted out the door.

"It's not important," she answered without turning around.

Annick returned to her call room, turned on the TV and plopped down on the couch. She knew the research facility was closed but she was quite confident she'd find the time tomorrow to act on Rick's advice.

If there were a tube of Justin's blood and she could somehow acquire it, she was sure Rachel Warren at the CDC would agree to run a botulism toxin assay on it. Assuming the sample was positive, it should be a simple enough matter to compare it to Michael Flannery's.

Chapter Twenty-three

"It's nice to see that smile on your face," Annick told Caryn Flannery as she packed up the last of Michael's things.

"I never thought this day would come," Caryn said with a look of tranquility and relief on her face.

"I won't try to kid you. He was a pretty sick guy," she confessed. "But I knew he'd make it," she added with all the confidence of a Monday-morning quarterback.

Several of the nurses and other physicians had gathered in Michael's room to say their good-byes to the biggest celebrity the hospital had cared for in quite a few years.

"I don't know how I'll ever be able to thank all you guys," Caryn said.

Annick quickly scanned the faces of the others in the room. "I think I speak for all of us when I say that just the fact that he's better is enough."

Caryn placed the last vase of flowers on a large metal cart the nurses had rounded up.

"What's your feeling, Dr. Clement? Do you think we'll ever know where he got botulism from?" Caryn asked.

"I hope so," she answered. "The CDC's still working on it.

I'm going to give them a call in the next day or two to see if they're making any progress."

"Are you ready, buddy?" Caryn asked her son. He nodded, grabbed his GameBoy off the bed and walked over to his mother.

"I guess we'll see you in Dr. Howe's office next week," Annick said as she extended her hand to Caryn.

Caryn looked directly at Annick and smiled. "I'm afraid that won't do it," she said, and then stepped forward and hugged Annick. After a few seconds, Annick could feel the warmth of Caryn's tears on her own cheek.

Putting her arm around her son, Caryn escorted him through the door. Annick was a couple of steps behind as they walked down the hall.

One of the nurses had already summoned the elevator. It took a minute or two for it to arrive and for the nurses to wheel the cart onto the elevator. With the doors starting to close, Caryn waved and said one last good-bye to everyone who had helped Michael recover.

As soon as the doors closed, Annick hit the up button. There were two newborns with seizures and temperature instability whom she wanted to check on.

"Excuse me, Dr. Clement," came a soft voice from behind her.

A young nurse with "Tracy Poston R.N." printed boldly on her name tag stood in front of her.

"Yes," Annick answered.

"The information desk just called. They thought you might be up here. They asked if you could stop down for a minute. They have a package for you."

"Okay," Annick said. "It's probably more propaganda from one of the pharmaceutical reps."

Hitting the down button and then staring at the elevators for a few seconds, Annick decided to walk down. When she arrived, the lobby was fairly crowded. The information desk was on the opposite side and she began to walk toward it. She frowned when she saw there was only one senior volunteer manning the desk and several people trying to get his attention.

"Excuse me, Dr. Clement."

Annick turned. A young nurse walked up and smiled. She was wearing a plain white uniform, which was a little unusual for Children's Hospital nurses, who usually opted for more casual outfits with bright colors. Annick also found her excessive makeup a little strange. Her Children's Hospital ID read "Danielle Sudor."

"Yes, Danielle," she answered, checking her identification badge for a second time, trying to recall if she'd ever met her.

"I was wondering if I might have a word with you."

"Of course. How can I help you?"

"I must have just missed you upstairs. I work on Four East. I've been taking care of Michael Flannery for the last few days."

"He just went home," Annick said.

"I know. They needed me in the emergency room, so I said my good-byes a little earlier."

"I see. What was it that you wanted to talk to me about?"

"Well, one of the employees took a particular interest in Michael and we . . . the nurses I mean, thought it would be nice to formally thank him. We were hoping that he'd be able to say good-bye in person but I guess he wasn't able to make it."

"That sounds like a nice idea. I guess it's something we should do more of."

"I'm so glad to hear you say that, because we felt it might be nicer if it came from one of the docs."

Annick smiled politely. "Who did you have in mind?"

"There aren't too many residents more popular with the nurses than you, Dr. Clement. We were hoping you'd be willing to do it."

"I'd be happy to," she said, pulling out her notepad. Danielle's request was a minor one. In general, many of the residents tended to diminish the importance of the nurses, but Annick was savvy enough to appreciate just how essential they were. She flipped open the notepad and pulled out a pen. "What's his name and what department does he work in?"

"Grady Simione. He works in the lab."

Annick looked up from the notepad with a muddled expression. "Grady Simione . . . but he's a tech in the microbiology lab."

"That's right," Danielle said. "He visited Michael several times, especially at night. He mentioned to me he was very much involved in the lab tests and was very concerned about him."

"That's a little unusual," Annick said.

"What's unusual, Dr. Clement?"

"Uh . . . nothing. I was just thinking out loud."

"Do you know him?" Danielle asked.

"Yes, I do, and I'll be happy to get in touch with him and thank him for you."

"That would be terrific. I'll mention it to the others." Danielle glanced over Annick's shoulder toward the elevator and then waved at a group of nurses. "I have to get going. Thanks again."

Annick watched as Danielle walked toward the elevator. She then turned and headed over to the information desk. The volunteer working behind the desk, an elderly man in white pants and a golf shirt with the Children's Hospital logo embossed on it, smiled as she approached. He was a slight man, slump-shouldered but still sporting a full head of thick white hair.

"I'm Dr. Clement. I was told you have a package for me."

"Yes, Dr. Clement. There was a young man here a few minutes ago with a large envelope but he's gone now."

"Did he leave the material for me?"

"No, he didn't."

"That's a little strange," Annick said.

"Maybe he had another appointment," the man said. "I think he worked for one of the drug companies. He had one of those big name tags on."

"Do you remember his name?" Annick asked.

The man scratched his head and smiled. "At my age, Doctor, you're happy to remember your own name."

Annick shared his grin for a moment, thanked him and then headed back across the lobby. Waiting for the elevator, her mind flashed back to her conversation and Danielle Sudor's request.

Why the devil was Grady Simione visiting Michael Flannery? From a medical standpoint, there was absolutely no

*reason for him to be anywhere near him—or, for that matter,
any other patient.*

Unable to dismiss the unsettling feeling, Annick tried to
conceive of any plausible reason to explain Simione's strange
interest in a twelve-year-old boy with botulism.

Chapter Twenty-four

Grady Simione was hunched over his microscope evaluating a blood specimen when Annick entered the laboratory. As soon as she walked through the door she noticed him, but she looked away to avoid catching his eye.

As usual, Bobbie's door was wide open. Her desk looked like a dozen kindergartners had just finished dumping three days' work on it, a fact Bobbie seemed to be oblivious to. Before Annick knocked, Bobbie noticed her and stood up.

"Don't be mad at me," Bobbie pleaded. "It's been a zoo around here and I haven't had a chance to track down the information you wanted on botulism toxin."

Annick took a seat. "Don't worry about it. I kind of put it on the back burner for now."

"I understand Michael Flannery went home," Bobbie said, sitting back down.

"He certainly did," Annick said as she peeked over her shoulder at Simione. His head was still buried in his work. "Actually, the reason I'm here has something to do with Michael."

"And what might that be?" Bobbie inquired.

"The nurses asked me to thank one of your techs for taking such a personal interest in Michael."

Silent for the moment, Bobbie pushed her delicate reading

glasses down until they perched on the tip of her nose, allowing her to peer over the top.

"Really," Bobbie said, "which tech?"

"Grady Simione."

Bobbie remained straight-faced. "I don't understand."

It was warm in the office. Before explaining, Annick stood up, removed her white coat and hung it over her chair.

"The nurses said Grady had taken a real interest in Michael and that they wanted to thank him. They thought it might be nicer coming from a doctor . . . so, here I am."

"What kind of an interest are we talking about?" Bobbie asked.

"I'm not exactly sure of the specifics, only that he came and visited Michael several times."

"I see."

"Is it a routine part of a lab tech's responsibilities to visit patients?" Annick watched Bobbie take a long look through the window at Simione.

"I guess it depends if it was for social reasons."

"What do you mean by social?"

"Maybe Grady knows Michael's mother from outside the hospital," Bobbie suggested.

"Supposing he didn't. In an official sense, under what circumstances would a lab tech's work require face-to-face contact with a patient?"

Bobbie thought for a moment and then shook her head. "None that I can think of."

"Caryn Flannery seemed quite comfortable with him."

"Well, I . . . I guess a lot of people are."

"But you're not one of them?" Annick stated.

"I didn't say that," Bobbie was quick to answer.

"Then what are you saying?"

"I guess he's just not my cup of tea."

Annick thought for a moment. "In what way?"

"He's just too helpful and too accommodating."

Annick laughed. "I thought that's what the hospital's looking for."

"They are but he's not sincere about it."

Annick smiled in agreement. "It's interesting you should say that. I spoke with him the other night about some spinal fluid cultures."

"And?"

"He seems to say the right thing, but in a strange kind of way, he's just so . . . patronizing," Annick said.

"I think we're saying the same thing. I just find him so damn polite that it's annoying. Even though he's always kissing ass and acting like he values your advice, you can just tell he feels intellectually superior to everyone. To tell you the truth, I'm a little surprised he'd have the interest to go visit a patient."

"Why's that?" Annick asked.

"Because, when it comes to children, I don't think there's a single drop of compassion in him."

"Did he ever say anything like that?" Annick asked in a voice that was, perhaps, too eager.

"No, not in so many words. It's more of an intangible . . . but I'll tell you this, he's different from most people who work in a children's hospital."

"Why?"

"Because he just doesn't fit in. That's the only way I can put it."

Annick sat forward in her chair. "How long has he worked here?"

"I'm not exactly sure, maybe about eighteen months."

"Is he married?" Annick asked.

Bobbie tapped her chin a few times before answering. "As I recall, he lives alone, but I could be wrong."

There were a dozen other questions that popped into Annick's head but a red flag went up warning her that she'd been inquisitive enough for one day.

"Well, what do you think, Bobbie? Should I thank him for Caryn Flannery or just forget it?"

Bobbie grappled with the question for a few seconds before answering. "Maybe I'm just being a little paranoid. I guess there can't be any harm in thanking the man."

"Okay, then, that's what I'll do."

"Sounds good," Bobbie said.

"Oh, yeah, I don't have time now, but I think I'll come back later, after his shift ends, and check those culture plates myself."

"I'll do it for you if you'd like."

Annick waved her hand. "Don't bother. I'll take care of it."

Annick stood up, thanked Bobbie and headed for the door. As soon as she stepped out into the main lab, she noticed Simione a few feet away at one of the computer terminals. She was quite sure he looked away quickly when she noticed him.

"Mr. Simione?" she asked.

He looked up and smiled. "Yes, may I help you with something, Dr. Clement?"

"We discharged Michael Flannery earlier today. The nurses wanted me to thank you personally for the extra attention you showed him. They were quite appreciative."

"That's very kind of them to say, but I would hardly call it extra attention. I ran some of the preliminary tests on his blood samples. I just needed a little additional information on his symptoms."

"That was very thorough of you," Annick responded. "A lot of lab techs would feel that was outside the scope of their duties."

Grady opened the incubator and placed three culture dishes on the top shelf. He noted the time on the log and then closed the door.

"I don't feel that way, Dr. Clement. I believe I'm part of the team. I really try to stay on top of things. I bet I have the same medical books in my library that you do."

"It's certainly refreshing to meet someone as committed as you are, Mr. Simione."

"Please call me Grady, and thank you. If you speak with Mrs. Flannery, please tell her how happy I am that Michael recovered."

Annick nodded as he spoke. His words were genuine enough but she was far from convinced about their sincerity. "I should see her next week in Dr. Howe's office. I'll pass along your message." Grady extended his hand and Annick shook it. She watched as he ambled back to his lab station, selected a slide from a small box and slid it on the platform of his microscope.

Annick waved at Bobbie and then gave her a quick thumbs-up as she turned and walked by her office. There could be no question that Bobbie was not alone in her uneasiness about

Grady. Even in the absence of hard evidence, Annick suspected he had a dark side.

Waiting for the elevator, she remained lost in thought about Grady. His explanation about the time he spent with Michael was ludicrous. His job was to run lab tests, nothing more. The child's symptoms were irrelevant to his purpose. If his visits to Michael were nothing more than thrill seeking, he was way out of line and should probably be counseled by one of his superiors.

Looking up, Annick groaned as it became clear the elevator was stuck on the fifth floor. Her mind was filled with many unanswered questions, but one thing was for sure: in the next few days, Annick was going to do everything she could to start finding some of the answers.

Chapter Twenty-five

The nursing station on Three East was one of the less hectic ones in the hospital. Annick walked around the large chart rack to a small work area specifically designated for physician chart review. As she'd hoped, there was nobody there. Picking up the phone, she asked the operator for a long-distance line and then dialed the number of the CDC. Fortunately, Rachel Warren was in the lab when she called.

"Dr. Warren, this is Annick Clement calling from Franklin Children's Hospital in New York. I know it's a little late but I was hoping to catch you before you went home."

"How are you, Annick? I hope you're not calling to report any new cases of botulism."

"No, thank goodness, we haven't seen any more. Actually, I was calling to see if you received the specimen we sent you."

"I received it early today. We finished up the analysis this afternoon. Hold on for a second while I grab the report."

"I'll be here," she said as calmly as she could.

In the thirty seconds it took Rachel to return to the phone, Annick had changed positions three times in her chair and twisted a small paper clip into an unrecognizable form.

"The toxin you sent is distinctly different from the type we isolated from Michael Flannery's blood."

"I see," she muttered.

"I'm not sure what answer you were looking for," Rachel said. "I hope this information is of some help to you."

Annick was crestfallen by the news. If the toxins were identical, it would have at least given her a place to start. She might have even entertained the possibility that by some bizarre hospital mishap the toxin from Dr. Kincaid's lab had reached the trays served to Michael and Justin. If that were the case, at least they would be dealing with a freak accident instead of some madman.

"I certainly appreciate you taking the time to run the assay," she said. "I may have another one to send to you in the near future. Would it be too much to ask you to have a look at it as well?"

"Absolutely not, but you said you had no new cases . . . so if you don't mind me asking, where would this next sample be coming from?"

"It's from a young diabetic who died recently. His cause of death was listed as overwhelming bacterial infection but I have my doubts."

"But you said he died."

"That's right."

"So, where's the sample coming from?" Rachel asked.

"He may have been on one of our diabetic experimental protocols. If he were, the lab probably froze a tube of his blood. They're checking for me now."

"Well, if that's the case, I'll be happy to analyze it and let you know if it contains the same type botulism toxin as Michael Flannery's."

"That would be great," Annick said, her voice becoming more upbeat.

"I'll look forward to hearing from you . . . and if you're ever in Atlanta, drop by. I'd love to show you our facility."

"That's very nice of you to offer. I'll look forward to it."

Annick said good-bye and slowly replaced the receiver. The whole issue of Justin Silva's death reminded her of her strange meeting with his aunt, Joelle Parsons, in the hospital cafeteria. It took her only a moment to find her phone number. After several rings, an answering machine came on. Annick recognized Joelle's voice and left a short message that she was still working on things and would contact her as soon as she had some news. Annick felt like she was spinning her wheels. Crossing her fingers, she hoped for a little luck.

Annick checked the time and then jumped up and headed for the door. She had just over two minutes before afternoon card rounds started in Dr. Howe's office. As she walked toward the elevator, she made the firm decision to maintain a low profile during rounds. The last thing she needed at this point was to antagonize Dr. Howe.

Chapter Twenty-six

Annick Clement was more than furious when she knocked on Bobbie Whitman's door. It was 6:50 A.M. and approaching shift change in the lab. Bobbie had always made it a point to be at her desk at 6:30, even though most of the other lab supervisors didn't clock in until eight. She was a little startled by the intensity of Annick's knocking and motioned her in immediately. In spite of her invitation to have a seat, Annick stood in front of her desk.

"I almost called you at home last night," she told Bobbie.

"Calm down, Annick. What happened?"

"Remember our little conversation about Grady Simione?"

"I think so," she said dryly, "it was only yesterday."

"Do you remember I mentioned that I had spoken with him about some spinal fluid cultures on a little girl?"

"Of course I remember."

"Well, I came up here last night and checked the plates myself. The cultures are positive for *streptococcus* . . . and it's a heavy growth. This poor kid's got meningitis and Grady told me her spinal fluid was fine. Thank God I didn't stop the antibiotics. She might have died."

Bobbie listened closely as she dipped a tea bag into a steaming mug of boiling water in front of her. "Maybe the plates were negative when he checked them and all the growth took place afterward."

"I don't think so," Annick said in no uncertain terms. "I checked the log myself. The routine reading at six P.M. recorded heavy growth. That was hours before I spoke to Grady."

"Have you talked with him about it?" Bobbie asked.

"Absolutely not. He works for you. My responsibility is to bring it to your attention and that's exactly what I'm doing."

"And I'm glad you did. Listen, he's scheduled to work this afternoon. I'll find out what happened," Bobbie promised.

"I would appreciate getting some feedback on this thing."

"As soon as I speak with him, I'll call you."

"I'm starting not to like this guy very much. Why do we hire people like him?" Annick asked in complete frustration.

"Maybe he made a legitimate mistake. Let me get the facts before you go off the deep end."

"I'm afraid it's too late for that," Annick assured her.

"How's the little girl doing?"

"She's doing fine . . . but only because I didn't stop the antibiotics."

"Yes, you mentioned that. I guess that's the most important thing," Bobbie offered as the only saving grace. "I'll deal with Mr. Simione."

Annick had confidence in Bobbie—it was the system that worried her. With the new atmosphere of near total tolerance, disciplining employees was becoming more perilous by the day. Risks of formal complaints to state agencies and lawsuits had the administration's hands tied squarely in a knot.

A little calmer now, Annick thanked Bobbie and left. For the most part, she looked upon herself as a reasonable and understanding person, but giving Grady the benefit of the doubt and dismissing what happened to Mandy Coe as an unfortunate oversight was not something she was sure she could do.

Chapter Twenty-seven

It had been less than two weeks since Dana's funeral, making Annick's decision to call Linda Vitale a tough one. Much to her relief, Linda sounded relatively calm for the first few minutes of their conversation. Annick had her fingers crossed, hoping that she was starting to deal with her child's death.

"I was wondering if we might get together," Annick said. "I'd like to discuss some things with you regarding Dana's illness. If you think it's too early, I can always—"

"No. In fact I think it may be a good idea. Actually, I was going to call you this week. I guess I still have some unanswered questions."

"I'd be happy to answer any question you might have," Annick said. "When would be a good time for you?"

"Are you on call tonight?"

"No, I'm not on until tomorrow."

"How about tonight then? The evenings have been the toughest. It would be nice to have some company. I'll make dinner."

"Tonight would be fine. I should be off by seven. I'll see you then."

The remainder of the day was hectic but by seven-fifteen Annick was on her way to Linda's house. The directions were quite straightforward and she made the trip to Glen Cove in about fifteen minutes. Linda answered the door wearing brown corduroy overalls over a white turtleneck sweater. Linda extended her hand as Annick stepped into the foyer. She immediately noticed the wonderful aroma of fresh marinara sauce coming from the kitchen.

"I hope you haven't eaten yet," Linda said.

"Not a chance. I wasn't about to blow one of the few chances I get to have a home-cooked meal."

Linda smiled warmly as she took Annick's coat, hung it in the hall closet and then led her to the kitchen.

"It was nice of you to see me on such short notice," Annick said, pulling out one of the cherry-stained early-American chairs.

"As I mentioned on the phone, the evenings have been the loneliest. Believe me, I welcome the company. I'm going to open a bottle of Chianti. Can I interest you in a glass?"

"I think I'll pass for now," Annick said.

Linda opened the refrigerator, removed a bottle of the wine and opened it. After pouring herself half a glass, she walked to the stove, picked up a large wooden spoon and slowly stirred the sauce. For the first ten minutes or so, they both treaded softly and merely exchanged small talk.

Eventually, Annick took the initiative. "You mentioned on the phone you had some questions."

Linda was still at the stove attending to dinner, her back to Annick. She reached above the stove, opened a cabinet and reached for a box of spaghetti. "Actually, after we got off the phone, I got a little curious as to why you called," Linda said as she dumped about half of the box into a large pot of boiling water.

"Would you rather talk about that first?"

"I think I would," she answered.

Annick pushed her chair back slightly and crossed her legs. "The circumstances of Dana's illness have bothered me from the time she was admitted."

"In what way?"

"Plague is a pretty rare disease," Annick explained. "Some cases from California and the southwestern states are reported every year, but those are generally confined to people who live there and are in a high-exposure area."

"But Dana was in California," Linda reminded her.

"True . . . but where in California was she?"

"To my knowledge, she spent most of her time in L.A. and Malibu."

"Not exactly the places you'd expect someone to be exposed to plague."

"I don't understand," Linda said, turning back around, attending to the simmering sauce. "Are you suggesting Dana didn't have plague?"

Annick reached forward and began fidgeting with a beautifully hand-painted ceramic salt-and-pepper shaker set.

"No, the tests were pretty conclusive. I'm just trying to figure out how the heck she got it." Annick stood up and walked to the far side of the kitchen to have a better look at a colorful serigraph of the west coast of Ireland hanging on the wall. "May I ask you something?"

"Sure," Linda said. Her voice was a controlled monotone.

"Who else knew she was making the trip to California?"

"That's kind of a strange question. Uh . . . let's see. Well, her father, obviously. My sister, a few friends and I guess some people at the hospital." Linda's voice was a little perplexed when she asked, "What difference does that make?"

"I'm not sure. Maybe nothing. Did anybody in the lab know about Dana's trip?"

"I guess so. It's not exactly the type of thing you fight to keep a secret." Linda moved to a large cutting board and began chopping a long carrot for the salad.

"How much time do you spend in the microbiology lab?" Annick asked directly.

"I'm a supervisor. It varies from day to day depending on where the problems are." Linda stopped chopping for a moment, set the knife down and dried her hands with a small floral dish towel. "How does all this tie in with Dana?"

Annick made no effort to hide the exasperated look on her face. "I wish I had an answer for you, but for the moment I'm afraid I don't."

"I was hoping you might," Linda said.

"Do you know Grady Simione? He's one of the micro-biology techs."

"I know who he is if that's what you mean."

"What do you think of him?" Annick asked.

Linda stopped for a moment and looked up. "That's another strange question," she said. "He's conscientious, although somewhat of a brownnose and a snoop."

"That's hardly a resounding endorsement."

"He's average and he does his job," Linda said with a degree of caution. "I supervise a lot of people. I have to be somewhat flexible about their individual personalities and resist the temptation to be judgmental."

"I see," Annick said.

"What's your interest in Grady Simione?"

"Nothing really. He's been . . . helpful on several of our cases. That's all." She knew she had bungled the answer and wasn't too surprised when Linda glanced at her skeptically.

"Let me guess. Your next question is going to be if Grady knew Dana was going to California."

Annick smiled. "Not really, but as long as you've brought it up . . . did he?"

"He knew."

"Are you sure?" Annick asked, no longer foolish enough to think Linda believed her questions were either casual or innocuous.

"Absolutely, and the reason I'm sure is because a couple of days before Dana left, he overheard me talking to Maxine Kennard."

"About what?"

"Oh . . . how my schedule was all screwed up. I was trying to figure out how I was going to get Dana to the airport and pick her up the night she came home. I guess he overheard me."

"How do you know?"

"Because he offered to help me out if I needed someone to take her. I thought it was a little strange but didn't really give it much thought after that."

"What did you say?" Annick asked.

"I just politely blew him off."

"But it sounds like he knew Dana's travel itinerary."

"I guess so," Linda said with a shrug. "But so did a lot of people."

Annick detected a note of discomfort in Linda's manner and said, "I have an idea. Why don't we talk about what was on your mind?"

"Unfortunately, it doesn't appear as if you're any closer to figuring out what happened to my daughter."

"I can't say that we are."

"Do you know what I remember the most?" Linda asked Annick, who just shook her head slowly. "Well, it was the first evening Dana was sick. All she cared about was getting better quickly so she wouldn't miss any field hockey practice."

"Was she close with the girls on the team?" Annick asked.

"They were all great friends. Some of them wanted to come over and visit her but Dana said no because she was afraid they'd get sick." Linda stopped for a moment and quickly dried the drizzle of tears now resting high on her cheekbones. She took off her apron, tried as hard as she could to smile. "Let's have some dinner," she said.

"That sounds great."

"I hope you like pasta."

Annick walked across the room and put her arm around Linda's shoulder. The tears were gone but her face was somber again. "As a matter of fact, I love pasta," she said.

Annick helped Linda put the final touches on dinner and then the two of them spent the better part of the next hour talking and eating. Most of the conversation was on a lighter note, but Linda did ask a few more questions about Dana's illness. Annick was surprised how well Linda had maintained her composure. Hopefully, she hadn't stirred up too much suspicion with her questions about Simione. At the end of the evening, they agreed to meet in the next week or so for lunch.

The traffic was light. Annick was still thinking about the evening when she accelerated up the entrance ramp to the Long Island Expressway and her cell phone rang.

"Hello."

"How did your dinner go?" Mac asked.

"Actually, a lot better than I thought. Linda seems to be doing pretty well under the circumstances."

"She's a tough lady. There's no question about it."

"I wouldn't want to be walking in her shoes at the moment," Annick responded.

"I guess I wouldn't either. I just finished up at the hospital. I was going over to the Food Court for some dinner. I could use some company."

Annick glanced down at the digital clock above the speedometer. She was a little tired but the thought of spending some time with Mac was too appealing to pass up.

"I'm about fifteen minutes away," she said.

"I'll see you there," came his enthusiastic response.

Annick easily merged into the westbound traffic. Turning the radio to a light jazz station, she thought carefully about what Linda had said about Dana. The mellow notes of an alto saxophone filled the car, helping her to relax and, at least for the moment, diverting her attention from the strange events at Franklin Children's.

Chapter Twenty-eight

Just as Grady pulled into his parking space, he recognized Annick's silhouette passing under one of the bright floodlights. She was wearing a short wool coat with an oversized leather carry-on hoisted high on her shoulder. He got out of his SUV and caught up to her as she was approaching her car.

"Dr. Clement? Is that you?" he asked, making a fist to cover his mouth as he spoke.

She appeared to him only slightly startled. "Yes, it is."

Grady took a couple of steps forward and gently stroked the trunk of her BMW. "Now this is a driving machine," he said and followed it with a low whistle. "I'm glad I'm not the one making the monthly payments on this automobile."

She looked over at his Lexus with a degree of skepticism. "That's not exactly a Ford Escort you're driving."

"It's none of my business, Dr. Clement, but I know for a fact that a lot of the female residents have security escort them to their cars at night." He stopped and looked around cautiously. "About two years ago, right here in this parking lot—there were two nurses raped. Administration will deny it, but believe me, it happened."

"Thank you for your concern, but I have a black belt in martial arts and feel quite comfortable taking care of myself." She glanced down at her watch and smiled for just a moment.

"I'm really sorry about that communication screwup the other day. Bobbie and I spoke about it for quite some time. She said she was going to give you a call."

"I was kind of busy today," Annick said. "Maybe I missed it."

"I sure hope it didn't cause a problem for you. I know you guys are always under the microscope and could lose your job at the drop of a hat."

Annick folded her arms. "It's a big hospital. I guess these things happen. Fortunately the child did fine, in spite of the misinformation you gave me."

"Actually, we determined it was a specimen labeling error," Grady said. "So neither of us were at fault. If it's caused you a problem with Dr. Howe, I'd be happy to call him and—"

"That won't be necessary, Grady. I really don't think Dr. Howe accepts calls from lab techs."

"Sure he does." Grady corrected her in his most cordial voice. "I call him all the time with culture results. We're practically on a first-name basis. It would be kind of like me calling you Annick."

Disregarding his last comment, she said, "Hopefully in the future, we won't have any further problems communicating about culture results."

"I certainly hope not."

"Thank you," she said and got into her car.

Although Annick was an attractive woman, she did nothing for Grady sexually. Impotence was something he had learned to live with. A long string of performance failures with various women and prostitutes had done nothing to diminish his ego, and he instead blamed his inadequacy on their inability to arouse him.

Annick pulled out carefully and sped off without acknowledging his wave. Grady checked the time and then started across the parking lot. He had ten minutes to clock in before his shift started.

From a few rows away, a tall man with long straight black hair emerged from a dark minivan. He was dressed in a tan knee-length topcoat with his hands buried in the front pockets.

Expressionless, he rolled his shoulders, pulled his hands out and blew on them for warmth. Reaching in through the open window, he pulled a cell phone off the front seat and tapped in a number. The conversation was brief and as soon as it was over, he got back into his van and quickly left the parking lot.

Chapter Twenty-nine

Since coming to work at Franklin, Grady had made it his business to cultivate as many friendships with employees from other departments as possible. One in particular, Alan Mitchell, was a pharmacist's assistant. They never socialized outside the hospital but dined together frequently while at work.

It was nearly two A.M., when Grady tapped in the access code to the pharmacy. The buzzer sounded immediately, unlocking the door and allowing him to push it open. Six feet tall and looking at least a decade younger than his fifty years, Alan was a plain, unassuming man whose reach never exceeded his grasp. Every few years he'd wrestle with the idea of applying to pharmacy school but never did, remaining content in his present position, preparing medications for administration.

"How's it going?" Grady asked as he approached Alan. "What about that break we talked about?"

Alan glanced up at the clock. "You're about twenty minutes early. How's everything?"

"Same old, I'm afraid. Just taking it one day at a time," he said in a singsong voice as he patted Alan on the back.

Alan's bench was covered with dozens of medications. Most of them were pills but several were in liquid form in small plastic cups. Each group of medicines was laid out by its corresponding hospital unit. Grady looked at the desktop. The drugs being prepared for Four West, the gastro unit, where the children with severe vomiting and diarrhea of a contagious nature were hospitalized, were right in the middle.

"How's Kathy and the kids?" Grady asked.

"They're doing fine. Tess just got accepted to Duke, early decision. Everybody's delirious with joy about it."

"That's great."

"I guess," he said with a proud grin. "I'm still trying to figure out how we're going to pay for it."

Grady smiled and patted his colleague on the back for a second time. "These things have a way of working themselves out. And if not, that's what they have student loans for. And if that doesn't work, give me a call. I'll help."

"I appreciate the thought," Alan said after letting out a long breath.

"Are you ready to go?" Grady asked.

Alan looked a little perplexed. "I still haven't had a chance to go to the E.R. That's why I told you to come down at quarter after two."

Grady snapped his fingers. "That's right. You did tell me that. I think I'm getting senile."

"I should be back in about ten minutes. Do you want me to meet you in the cafeteria?"

"What about all this?" Grady asked, pointing to the mountain of unfinished work on the desk.

Alan sighed. "I guess it'll hold till we get back."

"I don't mind waiting," Grady offered.

After taking another long look at the half-filled medication orders, he said, "Okay, I'll stop back here and finish up before we go to the cafeteria."

As Alan grabbed his lab coat and headed for the door, Grady sat down and took a casual look around. This was not the first time he'd been in the pharmacy during the graveyard shift. Over the past several months, he had become quite familiar with the usual personnel and their activities.

In addition to Alan, there was a registered pharmacist and two other techs. As was generally the case, the pharmacist, Jobeth Childs, was in her office, seated behind a large bay win-

dow that overlooked the entire department. Having graduated
pharmacy school only eighteen months earlier, she was still a
little wet behind the ears. Serious and single-minded, Jobeth
was developing into an excellent pharmacist.

One tech, whose only job was to prepare chemotherapy
agents for the cancer patients, was secluded in a corner working intently under a sterile hood. The other tech was a trou-
bleshooter who spent most of her time out on the floors
assisting the nurses with medication questions and problems.

An easygoing glance over his shoulder revealed Jobeth to be
still sitting behind her desk. His back was directly to her. Grady
sat with his fist clenched and his eyes riveted on the medications intended for Four West. A mysterious smile crossed his
face as his hand opened slightly and moved ever so slowly forward.

Alan had been gone about ten minutes. Grady picked up a drug
advisory he had started to read earlier and flipped through the
pages. He found the soft music coming from the pharmacy's
stereo system too unsophisticated for his ear. Not minding the
characteristic odor of the microbiology lab, he found the distinctive medicinal aroma of the pharmacy offensive.

Looking up, he saw Alan coming toward him.

"How did everything go in the E.R.? You weren't down
there very long," Grady said.

"They only had one med for me to check. I'll be done here
in a few minutes. Do you have any time left on your break?"

"Things are quiet in the lab. They won't miss me. Take your
time. Hey, of all of us, you're the guy who can't make a
mistake."

Just before Alan sat down, Grady stole another peek in the
direction of Jobeth's office. She was no longer behind her desk
but had moved outside and was staring directly at him. Wearing
a knee-length white coat with a plain white blouse, she stood
there with an earnest face. He forced a smile, but instead of responding she turned and went back to her office.

Grady sat quietly for the next fifteen minutes while Alan finished up his work.

"I'm ready," Alan said.

Grady smiled and stood up. "Let's go."

The two spent only about twenty minutes in the cafeteria. The conversation was light, mostly about Alan's kids and Grady's ideas of how to reorganize the lab to give more authority to the techs, but from the time they had left the pharmacy for the cafeteria, Grady had had an uneasy feeling. Even after Alan left and Grady started back to the microbiology lab, he was unable to totally dismiss Jobeth Childs's strange look and spent the remainder of the shift wondering what she had seen and if she would become a problem.

Chapter Thirty

After a hectic three days that included twenty new consults, an unexpected outbreak of the flu and a near epidemic of bronchitis, Annick and Mac delighted in the thought that they both had Sunday off. Just before parting company at almost midnight, Annick invited Mac over for brunch in the morning. They had been spending a lot of their time off together, both enjoying the other's company more than they would care to admit. Mac had become comfortable opening up to Annick about the most personal parts of his life, but until this morning, the topics of Michael Flannery, Dana Vitale and bioterrorism had not been broached for several days.

"You're a big girl, Annick. I'm not going to tell you what to do." Mac's tone was serious, not confrontational, but Annick was still a little put off by it.

"I'm only asking for your opinion, Mac. I'm not going to hold it against you one way or the other."

Mac squirmed a little in the tan leather love seat that sat catty-corner to the matching couch. A beautiful burled wall unit with black trim stood against the far wall. Behind its curved glass doors, dozens of Annick's crystal collectibles were perfectly arranged under soft lighting.

"I've listened to everything you've said," he stated.

"I appreciate that, but that's a statement of fact, not an opinion."

"Listen, Annick. I can't say that any of your observations aren't interesting. You've certainly spent a lot of time gathering information, but all of it is probably coincidental and circumstantial." Mac leaned forward and placed his empty plate on a glass coffee table. "To be honest with you, the only thing I'm really happy about is that you've had the sense to keep this thing to yourself." His eyes drifted up as he wrinkled his brow. "I don't even want to think what Dr. Howe and the administration would do if they knew what you were up to."

"Is that what I'm supposed to be worried about?"

Mac waited a moment and then said, "Well, it might be something to give some serious thought to . . . especially if you're interested in the I.D. fellowship."

Annick moved to the end of the couch and propped her feet on the coffee table. Talking to Mac about her concerns was not a capricious decision. She appreciated his diplomatic nature, but she was hoping to spark some concern in him.

"I still think somebody's behind all this," she insisted.

"It's a little far-fetched," Mac offered.

Annick pulled her legs off the table and stood up. "It looks like the only way you're going to believe me is if some kid shows up in the emergency room with smallpox." Annick stopped for a moment. Even though her comment was impetuous, the hypothetical stirred a question in her mind. "Supposing we do see another bizarre case? Would that change your opinion?"

Mac reached for another piece of banana bread and set it on his plate. "That's a tough one," he answered.

"C'mon, Mac," she said, shaking her head. "Get off the fence for two minutes and answer my question."

"I thought I had," he said in an emphatic voice. "My conclusions would be based on the particular circumstances of the case. How's that?"

She leaned forward and shook her index finger at him. "I'm going to take that as a maybe, which implies that you still might have an open mind."

Mac raised his hands over his head, palms toward the ceiling. "If that's the implication you draw . . . so be it."

"You're a shithead, Mac," she said, picking up a small throw pillow and tossing it in his direction.

"You are certainly entitled to your opinion. But I remind you that I've been insulted by the best of them, and compared to them, mademoiselle, you are a hopeless amateur."

"Is that so?" she said.

"It is, and by the way, I love it when you call me dirty names. It stirs me . . . and one other thing: I certainly hope you're going to be a little more laid back in Paris than you have been for the last few days."

Annick fell forward on the couch in total frustration. "What do you say we watch a movie?"

"Sounds great."

"Pick one out," she said.

The conversation turned to less inflammatory topics as they enjoyed the remainder of the morning. Mac's conscience eventually got the best of him and he decided to spend an hour or two at the hospital just to make sure he didn't arrive back to work the next morning with a bunch of unexpected problems.

Lying on the couch, Annick wondered why she and Mac hadn't made love yet. It was probably because he sensed she wasn't ready. Maybe her conflict about becoming intimate with one of her fellow residents was more obvious than she realized. With her confidence slipping a little and being plagued by second thoughts, she even started to wonder if she should have thought the whole Paris idea out a little more carefully before asking him to join her. Inviting someone you were clearly attracted to to the most romantic city in the world must send a pretty clear message. She viewed herself as a fairly intuitive woman when it came to men, but she wasn't sure how she'd feel if she did sleep with Mac and soon became nothing more than another feather in his cap.

She reached over and tucked a small pillow under her arm. Her mind was still doing back flips, but she was more exhausted than she realized. She tried to put the matter of Mac Eastwick on the back burner for the moment, but he nonetheless remained on her mind as she slowly drifted off to sleep.

Chapter Thirty-one

"What the hell happened between you and Jobeth Childs when I went to the emergency room this morning?" Alan Mitchell asked Grady.

"Jobeth Childs?" Grady asked calmly as he sat on the side of his bed. It was just after nine A.M.; he had only been home a couple of hours, and the last person he expected a call from was Alan Mitchell.

"She was the pharmacist in charge," Alan said.

"I didn't even speak to her."

"Well, she sure had a bunch of questions about you."

"Really? What kinds of questions?" Grady asked.

"She wanted to know how long you've worked at Franklin. Why you come up to the pharmacy and how well I know you."

"That's strange," Grady said. "Is that information really any of her business?"

"She wanted to know if you had any experience in the pharmacy."

"What did you tell her?"

"I told her you didn't," Alan assured him. "She also wanted to know what department you worked in and for how long you've been there."

Grady stood up and paced. "You were only gone a few minutes. All I did was sit there and wait for you."

Alan went on, "Then she wanted to know if I thought you were trustworthy."

"Are you kidding?" Grady asked.

"Well, we are working in a pharmacy."

"So? Why would she ask that?"

"I have no idea. But she wanted to know what your usual schedule was. I got the feeling she was going to call your supervisor. Maybe she just doesn't want people she doesn't know hanging out in the pharmacy. I probably should have introduced you."

"Or maybe I should have introduced myself," Grady said, far from convinced that Alan's take on things was correct.

"I wouldn't take too much of this to heart," Alan advised. "She's always in a bad mood. Maybe it's the trip out from Manhattan every day."

"Living in the city can be a bitch," Grady said. "I wouldn't want to be making that commute every day."

"Me neither."

"Listen, Alan, it was nice of you to call. If I get hauled into Bobbie's office, at least I'll be ready. If she asks any more questions, put in the good word for me."

"I already have."

"Thanks."

"You'd do the same for me. I'll speak to you at work."

Grady hung the phone up, walked into the living room and tuned the stereo to his favorite classical music station. Using a pencil to conduct the orchestra, he found his way to the reclining rocker. Reviewing Alan's call slowly in his mind, he still wasn't convinced that there was a clear and present danger to his work. Even if a suspicion had been raised and he was questioned about it, he would be comfortable dealing with it. It wasn't like he'd never been in that position before. A confident smile came to his face when he thought about how easily he had handled the Delaware authorities when he was questioned about four of his coworkers suddenly becoming violently ill. He could still smell the fresh paint and see every stick of furniture in the detective's office. Calm and viewing the detective as intellectually unarmed compared to himself, Grady remembered almost welcoming the interview to toy with the man.

His eyes closed slowly as the images became clearer.

"I'm sorry I can't be of more help, Detective Calloway, but I barely know the people you're asking me about," Grady said.

Calloway, a serious man with a hulking physique and twenty years of experience, stared at Grady from across his desk. "I certainly appreciate you trying, Mr. Simione. We can't for the life of us figure out how these people all managed to turn up with very high levels of pesticide in their body."

Grady looked around, leaned in and lowered his voice. "It's a big organization we work for. Maybe they're having a rodent problem they don't want the whole world to know about. If I were you, I'd have an independent exterminator go in there and see if there's a family of rats living in the basement."

"Help me a little here. Why wouldn't the lab tell us if they were having a problem like that?"

Grady looked at the man as if he were a child stuck on a simple math problem. "I'm sure that would make for great publicity. I can just see the headlines now," he said with a touch of theatrics as he raised his hand in front of his face, moving it from left to right as he spoke. "'Highly sophisticated and sterile lab infested with rodents.'" Grady laughed. "I'm sure that would do wonders for their business."

Calloway nodded and then asked, "So you think these folks were accidentally poisoned?"

"Of course. Who the hell would intentionally poison four innocent people?"

"I'm not sure. All I know is that four apparently healthy people all ate dinner three nights ago in the lab's employee cafeteria between six and six-thirty and now they're all sick as hell."

"I'm sure it was an accident," Grady said again.

"According to the lab's records, you were working that night."

"That's correct," Grady said.

"You wouldn't have any reason for being in the kitchen that night, would you, Mr. Simione?"

"Only to cut through."

Calloway smiled. "What do you mean?"

"It's faster from my lab to the cafeteria if I take a shortcut through the kitchen. I do it all the time."

"I think you already mentioned this but you're sure you don't know any of the people who got sick?" Calloway asked.

"I'm sorry, I don't. I'd really like to help, but I—"

"I hope I haven't offended you with my questions, but we're asking everyone the same ones. And I'm going to look into your rat theory," he said with a chuckle.

"I think you'll find that I may be right," Grady said as he got up.

"I'll let you know," Calloway assured him as he escorted him to the door. When Grady was well down the hall, the detective, who didn't suspect him of a thing, shook his head and said to himself, *"What a fruitcake."*

When the Brahms symphony ended, Grady opened his eyes. When all the facts regarding the victims finally surfaced, a total of six people required extended hospitalizations and two were erroneously diagnosed with surgical illnesses and underwent needless operations. Grady was well aware that the lab he'd been working for in Delaware had hired an exterminator when one of the supervisors had reported seeing a mouse. When this came to light, the police assumed the poisonings were accidental and Grady never heard another word about it. It hardly surprised him when he considered the meticulous way in which he planned and executed the poisonings. An innocent flash of the hand was all that was necessary to taint the rice pudding with the toxic substance he had so carefully chosen. There was nothing personal involved—there never was.

His only regret was that he was unable to observe the horrific suffering he'd inflicted upon his fellow employees. To cause such devastating pain without offering your victim the escape that only death provides is a formidable goal, but one that he had attained.

The room was a little chilly but Grady hardly noticed. He reached for a manila folder marked RICIN, which lay on a small end table next to his recliner. Turning on a lamp with a pearl white shade, he opened the file and began reviewing in meticulous detail the specific characteristics of one of the most deadly and easily obtainable poisons known to man.

PART
Two

Chapter Thirty-two

Mac had left the hospital at four-thirty after spending over an hour with Kevin and the two residents who had offered to cover the I.D. service while he was overseas. The realization that he was within hours of boarding a private aircraft and jetting off to Paris with fabulously wealthy people left him with just a touch of apprehension. He packed twice, checked and then rechecked everything in his apartment before finally locking up.

It took him an hour and a half to make the trip from his house to Newark International Airport, making it just after seven P.M. when he arrived. He had offered to give Annick a ride but she had left earlier to meet her father in Manhattan for lunch and an afternoon of shopping before going on to the airport. Mac parked his car, grabbed his suitcase off the backseat and headed toward the terminal. He was dressed in his best gray dress slacks, a white button-down shirt and a blue double-breasted blazer.

The corporate travel terminal was nicely laid out with an operations desk on one side and seating for about twenty people on the other. There was a huge bay window overlooking the flight line. A bar, well stocked with snacks and drinks, occupied the far corner. The walls were painted pale blue and covered with large color photos of business aircraft.

A slender young lady working behind the desk in a dark green uniform was the only person in the terminal when Mac came through the doors. As he approached the counter, Mac took note of her name tag, which read "Jody Hopkins."

"Hi, my name is Mac Eastwick. I'm suppose to join Mr.—"

"Mr. Clement is expecting you, Dr. Eastwick." She gazed up at a large clock hanging above the automatic glass doors that led to the tarmac. "He phoned a few minutes ago. He should be here any moment."

"What time does the flight leave?"

"When Mr. Clement arrives," Jody said with a bright smile.

Feeling a little foolish for asking such a dumb question, Mac turned around and looked out the window. "I left my car parked against the fence. Is there someplace I should move it?"

"It will be fine there," Jody assured him.

"I probably won't be back for a few days."

"Don't worry, Dr. Eastwick," she said. "Most of our clients leave their cars with us until they return. Sometimes they're gone for weeks. The area's patrolled twenty-four hours a day."

Mac nodded with a plain expression. Above all, he was a realist, and it was quite obvious that Jody had not mistaken him for a seasoned corporate jet-setter.

"What should I do with my bag?" he asked.

"The crew will be here in a minute. They're just preflighting the aircraft. They'll stow all the bags when the rest of your party arrives."

Mac turned when he heard the whoosh of the electric doors opening and watched as Annick and two men entered the terminal. She was dressed in a fuchsia warm-up outfit that Mac estimated to be worth more than his entire wardrobe. A tan leather carry-on hung over her shoulder. Her arm was interlocked with her father's.

"Mac, this is my father, Luc Clement."

Mac extended his hand and caught himself swallowing hard. "It's a pleasure to meet you."

"And this is his associate, Philippe Descartes." Mac smiled and shook the rangy gentleman's hand as well. Mac gazed out the window. There was a large white limousine parked directly in front of the door with its trunk open. The area was brightly lit and Mac could see two men in white coveralls unloading the luggage and placing it on a cart.

"Why don't you and Mac get on the plane?" Luc suggested with an ample smile. "We have a long flight. There'll be plenty of time for me to get acquainted with Mac once we're on board. Philippe and I will join you in a few minutes. We have a couple of last-minute phone calls to make."

She smiled, kissed her dad on the cheek and waited until he and Philippe started toward the desk.

"Are you really going to travel in those clothes?" she asked Mac in a whisper.

Mac looked down at himself in despair, wondering why he spent forty-five minutes trying to figure out what to wear. "Actually, these are just my takeoff clothes. Once we're airborne, I'm going to change into my ballroom attire. Even as we speak, they're loading my favorite polo pony onto the plane."

"You're a funny guy," she said under a soft giggle while she flattened out the lapel of his sport coat.

Mac distinctly remembered Annick telling him that her father had just celebrated his fifty-third birthday. Not that Mac had a particular talent for guessing ages, but Luc didn't look a day over forty. His five o'clock shadow blended into his deep, ruddy complexion. At five feet nine with dark brown eyes and a pencil mustache, Luc tended toward the stocky side, but his fingers were tapered and delicate. Dressed in perfectly pressed black dress slacks, three-hundred-dollar Italian shoes and a thin gray cashmere turtleneck, Luc Clement was exactly what Mac would describe as the debonair and affluent European businessman.

Escorted by Jody, Mac and Annick left the terminal and headed across the tarmac. It was a cool, windless night with a luminous full moon. The relative silence was abruptly broken by the deafening roar of a large jet hurtling down the runway. Mac followed Annick up the short stairway and entered the Gulfstream V.

What he found himself gazing upon in no way resembled anything he'd ever seen on a commercial jet. The smack of the aircraft was one of fresh leather. The cabin was softly lighted with seating for fifteen. There were four berthable white leather club chairs toward the front of the cabin that faced a beautifully constructed handcrafted wood credenza. A mini galley and a small buffet occupied the area directly behind the flight deck.

The instant the four of them were aboard, the copilot secured the door, and two minutes later they were taxiing out to the active runway. Another fifteen minutes passed and they were at their cruising altitude of thirty-one thousand feet.

"How do you like the trip so far?" Luc asked Mac.

Mac couldn't help but smile. "It certainly beats flying Delta."

"Annick wasn't sure you were going to make it."

"It was an offer I couldn't refuse. I've always wanted to see Paris."

"Well, you'll have three solid days to do it. I'm returning to the States on Friday. We'll drop you and Annick in New York on our way to Washington, D.C."

"How often are you in the States?" Mac asked, trying to keep the conversation going.

"I'd say about twice a month," he answered, unbuckling his seat belt, walking over to the galley and opening the refrigerator. He removed a bottle of imported beer and then poured it slowly down the side of a pilsner glass. "Can I get you anything, Mac?"

"No, thank you." He stole a peek at Annick, who was sitting in the back of the cabin talking and giggling with Philippe.

"Don't be jealous," Luc told him. "Annick has known Philippe since she was fourteen. He adores her but I'm afraid she'll always see him as her big brother. Nothing romantic will ever come of their relationship. Philippe's been with me ever since he got his master's from Wharton. He's got an uncanny gift for research and development. He's headed up our division for the last six years."

"He sounds like an interesting guy."

"His real passion is flying. If he could make the same money he's making now flying for a living, I don't think I'd ever see him again. He's probably got more hours in jets than the guys up front right now. Generally he does some of the flying, but he seems a little preoccupied tonight."

Mac nodded and then looked out the window for a moment.

It was a clear night and the lights along the eastern coast of New England were clearly visible.

"My daughter tells me you're an excellent physician."

"Your daughter's prone to exaggeration, sir."

"Sir? Let's stick with Luc. She may tend to shoot from the hip from time to time but she's an excellent judge of character, and she certainly speaks highly of you." Luc took a long swallow of the beer and then wiped his lips with a small cocktail napkin. "I've been looking forward to meeting you."

Mac gazed at Luc politely, feeling a little like an object of art at Sotheby's on display prior to the auction. He looked around the cabin. "Your jet is beautiful."

"Thank you. We just recently acquired it."

"Your daughter's an exceptional person," Mac said.

Luc had just raised the glass to his lips, then pulled it back and laughed. "I couldn't agree more. She's the light of my life, but I'm afraid I spoil her too much."

"I didn't mean to sound so direct," Mac explained.

"Don't give it another thought. As a matter of fact, I could use more of that kind of honesty in my corporation. Maybe you'll consider coming to work for me when you've completed your medical training."

Mac swiveled in his chair and decided to go along with Luc's offer. "In what capacity? You couldn't have much need for a near destitute pediatric infectious disease specialist."

"To the contrary. We're always exploring new ideas and developing new companies. We even have a couple on the cutting edge of health care."

"Well, I'm afraid there's nothing cutting edge about infectious diseases." Mac could already understand why Annick felt the way she did about her father. He was obviously an extremely perceptive man with a disarming personality. It was hardly a mystery why he had achieved such enormous financial success. "What business would I have to learn?" Mac asked.

"We are an international group of highly specialized investment bankers. We concentrate on acquiring companies and pursuing ideas that other more . . . shall we say, traditional financial conglomerates have passed on."

"Sounds complicated," Mac said.

"Everything's relative. What's complicated to one man is elementary to the next." Luc placed the pilsner on the small writing table in front of him. "It's just a matter of what you become accustomed to. I've been doing this for a long time . . . perhaps too long."

"What would your second choice have been?" Mac asked.

"That's a good question. You can oftentimes judge a man by the questions he asks. Let's see . . . probably to have conquered Mount Everest."

"It might be difficult to make a living doing that," Mac offered.

"Perhaps, but not when your grandmother died when you were nineteen and left you twenty million dollars."

Mac whistled almost as a reflex and then shook his head. "You could probably buy Everest for that."

Luc laughed. "I'm a very wealthy guy, Mac. I'm sure my daughter has told you that. But there are a lot of men out there who started with nothing that have made more money in their lifetimes than I'll ever see." Luc paused for a moment before adding, "Don't be fooled. Not everything that glitters is gold. Ours is a tough business. Million-dollar decisions are often made on a whim or a flash intuition, and at times things can get pretty cutthroat. It's not a profession for the faint of heart."

Luc and Mac spoke easily for the next two hours on everything from the arts to global warming. Mac had to confess that whatever his first impression had been about Luc's intellect was probably a gross underestimate. The flight proceeded smoothly thanks to an eighty-mile-an-hour tailwind. Not the most comfortable of flyers, Mac was gratified that there wasn't a bump of turbulence.

Mac turned around and looked at Annick. Philippe was already asleep. She was curled up on a short couch under a halogen spotlight reading a medical journal. An empty wineglass sat on the small table next to her. Mac looked over at Luc, who was also looking toward the aft section of the jet. When she saw them both staring at her she made a silly face and then returned to her journal.

"I really love that girl," Luc said.

"She's pretty crazy about you too."

He looked at his watch. "I think I'll get some sleep. I have a meeting in the morning. Maybe you ought to spend some time with her. She can pout with the best of them when she's ignored."

Mac extended his hand. "That's an excellent suggestion. I enjoyed speaking with you."

"We'll spend more time together in Paris," he promised.

Mac got up and walked to the back of the plane and took the seat across from Annick.

"I'm glad you two didn't have anything to talk about," she said sarcastically. "I didn't think you'd ever come back here."

"He's an interesting guy."

"What's that you were drinking?" she asked, pointing to an empty cocktail glass.

"I had a little scotch," he confessed. "Your dad insisted."

"That was very politically correct of you."

Mac looked over at Philippe, who was fully reclined and sound asleep. He was a thin man with deep-set eyes, casually dressed in jeans and a black shirt. Mac couldn't help but wonder if there really wasn't anything between him and Annick.

"What did Dad tell you about him?"

"Who?"

"Him. That's who," she said, pointing at Philippe.

"Not too much. He mentioned in passing that you two have been lovers for years."

"I don't think so but try again," she encouraged as she rolled up her journal in a tight spiral and held it in front of his face.

"He said he was a superb businessman who was very loyal," Mac said.

"Is that all?"

"Pretty much." Mac thought for a moment before asking, "Are you afraid he divulged something about you two?"

Annick covered her mouth to smother a laugh. "Hardly. He knows better than that. Philippe's a pretty creative guy but even with his imagination there's no way."

Philippe opened his eyes, yawned and then smiled. "It's too noisy back here to sleep, plus I find it boring when people talk about me." He looked over at Mac as he popped a piece of hard candy into his mouth. "Do you have any idea what you're getting yourself into?" he asked with the most dramatic, serious expression he could muster.

"I can't tell you how many times I've asked myself that same question."

"Well, at least you're more insightful than those that have preceded you," he joked.

Annick looked scornful. "Did you miss the announcement, Philippe?"

"I beg your pardon?"

"The pilots said they needed some help up front," she explained, trying to hold back a smile.

"Our crew doesn't make announcements, Annick, but perhaps I will go forward for a bit." Philippe stood up, leaned over as if he were going to pick something up, and instead kissed Annick on the top of her head. "We'll have to have a lengthy talk when I return," he said to Mac.

"I'll look forward to it." Philippe made his way past them. Mac looked at the clock above the entrance to the flight deck. "Five more hours. When does the movie start?" he joked.

"Actually, that center portion of the buffet opens and a TV pops up. There's about twenty movies to pick from in that bottom drawer," she told him.

"I was kidding, Annick."

"I'm not."

"What are we going to do tomorrow?" he asked.

"Not go to sleep."

"I beg your pardon?" he said.

"On your first day, you have to stay awake until at least nine P.M. Paris time or it will screw you up for a week."

"Okay," he agreed. "So what do we do?"

"We'll go out and see some of the sights and then go out to dinner with my father."

"Sounds great," he said.

They talked for about a half hour before Annick picked up a phone and asked the captain to make the cabin a little warmer. Pulling a light woolen blanket over her, she pointed to one of the bigger chairs. "Why don't you get some sleep. We started rounds at six-thirty this morning."

Mac found his way to the chair, rocked it all the way back and closed his eyes. The drone of the engines was soothing and any doubts he had about falling asleep were more imagined than real. The next sound he heard was the captain requesting they fasten their seat belts for their landing at Charles de Gaulle Airport.

Chapter Thirty-three

After clearing customs and making their way out of the terminal, Luc's Mercedes limousine was waiting for them. The drive in from the airport took only about a half hour. There was a bit of traffic on A106, but once they began traversing the city, Mac had the opportunity to get his first real view of the quintessential Parisian architecture. Small streets with paved stones led to wide boulevards and modern squares. When they passed over Pont de l'Alma, Mac watched as lazy barges filled with goods gently navigated their way down the Seine.

Moving quickly around L'Etoile Circle, Mac marveled for the first time at the imposing arches and perfect symmetry of the Arc de Triomphe. The limo made a quick turn down Avenue Foch and came to a stop in front of the Clements' apartment, an impressive example of French gothic architecture created with cut-stone masonry placed with meticulous attention.

An elderly uniformed doorman with snow-white hair opened the door and welcomed the Clements back to Paris. Mac was the first one out of the car. It was a crystal-clear day with a mild breeze and warmer than he'd expected.

The apartment itself was located on the fourth floor. Mac was a little too tired to appreciate the detail of its magnificent furnishings and spacious nature, but even in his fatigued state he knew he was in a place like no other he'd ever seen. In spite of Annick's warning and, as accustomed as he was to staying up all night, the thought of a brief nap did cross his mind.

"Why don't you grab a shower and we'll do some sightseeing?" Annick suggested.

Mac agreed and she showed him to his room. Thirty minutes later they left the apartment. Once Mac was out and exploring what some would consider the most beautiful city in the world, the thought of sleep was the furthest thing from his mind. As the day progressed, he became awestruck and enthralled by Paris. Their last stop was the Museum d'Orsay, perhaps the finest collection of impressionist paintings in the world. Mac never fancied himself an art connoisseur but he found the museum, which was once a train station, captivating. After two hours, Annick had to drag him kicking and screaming back to the apartment in time to get ready to meet Luc for dinner at his favorite restaurant.

As soon as they had showered and dressed, they were on their way again. After a short cab ride, a squatty man with a broad smile opened the double glass doors to the restaurant. With Annick leading, they descended a narrow sloped staircase that led to the center of the modernistic dining room. On the far wall, a series of booths were divided by sloped green leather partitions. On the opposite side, a bar ran the entire length of the restaurant. Perfectly arranged bottles of alcohol stacked in racks were only partially visible because of the expansive frosted glass doors that slid back and forth in front of them. Luc was already seated at a glass table.

"Tell me about your first impression of our city," Luc said to Mac.

Mac reached for the napkin in front of him and placed it on his lap. The hand-painted china sparkled. "You live in an incredible city," he told Luc.

Luc winked at his daughter. "A man of great insight, I see. What were your favorite sights?"

Mac answered without hesitation. "Napoleon's tomb and the impressionists' museum. I'd love to go back and see them again."

"We still have some other things to see," Annick reminded him. "It's a little hard to cover the entire city in three days."

"Are you going to see Professor Aaron?" Luc asked his daughter.

"Absolutely," she said. "I called him this afternoon. We're going over there the day after tomorrow. He's arranged a tour for Mac."

A young man dressed entirely in black placed large menus with gold embossed borders in front of them.

"I'm sure you'll enjoy that. The Pasteur Institute is quite a place."

"I've read a lot about it," Mac said.

Luc took the liberty of ordering and the conversation flowed easily. Any apprehension Mac had about the evening soon evaporated. They were already on their second bottle of wine when the waiter served them each a delicate vegetable soup, which Mac found to be like none he had ever tasted. Engrossed in the ambience of the restaurant, his head swirling a little from the wine, he took no note of Annick and Luc's amused expressions at Mac's obvious excitement by all that surrounded him. Mac had hardly finished his soup when the waiter returned with the main course, chateaubriand with bearnaise sauce that was cooked to perfection.

When they finished dinner, they returned to the apartment and went into the library. On three of the four walls, oak floor-to-ceiling bookshelves with a sliding wooden ladder were filled to capacity with books from the last two centuries. As soon as they sat down, Marcel brought them each an after-dinner liqueur.

"Where do you think you'd like to live after you finish your training?" Luc asked Mac.

"I haven't really given it much thought. From what I've seen today, I wouldn't mind working here," he said. "But I guess I'll probably wind up wherever the best job is."

"Are you saying you could be happy anywhere?" Annick asked.

Mac reflected for a minute and then took a small sip of his apricot liqueur. "With the right person," he finally said.

Luc laughed. "It's nice to finally meet someone who can match wits with my daughter."

"Actually, when I talk to Annick, I feel like I'm in a chess game with a grand master who's always a dozen moves ahead of me."

"Well put," Luc said with a chuckle and then raised his glass in a toast. "With the present climate, I think you two are lucky to be physicians and not out in the business world." Luc took a second sip of the apricot liqueur and set the glass down on a small end table. "Many of my days are spent trying to outfox cutthroat individuals who possess neither the soul nor the understanding for our chosen profession. Survival with dignity is becoming more and more difficult."

Mac listened carefully, taking particular note of the somber and serious look in his eyes. For the first time since he'd met Luc, he saw the fatigue in his face.

"I'm not sure medicine hasn't taken its shots over the last twenty years," Annick observed.

Mac nodded in agreement. "I can't speak for France but according to a lot of thoughtful senior physicians, medicine's certainly not what it used to be."

Annick nodded.

"Perhaps," her father said.

They talked for about an hour before a lavish grandfather clock with etched glass doors and a beautiful brass mechanism chimed softly.

"I don't know about you two," Luc said, "but I've had a long day. I'll see you for breakfast." He turned to Annick. "I'm going to Prague tomorrow afternoon. I'll be back Thursday morning."

Annick crossed her arms in her signature pouting position. "We're only here for three days, Daddy. I thought you'd be here the whole time."

"I just learned today I have to go. We'll see each other for dinner Thursday and then we'll have the entire flight back to the States on Friday." He walked over and kissed his daughter on the forehead and then shook Mac's hand.

"Your dad's quite a guy," Mac said as soon as Luc closed the door.

"You don't have to convince me," she said with a look of affection. "He's always been there for me, trying to be both a mother and a father." Annick moved to the couch and curled up next to Mac.

"He certainly does a lot of traveling."

"Oh, I'm sure he didn't have to go to Prague tomorrow," she mentioned.

"What do you mean?"

"He just wanted to give us some privacy," she said.

Mac moved forward, forcing Annick to sit up.

"I beg your pardon?" he said.

"I'm almost thirty years old. I think he understands that."

Mac just shook his head. "I hope I'm so open-minded when it comes to my daughter."

"Don't worry about it," Annick said. "You won't be. Let's get some sleep." After a long kiss, Mac took Annick's hand and they walked slowly from the library to their bedrooms.

Mac changed into a pair of surgical scrubs for sleeping attire and walked over to the large window and pulled back the curtains. The view of Paris was striking, especially to the south, offering him a perfect image of the spectacularly illuminated Eiffel Tower. He stood there for twenty minutes, still in disbelief that he was actually in Paris. After getting into bed, he thought about Annick and how comfortable he was with her. It was a soothing feeling, and before long he was lulled into a deep sleep.

At the other end of the hall, Annick had decided to take a hot bath. Her bathroom was enormous, with ornate mirrors, shag carpet and a large marble tub. The smell of her lilac bath oil filled the air. Turning down the lights and easing her way into the tub, she closed her eyes and thought about Mac, still conflicted by good sense and what her heart wanted to do. She was hardly in the mood to lecture herself again about the inadvisability of getting romantically involved with a fellow resident.

She knew she'd been weakening over the past week or so, but just since the short time they'd been together in Paris, her protective barriers were tumbling left and right. Good sense aside, she was a very normal woman with very normal desires.

Her instinct told her that Mac cared for her deeply and she was sure she had profound feelings for him. Sweeping a handful of the warm water over her neck, her mind drifted to thoughts of being made love to by Mac Eastwick.

Chapter Thirty-four

Grady stood on the northwest corner of Seventh Avenue and Forty-first Street dressed in a tan corduroy coat, sunglasses and a sun-bleached Mets baseball cap. It was a gloomy afternoon, but by New York City standards it was only mildly overcast. Two men standing a few feet from Grady in flannel shirts and heavy industrial boots hovered around a hot dog cart inhaling their chili dogs.

Grady had learned two important facts from Alan's phone call. The first being that he should have trusted his first impression that Jobeth Childs suspected something. And secondly, she lived in Manhattan, a city with millions of preoccupied inhabitants pushing and shoving down the streets and avenues with little else on their minds except getting from point A to point B.

The file he so carefully reviewed on ricin was quite extensive. The poison was one of Grady's favorites because it was so easily extracted from the castor bean and was one of the most potent toxins known to man. During the summer of his junior year in high school, he acquired enough castor beans to become quite proficient in extracting the poison. It wasn't half the chore he thought it would be. When he finally convinced himself that he'd purified the poison, he proved the point by feeding the substance to his aunt's new litter of beagle puppies. Becoming violently ill from the massive overdose, none of them survived more than a few hours. Inconsolable and consumed with despair, his heartsick aunt accepted Grady's offer to take the puppies out to the woods and bury them respectfully near her favorite lake. After pouring alcohol on them and torching their tiny bodies, that's exactly what he did.

Grady had read that ricin had been identified as the agent used in a well-publicized political assassination in Europe. He had saved a report from London postulating that an injection device, loaded with a ricin pellet, had been fitted inconspicuously to an umbrella. The makeshift apparatus, which was actually quite easy to construct, was then used to assassinate a foreign diplomat. The diagram of the device was still vivid in his mind.

It had taken Grady two days of fairly intense surveillance to find out that Jobeth lived in midtown Manhattan, preferred to walk to Penn Station to catch the Long Island Railroad and seemed to take the same route each day. Holding his new umbrella tucked loosely under his arm, he glanced down at the thin plastic sheath that covered the specially modified tip. If his calculations were correct and Jobeth was only half as anal as Alan Mitchell had claimed, she would appear across the street at any moment on her way to catching the 4:49 train to Great Neck, which would give her more than adequate time to get to the hospital and set up for the evening shift.

Keeping a sharp eye open, Grady caught the first glimpse of her as she walked quickly down Seventh Avenue. Dressed in a purple business suit and a light coat, she carried a small attache. As soon as she was past him, he started across the street and fell in about thirty feet behind her. Continuing at exactly her pace, he looked ahead and smiled when the light on Fortieth Street turned red. A large group of anxious pedestrians came together in a herd, waiting impatiently for the light to turn green. With a few seconds to spare, Grady closed the distance between himself and Jobeth. Looking down, he could clearly see the bottom of her suit just above her plump calves.

Having timed the light and knowing it was about to change, he slowly lowered the umbrella tip to about one foot off the pavement. The mob of pedestrians waiting to cross the street grew—an impatient group of New Yorkers, all more preoccupied with their own agendas than an average-looking man with an umbrella.

The cars barreling east on Fortieth stopped quickly as the light turned red. The pack surged forward as if it were the beginning of the New York City Marathon. At the moment Grady stepped up on the opposite curb, he quickly jabbed Jobeth just below the knee and withdrew the fine needle. The tiny pellet it left behind buried in her muscle contained enough ricin to kill a man three times her weight. Without breaking stride, he immediately turned left, heading east on Fortieth Street while listening for a scream. He heard none and never looked back. The rush of adrenaline and pure maniacal excitement of what he had just accomplished consumed him like an overpowering religious revelation.

The moment he reached Sixth Avenue, he hailed a cab and took it to a parking lot on the Upper West Side where he'd left his Lexus. He never gave Jobeth a single thought on his way home. She was small potatoes . . . an insignificant player in a game she had neither the stomach nor intellectual capacity to understand. Annick Clement was a horse of a different color, possessing a mental level approaching his own. He couldn't help but grin when he thought about her little tirade after he'd set her up with those bogus spinal culture reports on Mandy Coe. If only she had stopped the antibiotics and the little girl had died. It would have been wonderful to watch her career come tumbling down like a bamboo hut in a monsoon.

"A patient with meningitis and Dr. Clement screws up the diagnosis," he said in a singsong voice that was followed by an immediate chuckle.

He would have given anything to be a fly on the wall when she tried to explain that dumb mistake to Dr. Howe. If she tried to shift the blame to him, he would have simply acted woebegone and suggest Dr. Clement must have misunderstood him. He wouldn't even take the opportunity to claim she bungled the case and was now trying to shift the blame to him. He could only imagine what Dr. Howe would have done with her. Wouldn't it have been perfect if she had gotten fired and sued for malpractice all in the same day. With a little bit of luck, An-

Chapter Thirty-five

It was Mac's third morning in Paris. Looking out through the enormous bay window of the Clements' breakfast room gave him a spectacular view of the city. Awakening with Annick in his arms less than an hour ago had left him in a dreamlike state. Any awkward feelings of uncertainties he harbored about sleeping with Annick melted away. Nothing could have been more natural or spontaneous.

It was nearly eight-thirty and the sidewalks below were already bustling with harried Parisians, some with the ends of freshly baked baguettes peeking out of long paper bags, on their way to work.

"How do you like the way the eggs are prepared?" she asked him as she finished her second helping.

"They're excellent."

She looked up from her plate for a second and then reached for a chocolate croissant. "You look content," she said.

He stopped eating his eggs Florentine for a moment and answered, "I've never felt better."

"I'm glad to hear that, because I thought you were worried that our relationship was going to wind up like all your others as soon as we made love."

Mac placed his sterling silver fork on his plate and tilted his head to one side. "I'm not sure I follow," he confessed.

"Sometimes making love changes things between friends."

Picking his fork back up, Mac pushed his eggs from one side of the plate to the other. "I can't think of a more perfect situation than making love to your best friend. It's something I've always looked forward to."

Annick plucked a couple of pieces of diced melon from a large fruit bowl in front of her. She had no regrets about her decision to sleep with Mac. She knew his feelings for her were genuine. "So you're saying you enjoyed last night?"

He looked up with a surprised expression. "Didn't it seem like it?"

"Of course," she assured him.

"What . . . what about you?" he asked in a way that seemed to be putting his machismo on the line.

"It was wonderful," she whispered. She got up, walked around the table, put her arms around his neck from behind and kissed him on the cheek. "It was more than sex, Mac. You made love to me. It doesn't get any better than that." A few moments of silence passed before Annick glanced over at the antique clock on the bureau. She knew Mac's silence spoke volumes. "We should get going," she said. "It will take us a good twenty minutes to get to the Pasteur Institute. I don't want to keep Dr. Aaron waiting."

Chapter Thirty-six

The Pasteur Institute is one of the most famous scientific facilities in the world. Equivalent to the CDC in Atlanta with respect to its mission, the institute remains on the cutting edge of scientific research and treatment in the field of infectious diseases.

For the third morning in a row, it was unseasonably warm and clear. Mac and Annick climbed the two flights of stairs, exited the metro station and walked at a brisk pace to the institute.

They walked through the institute's large main gate, which led to a pleasantly landscaped campus composed of several buildings varying widely in their architectural design, from beaux arts to Roman. Curved pathways crisscrossed the campus, connecting the various buildings.

Dr. Aaron's office was on the fourth floor of one of the basic research facilities. Having spent three months working in his lab, Annick was quite familiar with its location. They walked through the small lobby and took the elevator up.

The door to the office was open and Annick immediately spotted her favorite professor sitting behind his computer terminal with his usual curmudgeon scowl on. He was wearing his favorite gray sweater vest with a white shirt and no tie. Paunchy and round-faced with a full white beard and pale blue eyes, Dr.

Aaron more resembled a department-store Santa Claus than a distinguished scientist.

As soon as he saw her he stood up, came out from behind the desk and kissed her once on each cheek.

"Dr. Aaron, this is Mac Eastwick. He's a friend and colleague of mine, and a very gifted infectious disease specialist."

Red-faced from her comment, Mac immediately cleared his throat and tapped Annick's foot twice with his own. Being in the presence of a man who had accomplished far more in his career than Mac had even thought about was a bit intimidating.

"It's a pleasure to meet you," Aaron said in a deep French accent as he extended his hand.

"The pleasure's mine," Mac responded, shaking his hand. "I've long been an admirer of your work."

"That's kind of you to say. It's nice to see that a younger member of our profession still takes the ravings of an old man seriously. Luc Clement tells me that you're completing your training this year."

"That's correct."

"Have you decided on a position yet?"

"Not as yet," Mac said. "But I'm hoping to start interviewing this winter."

Aaron smiled. "I know you'll find just the right opportunity. Would you like to see the institute?"

"Very much."

"Good. I've asked one of my graduate students to take you on the royal tour. He's just across the hall. Come," Aaron said, motioning to Mac. "I'll be right back," he whispered to Annick in French.

Dr. Aaron's office hadn't changed a bit, being just as bare, musty and uninviting as she remembered it. Annick sat down on a lumpy and hideously upholstered love seat. Just above the love seat, a set of bookshelves filled with historic medical texts rose almost to the ceiling. A moment later, Aaron returned and took a seat behind his desk.

"Your young man is very nice," he said with a paternal tone to his voice.

"He's not exactly my young man, Professor."

"I'm an old man, so please don't try to pull the wool over my tired eyes."

Jacques Aaron was a respected scientist in the French medical community. After acquiring his M.D. from the Medical Faculty in Lille, he enrolled in a Ph.D. program in microbiology at the University of Wisconsin. When he completed his studies in 1965, he was offered a position at the Pasteur Institute, accepted it gladly and had been there ever since. A dedicated researcher, Jacques Aaron was a man who couldn't take no for an answer and still welcomed every new challenge that presented itself.

"Mac's a great doctor," she said. "I'm sure he'll do well wherever he chooses to settle."

"Is he interested in doing basic research?"

"I'm not sure." Annick gazed into the eyes of her mentor and old family friend. "You wouldn't be interested in offering him a position?"

Aaron rocked back, crossed his arms in front of himself and smiled modestly.

"We're always interested in cultivating new talent. A one-year fellowship might be just the thing he needs."

"Except for the fact that he doesn't speak French," she pointed out.

"I was going to leave that to you. If my memory serves me correctly, you are planning to do your chief residency at Enfant Malades right here in Paris before returning to the U.S. for your fellowship. The timing would be perfect."

"It sounds like you've been speaking to my father."

"Not a word," he said in all sincerity and then slapped his thighs. "Now, tell me about yourself. Are you enjoying your time in the U.S.?"

"So far, it's been a wonderful experience."

"Have you spent much time with my old friend David Howe?"

Annick frowned. "I'm on his service right now."

"From the look on your face, you don't seem very happy."

"He's a bit rigid and not very open to suggestions."

"I see," he said, stroking his wiry whiskers. "Are you sure you're not confusing rigidity with responsibility?"

Annick half closed her eyes and leaned in. "I'm not sure I understand what you're saying."

"He holds an important position in your hospital. He has to

make sure things get done efficiently and expeditiously, while at the same time assuring excellence in patient care. Maybe he doesn't have the time to listen to every new resident's suggestions about how he should do his job."

"We're getting along well and I've kept my opinions to myself."

"A wise approach," Aaron said.

Annick knew Mac would be gone for only about thirty minutes and she desperately wanted to broach the topic of the real reason for her visit today. "We've recently had some interesting cases," she began.

"Tell me about them," he encouraged.

"We treated a child for pneumonic plague and another for botulism, both within a week of each other."

"Where was the child with pneumonic plague from?" he asked.

"New York, but she had recently made a trip to California."

Aaron nodded. "And the case of botulism?"

"It was an isolated case. We've been unable to identify the source, and what's more interesting, the CDC in Atlanta can't identify the specific serotype."

"That is very interesting," Aaron said, pushing his delicate wire-rim glasses a little higher on the bridge of his nose. "You're sure there were no other cases of botulism . . . perhaps at another hospital or—"

Annick moved farther forward in her chair. "None. I checked with the New York State Health Department."

"Perhaps there were other cases that went undiagnosed," he suggested.

"That's kind of what I wanted to talk to you about. At about the same time, there was another child in the hospital who died. The cause of death was listed as septic shock resulting from diabetes but I've reviewed the chart and spoken with his aunt."

Aaron's smile was a guarded one. "And why did you do that?"

"Because I think he died of botulism."

"Why?"

"His symptoms were very specific for the disease. He was also a patient in the emergency room the same night the other child with botulism was admitted."

"Interesting, but that could be nothing more than a coincidence," he said.

"Maybe, but they both received a clear liquid tray in the E.R. and they both developed symptoms the very next day."

Aaron reached forward, picked up a pack of cigarettes and stared at them for a moment. Annick knew he hadn't smoked in years but always kept a pack on his desk. He tamped the pack down and slipped one of the unfiltered cigarettes into his mouth.

"You're not going to light that?" she asked with the correct blend of affection and respect.

"Of course not," he said, obviously in deep thought. "I don't even keep matches in the office. Was the boy with diabetes tested for botulism?"

"No."

"Why not?" he asked.

"Either nobody thought of the diagnosis or . . ."

"Or what?" Aaron inquired.

"If it was an afterthought and there was nothing that could be done for the boy . . . then I think there may have been pressure from the hospital administration not to pursue the real diagnosis."

"And why would they do that?"

"The possibility of bioterrorism was raised and it seems the thought of such negative publicity has made them all gun-shy. The competition for children's health care on Long Island is very keen. If word ever got out that two children had been poisoned with botulism toxin while awaiting care in our emergency room . . . well, the hospital would be devastated."

Aaron shook his head slowly in obvious dismay. "It's always disappointing to hear that scientific ignorance has no geographic boundaries." He paused for a moment and tossed the cigarettes back on the desk. "At the present time there are estimated to be at last sixty different types of bacterium, viruses and fungi that can be engineered into bioweapons. Our best estimates would tell us that we can only treat about a quarter of them." Aaron gazed upward and again stroked his beard rhythmically. "Have you discussed any of this with Mac?" he asked.

"I have," she said disappointedly.

"What did he say?"

"He's been polite but leery," she offered.

"It's easy to be skeptical when considering such a terrible thing."

Annick spent the next fifteen minutes relating every unusual event at Franklin Children's Hospital and then, in painstaking detail, she related Grady Simione's suspicious behavior.

"Dr. Aaron, you're an expert in bioterrorism. Do you think there's any possibility that we have a problem?"

"I'm not sure, Annick. We live in strange times. We have certainly failed to get the public's attention regarding the bio-hazards that exist in the world. With just a little bit of ingenuity and resources, almost anyone can acquire deadly biologic weapons." Annick watched his eyes as he stopped for a moment to stare with pride at an eight-by-ten portrait-style photograph of his three grandchildren.

"Do you think I'm being overly melodramatic about this whole thing?" she asked, knowing in her heart she was looking more for reassurance than a candid answer.

"I wouldn't be comfortable telling you there's absolutely no chance that these children have been the victims of a biologic weapon."

"Is there anything I should do?"

"I don't want to give you any advice that might place you in difficulty. If I should take the initiative and say something to David Howe, he might be very angry with you."

Annick sighed. "I feel like I'm between a rock and a hard place."

"Do you think you could send me a sample of the blood of the young man who recovered from botulism?"

"I don't see why not."

"And if you are able to acquire a sample from the other boy, I would like to analyze that as well."

Annick looked toward the door as she heard Mac's voice. She quickly looked back at Aaron. "I didn't mention to Mac that I was going to speak to you about all this. Maybe we should—"

At the same moment that Mac appeared in the doorway, Aaron raised his finger to his lips.

"This is quite a place," Mac said. "I can't thank you enough for arranging the tour."

Aaron extended his hand across the desk to shake Mac's. "Paris is a beautiful city. You might want to think about spending some time with us."

It was a subtle change, but Annick was sure Mac's cheeks got a little rosy from Dr. Aaron's proposal.

"I'm flattered," Mac answered. "I'll certainly give your generous offer serious consideration."

Aaron nodded and then smiled at Annick.

"We better get going," she told Aaron. He stood up, joined her in the middle of the room and again kissed her once on each cheek.

"When will you be back in Paris?" he asked.

"Probably not until Christmas, but I'll call you."

Aaron turned to Mac, shook his hand again and said, "This is a very special young woman. You're a lucky man."

"Thank you," Mac said.

Mac and Annick took a cab back to the apartment. It was still early and Mac wanted to get in as much sightseeing as possible before the end of his last day in Paris. Luc had mentioned to them before he left for Prague that they would be leaving for New York early on Friday.

That evening Luc joined them for a quiet dinner at home and some interesting conversation, and then recommended a decent night's sleep before their flight back to New York.

At exactly 7:30 A.M. the wheels of the Gulfstream V retracted, and under full throttle the elegant jet climbed out over Paris. A few broken clouds obscured Mac's view but his brief glimpse of the Eiffel Tower was still exciting, reminding him of the same scene he had seen so many times in books and movies. Within a few minutes they were over the English Channel and setting a course for the United States. The flight was a smooth one and they touched down in New Jersey at a few minutes past nine.

Much to Mac's relief his car was exactly where he'd left it with no additional dents or scratches. Fortunately, they weren't due back at the hospital until the following morning, allowing them the luxury of spending a lazy day together getting over the jet lag.

Chapter Thirty-seven

Mac awoke at five A.M. and looked over at Annick. The only light in the room was a splash from a large digital clock she kept on her night table. Sleeping on her stomach with her favorite down pillow pulled halfway over her head, her breathing was soft. After kissing her softly on her bare shoulder, he slid out of bed and headed back to his apartment to shower and get ready for work.

By six-thirty, Mac was in the hospital seated in front of a computer catching up on the new patients. Rounds weren't for another hour but he wanted to have a handle on the service before meeting with the other residents and students. He was just about finished jotting down some notes when Annick arrived.

"What time did you leave this morning?" she asked.

"It was about five. I guess I'm still on Paris time."

"It was a great trip," she told him softly. "I was glad to see the romantic note Paris struck in you wasn't lost as soon as you got back."

Mac looked around quickly and then cast her a flustered glance. "Do you mind keeping your voice down?" he asked in a whisper.

Annick looked around, saw there wasn't a soul in sight and

rolled her eyes. "I'll try to be more careful," she promised. "What's new on the service?"

"It looks like things were pretty busy while we were gone," he said, pointing to the monitor. "Kevin saw a bunch of new consults, which means we should probably go back and take a careful look at each of the charts."

"Okay. Which ones do you want me to take?"

Mac studied the list for a few seconds and then said, "We'll probably see each of them briefly on rounds, but as soon as we're done, go back and check on these two newborns with sepsis and the three gastroenterology consults that were called in the day before yesterday."

"Do you have their names?"

"I'm printing you up a list of the whole service now. After you have a chance to see them, give me a holler. I'll go over them with you so we're both up to speed before card rounds with Howe this afternoon."

By the time Annick and Mac shared a cup of coffee and reminisced about their trip to France, Kevin and two medical students arrived for rounds. As Mac had planned, they spent a couple of hours seeing each patient on the service. When they were done, Mac and Annick set out on their own to review the charts of the more complicated patients.

When she arrived on Four West, the unit was teeming with activity. Three medical students were busy writing notes while the residents were going over the latest orders with the nurses. Annick spotted Sam Gideon, a second-year resident she had rotated with on hematology. Sam was from the mountains of West Virginia, built like a Roman gladiator but as mellow and gentle as they come. He was dressed in scrubs with a white coat that was at least two sizes too big for him.

"Sam," Annick said, tapping him on the shoulder.

"Dr. Clement," he answered without turning around. "I'd recognize that seductive French accent anywhere."

"Foolish of me to think I could pull the wool over the eyes of such a cultured linguist such as yourself."

Sam turned around, tossed a clipboard on the desk and grinned. "What brings you to my world?"

"Kevin mentioned to me that he had seen three kids on your service. Mac sent me down to have a look at them."

Sam sat down in a small wooden chair and rubbed the back of his mountaineer neck for a few seconds. Ever since the first day she'd met him, Annick had always gotten a kick out of his country bumpkin ways but had long suspected his manner was more theatrical than real.

"Two of them are brothers and the third's a little girl," Sam said.

"How old?" Annick asked.

"The girl's three. The boys are older. Brad's seven and Kyle's nine."

Annick looked down at the list Mac had given her. The boys' last name was Bartlett. The little girl's name was Christy Morgan.

"What's going on with them?" she asked.

Sam spun the large chart rack until he located all three charts. Pulling them out and then stacking them on top of each other, he handed them to Annick. "All of their stories are similar," he began. "They were all admitted as routine GI bugs with mild dehydration. Nothing out of the ordinary. We admit ten just like them every week."

Annick set two of the charts down on the counter and then opened Christy's. "Were they all admitted the same day?"

"The boys were admitted the same day but about twelve hours apart. Christy came in the following day."

"Sounds pretty routine," Annick said, flipping through the medical record and then looking up. "You don't usually consult us on these types of cases."

Sam raised his hand as she had seen him do so many times to slow the pace. Having worked with him on some very difficult cases, Annick knew he was a bright guy with a better than average diagnostic instinct.

"Normally, we wouldn't, but these kids got sick as hell, and to be honest with you, we weren't exactly sure why."

"What do you mean?" she asked.

"They all developed horrible diarrhea. Christy got so sick she had a few seizures. They were pretty miserable."

"Because of the abdominal cramps?"

"That's just it," he said, pulling his oversized black pen out of a top pocket and using it as a pointer. "They didn't have any cramps. They were just wiped out from all their fluid losses.

We had such a bad time with their blood pressures and electrolytes we had to put them in the ICU for a day until we finally got things straightened out."

"ICU? Are you kidding?"

"These kids were really sick, Annick. I've never seen anything quite like it."

Annick set the chart down and took the seat across from Sam. "How about fever?" she asked.

"Nope, not a degree."

"Maybe it was food poisoning. Anything in their dietary history?" Annick asked almost before he could finish his answer to the last question.

Sam shook his head. "No common denominator there. Not even between the two brothers."

"Anything growing out on their stool cultures?"

"We sent several samples for routine bacteria and viruses but so far they're all negative."

There were several more questions Annick could have asked but Sam had provided enough basic information for her to start studying the charts in detail. She was already convinced the illness Sam had described was a bit unusual. Most kids with routine GI viruses experience severe abdominal cramps, fever and vomiting—symptoms that were distinctly absent in these three children.

Annick spent the next forty-five minutes going over each of the charts. She actually had trouble keeping the cases separate because they so closely resembled each other. When she was finished with the last one, she replaced all three charts and headed down the hall to examine the Bartlett brothers and Christy. Before she reached the little girl's room, Carli Tabor, the charge nurse, stepped out from the medication room. Carli was one of the more visible nurses in the hospital and one of the youngest to hold a charge position. She was bright, efficient and totally committed to her patients, making her the type of nurse any children's hospital in the country would be proud to have on its payroll.

"Dr. Clement. I haven't seen you in a while. I heard you were on the I.D. service. How are you enjoying it?"

"I can't complain. Listen, I was just about to see the Bartlett brothers and Christy Morgan. Have you been taking care of them?"

"Night and day."

"How are they doing?"

"They're getting better slowly," she said with concern. "They've had so much diarrhea. I don't think I've ever seen anything quite like it."

Annick leaned against the wall and then centered her stethoscope around her neck. "I just spoke with Sam. He said all the cultures have been negative."

"Something will grow out," Carli stated confidently. "This is not routine gastroenteritis."

"It sounds like you may be right. I may want to talk to you again after I see them."

Carli pointed to the other side of the door. "I'll be here. The gowns and gloves are right over there."

Annick thanked her and then donned a yellow disposable gown and a pair of latex gloves. The unit was smaller than one would expect and its drab gray walls were a contrast to most of the other bright and upbeat units in the hospital.

Christy had been moved to a private room for isolation purposes. When Annick peeked in she saw the child sleeping on her back. The room had a distinct stale odor of sickness. A young woman wearing a baggy white sweatshirt sat in a club chair reading a novel.

Annick took a few steps in and smiled. "I'm Dr. Clement. I'm from the infectious diseases service."

"It's nice to meet you. My name is Merrilee Morgan. I'm Christy's mom."

They both glanced at the little girl at the same time. Her breathing was rhythmic but her forehead was lightly dotted with droplets of sweat. Even in the poor light, Annick could see there was no blossom in her cheeks.

"How's she doing?" Annick asked in a whisper, noticing how exhausted and pale Merrilee looked. Her thick auburn hair was pulled straight back in a ponytail and she was wearing no makeup.

She took a deep breath before answering. "I'm afraid she's a lot worse than when we got here."

"Can you tell me about when she first got sick?" Annick asked.

"Our pediatrician sent us to the emergency room because Christy was having severe vomiting. But that got better the first couple of days she was here. The doctors were even talking about sending us home until this awful diarrhea began. If it weren't for the IV, I'm sure she would have died. When they moved her to ICU . . . she had those awful seizures. The doctors said it was because of her low blood sugar." Merrilee turned away as her voice started to strain. "I wish they would figure out what's wrong with her."

"All the appropriate tests have been done. It's just a matter of waiting for the lab to report the results. Hopefully within the next twenty-four hours we'll have an answer."

"What about antibiotics? Have they started any yet?"

"No, and I agree with that decision. If we don't know what we're treating, they could actually make her worse."

Annick stepped to the bedside and gently pulled the covers down. She was a pretty child with the same dark red hair as her mother. Her face was peaceful, her tummy flat. Beginning gently in the upper part, Annick examined her entire abdomen. There were absolutely no signs of peritonitis but Annick was taken by her cool, moist skin. When she had completed her examination, she slowly slid the blanket back up to just below Christy's chin. Merrilee had remained quiet, watching Annick's every move.

"What do you think, Dr. Clement?" she asked with her fingers crossed.

"Her belly's fine. There's no peritonitis, but she's obviously picked up a really bad bug. We're just going to have to be patient until the lab's identified it."

Merrilee sighed with disappointment and then set her book down on a small table next to the bed. "I overheard two of the nurses talking. They said there are two brothers across the hall with the exact same symptoms, but none of the other children on the unit have come down with it."

"That may be just a coincidence," Annick explained. "Do you mind if I ask you a few more questions?"

Merrilee forced a smile. "I've spoken with so many doctors and answered a million questions . . . but if it will help."

"I can't make any guarantees," Annick said.

The two women spoke for another fifteen minutes or so, especially as it pertained to Christy's diet in the days that immediately preceded her illness. The thought of botulism did cross Annick's mind, but she quickly dismissed it because the symptoms were not typical of the disease. When they were finished talking, Annick mentioned to Merrilee that she would return the next day.

As soon as Annick had removed her gown and gloves, she thoroughly scrubbed her hands, put on a new gown and went across the hall. The Bartlett brothers were sharing a room and were both awake. A ceiling-mounted TV was set to the Disney Channel. They were alone in the room.

"How are you guys doing?" she asked in an upbeat voice. "Are they treating you okay around here?" The boys shared the same bleached complexion, sunken eyes and look of exhaustion. After they had exchanged a cautious glance, each was able to manage a smile. "My name's Dr. Clement. Your doctors asked me to stop in. Is your mom around?"

Brad, who was in the bed closer to the door, answered, "She just went downstairs for a few minutes." His voice was strained. In spite of the two-year difference in their ages, the boys could have been easily mistaken for twins. Similar in size, they both had straight jet-black hair that laid obliquely across their foreheads.

"Are you guys feeling any better?" she asked. The response from each of them came in the form of a shrug and a mild groan.

Annick spent the next few minutes examining them from top to bottom. As was the case with Christy, there was no reason to suspect peritonitis. The dehydration had obviously taken its toll, leaving them washed out and dispirited. She was anxious to speak with Mrs. Bartlett and mentioned to the boys that she would return later.

Annick finished removing her gown and gloves and was making her way to the sink when Merrilee Morgan appeared in the hall.

"Do you have a moment?" she asked Annick. "I'd like to show you something."

"Of course. Just let me wash my hands."

While Annick finished up, Merrilee disappeared into the room and quickly emerged with a small plastic specimen container. It was about half filled with a clear fluid with dozens of white flecks of mucus in it.

"Christy just went to the bathroom," she said, holding the container up for Annick to see. Annick stared at the cup for a second and then put a glove back on. She turned the container slowly in her hand. There was something sparking her memory but she just couldn't put her finger on it. Her eyes remained transfixed on the specimen until they suddenly widened.

Oh my God. How could I have been so dumb? Painless diarrhea and no fever. Add those symptoms to *rice water stools*. Her pulse began to race.

"I'm going to take this over to the lab," she told Merrilee as calmly as she could. "Maybe with this we can figure out what's going on."

"They've already taken about ten samples of it," she said in a discouraged voice with a slight sigh.

"Maybe the eleventh one will be the charm," Annick said with a smile. She left Merrilee and walked down the hall looking for Carli. Poking her head in the small medicine room, she spotted Carli preparing an IV.

"Hey, Carli, do you have a sec?"

"Sure," she said, turning around. "What can I do for you?"

Annick held the specimen cup up. "This is a stool sample from Christy Morgan." Carli took a step forward, moving her head slowly from side to side as she studied it. "Is this the same type of stool that the Bartletts are having?"

"Identical," she said without hesitation.

Annick didn't even stop to write a note on Christy's chart or have a word with Sam. She flew out of the unit and headed straight for the stairwell. When she was about halfway to the microbiology lab she stopped in the Radiology Department and paged Mac. Staring at the phone, tapping her foot, she grabbed for the receiver when it finally rang.

"Meet me in the micro lab right away," she told him.

"What's going on?" he asked. "You sound like a madwoman."

"Well, this madwoman has something to show you."

"Can't it wait? I'm kind of tied up with—"

"Now, Mac. It's important."

"Okay, okay . . . I'm on my way."

Annick hung the phone up quickly, left the Radiology Department and headed for the lab. She could feel her heart pounding. If her hunch was correct the naysayers and skeptics of Franklin Children's Hospital were in for the shock of their lives.

Chapter Thirty-eight

Just as Annick was about to enter the microbiology lab she saw Mac get off the elevator and start lumbering down the hall. When he was a few steps away, Annick removed the specimen container from her pocket and held it up to within inches of his face.

He raised his hand and took one step back. After studying the plastic container for a few seconds, he shrugged. "Okay, I give up. What is it?"

Annick wrinkled her forehead and then shook her head slowly. She had already called Bobbie to make sure Grady wasn't in the lab.

"It's a stool specimen," she informed him.

"It's a little strange-looking," he offered without any further comment.

"I just saw three kids on the gastro unit—all with stools that look like this."

"Are their symptoms similar?"

"Identical. They were all admitted with mild gastroenteritis, and were all getting better until developing serious diarrhea."

"Do they have fever?" Mac asked.

Annick's expression intensified as her eyes narrowed their

focus on Mac's. "No fever, no belly cramps and no vomiting. The little girl had at least two seizures."

Mac looked directly at Annick and then studied the container for a second time. "What about a dietary and travel history?"

Annick smiled for a moment. She had anticipated the question and knew exactly where Mac was going. "Are you going to ask me if they have been to Latin America or Asia, or have they eaten any shellfish from the Gulf Coast?"

"It crossed my mind."

Annick had done her homework and knew that shellfish from the Gulf Coast of the United States could harbor an unusual strain of cholera. Persons who consumed improperly cooked shellfish were at risk of contracting the disease. She was also well aware that in the absence of such a dietary history and with no foreign travel, there was no way Mac or anyone else could explain why three kids in a children's hospital in New York should be suffering from cholera.

Annick looked up and down the hall and then whispered, "C'mon, Mac, we both know what's going on here. Have you ever seen a case of cholera?"

"I have," he responded calmly.

"Here?"

"No. During my second year of residency, I did a three-month rotation at Jackson Memorial in Miami. We treated a lot of patients who had recently arrived from Latin America. It wasn't uncommon for them to have brought contaminated food. In some cases they had consumed contaminated water tainted with raw sewage."

Annick stood silent for a few seconds and then slowly raised the specimen container again. "So then you know what this is."

"Rice water stools? I think so. There aren't too many things that have that appearance," he observed while pointing at the container. "Let's let the lab have a look at it before going off half-cocked and starting a panic."

"Should we send a sample to the CDC?" she asked.

"That might be a little premature, but I would definitely send it to the state lab. I would also call Sam and tell him to start those kids on tetracycline right away. He may want to start the three-year-old on sulfa. If we are dealing with cholera—"

"If?" Annick demanded in a raised voice.

Mac looked around and then gently took her arm. "We're doctors, Annick. We deal in scientific facts. It's a simple enough matter to have the stool analyzed to see if the bacteria that causes cholera is present. I'm only asking you to be a little patient."

"I have no problem with that . . . just as long as you're not asking me to overlook it."

"Of course I'm not asking you to do that," he said.

"Are you going to discuss this with Dr. Howe?"

"Absolutely. We're playing this one by the book. He mentioned to me that he'll be out of the hospital until mid-afternoon. We'll talk to him about it as soon as he gets back."

Annick could feel every muscle in her neck tighten. "By that time the hospital will probably have passports for all three of the kids stamped from Peru and claim they just returned from an earthquake zone."

"Save that biting wit for a more appropriate time, Annick. This is a delicate matter. It doesn't call for a bull-in-a-china-shop approach."

"Always the diplomat, huh, Mac?"

"That's why you love me so much," he said in a voice meant to defuse the rising tension. "Why don't we get some lunch?" he suggested.

Annick rolled her wrist over and checked the time. "I'll meet you in the cafeteria in ten minutes. I have to do something first." Mac looked at her skeptically, but before he could say anything she covered his lips with her finger. "I'll meet you in ten minutes," she repeated calmly, to which he just nodded cautiously.

Annick watched as Mac got on the elevator. She turned and faced the entrance to the microbiology lab. With the first step she was through the door, with the next she was standing outside Bobbie's office. Annick was resolute about one thing. Before she left Bobbie's office she would have her promise that Grady Simione would not have any knowledge of or go anywhere near the specimen container she held tightly in her hand.

Chapter Thirty-nine

Annick had just finished giving a lecture to the two new medical students about the appropriate use of antibiotics in newborns when her pager went off. She made her way to the back of the small classroom and picked up the receiver of a wall-mounted phone. The operator picked up immediately and told her that Rick Van Owen from the laboratory was trying to get in touch with her. Annick wrote down his extension on a three-by-five card, thanked the young man and dialed the number.

He answered on the first ring. "Van Owen."

"Rick, it's Annick Clement."

"Hi. I was calling about that tube of blood you were after last week."

"I went over to the lab but basically got the runaround. They said they'd call me back but the supervisor didn't seem real thrilled with my request. I've left two messages for her but she hasn't called me back."

"Was it Carol Myers?"

"Uh-huh."

"Did you mention my name?" he asked.

"I think so. Why?"

"Because she called me a little while ago. I'm not sure if she was genuinely interested in your motives or just snooping. Carol can be like that."

"So where does that leave me?" Annick asked.

"In great shape. She's going to give you the blood."

Annick pressed the phone firmly against her ear. She had assumed acquiring a tube of Justin's blood was a lost cause.

"That's great," she told Rick. "I'll call the CDC to get shipping instructions. How do I handle getting the blood from her?"

"Actually, she said she'd drop it off with me. If you give me the name of the person and the lab you want it sent to at the CDC, I'll be happy to take care of it for you. I've already checked the protocol. It's no big deal."

Feeling the excitement build, Annick said, "I'll give you a call later with the specifics. I owe you one for this, Rick. I don't know how to thank you."

"I'm happy to help. I hope you find what you're after."

By the time Annick was off the phone, the students had already left the room. The heater kicked on, throwing an immediate gust of warm air across the back of her neck. She cautioned herself about getting her hopes up that Justin's blood would contain traces of botulism toxin. The first order of business was to call Rachel Warren at the CDC and advise her the sample would soon be on its way. The second call would go to Joelle Parsons, letting her know that she hadn't forgotten about her and was getting closer to finding out what really happened to her nephew.

Annick closed her eyes and filled her lungs with a deep breath, and then slowly let it escape. *What would she do with the information if Rachel Warren was to discover traces of botulism in Justin Silva's blood sample, and it turned out to be the exact same type that had almost killed Michael Flannery?*

Chapter Forty

"Are you crazy?" Paulette Davis asked Annick in a whisper as she looked around quickly. "I could lose my job."

Self-assured, attractive and at times a little too direct, Paulette had worked in the human resources division at Franklin Children's Hospital for the past three years. Divorced with two children, she suddenly found herself between a rock and a hard place. Annick had treated Paulette's kids on several occasions for minor problems, such as earaches and the flu, saving her from marathon waiting times in her pediatrician's office. Annick and Paulette had developed a casual friendship and had even met for dinner a couple of times.

"I was just asking," Annick clarified in a calming voice. "I'm not aware of all the rules."

Paulette adjusted the collar of her red turtleneck sweater. "Cut the crap, Annick. The personnel files of the employees are strictly confidential. You know that. How would you like it if someone strolled into the medical staff office and started perusing yours?"

"I've got nothing to hide."

"That's a lame answer," Paulette pointed out. "You know what I'm saying."

"As I said, I was just asking."

Annick watched as Paulette fidgeted with her gold channel bracelet and then began stacking a dozen or so personnel files that were scattered across her desk.

"What the hell's your interest in Grady Simione anyway?"

"I . . . I'd rather not say," Annick said.

"Oh, I see," Paulette countered and then raised her hands over her head in disbelief. "You want me to let you review a confidential file and you won't even tell me why."

"It's probably better if you don't know," Annick offered.

"You'll have to do better than that if you want me to put my ass on the line."

Annick thought about her position for a moment, realized how important Grady's personnel file might be and decided to take the plunge. "He may be a risk to the children of this hospital."

Paulette stopped what she was doing and looked directly at Annick. "I'm not quite sure what that means, but have you ever heard of going through normal channels?"

"I've already tried that," she exaggerated. "But I suspect that in the absence of hard proof they wouldn't be interested in hearing what I have to say."

Paulette tilted her head to one side, her demeanor more controlled. "Hard proof? Is that what you're after? C'mon, Annick, just how important is this?"

"I wouldn't be asking if it weren't."

Paulette stood up and boosted her knee-length charcoal skirt up an inch or so.

"Dr. Clement, you have twenty-four incomplete medical records. I saw your name on the delinquent doctor's list this morning."

"I know," Annick said, not knowing exactly where Paulette was going with this. Medical records, the bane of most physicians' existence, required a monthly trip to the Medical Records Department to sign endless chart entries and dictate admission histories and physicals. Since her first month at Franklin, Annick had frequently found herself on the delinquent list.

"I'll have your charts pulled for your signatures," Paulette said. "They'll be in a stack in booth number three. I would appreciate it if you could get to them by no later than four today."

Annick nodded without uttering a word. Nothing else needed to be said. She knew Grady's file would be in the stack.

"Thanks, Paulette," she said sheepishly.

"Don't thank me, just don't complain when I call you at two in the morning about a stuffed nose."

"It will be my pleasure to be on call to the Davis children twenty-four hours a day."

"I assume that includes house calls."

"Was there ever a doubt?"

With a huge smile on her face, Annick left Paulette's office in great anticipation of her next trip to Medical Records.

Chapter Forty-one

Whatever doubts Annick may have had about Paulette's ability to arrange for a clandestine review of Grady's personnel file were quickly dispelled when she pulled up a chair behind the stack of her delinquent medical records, thumbed through the pile and quickly came across his file. Even though the booth provided a more than reasonable amount of privacy, Annick cast a guarded glance over her shoulder before sliding Grady's file out.

The folder was hardly voluminous. It included standard biographical information, past employment history, two letters of recommendation and a background check provided by a company that was headquartered in Chicago.

Annick quickly turned to the background information, which listed, among other general areas, major criminal record, bankruptcy and military service. She reviewed it carefully and then frowned. Grady Simione was clean.

His biographical profile was straightforward and unenlightening. Raised in Virginia, he graduated high school when he was eighteen. Never married. He denied ever being convicted of a crime. In the section designated for the name of an individual to notify in the case of an emergency, he left it blank. He had a Port Washington address and had attended college in Wisconsin. His last address before moving to Long Island was in Wilmington, Delaware.

Still a little nervous, Annick continued to move cautiously through the file. One letter of recommendation was from a hospital while the other was from a private lab. Both were located in Wilmington. She took her time and read the letters in extreme detail. They were hardly enthusiastic endorsements, but were solid letters that did support Grady for employment at Franklin Children's.

Shuffling through the file one more time, Annick was consumed by a feeling of disappointment. For all intents and purposes, the man's file was unblemished. It had been a long two days and she welcomed the night off that lay in front of her. She sat back in her chair for a moment and closed her eyes. Before she opened them, her pager went off. She reached for the phone and dialed the number displayed on the screen.

"Where are you?" Mac asked.

"Uh . . . I'm in Medical Records. I got a nasty call from one of the secretaries that I was on their most wanted list and I better get my charts signed."

"Why are you so bad about getting your charts done? Dr. Howe's a fanatic about tidy medical records. If you're really interested in landing this fellowship, then—"

"Mac, I appreciate your profound interest in my career, but it has been a bad two days and the last thing I need at the moment is a lecture about being anal retentive when it comes to my medical records." Her tone was calm, but she regretted the comment almost before she'd uttered the last few words. It didn't take a genius to realize she was taking out her frustration regarding Grady's dead-end personnel file on Mac.

"We're a little testy this afternoon," Mac said. "Does this mean you're not interested in having dinner with me and then letting nature take its course?"

She smiled. He had her and she'd known it since Paris. She loved everything about him, right from his kind heart straight down to his typically male attitudes about sex.

"I appreciate the offer," she told him. "I'll try to be a little more civil. I guess doing medical records always puts me in a grouchy mood."

"I forgive you. Don't forget about four o'clock rounds," he reminded her.

"I'll be there."

Annick hung up the phone, drummed the top of the chart pile with her fingers and thought about Grady. The hum of the copy machine droned in the background. She was just about to return the file to the center of the stack when she gazed over her shoulder at the photocopy machine. Feeling as if there were a miniature devil on one shoulder while a tiny angel was on the other, she slowly stood up.

Conflicted but undaunted in her pursuit of Grady, Annick lifted the two letters of recommendation from the chart, pushed her chair back and made her way innocently over to the copy machine. After a nonchalant look around and convinced that there was indeed a method to her madness, she made a single copy of each letter. Returning immediately to her chair, she jotted down Grady's social security number and then replaced his file back in the middle of the stack. She then reached for the phone and dialed Paulette's extension.

"I'm done with my medical records," she told her.

"I appreciate the call," Paulette said. "I'll make sure everything gets put back where it's supposed to."

"Thank you for your help."

"I hope you know what the hell you're doing," Paulette said, falling out of character for the moment.

"Trust me," Annick said with total resolve, checking her watch and realizing she only had five minutes to get to Dr. Howe's office or she'd be late for rounds. "I know exactly what I'm doing."

Chapter Forty-two

Mac had just completed examining a twelve-year-old boy with an unexplained fever and an unusual facial rash when he received a page from the operator that Dr. Howe wished to see him in his office at his earliest convenience. From the nature of the message, he decided to comply with the request as soon as possible.

"I'm not trying to put you on the spot, Mac," Dr. Howe explained in his usual Dutch uncle tone. "It's just that I . . . and the administration have some concerns about Annick."

"Concerns? I'm not quite sure I understand. She's doing a great job. She's here every day at six-thirty, sees every consult immediately, follows up in the lab and—"

"I'm not questioning her clinical competency," Howe stated, rubbing his chin and then sitting up a little taller in his chair. Mac was a little confused. Howe was usually more direct and articulate. "She just seems to be a little too preoccupied with both Dana Vitale and Michael Flannery's cases. She may even be pushing the edge of the envelope a little with respect to her inquiries. Both of the cases are over."

"I'm not quite sure I understand, sir."

Howe smiled. "C'mon, Mac. It may be a big hospital but the

walls have ears. I'm well aware of Annick's . . . let's just call it interest in some of our recent cases."

"I'm not sure—"

"We're talking man-to-man here, Mac. My eyes and ears are still working. Just because I'm head of a department doesn't mean I'm oblivious to what's going on. And I'm not trying to tell you how to run your personal life . . . it's just that I'm a little worried about Annick. That's all."

The awkward conflict before Mac was testing every diplomatic bone in his body. He realized he was hardly in a position to be uncooperative. He was talking to the chief of Infectious Diseases, a man he revered and who had always bent over backward to help him. On the other hand, his relationship with Annick had grown into the most personally rewarding experience he'd ever had. He knew it would be foolish of him to play completely dumb with Dr. Howe, but if he could carefully sidestep some of the more delicate aspects of Annick's activities, that might be his way out.

"Annick has a particular interest in diseases that have been identified as possible bioweapons," Mac explained. "She spent several months at the Pasteur Institute in Paris with Dr. Aaron, who has a particular interest in matters relating to bioterrorism."

"I'm well aware of Professor Aaron's work, but are you suggesting that she believes that Dana and Michael were victims of a biological weapon?"

"I can't answer that," Mac replied.

Howe's temperament and patience remained indulgent. "Annick has spoken to several family members, doctors and hospital employees regarding Michael and Dana's illnesses. Some of her inquiries and actions may border on unprofessional." Howe paused for a moment before adding, "I'm just curious as to why she's behaving in such a manner. You're her senior fellow. I thought perhaps you could shed some light on the problem."

"Not really, Dr. Howe. I am aware that she's interested in these cases, but apart from that . . . I haven't really discussed it with her."

Howe appeared unconvinced. "As we've discussed in the past, the hospital is extremely anxious to avoid any sensationalistic publicity regarding the care of these or any patients at Franklin. I'm sure you can understand their concerns."

"Absolutely. And I'm totally comfortable telling you that Annick would never discuss the details of her patients with anybody from the press or other media."

Howe picked up a neatly sharpened pencil and tapped the top of his desk with the eraser end.

"I was considering talking to her, but if you're sure she will conduct herself in a totally professional manner, then I'll be satisfied just to . . . shall we say, monitor the situation."

Mac was nobody's fool and realized that Howe had left his real agenda intentionally unspoken. He obviously expected him to carry the message to Annick to tread a little more gently.

"Is there anything I can do?" Mac asked.

"No." Howe was already looking down at a stack of papers when Mac stood up. He gazed up for a moment just as Mac got to his feet. "Well, maybe there is one thing. Try and keep me in the loop. I'd appreciate it."

"I understand," he assured him and then left the office.

Mac was not one to easily rattle, and perhaps the anxiety he was feeling standing in front of the elevator was more for Annick than for himself. He would have to be tactful when he talked to her about his conversation with Dr. Howe.

The elevator door rolled open, allowing Mac to step on. He thought about Annick as the car slowly made its way back to the ground floor. Besides an enormous passion for medicine and children, she was unquestionably one of the most motivated and goal-oriented residents he'd ever worked with. He closed his eyes, shuddering at the thought that something terrible could happen to her fledgling career . . . or even worse, to Annick herself.

Chapter Forty-three

It was twenty minutes past two when the bell rang at Great Neck South Junior High School, opening the floodgates to the hordes of students pouring out of the exit. Annick had arrived about thirty minutes earlier and was seated on the same bench that Dana Vitale had sat on the morning Grady Simione intentionally infected her with pneumonic plague.

Dressed in a white sweater and blue jean overalls, Annick sat quietly, looking over the athletic fields, waiting for the girl's field hockey team to emerge from the gymnasium for practice. It was a long shot, but the chance of speaking to some of Dana's friends about her last day at school was enough for Annick to tell Dr. Howe that she needed a few hours off for a doctor's appointment.

It was a clear day. The moisture in the air from a late-morning shower had just about evaporated. Every few seconds, the wind would gust, sending dozens of crisp-smelling, multicolored leaves swirling over Annick's sneakers. It couldn't have been more than fifty-five degrees, but the mid-afternoon rays of the sun were still strong enough to warm her face.

Annick heard a door slam open and then watched as a group of girls dressed in field hockey uniforms jogged from the gymnasium and made their way up a small grassy hill that led to the athletic fields. Stopping not more than thirty feet away, they formed two groups and began a series of stretching exercises.

Annick was just about to wander over when she noticed one of the girls staring at her with an uncertain look on her face. In the next moment, she broke into a quick walk and headed straight for Annick. Softly complected with ample brown eyes, the girl wore a smile bright enough to match her orange-and-blue uniform.

"Weren't you one of the doctors who took care of Dana at the hospital? I remember you from when I came to visit her."

"Yes, I am. My name's Annick Clement. I'm surprised you recognized me."

"Most doctors don't look like you. You look more like a TV doctor."

Annick turned away for a moment and grinned. "That's very kind of you to say . . . I think."

The girl sat down in front of Annick, first crossing her legs and then placing her hockey stick on her lap. In a strange way, she reminded Annick of herself when she was that age.

"My name is Jamie Sutton. Dana and I both played defense. She was going to be my best friend." Jamie looked around and then asked, "Do you have a sister or brother here?"

"No, I just wanted to spend some time in one of Dana's favorite places. I miss her. I guess you do too."

"Everybody on the team does. I had lunch with her the day she got sick."

"How did you know she wasn't feeling well?"

"Because she was coughing a lot. She said she was getting the flu."

"It must have seemed that way," Annick offered. "Did she say anything to you about how she got sick?"

Jamie glanced down at the ground, picked up a leaf by its stem and then tossed it up in the air and watched it spin gracefully to the ground.

"I already know how she got sick."

"Really?" Annick said.

"Uh-huh. She sat right where you are, studying in the cold," Jamie said, pointing at the bench.

"You mean that morning?" Annick asked.

"Yup. It was right before homeroom. It was really cold. She

said it was the best place to study because nobody bothered her . . . except for that weird guy."

"What weird guy?" Annick asked nonchalantly.

"Some substitute teacher. I saw her talking to him so I asked her who he was."

"Well, that's not so weird. They must have several substitute teachers a day in a big school like this."

Jamie covered her mouth as she chuckled. "Yeah, but most of them don't chicken out before the first bell."

Annick crossed her ankles in front of her and then slid down on the bench a couple of feet.

"What do you mean, chicken out?"

"After he spoke to Dana, he went straight to his van and left." Jamie tried to smother another laugh with her hand. "When I asked her about him during first period, she told me he was a substitute. That's when I told her she probably scared him off."

Annick could feel her senses heighten as Jamie spoke.

"Did you see the man?" Annick asked in a ho-hum voice.

Jamie narrowed her eyes in concentration. "Not very well. He was pretty far away."

"Do you recall anything about him?"

"It's hard to remember," she said, but then smiled. "He was real thin and walked quickly."

"What about his van?" Annick asked. "You said something about a van."

"Uh . . . it was one of those fancy ones."

"Do you remember the color?"

"Yeah, it was black. It looked pretty new."

Suddenly, the shrill of a whistle filled the air and Jamie jumped up. A portly woman wearing a gray sweatshirt and white shorts stood with an impatient expression along the side-lines of the hockey field. Her hands were squarely on her hips. Annick and Jamie both looked at her at the same time.

"I think you're being paged, Jamie."

"That's just Mrs. Winthrop. She's right out of the dark ages . . . very uncool."

Annick couldn't help but laugh. "I had a few teachers like that myself. Hey, how do I get ahold of you if I want to talk with you again?"

"We live in Great Neck. We're like the only people in the whole town whose phone number isn't unlisted. My dad's first name is Guy." She waved and started away. "It was nice talking to you, Dr. Clement. I think I want to be a doctor someday."

"Come talk to me about it anytime," Annick yelled back as she started down the hill.

For a few minutes, she watched the girls practice. Perhaps Jamie's recollection about the man speaking to Dana wasn't even accurate. Maybe she wasn't even right about the day. Annick stood up, caught Jamie's eye and gave her a quick wave and a smile.

Walking to her car, she thought more about the man. A tall guy with a new black van. She resisted the temptation to jump to any conclusions but the possibility that it was Grady Simione stuck in her head. Reaching her car in just a few minutes, she opened the door and got in. With her mind still racing, she remained uncertain about her next move. She stared out the windshield. Taking a long look around, she realized for the first time she felt a little frightened.

The moment Annick pulled away, Grady Simione emerged from behind a stand of trees. He couldn't have been more than fifty feet from where she had parked her car. He snugged his wool Kangol cap a little farther down on his forehead. There was no self-satisfied smile on his face this time, no thoughts of playing little mind games. Tapping his lips rhythmically with his finger, he stared at her car until it disappeared, the entire time asking himself why she would come to Dana Vitale's school.

Annick Clement was quickly becoming more than just a mere nuisance. It was hard for him to determine just how much she really knew and how much she was guessing. Irrespective of the answer, Grady still couldn't figure out how a lackluster, run-of-the-mill pediatrics resident could be so perceptive about his activities. Still a little in awe of her astute nature, Grady decided not to underestimate this woman.

Chapter Forty-four

Annick sat alone at a small round table in the back of the cafeteria. It was two o'clock and she had just finished seeing her last consult of the day. Lamenting about another late lunch, Annick picked slowly at her chicken Caesar salad.

Lying on her tray, folded in half, was the photocopy of Grady's letter of recommendation from the Continental Bioculture Laboratory in Delaware. Placing her fork down for a moment, Annick unfolded the letter and read it for the fourth time. There was no question that it was a good letter, containing words such as "competent," "responsible" and "punctual," and phrases such as "well organized" and "appropriately motivated." But the letter lacked the personal touch, and what was even more disturbing was the complete absence of any references to Grady's moral character.

Annick gazed up at the phone on the wall just above her table. Without getting up, she plucked the receiver, dialed the operator and requested a long-distance line. Glancing back at the letterhead, she dialed the laboratory and asked for Elizabeth Emory, the woman who had written the letter.

"This is Liz Emory," came a voice with a strong New England accent, after only one ring.

"My name is Dr. Annick Clement. I'm calling from Franklin Children's Hospital in New York."

"On Long Island?" Liz asked.

"Yes. We're located in Great Neck."

"What a strange coincidence," she began as if she and Annick were old friends. "My sister lives in Douglaston. Her son's under the care of Dr. Charles Sweet in the pulmonary medicine department."

"I know him well," Annick answered. "I spent a month working with him in the cystic fibrosis clinic. He's a great doctor. What's your nephew's name?"

"Thomas Bryer."

"I . . . I don't think I've met the family," Annick said.

"Well, I'm sure you have a lot of patients there, but I'll mention your name to my sister the next time I speak with her. It's such a small world," Liz said. "How can I help you?"

"We have an employee in our microbiology lab by the name of Grady Simione. He listed you as a past employer. He's recently won one of our resident awards and we were trying to find out a little more about him . . . as kind of a roast when we present him the award."

"I see," Liz said in a much more serious tone. "What's this award for?"

"It's to recognize him for going above and beyond with respect to helping the residents," Annick said confidently, adding to her story as she went along.

"I'm not sure I can help you, Dr. Clement."

"Any little tidbit will help. I can assure you it's all being done in the right spirit. I thought Grady mentioned that you wrote him a very nice letter of recommendation when he applied for a job here at Franklin Children's."

"Is that so?" she asked quite incredulously. "I'm director of Human Resources and I'm pretty careful about whom I provide glowing letters of recommendation for."

"My goodness," Annick said. "This is a little embarrassing. I . . . I don't know what to say. Grady spoke so highly of you."

"We got along for the most part. It sounds like he's doing fine up there."

"From your tone," Annick responded, "it doesn't sound

like he was nominated for any awards while he worked for you."

"Not that I recall," Liz answered.

Annick's mind was trying to stay at least a couple of steps ahead of her mouth. It was obvious that the letter she held in front of her must be a forgery.

"You mentioned that he's working in your microbiology lab," Liz said.

"Yes," Annick answered. "In fact, he told me when he resigned from your company that—"

"Resigned? He told you he resigned?"

"Uh . . . yes."

"Unbelievable," Liz mumbled just loud enough for Annick to hear.

"That's not the way it happened?" Annick asked.

"Hardly, but to tell you the truth, Dr. Clement, I've probably said too much already."

Annick heard her words plainly but her instinct told her that Liz could be prodded to say more. "May I call you Liz?"

"Of course."

"We work at a children's hospital. As the representative of the resident staff, I can say with a reasonable degree of certainty that we have no interest in honoring an individual who is not worthy of the recognition."

"Mr. Simione did not resign and it was only by an enormous amount of pressure from our legal department that certain unexplained irregularities in this laboratory were not reported to the authorities."

Annick hung on every word as she felt her breathing becoming more rapid. Her chest tightened as it had when she was a child suffering from asthma. She was desperate to keep Liz talking. What started out as a shot in the dark now appeared to be the map to the mother lode.

"I certainly appreciate your candid comments, Liz. I will of course keep your confidence. Rest assured that your input has been very important and I am going to recommend against giving Mr. Simione the award." Annick reached forward, picked up a napkin and crumpled it in her hand. "What kind of work does your lab do? If you don't mind me asking?"

"Mostly routine microbiological cultures, but we are involved with some sensitive research and development."

Annick then said, "You might be interested to know that I have a particular interest in bioterrorism. I hope to work at the CDC when I've completed my training."

"That's very interesting," Liz said. "Then I'm sure you're very careful about keeping track of your potentially dangerous bacterial cultures. We live in strange times and things can sometimes disappear . . . especially when certain people are around."

"I appreciate the advice."

"I don't suppose he mentioned his misdemeanor conviction for cruelty to animals?" Liz asked.

"No . . . no, he certainly did not," Annick said. The obvious implications of Liz's revelation were frightening.

"When he was seventeen, he was convicted of killing dogs with ricin. He extracted the poison himself and had killed over thirty pets around town before the authorities figured out that this sudden rash of deaths wasn't some weird canine epidemic."

"What happened?" Annick asked.

"He got off with community service hours and a slap on the wrist."

"If you don't mind me asking, how do you know this?"

"Let's just say our company felt it was in their interest to gather all the data they could on Mr. Simione. Enough said?"

"Enough said."

"By the way, Dr. Clement, I've worked at several teaching hospitals over the years, and as I recall, the residents' awards were always given out in June, just before the new interns started." Annick smiled but didn't respond. It was obvious that Liz Emory was nobody's fool. "Take good care of my nephew. It was nice talking with you."

Annick said, "We'll take excellent care of Thomas. I can't begin to tell you how helpful you've been."

Staring at her salad, Annick's mind remained focused. It was obvious that while he was employed in Delaware, Grady had been suspected of tampering with or perhaps even stealing dangerous bacterial cultures. There was probably no proof and Annick guessed the risk of him suing over the accusation was enough for Continental Bioculture to take the path of least resistance and just simply fire him.

Annick stood up and slowly made her way over to the large trash bins. As she tipped her tray into the receptacle, she thought about Grady Simione and the vulgar trail of behavior he'd left from Virginia to New York.

Chapter Forty-five

Dressed in black warm-up pants, a T-shirt and an old navy pea coat, Grady covered the three blocks to Annick's house in about five minutes. It was two o'clock and the early-morning air was still damp from an earlier deluge. The wind was cool, coming in gusts instead of the usual steady stream. After two nights of surveillance he concluded she had no alarm system and he felt comfortable that gaining access to her town house would not be a difficult task.

When he reached her driveway, he stopped and bent over to tighten the laces of his work boots and scan the block in both directions. It was a moonless night but broad floods from the neighboring homes threw out a considerable amount of light. Pulling up the collar of his coat, he made his way along a tall ficus hedge that ran the length of her driveway and through a white wooden gate that led to her backyard. Grady slid along the side of the town house until reaching the back patio.

Using a very thin screwdriver, Grady easily flipped the latch of her sliding glass doors to the open position. With just a slight push, the door slid open and Grady found himself standing in Annick Clement's kitchen. Wearing latex gloves, he quietly closed the door, drew the venetian blinds and then withdrew a small flashlight. Grady always believed that he possessed a heightened sense of smell and could have sworn he detected just the slightest aroma of vanilla.

Panning the room with the narrow beam of light, he took an extra moment to study the long row of cupboards that hung over the sink and long granite countertop. He then approached the stove and turned on a small light at the top of the oven. It didn't take him long to spot what he suspected would be sitting right there on the counter—an automatic coffeemaker. He smiled, thinking about the numerous times he had seen Annick racing around the hospital with a cup of coffee in her hand. Just to the side of the coffeemaker sat a hand-painted ceramic sugar bowl. Even before lifting the lid, he suspected he'd found the perfect means to poison Annick Clement.

Turning the flashlight off and then placing it on the countertop, Grady reached into his pocket and pulled out a plastic pill bottle. He held it up to the light and looked at the ricin powder that filled about a third of the bottle. He had already decided that Annick would not be a victim who slowly suffered from the ingestion. She would die from it as quickly as Jobeth.

It took him only a few seconds to tap about half the contents of the bottle into the sugar bowl. As he stirred in the deadly ricin with his finger, he considered the irony and pure beauty of interlacing the potent poison so inconspicuously between the grains of harmless sugar. Grady replaced the lid to the sugar bowl, picked up his flashlight, took a final look around and started toward the sliding glass doors. Just as he reached for the handle, he stopped, turned and pointed his flashlight at the sugar bowl. He rubbed his chin for a few seconds before a broad smile covered his face. The usual surge of excitement he felt the moment a perfect poisoning was set into motion was distinctly absent. There was no indescribable rush or high and he knew why. Annick Clement was different from his other victims, who offered him no measurable intellectual challenge. The thought of killing her this easily and being unable to watch her suffer was totally unsatisfying. She deserved more respect than that—she had earned it. Timing was everything and he'd made a mistake coming to her house at this time. Annick Clement was due more—she deserved his best, and when the right moment came . . . she'd get it.

Returning to the sink, he turned on the cold water. Reaching over, he picked up the sugar bowl, lifted the lid, turned it upside down and watched as the entire mixture of ricin and sugar swirled rhythmically before disappearing down the drain. He spent the next few minutes scrubbing the bowl with detergent and hot water. When he was done, he carefully refilled the bowl from a bag of sugar he found in a pantry alongside the refrigerator.

He opened the glass doors without penetrating the silence, raised his flashlight for one final sweep of the kitchen and then slid out.

"Let's just call this little visit a preview of things to come," he whispered with a sneer. "However many additional days you now have left on earth, Dr. Clement, are only the result of my good graces."

Chapter Forty-six

By eleven A.M., Annick finished seeing her last consult. Mac had called around an hour before and they agreed to meet for lunch at noon, which left her just enough time to head up to the residents' lounge and catch up on some reading. It had been a busy night on call and she welcomed the hour to relax.

She had seen the Bartlett brothers and Christy Morgan earlier and all three were within a day or two of going home. As the elevator climbed slowly to the fourth floor, it occurred to her that it had been several days since their specimens had been sent to the state lab. Having become an expert in the bureaucratic delays commonly associated with the state lab, Annick decided to cut through the red tape and call them instead of waiting for the written report.

The lounge was empty. Annick plopped down on the large leather couch and reached for the phone. A fast shuffle through her stack of three-by-five cards produced the lab's phone number. A pleasant-sounding woman answered on the second ring and quickly connected her to the bacteriology section.

"This is Dr. Killington. May I help you?" came a husky but friendly voice.

"My name is Annick Clement. I'm a resident at Franklin Children's. We sent you three specimens a few days ago looking for cholera. I was wondering if you had the result yet." Annick leaned her head back against a soft throw pillow in anticipation of the lengthy wait.

"They're positive," he said calmly.

"I beg your pardon?"

"They're positive," he repeated. "Where have these kids been for God's sake?"

Annick had already moved to a bolt-upright position. "None of them have been out of New York in months."

"Really," he said. "Well, I'm afraid they picked up cholera somewhere."

Annick switched the phone to her opposite ear. "Is there any chance there could be a mistake?"

"Dr. Clement, I'm the director of the lab. I'm as positive as the cultures. In fact, we just read the plates about an hour ago. We already put a call into Atlanta. The CDC's expecting the specimens by tomorrow to start on the biotype and serotype determinations."

"Do you have any idea of which type we're dealing with?" she asked.

"In general, there are two main types. El Tor, which was responsible for the epidemics in Peru and India in the early 1990s. The samples you sent us clearly aren't El Tor. The other, termed oh-one, causes sporadic cases and is usually caused by eating contaminated food from South America or shellfish from the Gulf Coast of the U.S."

Annick listened politely, deciding not to point out that the classification system of cholera toxin was, in fact, far more complicated than Dr. Killington had explained. Suffice it to say, she was not surprised to learn the samples were not consistent with El Tor.

"Do you have any idea how long it will take the CDC to complete their analysis?" she asked.

There was a moment's hesitation before he responded. "Actually, I don't, but my best guess would be a few days."

"When do you anticipate we'll be receiving your official report?"

"We'll fax it late today or tomorrow," he answered.

Annick thanked Killington for his assistance and slowly replaced the receiver. Frozen in thought, she barely noticed when the door opened and Mac came in. His white coat, which he normally wore buttoned all the way up, was open. His color was a little pale and his expression haggard.

"What the hell's wrong with you?" she asked.

Mac took the seat next to Annick, his eyes locked in a daze across the room.

"I have a feeling you already know," he said, sitting down next to her.

It never occurred to Annick that Mac had also called the state lab. "I'm not sure what you're referring to but I was just about to page you."

"I assume you called the lab."

Annick nodded slowly as the reason for Mac's strange appearance and behavior suddenly became clear.

"I just got off the phone with them," she said in a soft voice, making every effort not to appear as if she were gloating or preparing to make an I-told-you-so speech. "What do you think we should do?"

"I know exactly what we should do. We're meeting with Dr. Howe in forty-five minutes." Mac stood up, buried his hands deep in his waist pockets and began pacing in front of the couch.

"What do you think he'll do? If you remember, he was pretty skeptical when we told him we were sending the specimens to the state lab."

"But he didn't tell us not to send them. He may have been skeptical but I think his mind was open."

"How do you think he'll handle all of this?"

"I'm sure it won't be his decision alone." Mac closed his eyes and rotated his head as if he was working a bad spasm out of his neck. "The medical staff leadership and administration will just have to decide what to do." Mac cleared his throat and added, "I'm sure they'll do the right thing."

Annick didn't share Mac's optimism, but his intuitive sense of timing was beginning to rub off on her and she quickly decided this was not the time to debate the issue of how the administration would react to the news.

Before she could think of something to say, her pager went off. She looked at the long-distance number with the 404 area code for several seconds before she realized it was Rachel Warren at the CDC. Immediately reaching for the phone, Annick dialed the operator, obtained a long-distance line and called the number on her beeper.

"Hi, Rachel. It's Annick Clement. I just got your page."

For Mac's benefit, Annick remained outwardly calm as she listened to Rachel. She closed her eyes at the same moment her grip tightened on the phone. "I appreciate you calling," she finally said. "I'm sure the appropriate people will be back in touch with you by this afternoon." Annick quietly replaced the receiver and then stole a look at Mac, who stared at her with wide eyes.

"Who was that?" he asked.

"It was a physician from the CDC. Her name's Rachel Warren. She's been working on the Michael Flannery case."

Mac interlocked his fingers and held his clasped hands just above his waist. He looked somewhere between frustrated and baffled. "What did she want?" he asked.

"Why don't you sit down?" she suggested as she patted the seat next to her.

Mac raised his hand, indicating he'd prefer to stand. He repeated his question. "C'mon, Annick. What did the CDC want?"

"Do you remember a while back when we talked about that boy who died of complications relating to diabetes?"

"Yes, I remember. You were suspicious that he really died of botulism."

"According to the CDC, he did," she said in a voice barely above a whisper.

"Did what?" he asked abruptly, but before she could answer, his shoulders suddenly slumped. "Die of botulism?"

"I'm afraid so. They just finished running the assay. The toxin was the exact same serotype as Michael Flannery's."

Mac, who had not stopped pacing, now stopped dead in his tracks and sat down on the edge of the coffee table. The remainder of the color in his face drained in a matter of moments. "I feel like I'm in the middle of a bad joke," he finally said.

"Are you going to tell Dr. Howe?"

"About the diabetic kid?"

"His name's Justin Silva."

"Of course," he said with the first hint of impatience in his voice.

She sighed. "In that case there may be something you want to know."

"Would this be a good time for me to start pacing again?"

"It might not be a bad idea," she told him. "Howe doesn't know I sent the sample."

Mac shook his head as Annick sighed. "I beg your pardon?"

"It was one in a million."

"What the hell's that supposed to mean?"

"Take it easy, Mac."

"I'll take it easy as soon as you start explaining."

"Justin was on one of the diabetic research studies . . . so the lab happened to have an extra tube of frozen blood. When they offered to give it to me, I jumped at the chance and sent it to the CDC."

"Oh, well, that explains it. The lab just happened to call you up and offer you a tube of this kid's blood?"

"Of course not. I asked for it."

"How come that doesn't surprise me." Copying Annick's inimitable style, Mac crossed his arms in front of his chest. "Well, I guess under the circumstances Dr. Howe's going to have bigger problems to deal with than worrying about one little unauthorized lab study."

"What do you think Howe and the administration are going to do?" she asked him.

"I guess they'll have to notify the appropriate law enforcement authorities. . . . I assume that will include the CDC."

"And their bioterrorism team."

"I guess so," he muttered, looking at his watch. "Let's go get a cup of coffee before we see Dr. Howe. I could use it."

For the first time since Michael Flannery was admitted, Annick felt vindicated. It was as if an enormous burden had been lifted from her shoulders.

There was no question that the authorities would have their work cut out for them, but she would have to avoid getting caught up in the turmoil that was about to consume Franklin Children's, and take every precaution to proceed with extreme care.

PART
Three

Chapter Forty-seven

David Howe was already seated at his desk when his secretary ushered Annick and Mac into his office. He was leaning back with the telephone wedged between his shoulder and ear. He smiled, pointed at the two chairs in front of his desk and held up his hand, indicating he'd be off the phone in a moment. As usual, he was dressed to the nines, this time in a light wool gray pinstripe suit.

Before they left the cafeteria, Mac had made it crystal clear to Annick that he would do the talking. Annick understood as well as anyone the time-honored protocols of a residency program and she accepted his decision without too much of a protest.

"It's not like you to call an urgent meeting, Mac," Howe said as he hung up the phone. "What's going on?"

Mac sat with his forearms flush on the leather rests of the chair with his right leg crossed over the left. "I think we may have a major problem, sir."

Howe removed his reading glasses and set them in a black leather case. "I'm listening," he said calmly.

"The samples we sent to the state lab on the three kids from the gastro unit came back positive for cholera."

"C'mon, Mac. There must be some mistake."

"I'm afraid not."

"Are they absolutely sure?" Howe asked.

"One hundred percent. There's no doubt. We should have the faxed report this afternoon."

"Did you speak with a supervisor?" Howe inquired.

"I did. He assured me that they ran it three times. They've already sent a specimen down to Atlanta for further subtyping."

"Have these kids been out of the country?"

Mac shook his head. "I'm afraid not. They've been right here on Long Island for months."

"Do they have any friends or relatives who might have brought them contaminated food?"

"No. Annick took a very careful history from both parents."

"How are the children doing?" he asked.

"They all had a rough few days but they should recover. One had a couple of seizures."

Mac was calm and noticed Dr. Howe had barely acknowledged Annick's presence. He sat forward in his high-backed manager's chair. His expression was somber. Turning in his chair, he remained silent while he stared at the bookcase along the far wall.

"I'll have to make some phone calls," he finally said. "Obviously we're in a situation that calls for the involvement of more than one state agency. I can't do anything until I speak with administration."

"I'm afraid there's one other thing, sir."

Howe did his best to smile. "I think I've had enough bad news for one meeting, Mac."

"I'm sorry."

"Let's have it," he said.

"It involves a patient Annick and I spoke to you about a week or so ago. You may not remember him."

"What was his name?"

"Justin Silva. He was a child admitted with diabetes who died a couple of days later. The cause of death was listed as overwhelming sepsis but that now appears to be an error." Mac changed positions in his chair, cleared his throat and went on. "We never officially saw the child in consultation but Annick heard about him through the hospital grapevine and ... uh, well, felt that his symptoms were consistent with botulism."

Howe rotated his chair back around. He was slowly rubbing his chin. "Yes, I remember her mentioning the boy."

"As it turned out, we were able to acquire a tube of his blood and sent it off to the CDC for analysis."

"Don't tell me," he said, shaking his head slowly.

"I'm afraid the CDC confirmed the presence of botulism."

"Was it the same type as Michael Flannery's?"

"No question about it."

Howe stood up and walked out from behind his desk until he reached the bookcase. Reaching down, he pulled out two large three-ring binders.

"Bioterrorism has become an increasingly important issue in infectious diseases. We've all attended seminars, read the latest journal articles and stayed current with the newest developments." He walked back and placed the binders on his desk. "I guess we all hoped that it would not happen here." He placed his palms flush on his desk and leaned forward. It was obvious to Mac he was still a little shell-shocked. "Have you discussed this with anyone?"

"Absolutely not."

"What about you, Annick?"

"No, sir," she assured him evenly. "Not a word."

"Good. I want you to keep it that way." He checked his watch and then sat down. "Mac, I want the phone numbers and names of the people you spoke with at the state lab . . . and at the CDC as well. Don't be offended. It's just something I'm obligated to do."

"I understand," he said.

"As soon as I've confirmed all this, I'll call an emergency meeting of the hospital's executive committee."

"Is there anything we can do?" Mac asked.

"As a matter of fact, there is. I want things to remain business as usual," he said. "We'll meet later today after I've had a chance to speak with the powers that be." For the first time he looked directly at Annick. "I think I owe you an apology, Dr. Clement. I dismissed your suspicions as melodramatic claptrap. I . . . I was wrong. Obviously, we're facing a serious problem. I'm just hoping that we're dealing with just one crackpot as opposed to some fanatic political group."

"I think it's the former," Annick said.

Howe replaced his glasses. Peering out from behind them, he said, "Well, seeing how nobody's taken credit for any of these atrocities, hopefully you're right."

"Will I have the opportunity to speak with the authorities?" Annick asked.

"Is that what you want?"

"Yes, sir."

"Well, I can't imagine they won't want to speak with you. I certainly won't do anything to prevent it."

"Thank you, sir."

Howe escorted them to the door and then returned immediately to his desk. Annick and Mac walked through his outer office and headed back to the residents' lounge.

"He seemed pretty sincere to me," Annick said.

"There's no question about it," Mac agreed. "I told you he'd do the right thing. By tonight this place will be a madhouse. Between the media and all the health and law enforcement personnel . . . well, it's going to be a three-ring circus. If I know Howe, he'll schedule a press conference as soon as possible."

"A press conference?" she asked. "I guess I'll never understand these people."

"What's that supposed to mean?"

"I thought their goal was to avoid publicity."

"C'mon, Annick. It's a little late for that. They'll be thinking about damage control and preventing a panic at this point."

"Well, if they're worried about a panic, I can't think of a better way to get one going than to hold a press conference."

Annick picked up the pace to keep up with Mac, who always seemed to walk quickly when his mind was racing.

Chapter Forty-eight

Since around the time of his twelfth birthday, Quinton Thorne had never given serious thought to pursuing any career other than being a special agent with the FBI. Now thirty-three years old, he had been assigned to the New York City office for the past ten years. Soft-spoken, mild mannered and never pretentious, Thorne had turned many a head in the bureau with his rapid advancement. A husky man with distinctly high cheekbones and muscular hands, he had compiled an impressive arrest record. Over the last several years, he had developed a particular interest in bioterrorism and had been selected to lead a team to Bosnia to investigate the use of bioweapons. As soon as Franklin Children's reported their suspicions to the FBI, Thorne became the logical choice to head up the investigation.

By seven P.M., the large administrative conference room had been commandeered by the Nassau County Police Department and the FBI for the purposes of conducting interviews. It was almost eight when Annick was summoned to speak with the authorities. In addition to Special Agent Thorne, who was dressed neatly in gray dress slacks and a black blazer, two other agents from the FBI and two Nassau County police officers were present. They were all seated around the large conference table.

The door was ajar but Annick decided to knock. Thorne

looked up, smiled and signaled her to come in. The atmosphere was hardly that of a smoke-filled room with harried police officers scurrying back and forth. Thorne walked toward the door to greet her.

"Dr. Clement, I'm Special Agent Quinton Thorne with the FBI." He half turned to face the others, and then introduced Detectives Peterson and Kozlov of the Nassau County Police Department, who each nodded politely. Annick returned the nods, noting that the two men appeared to be about the same age, both with short-cropped hair and average looks.

"It's nice to meet you," she said, feeling more like she was being interviewed for a job than a criminal investigation.

Thorne then introduced the two other special agents as Gina Dandridge, a young, pleasant-looking woman with a natural smile, and John Abernathy, an all-American-looking man who Annick thought probably fit everyone's image of what an FBI agent should look like.

"Have a seat," Thorne said. "Do you have any objection to us taping this interview?" he then asked, holding up a small recording Dictaphone similar to the one she used in the clinic.

"I have no objection," she said.

For the next thirty minutes, Thorne asked dozens of questions regarding Annick's basic role and activities in the hospital. He stood the entire time and never broached the topic of the poisonings. Some of his questions skirted the edges of personal information, but she opted to answer all of his inquiries fully and openly. As the interview proceeded, it struck her as odd that none of the other members of Thorne's team asked any questions.

"It's our understanding that you cared for all the children who became ill," Thorne finally stated as he flipped through several pages of handwritten notes on a yellow legal pad. His demeanor and tone were no different from when he asked her what her role as a resident was.

"I cared for all of them," she said. "Except Justin Silva."

"We were told that you were the one who first became suspicious that these children had been intentionally poisoned. Would you say that's accurate?"

"In a manner of speaking."

He looked up for a moment, and in the first change in the

tone of his voice she had noticed, he asked, "I don't understand. Wasn't it you who sent the specimens to the state lab and the CDC in Atlanta?"

"Yes, it was," she answered without elaborating.

"What made you suspect that these children might have been poisoned?"

Annick looked up. "They weren't exactly poisoned, Special Agent Thorne. They were the victims of a biologic weapon."

He frowned. "You'll have to excuse me. I'm a cop, not a doctor. But you haven't answered my question. What made you suspicious?"

"A lot of things, I guess."

"For instance," he said, moving around to the other side of the conference table and then taking a seat next to his colleagues.

"The nature of their symptoms. Maybe a little instinct, maybe a little luck, and the fact that there wasn't a rational explanation for their illnesses based on exposure, travel or food consumption."

Annick could see from his eyes that Thorne was listening to her carefully. She wondered if he was dismissing her answers as vague. She was even starting to fear he was doubtful about the accuracy of her answers.

"It's hard to imagine anyone would be capable of such a thing," he said to her.

Annick found his comment a bit transparent. She assumed an FBI agent with special training in bioterrorism would have no trouble believing that there were scores of people out there who would be more than capable of such a thing. Thorne's coy expression made her suddenly quite uncomfortable.

"I'm sure you've been to as many conferences as I have, Mr. Thorne. If we've learned anything about bioterrorism in the last dozen years, it's that any individual with a moderate amount of training in any number of medical fields could acquire the knowledge to construct a biologic weapon."

"Unfortunately, that's true."

"Open up any *Soldier of Fortune* magazine or biologic supply catalogue. Seed cultures of the most deadly bacteria are readily available to anyone who wants to purchase them."

"In a manner of speaking, but as I recall, some documentation of your credentials and intentions are required," he pointed out.

"You're absolutely right. You'd have to invest in some phony laboratory stationery to make your request on. That would probably cost about thirty dollars."

Thorne cleared his throat. "We understand the need for constructing and implementing a reliable national bio-defense system," he offered as an explanation, but Annick looked past him. They were both well aware of the extremely poor state of preparedness in the United States against such an attack. "You seem to be quite . . . conversant on the subject of bioterrorism. Would someone with your training be able to construct a bioweapon?" he asked.

She resented the implication of his question but resisted the urge to smile as she now realized where Special Agent Thorne was going with all this. In spite of his authority, she was neither intimidated nor threatened by his tacit accusation.

"That's a strange question, Mr. Thorne."

"How about an answer?"

"I don't know. I've never thought about it. I guess I always viewed myself as someone trained to prevent or treat bioterrorism, not cause it. Does that answer your question?"

"For now," he answered.

"Good."

"We're just asking questions, Doctor. You seem a little annoyed. What happened here at Franklin is potentially a terrible act of bioterrorism. We have to keep an open mind. Please don't be offended by my questions. We're asking everyone the same ones."

"Instead of focusing on asking the right questions, maybe you should concentrate on asking the right people," Annick blurted out with a bit more antagonism in her voice than she should have permitted. It wasn't quite the way she had planned to ease into the topic of Grady Simione. When she looked around, it was quite obvious she now had everyone's attention.

"Dr. Clement," came Thorne's exacting response, "is there someone in particular you believe we should be talking to?"

When she had first entered the room, she was certain of her facts and intent to implicate Grady. She paused for a moment when she considered that in a recent conversation with Mac, he had reminded her of the security guard at the Olympic Village in Atlanta who was all but convicted of planting a bomb before the authorities eventually determined he'd played no role in the crime; nevertheless, his life was nearly ruined.

"Grady Simione," she answered evenly. Almost before the words were out of her mouth, each of the officers began rifling through their notes and papers. Thorne never moved. Annick could feel his eyes fixed on her, studying her every move and expression. A moment later, he scanned the group and was met with four consecutive negative shakes of the head.

He smiled, pushed his chair out a little and crossed his legs. "Who is Mr. Simione?"

"He works in the microbiology lab. He's a tech."

"And why do you think we should talk with him?"

Annick looked at each of the officers before asking, "Are my comments confidential?"

"Completely," he said. "I just want to know what you think you know."

Annick wasn't buying into his unruffled, easygoing routine, and just assumed that every profession had its own bedside manner.

For the next hour, while the other officers in the room took notes feverishly, Annick told Special Agent Thorne everything she knew about Grady Simione. Remaining stone-faced, Thorne's questions progressed in an orderly and logical manner. There were many answers Annick didn't have and she made no effort to theorize or guess about things she clearly wasn't sure of.

"I'm still a little confused about Grady seeing Dana the morning she became ill. You said something about the van he got into."

"As best as Dana's friend could remember, it was black." She looked over at Thorne, who appeared as if he were waiting for her to complete her answer. "Grady Simione drives a black Lexus SUV."

"There are a lot of black SUVs out there, Dr. Clement. Did you say his truck was parked directly across from the main entrance to the school?"

"That's right."

Thorne glanced at Special Agent Dandridge, who nodded. "Anything else?"

"I think he probably forged at least one of his letters of recommendation that he used to get his job here."

"Now, how would you know something like that?" Thorne asked with a baffled expression.

Annick knew she'd slipped but there was no way she was going to tell him she'd been through Grady's personnel file. For the first time since she'd entered the room, she found herself scrambling for an answer. "Let's just say I heard it through the grapevine."

"Not exactly what we call an accurate source of evidence." Thorne paused, then said, "So apart from the school thing, we have a guy who works in a microbiology lab, was convicted of cruelty to animals as a juvenile and has a real interest in poisons. He seems to be a loner but has taken a peculiar interest in a young man admitted with botulism and he may have forged a letter of reference. Anything else?"

"Well, instead of one, we have two victims of botulism, both seen in our emergency room on the same night, both of whom consumed a clear liquid tray. Mr. Simione also made it his business to know every detail of Dana Vitale's travel plans and purposely gave me erroneous data about a patient with meningitis."

"I forgot you mentioned that," Thorne said. "Why do you think he would do that?"

"I guess he either wanted to get me fired or have the sick pleasure of seeing another child suffer."

Thorne walked over to a large automatic coffeemaker and poured himself a steaming cup. He offered Annick the same but she declined with a quick hand gesture. "All of this could be nothing more than happenstance and coincidence," he postulated with his back to her, slowly stirring his coffee.

"Which is exactly what the administration and Dr. Howe believed." She sighed loudly. "Apparently, they don't see it as a strange happenstance any longer."

"What makes you so sure it's not?" he asked.

"Simple. You wouldn't be here."

"Touché," he said, raising his cup.

"Look, Mr. Thorne. Believe what you may, but I'm not buying Grady Simione's bizarre activities add up to nothing more than a coincidence."

Thorne turned back around and faced Annick. He smiled for the second time since she entered the room. "I certainly appreciate your cooperation in all this, Dr. Clement. We may want to speak with you again. You're not planning on leaving Long Island, are you?"

Annick was stunned. "No, I'm not."

"Good," he said.

She looked at Thorne and then the other agents. "Is that it?" she asked.

"That's it," he said plainly as he walked toward her. "Unless you think of anything else, that is. Here's my card." He waited for her to stand up and then escorted her to the door.

As soon as she was in the hallway, he closed the door and walked back to the conference table.

"Pull the personnel file on this guy Simione right now. I want to take a look at it. See if someone has a photo of him and let me know if he's working tonight. I want him checked for priors. Get me a list of the substitute teachers assigned to Great Neck South that day . . . and find out who's in charge of security there. Let's find out if the area across the street from the main entrance is covered on their security scan."

"And if it is?" Abernathy asked.

"Then meet him over at the school and go over the morning tapes from Dana Vitale's last day in school."

Abernathy took a deep breath. "Do you mean . . . tonight?"

A severe glance from Thorne was all that was necessary. He got up, walked to the other side of the room and picked up a telephone.

As soon as Annick started down the hallway, she spotted Kevin standing against the far wall. His face was one shade lighter than the color of chalk.

"What's the matter?" she asked.

"They sent for me. I feel like a common criminal."

"Relax. They're talking to everybody, Kevin."

"How was it in there?"

"It was okay. They're just doing their job."

He wiped his brow with the back of his hand. "What did they ask you?"

"Just routine stuff. They're trying to find a murderer, Kevin. They're not looking for you."

A moment later the door opened and Special Agent Thorne appeared at the door.

"Dr. Killpatrick?"

"Yes, that's me," Kevin answered as he stepped forward and entered the conference room. "I'll speak to you later," he told Annick just before the door closed.

Annick found Kevin's demeanor a little perplexing. He had always seemed so cool under fire. He handled Dr. Howe better than most interns and was a fairly calm problem solver. Starting down the hall, she couldn't help but hope that Kevin would regain some of his composure before Thorne lobbed in the first salvo.

Annick started down the hall with a strange disquieting feeling nagging at her. The interview was hardly what Annick anticipated but she had been extremely open. Nobody in that room could possibly accuse her of being evasive or uncooperative. Praying her concerns about Grady Simione had not fallen on deaf ears, she suddenly stopped, turned and looked back in the direction of the conference room. Could Thorne possibly believe that she concocted everything she told him about Grady? For what purpose? It made no sense. Unless he truly considered her a suspect.

Chapter Forty-nine

Annick was sitting at a small table just inside the entrance to the doctors' dining room sipping a cup of coffee when Kevin came through the door. Whistling a Broadway tune, his color had returned to normal and his manner seemed quite relaxed. He waved at Annick, walked to the back and removed a piece of carrot cake from the refrigerator.

"That wasn't so bad," he said, sitting down in the chair directly across from her.

Looking down at her watch, Annick said, "You weren't in there very long."

"It was pretty benign," Kevin said easily, then laughed.

"What did they ask you?"

"It was pretty general stuff," he said, taking the first bite of the cake and chewing it as he continued to fill her in. "Actually, they didn't ask me very many questions."

Annick's level of concern began to escalate when she considered the entirely different manner in which her interview had gone. "I'm glad to hear it," was all she could think of to say.

Kevin continued to look down at his plate as he took another forkful of the moist cake. "Oh, they did mention your name."

"I beg your pardon?"

"Yeah, it was right at the end. One of the agents came in,

whispered something to that Thorne guy, and then I heard him say something like, 'That's what Dr. Clement said.' "

"Did he say anything else?"

Kevin's already shallow eyes squinted as he thought. "I'm not sure. It was kind of hard to hear, but I think they said something about going out to some guy's house tonight. They were talking about a search warrant . . . I think."

Annick stood up immediately, and without saying another word, she headed straight for the door. Consumed by confusion, an instant wave of nausea overcame her. Her first impulse was to stop and compose herself but she kept going. Once out in the hall, she slowed her pace and forced herself to breathe more deliberately. The nausea passed quickly and she felt her mind starting to focus.

She had little reason to suspect that Kevin had misinterpreted what he'd heard, and for reasons she wasn't exactly sure of, and without any further reflection on the matter, she made the decision to see if she could find out what Special Agent Thorne had on his mind.

Chapter Fifty

Parked at the end of Grady's block for the last five minutes, Annick took a slow breath and finally mustered the courage to squeeze the accelerator. Teasing the BMW forward, she checked the address on each house until she spotted Grady's. It was eleven P.M. and the driveway and front lawn were brightly lit by two sets of floods above the garage. His SUV was parked in the center of the driveway.

Circling the block quickly, she started down his street again, this time pulling over to the curb under a large oak. She was about fifty yards from Grady's house. Still not exactly sure what she was doing made any sense, she hoped her instinct about Thorne was correct and that he'd use the information she'd given him about Grady and decide to act.

She lowered the window and gazed in the direction of his house. It was a cool night with a steady wind that nudged amorphous clusters of clouds steadily across the sky. Every few seconds, a bright crescent moon peeked out between the cloud banks.

The street was quiet. After setting the radio to a classical station, Annick leaned forward on the wheel, resting and watching the house. It had been a long day, and after about forty-five minutes, a soothing Mozart sonata relaxed her to a point where she had to fight to keep her eyes open.

At first, the three SUVs that turned the corner like a precision marching band were just a haze. A moment later, her brain made the connection and her eyes snapped open. The three vehicles stopped in unison across the street from Grady's house, the side doors slid open and three men in sport coats jumped from each truck. At a brisk pace, six of them crossed the lawn. Two peeled off and headed down the driveway while the last circled the house from the opposite side.

Annick crossed her arms in response to a sudden chill. Straining to focus her eyes, she was fairly certain that Thorne was one of the men at the front door. His three consecutive pounds with the back of his fist on the front door were barely audible from where she sat. The two men behind Thorne stood with their feet wide, their eyes focused straight ahead.

First twenty, then thirty seconds passed without the door opening. Thorne glanced back at one of the men behind him, pointed toward the window and then twirled his index finger slowly in a circle. The stockier of the two men jumped off the front stoop and made his way to the large bay window. From Annick's vantage point, she could see the blinds were drawn. The agent slipped off to the side, apparently trying to peer into the living room. After only a few seconds, he left his position and trotted back to the front step. The second agent pulled out a walkie-talkie, raised it to his mouth and then replaced it on his hip.

Having moved to a straight upright position, Annick was frozen in place. She could feel her throat tighten with anxiety. Instinctively, she reached forward and turned off the radio. In the next moment, the three agents on the front step nodded at each other, withdrew their weapons and plowed through the front door as if it were made of papier-mâché. Without knowing why, Annick covered her mouth as if to smother a scream. Every muscle in her neck was squeezing down in spasm. Several other agents followed Thorne and the other two men in. Annick found herself raising her hands to her ears in anticipation of gunfire but none came. Through the sheer curtains of Grady's window, she could see the silhouettes of the agents crisscrossing the living room.

For the next thirty minutes, apart from two more SUVs appearing on the scene, nobody entered the house and nobody exited it—at least through the front door. Annick was now relaxed and heavy in thought trying to figure out what was going on.

When the two brief knocks at her passenger-side window came, she gasped, grabbed the steering wheel and almost jumped out of her skin. She whirled around to the smiling face of Gina Dandridge, holding up her FBI shield. Annick was still trying to catch her breath when Gina signaled her to lower the window. More embarrassed than anything, Annick reached for the center console and lowered the window.

"Nice evening," Gina said.

"Probably as close to perfect as I've ever seen," Annick answered, looking up at the sky.

"Do you live around here?"

Annick let her chin drop to her chest. "I think we both know the answer to that one."

"Well, instead of playing junior G-woman on a stakeout, Special Agent Thorne has invited you to join him in Mr. Simione's house."

If her throat weren't so dry, Annick would have swallowed. "Do you really think that's such a great idea? The last thing I need is that lunatic to realize I tipped you guys off."

Gina nodded politely. "Why don't you let us worry about that?"

Gina was being evasive but her expression and eyes spoke volumes. Annick grabbed her purse and got out of the car. Shoulder to shoulder, the two women crossed the street, walked straight up the driveway and through the front door.

Chapter Fifty-one

As soon as they walked into Grady's house, Gina spotted Thorne and motioned to him. He acknowledged her with a nod but his eyes quickly shifted to Annick. He finished his conversation with a young agent in a blue FBI windbreaker and started toward them. Thorne greeted Annick politely and then escorted her into the kitchen. She watched in amazement as dozens of agents with electronic equipment, plastic bags and cameras scurried from room to room. Thorne pointed to a chair, waited for her to be seated and then sat down across from her.

"Since you appear to be so interested in Mr. Simione, do you have any idea where he might be?"

She shook her head. "I'm sorry. I don't have the first clue, but from your tone, I have the feeling you think I do."

"It was just a hunch. You can't really blame me. You do seem to know quite a bit about him."

"I guess I wasn't inclined to stick my head in the sand like a nearsighted ostrich and turn a blind eye to everything that was going on."

"Like the administration?"

"I didn't say that."

Thorne's smile was genuine but guarded. His eyes were red from fatigue. Taking a moment, he opened the middle button of his sport coat. Annick noticed his manner to be more relaxed than the first time they'd spoken.

"Do you mind telling me what you think you were doing out there?" he asked.

Annick had anticipated the question but at first drew a blank. When she gathered herself, she answered, "I don't know. I had a feeling you might show up, and . . ." Annick stopped, waved her hand for a moment and then said, "To tell you the truth, Mr. Thorne, I guess I don't know why I came over here. Why don't you just chalk it up to morbid curiosity?"

Thorne looked dubious as he took a moment to loosen his tie. Before he could respond to Annick, two of his agents entered the room with a large cardboard box filled to the brim with notebooks, photos, books and magazines. Thorne crossed his arms in anticipation as they placed the box on the kitchen table in front of him.

"All of this stuff is pretty much the same," the first agent said, picking up an amateurishly published book on physical torment and then tossing it back in the box. "I'm glad we spotted that false wall in the attic. The room behind it looks like a terrorist stronghold. I've never seen so much information on poisons, torture and bioweapons."

"Have you found anything else?" Thorne asked.

"There's all kinds of technical stuff and equipment that the lab boys are gathering up."

Thorne rubbed the back of his neck. "Just tell them to do everything by the book. I don't want one of those slippery Ivy League lawyers getting this psychopath off on some obscure technicality." The two men nodded in unison, picked up the box and headed toward the living room.

"Are you sure Simione's gone?" Annick asked.

"Well, his drawers and closet have been cleaned out and we can't find a suitcase anywhere. He had the brains to leave his car here. He's obviously smart enough to make our job a little harder. Somebody must have tipped him off," he added.

"Do you think that somebody was me?" Annick asked.

"Dr. Clement, I have lots of questions at this time. What I'm a little short on is answers. But don't worry. We'll find him."

"The good guys always win. Right?"

"Not always, but this time we will. Listen, why don't you

get going?" he suggested. "You probably shouldn't even be here." He stood up and looked down at Annick. "You're not planning on going out of town, I hope."

"That depends. Are you telling me not to?"

"Let's just say I'm asking."

"Am I a suspect, Mr. Thorne?"

"That's a funny question. Should you be?" he asked.

"I got the feeling from our talk at the hospital that you believed I might be mixed up in all this. Am I suffering from an overactive imagination?"

"Dr. Clement," he began slowly, appearing to take caution in what he was about to say. "This is off the record and I'd appreciate your discretion in what I'm going to tell you. We've already been over to Great Neck South and reviewed the surveillance tapes. We also pulled the names of the substitute teachers who were working the day Dana Vitale got sick. There were no male subs that day."

"What did the tapes show?" she asked, assuming he'd dodge the question.

A brief look of reservation covered Thorne's face. "Let's just say that I'm comfortable that I can place Mr. Simione at the scene of the crime."

"You're obviously very thorough," Annick said.

"As are you, Doctor. Since I'm not sure what the hell's going on around here, I'm going to have one of my agents follow you home and tag along with you for the next few days."

"Is that for my protection or to keep an eye on me?"

Thorne just smiled. "I don't know, but until we nail this guy there'll be someone . . . nearby. That's the best answer I can give you. Okay?"

Annick stood up and faced him across the table. "For the record, Mr. Thorne—I'm not involved and I think having me escorted or under surveillance . . . or whatever you want to call it, is completely unnecessary."

Thorne's expression never changed. "Maybe, but I'm going to do it anyway. If you've done nothing wrong, you have nothing to worry about. As far as my agents are concerned, they're watching you for your personal protection."

"That's comforting," she said.

"I'll probably want to speak with you again tomorrow. I'll track you down at the hospital—if that's okay."

"I'll be there," she said.

Thorne peered into the living room and motioned Gina to come in.

"C'mon, Dr. Clement. I'll follow you home," she offered.

Annick stole a final glance at Thorne. He was obviously a man with a lot on his mind and Annick found herself praying that he wasn't seriously entertaining the possibility that she was mixed up in this thing with Grady Simione.

The ride home was uneventful. Annick invited Gina in and the two of them shared a pot of coffee and an hour of conversation, which helped to allay a lot of Annick's anxiety. There was no discussion of either medicine or law enforcement, and in spite of their profound differences in background and vocation, their two personalities meshed well. At about one-thirty, Gina excused herself and Annick went straight to bed.

The first thing she did when she awakened was to look out her window. A relaxed smile crept across her face when she saw a dark brown Ford parked in her driveway with Gina behind the wheel sipping from a large Styrofoam cup.

Chapter Fifty-two

"What the hell happened last night?" Mac asked Annick the moment he saw her approaching the nursing station. "You never called me back."

"By the time I got home it was after midnight. I decided not to wake you."

Mac's eyes narrowed. "I'm a little confused here, Annick. The last I heard from you, you told me you had something real important to do . . . and then nothing."

"Things got a little crazy, Mac."

"I'm listening."

"The FBI got to Grady Simione's house right after I did. They broke in—"

"Wait a minute. You went to the guy's house?"

Annick took a moment to collect herself before answering. "Let me finish," she said. "When the FBI broke in he was already gone. They must have seen me sitting there because they came and got me." Mac sat down on one of the small wooden chairs, extended his legs and crossed his ankles.

"And then what happened?" he asked.

Annick blew out a long breath. "Thorne spoke to me and

said they were going to assign an agent to watch my house while I'm there."

"Why are they doing that?" he asked.

Her shoulders slumped and her expression became blank. "Thorne kind of said that Simione might try and . . . uh—"

"Try what?" Mac said with a distinct edge to his voice.

"Relax, Mac. They're just being cautious."

"I'm not sure I like the sound of all this. Did you call your dad?"

"Not yet, but I will. Listen, can we talk about this later, please?"

Mac took a deep breath and a hard look at Annick before answering. "I guess so . . . but not too much later."

"Good."

"Are we having dinner tonight?" he asked.

"I'm looking forward to it."

"Should I make the reservation for three or does your FBI escort eat alone?"

Annick made a fist and shook it at him. "I have a call to make. I'll see you later."

She walked around to the other side of the nursing station to a row of four booths designed for the doctors to review and write notes in the charts. She sat down, reached into the breast pocket of her lab coat and pulled out a small spiral notepad. It took her only a moment to locate Joelle Parson's phone number and dial it. She leaned back in her chair and listened as one ring led to the next until the answering machine connected.

"Joelle, this is Annick Clement. Please give me a call when you pick up your messages. I have some news for you."

Annick replaced the receiver. Anxious to speak with her and too impatient to wait for Joelle to call back, Annick turned to the computer and tapped in Justin Silva's medical record number. Scrolling to the face sheet, she easily located the Silvas' home phone number. A moment later, she was back on the phone.

"Hello, this is Dr. Annick Clement calling from Franklin Children's Hospital. May I please speak with Suzanne Silva?"

"This is she," came a soprano voice with a distinct Southern accent.

"I'm sorry to disturb you. I'm calling in reference to your son. Is this a bad time?"

"No, Dr. Clement. Everybody at the hospital was wonderful. I'm happy to speak with you."

Annick heaved a breath of relief. "Your sister recently came to the hospital to discuss Justin's care. She asked me to look into something for her. She mentioned you were aware of it. I've been trying to locate her but haven't been able to."

After a few moments of silence, Suzanne answered, "I'm a little confused, Dr. Clement. My sister did visit us for a few days just after we lost Justin but I wasn't aware she had come to the hospital." Suzanne's manner was poised but there was an obvious degree of uncertainty in her voice.

"I'm not sure I understood you correctly," Annick said. "Did you say Joelle visited you after Justin passed away? I thought she lived locally."

"Doctor, I'm not quite sure where you're getting your information from, but I don't have a sister named Joelle. My sister's name is Chris and she lives in Fort Worth, Texas."

Annick's eyes flashed to the computer screen to make sure she was looking at the correct face sheet. Unable to make sense of any of this, it occurred to her that maybe Joelle was a friend of the Silvas' and had only claimed she was related to Suzanne to make it more likely that Annick would be sympathetic and cooperate with her.

"Excuse me for asking, Mrs. Silva, but do you have any friends or other relatives named Joelle?"

"I'm afraid I don't."

Annick closed her eyes and pressed her lips together. "I'm so sorry, Mrs. Silva. I've obviously made a terrible mistake. I hope my call hasn't upset you."

"Not at all, Doctor, but does this have anything to do with the news we received yesterday from the hospital regarding the botulism?" Suzanne asked.

"Yes, it does. I thought the woman I spoke to was your sister but I've obviously made a mistake."

Annick said good-bye and hung up. Her recollection of her conversation with Joelle was quite vivid and there was absolutely no chance she could be mistaken about what Joelle had told her. Suzanne Silva had absolutely no reason to lie, so who the hell was this woman who called herself Joelle Parsons? Annick gently massaged the bridge of her nose, trying to remember any additional facts that might help.

Suddenly, her eyes opened wide as she recalled that Joelle had mentioned she was a registered nurse and had worked in the area until about five years ago. If that were the case, there should be some record of her nursing license. The only question was how to get the information. Engrossed in thought, she didn't notice when Mac walked up.

"Are you ready?" he asked.

Annick's response was delayed. "Ready, what do you mean?"

"Are you okay? We have three new consults to see . . . that is, if you'll come back from whatever galaxy you're visiting at the moment."

"Gimme a break, Mac."

"Absolutely, Captain Video. Let's start in Radiology."

Annick scowled at him, stuffed her stethoscope back in her pocket and stood up. As they walked away, she heard Mac jabbering away about the patients, but for the moment, her mind was elsewhere.

Chapter Fifty-three

It was nearing two P.M., and apart from checking the lab results on a five-year-old girl with the chicken pox, Annick was free until four-o'clock rounds. The strange matter of Joelle Parsons remained paramount on her mind. Rechecking the phone number, she decided to try one more time. After four rings, the answering machine came on. It was a woman's voice:

> Gardner and I have decided to make a last-minute trip. We will be out of the country for several weeks. We'll be checking our answering machine from time to time, so, if you'd like, please leave us a brief message and we'll get back to you just as soon as we can.

Annick's brow crinkled as she hung up the phone. After reflecting on the matter, she decided to move on to plan B. Since being asked to serve on a committee that looked into nursing complaints, she had gotten to know Jane Kirby, the director of nursing, fairly well. Jane's office was located in administration, where she could usually be found behind her desk muttering to herself and up to her eyeballs in work. With thirty years of front-line experience behind her, Jane was fair-minded, articulate and an excellent manager.

"Anybody home?" Annick asked as she spotted Jane with her most serious face on no more than six inches from her computer screen.

Jane looked up and shook her head. "C'mon in. Do you know anything about computers?"

"I can send e-mail and order costume jewelry on-line."

"Strike three," she mumbled. "What's going on?"

"I have a little problem that I was hoping you could help me with," she told Jane as she sat down directly across from her.

"Which one of the residents has been yelling at my nurses this time?"

"I'm afraid it's nothing that important. And if I were here for that reason it would probably be because one of your nurses yelled at a resident."

"That's because I only hire the aggressive ones," she said. "Let's have it. What's on your mind?"

Annick took a deep breath. "I recently met a woman who claimed to be a nurse. I assumed she was telling the truth and discussed one of our patients with her. I now have reason to suspect she was probably lying to me."

Jane turned off the computer screen and rotated her chair toward Annick.

"Was she a family member and just trying to get more info out of you? It's been done before, you know."

"Possibly, but I don't think so. I spoke with the child's mother recently, and she has no idea who this person was."

"And how is it that I can help you with this problem?"

"You know everybody in this state who is even remotely connected to nursing. Do you think if I gave you her name you could work some magic?" Annick pushed her palms together as if she were praying, tried to look as pitiful as she could and added in a baby voice, "Pretty please."

"Enough. What's her name?"

"Joelle Parsons. I think she lives in Garden City. I tried information but they didn't have anything."

Jane wrote down the name on a scrap of paper.

"I may be able to do something right now." Jane flipped through her Rolodex until she found the number she was after and then reached for the phone.

"Hi, it's Jane Kirby. Can you connect me to Dawn McCarthy,

please." Jane smiled at Annick, covered the mouthpiece with her hand and began making small talk. In mid-sentence she stopped. "Dawn, hi, it's Jane Kirby. How's everything in Albany?" After listening for a few moments and making a few sarcastic faces at Annick, she answered, "I agree. It was a wonderful meeting. The leadership seems to be on the same page for a change. Listen, I have a favor to ask you. We're trying to locate an R.N. by the name of Joelle Parsons. She lives down here on Long Island. Can you see if you have an address or phone number?" Jane covered the receiver again with one hand and gave Annick the thumbs-up with the other. A few seconds later, Jane's attention shifted back to the phone call. "I see. Nothing at all. Well, I guess we'll just have to keep trying. Thanks a lot for your help. I'll see you in Boston next month." Jane replaced the phone and shook her head. "I'm sorry, Annick, they don't have anything on a Joelle Parsons. Whoever this woman is, if her name is Joelle Parsons, she's not licensed to practice nursing."

"How far do their records go back?" Annick asked.

"Eleven years. If she's an R.N. and worked in New York in the last decade, we should have something on her. I think you've been had."

Annick stood up, thanked Jane and left the office. She turned down a long corridor that led back to the main lobby.

For what reason would anybody pretend to be a nurse and make up that story . . . and where did she get her information about Justin Silva? The answers were still unclear, but the most bizarre part of the whole thing was that the woman's theory about Justin Silva dying of botulism turned out to be right on the money.

Annick stopped in front of the hospital gift store window and gazed at the floral arrangements. The more she thought about it, the more she realized that it was her encounter with Joelle that turned out to be the key factor in convincing her that a bioterrorism plot did indeed exist at Franklin Children's.

It seemed odd, but if she didn't know better, it was almost as if someone knew she was lost in a complex maze and had summoned Joelle Parsons to lead her out.

Chapter Fifty-four

The press conference was already well under way when Annick entered the auditorium through the rear doors. In addition to the hundred or so permanent theater-type seats, four extra rows of folding chairs had been set up in the back. Dozens of technicians walked over the thick cables that crisscrossed the rear of the auditorium. Cameramen, mostly in T-shirts and baseball caps, with their cameras hoisted on their shoulders, flanked the podium, while other technicians holding mikes on long booms circled behind them.

Dr. Howe, dressed in a dark blue three-piece suit, sat in the middle of a long rectangular conference table with a microphone directly in front of him. Representing the hospital administration and sitting immediately to his left was John Scanlon. To his right, Dr. Ira Myers, an anesthesiologist and the current medical director, gazed out over the audience. At least thirty reporters with notepads were out of their seats pushing toward the front.

The auditorium was so brightly lit that Annick found herself squinting. After a few moments, she spotted Mac about three quarters of the way back and sitting on the aisle. She quietly walked over and took the seat next to him.

"Where the hell have you been?" he asked.

She raised her eyebrows at the question. "The last time I checked, we still had patients to take care of. I was looking in on some of them."

He whistled very softly. "You're so compulsive and dedicated. I think that's what I love most about you."

Annick elbowed him in the ribs. "What have I missed?"

"It just started. Howe's making a brief statement and then he's going to take questions." Before she could say another word, Mac raised his finger to his lips. "Why don't we just listen," he suggested, pointing to the stage. "I think he's finished with the statement."

Howe reached forward and pulled the microphone a few inches closer and offered to entertain questions. His hair looked like it had been professionally coiffed for the press conference. There was a steady murmur in the crowd that was accompanied by a throng of waving hands.

A portly man with a rumpled dress shirt and a tie to match his loud voice got Howe's attention first.

"Assuming this was the act of some maniac, what's going to prevent something like this from happening again?" he asked, holding his pen up in the air as he spoke.

Howe took a deep breath and nodded. "That's an excellent point and underscores the question—just what is the state of this country's preparedness against those individuals or terrorists who would use bioweapons against us?" He looked down with a grim face. "I'm afraid the answer is that we are still grossly unprepared." Howe paused for a moment to let the buzz of the crowd pass. "The truth is it's a lot easier to make bioweapons than to defend against them. The majority of these devices are either colorless, tasteless, silent or invisible. As a nation, we are far too complacent about the risk." He stopped for a moment, cleared his throat and then reached for a glass of water. After two quick sips, he continued. "Much more research is needed, especially in the areas of vaccines, immunology and antibiotics. We also need more sophisticated detection and early-warning technology."

A woman with a black scarf in the front row jumped in before Howe could say anything more. "Can you be more specific about vaccines?"

"Certainly, and I'll just give you one example, but I assure you there are many others. In 1980, the United States suspended its program to vaccinate all children against smallpox. This disease, which is one of the most deadly known to mankind and extremely suitable to be weaponized, is perhaps the greatest risk to us." He again stopped and surveyed the audience, Annick assumed for emphasis, and then went on in a very stern voice. "It is presently estimated that at least half of our population would be prone to smallpox infection and a large number of those people would perish as a result of such an attack."

Annick leaned over to Mac and whispered, "This is getting a little too melodramatic for me. By tomorrow, Howe will probably have a Hollywood agent. I'll see you back out on the floor."

Mac scowled for a moment. "Do you have to be so cynical?"

"When he stops being so pompous, I'll stop being so cynical." Annick stood up, glanced behind her and walked straight to the exit.

For the next thirty minutes, Howe continued to answer questions. Finally, the press conference was called to a halt. Howe stepped down from the stage only to be confronted by a rabble of reporters who had positioned themselves to further question him. Mac watched as Howe oiled his way around them, and after thinking about it for a few seconds found himself agreeing with Annick that their department chief was enjoying these proceedings just a little too much.

Chapter Fifty-five

Annick left the hospital through the emergency room, walked past the loading docks and toward the parking lot. The sun was almost down but a lingering warmth remained in the air. As she approached her car, she saw a stocky man with his hands in his pockets leaning against the trunk. He was wearing a black top-coat and was gazing off in the opposite direction. It didn't take her more than another moment to recognize Special Agent Quinton Thorne. When she was about ten yards away he turned and waved.

Annick shook her head and then stopped directly in front of him.

"If you're following me, you're not being very sly about it."

"Actually, I'm just the decoy," he said. "The real surveillance team's on top of the hospital with telescopic cameras."

She tried but was unable to hold back one short chuckle.

"An FBI agent with a sense of humor. I'm impressed."

"How about a truce?" he suggested.

"A truce? How can you offer a truce to even the most insignificant of suspects?"

"I've been giving that theory some thought," he said, scratching his head.

"Really."

"We figure Simione might not have been working alone, but my instinct tells me you're not the Ma Barker type."

Annick wiped her forehead and let out a deep breath, making sure it was loud enough for Thorne to hear. "A man with a highly developed instinct. They're becoming rare," she said.

"So, how about that truce?"

Annick extended her hand and smiled. This was the first human side of Thorne she'd seen. His hand was large but his grip gentle.

"Do you have a family?" she asked.

"No kids yet," he admitted. "I'm having a little trouble finding the right wife."

"Maybe she doesn't exist." Before he came up with a clever response, she added with a laugh, "It couldn't be your job, could it?"

"Actually, I've been asked that very question by more than one woman."

Annick shook her head. "How come that doesn't surprise me?" She studied his face for a moment. It looked like he hadn't shaved in a day or two. "Have you had any luck finding Simione?"

"Not yet. But we've got a number of people working on it. I don't know how he did it, but for the moment he seems to have vanished into thin air . . . as they say. Are my agents bothering you very much?"

"They seem to keep a safe distance and I love Gina. I told her she should move to Paris and join the French National Police."

"She'd probably do great."

"What do you think your chances are of finding Grady?" she asked.

"We'll get him. It's just a matter of time." Annick listened carefully, noticing the confidence in his voice. "He's not as bright as he thinks he is."

"He probably thinks the same thing about the FBI." Annick placed her purse on the trunk of the car and thought for a moment. "Maybe you don't know him as well as you think."

"That's kind of what I wanted to talk to you about," he said. "You seem to be the only one who ever took the time to think about this guy. To everyone else I've spoken to he was just kind of a brownnose who did a semi-decent job. Is there anything else you remember about him that might help us? Something he said that might give us a hint why he poisoned those kids?"

"Did you ever consider the fact that maybe he's just a psychopath?"

"I might buy that if it weren't for all that money."

Annick looked surprised. "What money?"

"His bank account was pretty plump and he didn't seem to lack for anything. He had all the toys, an expensive house and a nice cash flow. It doesn't appear that he inherited some great sum of money or that he had an alternative source of income."

"What kind of money are we talking about here?" Annick asked, never even considering that her question might be crossing the line.

"A lot."

"Well, this is the first I've heard about the money and I don't have the first clue where he got it from. I'm sorry."

"It was a long shot," Thorne said. "Where do you think he got all of this stuff in his attic he was messing around with?"

"I don't know, but from what I guess we both know, it's not that hard to get almost anything. Being a microbiology tech, he's got the basic fund of knowledge. One of the biggest suppliers of bacterial cultures is right here in the U.S."

Thorne took out a pack of gum and offered Annick a stick. She indicated no, thank you, and he slid a piece into his mouth. She got the distinct feeling he was minimizing the magnitude of the problem that was before him. Annick suspected that deep down, Thorne gave Grady Simione more credit than even he wanted to admit to.

"He's certainly a strange duck," Thorne said.

"I wish I could tell you more."

"Don't worry about it. We'll eventually put the whole thing together. We just need a little more time."

Annick said, "I guess in the big picture, it was kind of nice and tidy the way it ended. With the kind of evidence you found it would have all been over if Grady were only there."

"Well, it doesn't always have to be hard. Every now and then even the FBI gets a break."

Annick's look was more coy than anything else. "I guess so, Mr. Thorne."

"I may want to speak to you again," he said, picking up her purse and handing it to her. "Here's my card."

"You know where to find me," she told him and then got into her car. As she pulled away, she looked in her rearview mirror. Special Agent Thorne was just standing there staring at her as she drove off.

Chapter Fifty-six

Annick was still thinking about her conversation with Thorne when the alert on her cellular phone chimed the "William Tell Overture."

"Hello," she said.

"How are you, Dr. Clement?" came the response in a very distinct but monotone voice. Annick recognized it in a flash. There was no doubt in her mind. It was Grady. She swallowed hard and found herself clenching the phone so tightly that her fingertips began to tingle.

"Why are you calling me?" she asked, fighting to hide the anxiety in her voice.

"I'm flattered you recognize my voice," he said.

"Where are you?"

He laughed. "In a safe place. With no FBI or meddling pediatric residents about."

"Why don't you give yourself up, Grady? They're looking for you everywhere. It's just a matter of time until they—"

"Catch me?" he interrupted. "I don't think so. Staying two steps ahead of those dim-witted bureaucrats barely classifies as a challenge. Aren't you going to ask me how I knew they'd be coming to my house that night?"

"The question has crossed my mind," she admitted, realizing he was in the mood to crow a little regarding his escape.

"I always knew staying chummy with Howe's secretary would pay off. She's always been a wealth of information, but the day he called in the authorities, well . . . she just couldn't stop talking about it. Once I learned you were on the list to be interviewed, I knew the FBI wouldn't be too far behind."

"You're a clever man, Grady."

"Except for one thing."

"And what might that be?" she asked.

"Well, I had to leave in quite a hurry, which means we have unfinished business, Dr. Clement."

"Are you threatening me?"

Grady hesitated for a moment. "Let's just say for the time being keeping you healthy might serve my purpose."

"Why did you hurt those children?" she demanded, shuddering at the thought of what he'd done.

"There were many reasons but it's complicated and we don't have the time to discuss it right now. Someday you'll see I'm not the animal you think I am. We make certain sacrifices in the name of necessity every day. Maybe you're too fragile or lack the resolve to understand what I'm talking about."

"None of this is about me, Grady."

"Perhaps, and I'd like to discuss that with you further but I fear my time is almost up. I just called to tell you that I'll be watching things very carefully."

"If you're trying to—"

"I have to go now, Annick. Oh, and don't bother trying to figure out where this call came from, you won't be able to."

Before Annick could utter another word, the phone went dead. The fear she should have been feeling was conspicuously absent. Nobody appreciated more than Annick what a monster Grady Simione was, but there was something in his voice, a lack of malice or emotion, that led her to believe that, at least for the moment, he intended her no harm. He acted like someone who believed they were in complete control.

She took a deep breath, cautioning herself on relying too much on her intuition. She looked behind her. A couple of cars back and one row over, she spotted her escort. Reaching into her pocket, she pulled out Thorne's card. He had written his number on the back and she dialed it.

"This is Thorne."

"It's Annick Clement. I just received a call from Grady Simione."

"Did he threaten you?"

"Not in so many words," she answered. "He said he was going to keep a close watch on things. He also mentioned that he didn't think much of your chances of finding him, nor would you be able to trace the call."

"Don't use the phone again. I don't suppose there was a number on the caller ID?"

"It's blank," she said.

"I'm going to contact the unit that's escorting you now. Just give the phone to Special Agent Cass as soon as you get home, and write down everything you can remember he said. I'll call you later."

"Not a problem."

"Are you okay?" he asked.

"I'm fine."

Annick waited in her driveway for the white Ford sedan to pull up across the street. A stiff-looking man wearing a blue ski jacket stepped out of the car and crossed the street. Annick handed the phone to Special Agent Cass, then let him escort her into her house. He spent the next ten minutes checking out the house and then left the same way he'd come in.

Annick looked out front through a large bay window. Apart from the Ford and two kids on scooters, there was nobody else in sight. She checked the time. Mac was due in about an hour. Glancing down at the phone, the thought crossed her mind to contact her father, but for the moment she decided against alarming him.

Chapter Fifty-seven

Annick was sitting on the end of her couch watching the late news when the phone rang. Asleep for the past two hours, Mac was sprawled out on her recliner breathing deeply. He didn't even stir when the phone rang.

"Hello," she said softly.

"Dr. Clement. This is Quinton Thorne calling. I hope I didn't wake you."

"Actually, I was just watching the news."

"I think I have some good news for you," he said. "We've just taken Simione into custody."

Annick closed her eyes, looked upward and mumbled a few words of thanks.

"Excuse me?" Thorne said.

"I said that's wonderful news." With a renewed spirit and great sense of relief, she asked, "Where did you find him?"

"Getting off of a plane in New Hampshire. An alert ticket agent at the Islip Airport out on Long Island spotted him. We had plenty of time to meet his connecting flight . . ."

Annick had remained fairly calm about Grady Simione being somewhere out there on the loose, but with Thorne's news came a measurable degree of relief. "Was anyone hurt?" she asked.

"No, he offered no resistance."

"I guess congratulations are in order. It looks like you've got everything all wrapped up."

"He said he wanted to talk with you," Thorne mentioned. "He claimed he admired your intellect."

"I guess that's one request I'll pass on," she said.

"I can't say as I blame you."

"Where do you go from here?" she asked.

"Well, we'll bring him back to New York to be arraigned. With the evidence we have on him, it shouldn't take very long to bring him to trial."

Annick glanced at Mac. He still hadn't moved.

"Will I have to testify?"

"We'll go over all that when I see you. We'll also be pulling our team off of your house."

"What about all that money Grady had that you were so worried about?" she asked.

"He's been pretty talkative. He claims he sold the technology he devised to others. He insists he's been working alone but I'm not sure he's telling the truth."

Annick picked her feet up and set them on the coffee table. "I'm glad you have him in custody."

"It's over, Dr. Clement. I'll speak to you when I get back to New York. Rest easy. We've got this maniac locked up tighter than the crown jewels."

Annick said good-bye and hung up the phone. She covered her mouth, yawned and then nudged Mac until he opened his eyes.

"Wake up, Mac. Thorne just called. They caught that miserable son of a bitch," she said with delight.

"That's great, Annick. You must really be relieved."

"I guess I'm more relieved for the children of the world than I am for myself with that misfit of humanity finally off the streets." She picked up a magazine, tossed it high into the air and tried to catch it as it fell. "Are you ready to go to bed?" she asked.

Mac looked down at his watch and rubbed his eyes. "I thought I was in bed," he groaned. It had been a long day and Annick could see how exhausted Mac was.

When he came out of the bathroom she was already in bed

wearing a pink Disney World nightshirt. "Can you set the alarm for six?" he asked with a perplexed look. "You'd think a girl from Paris would have sexier lingerie than you do."

Annick looked down at herself and pulled the covers up to her chin. "It hasn't seemed to stop you so far."

Mac slid into bed, reached across Annick, turned off her light and then slid his hand behind her. "You always give me something to look forward to," he whispered.

She kissed him once. "I wouldn't have it any other way."

Chapter Fifty-eight

Grand rounds was a conference that Annick made sure she attended every Friday morning. The entire medical staff, residents and medical students assembled in the main auditorium to discuss a particularly interesting case that had recently been seen at Franklin. The conference lasted one hour and Annick had always found it extremely informative and interesting.

Standing in the foyer just outside the main auditorium talking to some of the residents afterward, Annick looked up and caught Dr. Bart Kincaid's eye. She hadn't seen him since visiting him in his lab and persuading him to send a sample of his botulism toxin to Atlanta. As soon as the CDC called with the results that proved Dr. Kincaid's toxin was distinctly different from the one that had poisoned Michael Flannery, she called to inform him.

Kincaid was dressed in dark pants with a plaid shirt and a solid blue tie. His hair was disheveled. He nodded at her and then waved her over. Out of pure respect, she excused herself for the moment and walked the few paces to where he was standing.

"Hello, Annick."

"Dr. Kincaid," she said evenly.

"I've been meaning to call you to congratulate you. I guess your suspicions were correct."

"I guess I just got lucky."

"Maybe, but satisfy my curiosity for a moment. Did you really think my toxin was the one that poisoned those children?"

"I wasn't quite sure of anything at that point," she said, taking care to answer his question as nebulously as possible. She couldn't quite read his eyes but it was almost as if he were looking for some final form of exoneration.

"Now that it's all over, I don't mind telling you that I was a little nervous that you felt I was somehow involved in something sinister."

"It never crossed my mind," she assured him. Annick wasn't quite sure what was really on Kincaid's mind. Thorne had told her that they were trying to keep Grady's capture quiet for a few days so she didn't see any reason to share the information with Kincaid.

"Do you think he was working alone?" he asked.

"I don't know," she answered with a shrug. "I guess that's for the FBI to figure out."

"Are they talking to you about the investigation?" he asked in an offhand tone as he waved to one of his fellow researchers who had also attended the conference.

"No, Dr. Kincaid. I'm in the same boat as everyone else. All I know is what I read in the papers."

"I've been around a long time," he said, shaking his head, "but I've never seen anything like this. It's kind of exciting in a way. I hope I'm around to see how it all comes out."

Annick tilted her head a little to one side. "Are you leaving Franklin Children's?"

"I have a very tempting offer in the Midwest. I'm giving it serious consideration."

Annick studied his face and then looked down to check her pager. "I wish you luck if you decide to take the position. It was nice seeing you again."

They shook hands and Kincaid disappeared to join a small group of his colleagues who had congregated across from the auditorium. Annick watched him for a few seconds and then attributed his strange questions to the normal titillation that surrounds strange events. She walked to a phone in a small booth behind the main entrance to the auditorium and dialed the operator.

"This is Dr. Clement."

"We have an outside call for you, Doctor," the operator said in a scratchy voice. "Please hang up and I'll ring you right back."

"Hello, this is Dr. Clement."

The caller spoke in perfect French. "Dr. Clement, this is Claude Vincent with the *Figaro* in Paris. We've heard what a wonderful doctor you are and would like to interview you as soon as possible."

Annick giggled. In spite of his best efforts, she recognized Philippe's voice.

"That would be wonderful. But I insist that Philippe Descartes be there with me because he's my only reason for living."

"Very funny," he said, his voice dejected.

"How old are you, Philippe? You're still playing the same silly tricks on me you did when I was a child."

"Some would claim you are still a child."

"Yeah, you and my father. Where are you?"

"Actually, I'm in New York. I arrived yesterday. It's a nice change. I've been stuck in Venezuela for the last three days trying to pound out a deal with a bunch of very stubborn men."

"Is my father with you?" she asked in an excited voice. "I can't believe he would come without calling or—"

"Calm down. I'm here alone."

"Is he down in Nice at the house?"

"No, he's in Paris. Uh . . . I thought you knew he sold the house," Philippe said gingerly.

"No, I had no idea," she said in a puzzled voice. "I wonder why he did that. We both loved that house."

"I'm not positive but I think he felt nobody was using it and that it would be simpler just to rent a place when the two of you wanted to go down there."

Annick was still a little shocked. She spoke with her father at least twice a week. He loved their vacation home in the south of France. She couldn't believe he hadn't mentioned selling it to her. As crazy as it was, the thought even crossed her mind that perhaps her father was in financial difficulty.

"Well, he's the financial genius in the family," Annick finally said. "I guess I'll just have to defer to his opinion on real estate transactions."

"That's probably not a bad idea," Philippe told her. "How about some dinner Sunday night? Are you and Mac available?"

"Actually, we are. We'd love to have dinner with you."

"Great. I'll call you later and we can pick a place to meet."

Annick hung up the phone and turned around. As she glanced up, she caught Bart Kincaid staring at her. Instead of smiling, he looked away immediately. She was starting to wonder what kind of strange effect being cooped up in that laboratory was starting to have on him. It couldn't possibly be anything romantic, he was so much older than she. Whatever it was he found intriguing, she got the distinct feeling she hadn't heard the last from Bart Kincaid.

Chapter Fifty-nine

The Inn at Great Neck was a small hotel located in the central part of the downtown area just across from the railroad station. Immediately adjacent to the entrance, a patio with several tables adjoined a large bar located off the lobby. Annick and Mac had been there several times, enjoying the generally quiet atmosphere and comfortable decor.

"I figured you'd be happy," Mac said. "Simione's in jail and it looks like they've got him nailed dead to rights."

"I am happy."

"Then what is it?" Mac asked as a young waitress with black pants and a red vest approached to take their order. "I'll have an Amstel Light," he said and then looked over at Annick.

"A cosmopolitan, please."

"What's bugging you about all this?" Mac asked again.

She gazed past him for a moment, looking at the smartly crafted wood wine rack behind the bar. "I've already told you," she said flatly. "It just seems like everything ended almost as if it had been scripted."

"What do you mean?"

"Grady Simione's not that stupid. Why would he have all that stuff lying around his house?"

Mac slipped off his black sweatshirt and tossed it on the

chair next to him. A young couple walked past and sat down at the bar. "I thought you told me that *all that stuff* was hidden behind a false wall. That sounds pretty clever to me."

"And all this money he supposedly has?" she asked.

"You said the FBI is looking into that."

"They are."

"People get money in all kinds of ways, Annick." Mac waited for a few moments as the waitress placed their drinks in front of them. "He might have had some help but that doesn't necessarily mean that someone else was aware of what he was doing." Mac reached down, picked up the frosted mug and took a long swig. "This whole thing was the act of a crackpot, Annick. Why would anyone else be involved?"

"What about Joelle Parsons?" she asked.

"What about her?"

"Where did she come from?"

"I . . . I don't know, maybe—"

"If it weren't for the information she gave me, I never would have made the connection between Justin Silva and Michael Flannery," she said.

"She could have been anybody who worked in the hospital who had a hunch."

"If that were the case, she could have just called," Annick pointed out.

He raised his mug again. "Maybe she felt an anonymous phone call wouldn't have been taken seriously."

Annick listened carefully as she stirred her drink. She realized he was playing the devil's advocate, but his points were all well taken and his explanations quite feasible.

"You may be right, and I hate to sound pessimistic but I still think there may be something more to all this," she said.

"Let the FBI handle it, Annick. You've already done enough." Mac took another long swallow of the beer and then looked over at the couple at the bar who were laughing hysterically. "Have the press or TV people found you yet?"

"No. The hospital administration and the FBI have done a great job in keeping me out of it."

Annick leaned her head back and took the first quaff of her cosmopolitan. She listened to the soft jazz in the background, recognizing the mellow sound of a musician who could make a sax sound like something from heaven. The music changed her mood for the better, and as the drink passed her lips she decided to leave the matter of Grady Simione alone and concentrate on enjoying the rest of the evening.

Chapter Sixty

Annick picked up the patient chart she'd been reviewing and slid it back into the rack. The charge nurse, Daisy Saybow, sat a couple of seats away going over a recent update on the policies and procedures for disposal of medical supplies. Daisy was just starting her second year on the nursing staff, having transferred from Long Island Jewish, which was only a few miles away. Adaptable and low-keyed, Daisy's transition to Franklin had been a smooth one.

"We sure miss Michael Flannery around here," she told Annick.

"You always remember the winners," she answered. "I've seen him as an outpatient a couple of times. He's really doing great."

"We heard how sick he was from the ICU nurses, but he sailed right through once he was transferred to us."

"I think the antitoxin really helped. He certainly gave us a scare."

"Do you think things are starting to calm down around here?" Daisy asked.

Annick looked surprised. "What do you mean?"

"With that whole Grady Simione thing. Just the thought of him gives me the creeps."

"I guess you and Danielle must feel a little silly now about asking me to thank Grady for being so wonderful and attentive to Michael."

Daisy put her pen down and gazed over at Annick with an uncertain look. "You lost me, Annick. What are you talking about?"

"The day Michael went home. Danielle told me that the nurses got together and felt it would be nice to thank Grady for taking such an interest in Michael." Daisy's face remained blank. "She said you knew all about it."

Daisy removed her reading glasses, slipped them into her pocket and thought for a few moments. "I still don't know what you're talking about."

Annick stood up, walked the few paces over to Daisy and sat down next to her.

"It was my understanding that the nurses wanted me to thank Grady for his personal attention to Michael. If that has now become a source of embarrassment to your staff, I'm more than happy to forget it ever happened."

"Look, Grady was down here a few times but I wouldn't say he spent any extra time with Michael or any other patient. And I'm not aware of any of the nurses getting together to make sure he was properly thanked."

"Are you saying that Danielle didn't even—"

"Who's Danielle?" Daisy asked as the two women exchanged an equally bewildered glance.

"I thought she was one of your nurses," Annick said.

"I've never had anybody named Danielle work for me," Daisy assured her.

Annick sat back in her chair and crossed her arms. "Now, let's slow down for a minute, and I apologize for repeating myself, but are you telling me that you have no recollection of the nurses getting together and asking me if I would personally thank Grady for his special interest in Michael?"

"It never happened."

"And you have zero idea who Danielle Sudor is?"

"As I said, no such person has worked on this floor since I've been the nurse manager, and that was months before

Michael Flannery was admitted to the unit. What the hell's going on, Annick?"

"I wish I knew," Annick offered. She stood up and headed down the hall.

What the hell's going on around here? First there's no Joelle Parsons and now Danielle Sudor could turn out to be a myth.

Chapter Sixty-one

Having no reason to doubt Daisy, Annick found the nearest phone and immediately dialed Paulette Davis in Human Resources.

"Paulette, it's Annick. I need a favor."

"I beg your pardon but I think you've used up all your favors for one millennium," Paulette advised her.

"C'mon, this is important."

"Where have I heard that before?" she groaned.

"Flu season's coming up," Annick teased. "You better stay on my good side."

"Don't give me that crap," Paulette said. "You're already locked into being my kids' personal physician from the last deal we made."

"Don't make me beg," Annick said.

"Okay, what is it?"

"Actually, it's an easy one. Have we had a nurse by the name of Danielle Sudor working at Franklin in the last few months?"

"No."

"How can you be so sure? You didn't even check," Annick said.

"That's because I don't have to check. I prepare the file on every new nurse that's hired. I may not know every little detail about them but I'd certainly recognize all of their names."

"What about agency nurses?" Annick asked.

"Sorry, we haven't used any in the last six months."

"I can't believe it," Annick said, more to herself than Paulette. "What in God's name is going on around here?"

"What are you talking about, Annick?"

"Not more than a couple of weeks ago, I personally spoke with a registered nurse in the lobby with a big Franklin Children's ID badge pinned to her uniform that clearly stated her name was Danielle Sudor."

"You must be mistaken."

"I'm not mistaken, Paulette. I spoke with the woman face to face for five minutes."

"Maybe you got her name wrong," Paulette suggested. "Have you ever seen her since?"

Annick closed her eyes. Her stomach felt like she was halfway into the most turbulent roller-coaster ride of her life.

"Annick?" Paulette asked and then renewed her question. "Have you ever seen her since?"

"No," she mumbled. "I haven't. If she wasn't a legitimate nurse working here, where did she get the ID?"

"Anybody who is computer literate can make a phony ID, Annick. Every college kid under the age of twenty-one in the state has one. We've come across dozens of fake and altered hospital ID badges. Look, I guess I don't need to know the details of what's going on here, but maybe you should take this up with security." Annick barely heard her friend's suggestion and failed to respond. "Annick, are you still there?"

"Yeah, thanks for the information. I'll speak to you later."

Whoever Danielle Sudor was, she had led her right to Grady Simione. A situation very reminiscent of what Joelle Parsons had done with respect to Justin Silva. Annick tried in vain to calm herself.

Who were these women and what was their real connection to Grady Simione . . . and even more puzzling, why were they so anxious to help her uncover his depraved acts?

Chapter Sixty-two

After Grady Simione spent a couple of days in the Manchester, New Hampshire, jail, his paperwork had been completed and arrangements made for his transfer back to New York. It was exactly eight A.M. when he was led from the jail to a waiting black Chevrolet Tahoe. In order to avoid a giant media circus, the authorities decided to keep Grady's arrest confidential until he was returned to New York.

He was dressed in the same clothes he'd been arrested in, chino pants, a blue flannel shirt and his navy pea coat. The morning was damp with a stubborn fog that had rolled in the night before. The rising sun had done little to burn it off. Grady sat in the backseat with Special Agent Mel Pickering, a practiced agent who began his government service in the Treasury Department before transferring to the FBI. With a well-developed paunch and a dismal wardrobe, he probably would have been better looking if he cared about his appearance. A man with a limited imagination, Pickering was just marking time until the day his retirement arrived.

The two agents in the front seat said nothing as the Tahoe cruised at exactly fifty-five miles an hour toward the airport.

Deke Sanders, the agent sitting on the passenger side, glanced over his shoulder every minute or so.

Once they were in front of the terminal, Pickering covered the handcuffs that joined his right hand to Grady's left with his topcoat, waited for Sanders to open the door and led Grady out. Standing in front of the terminal, Pickering looked around and cursed the lousy weather and then told his partner, "We're flying commercial today."

"How come?"

"Our plane's down with a mechanical problem. I just found out about it a couple of hours ago."

"I hate flying commercial," Sanders complained.

The terminal was fairly modern but poorly heated. The two agents escorted Simione past a dozen boarding areas before reaching their gate, which was small, with the ticket counter immediately adjacent to the jetway. They hadn't been waiting for more than five minutes when an announcement was made that all flights were on hold because of the worsening fog. With the announcement of the indeterminate delay came the groans of the waiting passengers, followed by a mass exodus to the nearby gift shop and restaurant.

"Over there," Pickering said to Grady, pointing to three empty chairs located directly in front of an enormous window overlooking the tarmac. Grady nodded and walked with Pickering over to the seats.

"I'm going to the john," Sanders said, which met with a quick nod from Pickering.

Once seated, Grady extended his legs and glanced out the window. Through the thick fog he could barely make out the outline of the 737 that was scheduled to take them to LaGuardia Airport. He leaned his head back to better appreciate the enticing aroma of the fresh bread that was being baked in the nearby restaurant.

His eyes scanned the area. At the same time his mind began to act as a sponge acquiring bits of information. One airline agent remained at the ticket counter with his head buried behind a computer monitor and his fingers firing away at the keyboard. The few passengers that remained in the boarding area sat with their backs to Grady and Pickering. It had been about a minute since Sanders had left.

Grady took another deep breath, extended his head as far back as possible and stared at the ceiling. When he chuckled, Pickering looked over at him and then gazed up as well. His right hand free, Grady rotated his right shoulder forward, whirling his open hand around and catching Pickering directly in the throat with a pistonlike force that instantaneously shattered his windpipe and voice box. Pickering's last effort to gasp was muffled by Grady's hand covering his mouth. The entire move took less than a few seconds and attracted no attention. Grady held his hand in place until he felt the muscles of Pickering's neck go limp.

Letting his captor's head fall gently back against the chair, Grady reached into the waist pocket of Pickering's tweed sport coat and pulled out a small ring of keys. It was obvious which one would open the cuffs. Another twenty seconds passed and Grady was free. He stood up, pretended to stretch and looked around. Pickering's position was perfect but Grady couldn't resist the temptation to slide his hat just over his eyes, leaving the special agent looking like he was just taking an innocent catnap. Sanders was nowhere in sight.

Leaning over Pickering, Grady slid his hand into the inside pocket of the sport coat and pulled out his wallet. Without looking around, he pushed the wallet deep into the back pocket of his pants and strode out of the boarding area. When he had reached the next gate area, he looked back. There was Pickering, just the way he'd left him, with no one the wiser.

Grady exited the terminal and looked around. As he considered his options, a van from the remote parking area puffing great clouds of heavy charcoal smoke from a faulty muffler pulled up. The driver jumped out, opened the door and Grady got in with five other people. The van pulled away and circled the airport until reaching the long-term-parking lot. Peering out the window, Grady noticed the fog had become even denser. He watched as a young woman with an expensive leather carry-on stood up to exit at the first stop. When the van thumped to a stop, Grady got up and followed her out, but then immediately turned and headed down the next aisle from her. He was about fifteen feet away and the visibility was just enough to follow her silhouette as she strode down past a dozen or so parked cars until arriving at her own.

Moving in closer, he squatted down behind a black pickup and watched until she had her keys in hand. Sliding between two cars, he emerged just a few feet away from her. He heard her lock release and then quickly slid behind her. Before she could react, he grabbed her hair and chin and snapped her neck with one powerful twist. Her momentary scream was smothered by his hand.

Looking around for a moment, Grady let the woman's lifeless body slump to the pavement. Kneeling down beside her, he quickly found her keys and parking receipt. Emptying her purse of eight hundred dollars in cash, he then rolled her body under a white station wagon parked in the next space.

From the fresh smell of the Volvo's leather, Grady assumed the dead woman's car couldn't have been more than a couple of months old. Winking at the young lady in the cashier's booth, Grady handed her a twenty-dollar bill, said thank you for the change and exited the airport.

It took Special Agent Sanders twelve minutes to complete his business in the bathroom and answer a page from the FBI office in New York. The moment he approached the gate area, he sensed something was wrong. He quickly scanned the area again but still didn't see two men sitting together. In the next moment his eye focused on the man who was apparently asleep with his hat tucked over his eyes. Recognizing his coat this time, Sanders sprung forward. Arriving at his partner's side, he kneeled down and pushed back his hat and then shook him. Pickering's head fell forward as if it had no bony support. Without wasting another moment, Sanders felt for a carotid pulse but there was none.

He reached for his weapon but never removed it from the leather holster he wore under his sport coat. He then took a careful look around. Gazing toward the ticket counter, he saw the young man busy at work at the computer. Walking over to the counter and then displaying his badge, he said, "My name is Special Agent Sanders. I'm with the FBI. We have a situation here. As quietly as you can, I want you to call the paramedics and airport security to this gate. I'll explain everything when they get here. Don't ask any questions. Just do it."

Sanders's face was controlled but earnest. The airline agent paused for only a moment, looked over in Pickering's direction and then reached for the phone. At the same time, Sanders pulled his cell phone and dialed the regional office in Boston.

"Shit," he whispered to himself. Ten minutes later, when he received complete instructions, including an order to contact the Manchester Police Department, Grady Simione was already setting a course for Long Island.

Chapter Sixty-three

Grady followed the slow-moving line of cars and trucks through the exact-change lane of the Throg's Neck Bridge toll-booth. Listening to his favorite classical music channel for the last hour had done wonders to calm his nerves. He soon reached the Cross Island Parkway, which led him to the eastbound Long Island Expressway. After giving the matter quite a bit of thought, he figured the body of the woman he had killed had either been found already or soon would be.

Two months before he finalized his plans to poison Michael Flannery and Justin Silva, Grady rented a bay at a large storage facility in Smithtown on Long Island. It was clear to him from the beginning that to embark on such an undertaking at Franklin Children's without a carefully thought-out exit strategy would have been folly.

After exiting the expressway, Grady followed the streets until he spotted the series of prefab storage facilities. A winding gravel road led up to and then around the entire complex. Large floodlights mounted on the roofs of the two corner buildings illuminated the entire area.

Parking his car behind building A in a parcel of land that looked more like a junkyard than anything else, Grady got out and walked about a hundred yards farther until he reached building E. It was almost dark with just a wisp of an icy wind that was made foul by the odor of stale garbage from a nearby dump.

Grady tapped in the entrance code on the touch pad and pushed the door open. The building was poorly lit but he was familiar with the floor plan and easily navigated through the enormous warehouse until he found his bay. The cheap furniture he had purchased as a decoy was stacked exactly the way he'd left it. Entering the combination to the lock, he gently tugged down, sprung the lock and opened the door.

In the middle of the area, just in front of an old brown corduroy couch, sat a small trunk. Grady reached under the middle cushion of the musty couch, slid out a gold key and opened the trunk. There were only two items inside. One was a black garment bag; the other was a circular tin that once held an assortment of cream-filled cookies. Grady lifted the tin out of the trunk and then hung the garment bag on a small hook. Working his nails around the rim, he released the top of the tin and set it down on a small wooden end table.

Reaching in carefully, he removed a United States passport. He had paid a small fortune for it but the workmanship was extraordinary, including stamps from various countries with dates indicating travel over the past five years. He smiled at the photo of Father Sean Exelby, a man of the cloth who truly enjoyed traveling. Next, he removed a stack of cash and counted it out—three thousand dollars in twenties and fifties. Then on to the credit cards. There were two—both gold—one American Express, one Visa. Finally, the New Jersey driver's license, also a work of art.

Grady checked the time. It was five-fifty. He placed the items back in the tin just the way he'd found them and then turned his attention to the garment bag. Sliding the zipper gently down, he stood back to marvel at the perfectly pressed priest's wardrobe.

Taking a deep breath, he sat down on a lumpy old recliner that had lost its form years ago. He reached forward and slid his hand under the chair, exploring with his fingers until he found the corner of the New York State license plate he had stolen a few days before he first rented the storage space. Sliding the plate out, he picked it up and smiled, fully content that his meticulous planning for any eventuality had again paid off. He would only keep the dead woman's car another twenty-four hours and he'd probably be fine with the New Hampshire plate, but it was such an easy matter to switch it for the added degree of security.

Having spent most of the day on the road trying to keep his wits about him every mile of the way hadn't left him much time to consider his options. There were many uncertainties, but he was fairly sure the FBI would not credit him with sufficient brains to be prepared to leave the country.

He got up from the recliner and walked back to the trunk. The one strange fact that still plagued him was Annick Clement's role in this whole thing. Was she really as smart as she seemed or was she just the luckiest woman in the entire state of New York? There wasn't a sound in the entire warehouse. The distinctive odor of moist cardboard and must tickled his nose. He looked over at the recliner, walked back over and sat down. Almost immediately, his eyes closed and his breathing slowed. Exhaustion overtook him and within moments he was asleep.

Chapter Sixty-four

At about the same time Grady drifted off to sleep in Smithtown, Officer Roy White of the Manchester Police Department led Samson, a two-year-old German shepherd, down one of the central rows of the airport's long-term parking. Samson and Roy had trained together for almost a year, were inseparable and formed an excellent team, both relying on instinct and trust.

It had occurred to both the Manchester authorities and the FBI that it was a real possibility that Grady Simione had never left the airport grounds and had found a hiding place in a facility that was chock-full of excellent ones. Unfortunately, their exhaustive search had turned up nothing.

Roy pulled his collar up as a wet snow started to sprinkle his husky neck. He looked down at Samson, who seemed to be indifferent to the sudden change in weather. As they approached the white station wagon, Samson stopped and began barking and scratching at the pavement just below the passenger-side door.

"What do you have, boy?" White asked, pulling out his flashlight and kneeling down next to the dog. At first he didn't see anything and assumed Samson was off on a wild-goose chase, but as he edged forward a little, he caught the first view of Cora Treacher's hand. He pulled Samson back and laid down on his belly to have a better view. Pulling his gloves off, Roy reached for her wrist to see if he could feel a pulse. After a few moments, he closed his eyes. Her hand was frozen and pulse-less.

"Can you hear me, miss?" he asked, not really expecting an answer.

Wary about disturbing a possible crime scene, White had no choice but to move the body out from under the car to see if she were alive. Grabbing her hand and thigh and applying a gentle tug, he easily slid the body out. Her eyes were rolled up and her skin was icy-cold. He laid his ear on her chest but heard nothing. Before proceeding, he pulled out his radio and summoned both backup and medical assistance. As an act of desperation, he leaned over and blew three large breaths into her frozen mouth.

Another minute or so passed and he heard the wail of the sirens. The paramedics were the first ones on the scene. White immediately backed off as they began to work at a feverish pace.

A boxy man in a Manchester Police Department sergeant's uniform emerged from a brown cruiser, approached and then stopped right behind White.

"What do you got, Roy?" Carson Bradley asked.

"I'm not sure, Sarge. Samson found her. I'm pretty sure she's dead. She can't be more than thirty. Do you think this is tied into Simione?"

"I don't know, Roy . . . but then again, how many murders have you seen out here in the last dozen years? I called those FBI boys. They'll be here in a few minutes. I don't suppose her purse is anywhere around."

"I didn't see one."

White stood back and watched the paramedics. He didn't have much medical training but he did know what a flat line on a heart monitor meant.

"We'll go ahead and transport her but I think she's gone," the first paramedic said to White, who just nodded. They placed Cora gently on a stretcher and slid her into the ambulance. Roy White watched the ambulance speed away with its lights flashing. When it was out of sight, he reached down and rubbed

Samson's soft ears, which immediately made his tail start to wag.

"Sometimes I envy you, boy," he said.

Ten minutes later, Dr. Mark Ireland, the emergency room physician on call, pronounced Cora Treacher dead.

Chapter Sixty-five

"I was hoping Mac could make it for dinner," Philippe told Annick as he kissed her.

"He was planning on it but things got crazy this afternoon in the hospital and he wasn't comfortable leaving. After dinner I'll probably have to go back and give him a hand."

Philippe looked around, hung his coat on a brass hook and then sat down. "That must explains your choice of this elegant restaurant."

"Don't be such a snob," she said with total affection. "We commoners eat here all the time. The food's fine."

Philippe looked skeptical. "I'm sure . . . if you like bacon burgers," he said, opening the menu.

"Have you been doing much flying?" she asked.

"Whenever I can. I'd like to purchase an acrobatic plane but they're pretty expensive."

Annick looked horrified. "You're a great pilot, Philippe, but why don't you just stick to flying the company jet? It's probably a lot safer."

"But not nearly as much fun."

She smiled as she bowed her head and shook it slowly. "How's Daddy?"

"He's working too hard, as usual. I'm afraid he's burning the candle at both ends, as they say in the United States."

"He hasn't been talking about his business much lately. I'm a little worried," Annick said.

Philippe laughed. "Worried about Luc Clement, are you? I hardly think that's necessary. He's always one step ahead of the pack."

"I just spoke to him the other day. He didn't sound like himself," she said.

"We have a lot of deals cooking right now. He's got a lot on his mind." Philippe motioned the waitress, who came straight over to the table. They each ordered a glass of Chardonnay.

"I worry about him sometimes," Annick confessed.

"C'mon, Annick, he's healthy as an ox and he loves to work."

"Even oxen get tired eventually, Philippe. I can't remember the last time he took a real vacation. I was going to suggest we meet at the house in Nice in April but I guess that's not going to happen."

"Stop pouting. There are plenty of houses to rent on the Riviera."

"It's not the same. I still can't believe he sold our house. He loved that place so much."

"With your mom gone and you out of the country . . . well, I guess he just didn't see the need any longer."

"Maybe," she said, hardly noticing when the waitress placed her wine down in front of her.

Philippe raised his glass immediately and tapped her on the wrist to do the same. "To your continued success in the United States," he toasted.

She smiled, raised her glass and said thank you. Philippe looked as debonair as ever. His gray cashmere sweater and black dress pants fit perfectly. She had always been very comfortable around him, appreciating the special affection he felt for her. Her father still contended it was somewhat romantic but Annick chose to disagree.

As much as it offended his aristocratic taste buds, Philippe managed to put away the better part of his cheeseburger while Annick enjoyed a chicken and pasta dish. They each ordered a second glass of wine and spent the next hour reminiscing and talking about the future. Annick checked her watch and Philippe signaled the waitress for the bill.

"I'll meet you by the front door," he said. "I have to make a stop."

"I'll wait for the change," she said.

Just as she stood up, her pager went off. The number was familiar but she couldn't quite place it. She opened her purse and rummaged around until she found her cell phone.

As soon as she heard his voice, she knew it was Thorne.

"Good evening, Dr. Clement."

"Special Agent Thorne, how are you?"

"I've had better days," he said.

Annick sat down. "I don't like the sound of that," she said.

"As embarrassing as this is to tell you, it seems as if Mr. Simione has escaped. We expect to pick him up within the next few hours but I wanted you to be aware."

Annick struggled to gather herself. Thorne's news was the last thing she expected to hear. She hadn't forgotten Grady's pledge to cause her no harm, but she still felt endangered by the thought of him being at large again.

"I . . . I appreciate you calling to let me know," was all she could manage.

"We're going to have two of our agents meet you and escort you home. I assume you're still at the hospital."

"Actually, I'm out to dinner with an old friend."

"Where exactly are you, Dr. Clement?" he asked. His tone was clearly one of concern, not panic.

"We're at Friday's in Great Neck."

"Just stay inside by the entrance. I'll have somebody there in fifteen minutes."

It crossed her mind to tell Thorne she could stay at Mac's but she realized he'd never agree to the proposal. "Thank you," she said. "I guess Grady's not quite as dumb as you thought."

"We don't lose too many, Doctor. We caught him once, we'll get him again. It's still your feeling that he doesn't intend you any harm?"

"I'm not a mind reader, but, no, I don't think he'll come after me."

"I'll speak to you later this evening," he said.

Annick picked up her purse and then put on her coat.

The waitress returned with a small tray holding the change from Philippe's fifty-dollar bill. Glancing toward the front of the restaurant, Annick noticed a man standing by the entrance with a tan topcoat. His head was turned away and for a moment Annick was consumed by a strong feeling of déjà vu. Before she could make the connection, Philippe turned around and smiled at her. Feeling a little foolish and perhaps a little too alarmed by Thorne's call, she waved, picked up the change from the tray and walked up front.

"Why don't you go ahead," she said, not seeing any reason to burden him with the entire saga that surrounded Grady Simione. "I'm going to call Mac and see if he really needs me. If he doesn't, I'm going to head home. When are you going back to Paris?"

"I haven't finalized my plans as yet. It depends on when all the meetings are over."

"I'm still surprised my father isn't coming in to join you," she said.

"These are just preliminary conferences. When it's time to close the deal, he'll be here."

Philippe stepped forward, placed his hands on her shoulders and kissed her good-bye. She watched as he got into his waiting limo and pulled out of the parking lot. After staring out the door for a few more seconds, she sat down on a wooden bench, wondering how the FBI could have been so careless as to allow Grady to escape. It suddenly occurred to her that she hadn't asked Thorne what time he'd escaped or from where. Thorne's question regarding Grady's intentions was not a strange one and the more she thought about it, the more she had to face the possibility that he could be heading straight for Long Island at this very moment.

Chapter Sixty-six

Thirty minutes after Annick began morning rounds, she was summoned to Dr. Howe's office. The moment she arrived, she was escorted in by Howe's secretary. Her first sight was of Dr. Howe sitting behind his desk with a very solemn expression. Two more steps forward and she spotted Quinton Thorne sitting in one of the chairs in front of the desk. The look on his face wasn't much different from Howe's.

"Have a seat, Annick," Howe said. "I've just been talking to Special Agent Thorne, who has expressed some serious concerns about your safety."

Annick locked eyes with Thorne, giving him a look that was somewhere between exasperated and annoyed. His return look was neutral and accompanied by a slight shrug.

"While I truly appreciate Mr. Thorne's concern, I really think I'll be fine."

Howe looked unconvinced. "We both agree it might be a good idea for you to take a couple of weeks off."

"A couple of weeks? Dr. Howe, I really don't think this would be a good time for me to leave—"

Howe raised his hand to interrupt her.

"If Mr. Simione is apprehended sooner, we both see no reason why you can't return at that time."

"Your father agrees," Thorne said.

Annick turned her head slowly toward him. "I'm an adult, Mr. Thorne. I'm not sure I appreciate you contacting my father without consulting me. This is not his problem and I didn't want to worry him."

Thorne ran his hand through his hair and then sat up a little taller in his chair. "If I upset you, I apologize, but in view of your father's access to transatlantic transportation, we felt it would be the fastest way of getting you someplace safe."

"I'll have to give this whole matter some thought," she insisted.

Thorne looked at his watch. "I'm afraid you'll only have about eight hours to do that."

"And why's that?" she asked.

"Because your father has already sent his jet. They're going to pick you up tonight and turn right around and go back. We'll of course escort you to the airport."

"Oh, of course," she repeated and slapped the armrests of her chair and looked at Howe. "Sir, we're already one person short on the service and things have been crazy around here for the last few days. It's too much for Mac to handle by himself."

"Mac will be fine," Howe assured her. "We'll all help him. Need I remind you that you're here as an exchange resident? It's my responsibility to make sure you return to France safely. I'm personally asking you to leave for Paris this evening."

Annick crossed her arms. "I'm here in the United States at your invitation, Dr. Howe. I will go along with your wishes."

"I'm glad to hear you say that. Now, at the moment, Mr. Thorne and myself are the only two people on this side of the Atlantic who know about this. I don't suppose it would do any good to tell you not to say anything to Mac, so I won't bother trying. Other than him, however, I wouldn't say a word to anyone."

"If it would be possible, I'd like to finish today's work."

"Of course," Howe answered.

"Just don't leave the hospital," Thorne added.

Annick stood up and turned her back to Howe in such a way as to completely block his view of Thorne. When she was in the perfect position, she stuck her tongue out at the man from the FBI, whom she knew had a small crush on her. Being the true professional he was, Thorne's expression never changed, but it did take every bit of self-control he could gather not to break out in an enormous smile.

Chapter Sixty-seven

Annick landed in Paris at ten A.M. The flight had actually turned out to be more bearable than she expected. Using the time to relax, she read, watched a movie and eventually fell asleep for a couple of hours. When she stepped off the Gulfstream, she filled her lungs with a breath of the crisp Parisian morning.

By the time she went through customs, most of the morning traffic had dissipated, making the ride to her apartment a quick one. Her father had left her a message that he'd be in London until early evening but that he'd definitely be home in time to have dinner with her.

Setting her carry-on down in the foyer and just being in her apartment made Annick feel secure and at ease. As soon as she put her things away, she went to the dining room and enjoyed a late breakfast of yogurt, assorted fruits and a chocolate croissant the cook prepared especially for her. When she was done, she decided to give Dr. Aaron a call at the Pasteur Institute to see if he could meet with her.

"I'm back in Paris," she told him as soon as he said hello.

"And to what do we owe this stroke of good fortune?"

"A couple of things, actually. I was hoping we could get together later today to talk about it."

"It would be my pleasure. Why don't you come over at about half past eleven?"

"I'll look forward to seeing you," she said.

Annick had the doorman flag a cab for her and ten minutes later the late-model Peugeot rolled up in front of the Pasteur Institute. Crossing the campus quickly, Annick went directly to Dr. Aaron's office, where she found the old man watering a large potted plant.

"Hi, Professor," she said from the door.

He smiled, put down the glass of water and met her in the middle of the room. He had trimmed his beard since the last time she'd seen him and was actually sporting a new gray-and-black sweater vest. His eyes were a little puffy and his desk looked like there was two years of work piled on it.

"It's very nice to see you but I wasn't expecting you back so soon. This doesn't have anything to do with all that business at Franklin Children's, I hope."

"So you obviously heard about it?" she asked.

"It wasn't exactly earth-shaking news but it certainly drew some attention in the papers. Based on our brief conversation the last week, I was going to give you a call. I understand they apprehended the man responsible."

He escorted her to a chair, waited for her to be seated and then sat down on the corner of his desk. The office was a little warm and Annick took off her sweater.

"They caught him right away, but unfortunately he escaped, which they're doing their level best to keep a secret. I think they're underestimating how cunning and resourceful this man is."

The old man stroked his whiskers as he listened. "Which brings me back to my original question. Am I to understand that your presence in Paris has something to do with all of this?"

"Well, let's just say the FBI thought it would be safer if I disappeared for a few days until they caught him again."

"I assume your father knows about all this," he said.

"He knows I'm somehow involved but I've tried to leave the actual details a little vague."

"Do you think that's wise?"

"I'm not sure about anything anymore."

"Where's your father now?"

"He's in London. He'll be back tonight."

"I hope he's not regretting helping you get that position at Franklin Children's," Aaron said.

Annick looked a little surprised. "I wasn't aware he was involved with that."

Aaron closed his eyes and shook his head. "Please forgive the rambling of an old fool. I just assumed he told you."

Her curiosity was now stoked by Dr. Aaron's comment.

"Now that I think about it, I think he did mention it to me."

"I'm glad to hear that. I don't feel so asinine now."

She then said with total confidence, "You're referring to him calling . . . uh—"

"Professor Aguirre at Hôpital des Enfants Malades. A man in your father's position has influence."

"Well, you must have had some influence to get him to serve on the Children's Hospital advisory board. He's so busy."

"He was quite a help to us. He's very easy to work with."

"I'm not sure some of the people in his company would agree with you."

Aaron removed a handkerchief from his pocket and lightly blew his nose. "I am one of the people in his company."

"I beg your pardon," Annick said, tilting her head to one side.

"I'm on the consulting staff of his health care division. He's a delight to work with. He's given me carte blanche with access to information and has been extremely receptive with respect to my recommendations."

"Really," she said.

"Oh, yes, he's very accommodating, and as I said, a delight to work with."

"He has a great deal of respect for you as well. It doesn't surprise me that he'd ask for your opinion."

Aaron then said, "Now tell me, what are your plans for the next few days? If you'd like to spend some time with us, you're of course welcome."

"That's certainly a kind offer, Professor. I may take you up on it."

"How's that young man of yours doing?" he asked.

"Mac's fine. A little overworked, but otherwise fine."

"He's a bright fellow with a limitless future in our field. If he's half as smart as I think he is, he'll make you an important part of it."

She laughed. "I'll mention that endorsement to him as soon as I return to the States."

"How are his finances holding up? He mentioned to me he was anxious to complete his training to start putting a dent in some of his debt."

"He's keeping his head above water. I never worry about Mac," she said, a little surprised that he would discuss the state of his finances with Dr. Aaron. Whenever she brought it up, he dismissed her concerns as unnecessary.

Aaron opened the top button of his vest and then clasped his hands behind his head. "So tell me, what really brings you here to see me today? What happened at Franklin Children's?"

Annick's smile was guarded. She hardly knew where to begin. "So much has happened," she said with a sigh, "I wish I could figure it all out."

"I have nothing but time. I am very interested to hear your perspective on what's occurred there."

For the next hour Annick discussed every detail of what had happened at Franklin Children's with Dr. Aaron. His responses were insightful and his advice more than supportive. He assured her that Simione would be quickly apprehended but he agreed with Dr. Howe's and the FBI's recommendation that, for now, she'd be safer in Paris.

"There are still so many loose ends," she said.

"Meaning what?"

"I just think they're giving up too easily. I'm not sure Simione was working alone. I'm just afraid that as soon as they catch him they're going to close the file on this case, quite content that they solved it."

"Is that so bad?" he asked. "At least you can get back to being a doctor."

She frowned. "You're just like Mac. He thinks my imagination has gone crazy."

Aaron stood up, picked up a stack of medical journals and placed them on the lowest shelf of his bookcase. "When dealing with people who derive some sort of pleasure or financial gain by employing the use of biological terrorism, one can never be too careful."

"What I don't understand—"

He smiled and then raised his finger to his lips. "I agree with you. There's probably more here than meets the eye. You're dealing with a despicable monster and I'm sure the FBI recognizes that fact. Unfortunately, you're a physician, not a police officer, and it's probably best if you leave these matters to the authorities."

"But I was—"

"As difficult as it is for you to let go, that's what you should do."

Annick met his eyes across the desk and understood completely what he was saying. She had already done enough. The strange course of events that led her to Grady Simione probably weren't that important now, and whatever information she had was already in the hands of the FBI.

"Maybe you're right," she said.

"Of course I am," the old man said, rubbing his paunch. "All this talk has made me hungry. How about joining me for some lunch?"

Annick agreed and for the next hour they shared a hearty lunch across the street from the institute at a small brasserie. As Professor Aaron was paying the check, Annick promised to stay in close touch with him. Before trying to get a cab, she watched him cross the street. He was an unusual man and she was indeed fortunate to have such a wonderful relationship with him.

There wasn't a cloud in the sky and the temperature was approaching sixty degrees. If she were a tourist, she couldn't have ordered a better day.

The cab driver was a small man with a bony face. He puffed away on his unfiltered cigarette, and Annick tried to be polite as he prattled on about France's troubled economy. In spite of Dr. Aaron's advice, her mind was consumed with unanswered questions and inconsistencies about the children poisoned at Franklin Children's. The cab sped down Boulevard de la

Madeleine toward the Champs-Elysées. The driver droned on but his voice was becoming more distant. The long transatlantic trip was starting to catch up with her and she was feeling tired, but the thought of calling Mac when she got back to the apartment gave her a sudden burst of energy.

Chapter Sixty-eight

"How's Paris?" Mac asked.

Annick puffed up one of the oversized down pillows on her bed, pushed it up against the headboard and leaned back.

"Boring," she said. "I miss you."

"The feeling's mutual. I wish I were there."

"It was certainly a lot more fun when you were," she pouted.

Annick hadn't been honest with Mac about the reason for her sudden trip to Paris. She also didn't tell him about Grady's escape, but instead claimed the reason for her hasty trip was an unforeseen and immediate problem with her visa that could only be straightened out in Paris. Relying on Mac's inherent respect for privacy, she didn't heed Dr. Howe's suggestion to advise Mac to keep her whereabouts strictly confidential.

"Did you get your visa problem straightened out yet?" he asked.

"Uh, no, not yet, but I have an appointment tomorrow." She hated lying to him but realized she was in too deep at this point to change course. As soon as Grady was captured and she returned to New York, she'd explain everything to him.

"When do you think you'll be back?"

"I'm not sure. There's no bureaucracy in the world like the French. It could be days. What's new at the hospital?"

"God, I almost forgot," he said in an excited voice.

"Forgot what?"

"Kevin's gone. He's out on a leave of absence."

"Kevin? Our intern?"

"The very same," Mac said. "He's in a ton of trouble."

Whatever fatigue Annick was feeling was quickly replaced with a cautious sense of excitement. "What did he do?" she asked.

"Well, it's all kind of hush-hush, but Dr. Howe swore me to secrecy and then told me what he felt I needed to know. Evidently, Kevin was in possession of an enormous amount of really grotesque kiddie porn. Supposedly, it crossed the line into some pretty sadistic stuff. Somebody tipped off the cops and they searched his house while he was at the hospital. They think he was selling it in the schools."

"You're kidding," Annick said.

"It gets better. They also found a bunch of scrapbooks with all kinds of newspaper clippings and magazine articles about violent childhood deaths. He also had dozens of articles about the poisonings at Franklin."

Annick listened intently, loosening her grip on the phone only when she felt her fingertips start to tingle. After a few moments, she was able to collect herself.

"I assume the FBI knows about all this. Howe didn't say very much about that, only that he had heard they intended to talk to Kevin."

"My God," Annick mumbled. "It's not possible. Kevin? Is he in jail?"

"That I don't know," Mac informed her. "I think they arrested him but he may be out on bail."

"Has anybody been able to tie him in with Simione?" she asked.

"I was waiting for you to ask that, but I don't know. The rumors in the hospital are wild. I saw Dave Kaye today. He's working in the E.R. this month. He told me he heard the cops showed a picture of Kevin to a bunch of Grady's neighbors and one of them is sure he'd seen him talking to Grady in his driveway. He even told the cops what kind of car Kevin was driving."

Annick still couldn't believe what she was hearing. Her first impulse was to call Thorne but she was sure he'd deflect her questions in his usual polite form. She never thought much of Kevin as a doctor, but the more she thought about him, the more she considered the possibility that he was indeed tangled up with Grady. It certainly fit her theory that Simione wasn't working alone. What better accomplice than a physician in the hospital?

"Are you there?" Mac asked.

"I'm here," she answered. "I'm just a little shocked about Kevin."

"You and everybody else in the hospital. I'm not saying he was the best-liked guy around, but who would have ever figured him for a closet pervert?"

"Not me," she said.

They talked for another five minutes or so before Mac was paged by the hospital. She promised to call him tomorrow and slowly replaced the receiver on the white antique cradle. She closed her eyes, taking comfort in the fact that Quinton Thorne was an extremely thorough and competent FBI agent. If he hadn't already done it, he'd be all over Kevin at the first possible opportunity.

Annick felt herself breathing easily. For the first time in weeks, she truly felt that maybe things were finally coming together.

Chapter Sixty-nine

Luc Clement slid open the oak doors leading to his study and smiled broadly when he saw his daughter sitting on the sofa. He tossed his topcoat on a chair, walked over and kissed her.

"How was the flight?"

"It was fine."

"I was thinking of selling the company jet and getting a smaller one," he mentioned.

"It seems like you're selling a lot of things lately."

Luc furrowed his forehead, sat down on the arm of one of the large upholstered chairs and studied his daughter.

"So that's why you're pouting . . . the house in Nice."

"I loved that place. I thought you did too," she said.

"I wasn't getting much use out of it and it was expensive."

She smiled with her lips together. "I've never known you to be so concerned about money before."

"I've always been concerned about money, Annick. That's why we have so much. Why are you asking all of these questions?"

"I guess I'm having a bad day."

"Really? And why's that? You're in the most beautiful city in the world enjoying a nice break from work. It's practically a dream come true." Luc walked over to the bar, picked up a decanter of Johnnie Walker Blue and poured himself exactly two shots. Reaching into an elegant silver ice bucket he dropped a handful of cubes into his glass and then gently stirred the top of the ice with his finger.

"I'm afraid it's not that simple," she said.

He took the first sip of the scotch, shrugged his shoulders and asked, "What's troubling you?"

"It's that whole mess at my hospital. I just spoke with Mac and it looks like one of our fellow residents might have been mixed up in the poisonings."

"Are you sure?" he asked.

She pulled her legs up, crossing them in front of her, and turned her palms straight up. "It certainly looks that way but who knows?"

"I'm getting a little concerned about your involvement in this whole thing, Annick."

"Don't treat me like a child, Daddy. I know what I'm doing." He tried to hide his grin by taking another sip of his drink. "What's so funny?" she asked.

"The way you said that, you sounded just like your mother."

The corners of her mouth curled a little. "I know how much you loved her, so I'll take that as a compliment."

He raised his glass to her and said, "I have an idea. I'm going out of town in the morning. I'll be in Brussels but it's just for the day, so I'll be able to have dinner with you tomorrow night."

"What's your idea?" she asked.

"Who's the smartest man you know besides me . . . and maybe Mac?"

"Philippe," she answered.

"Without a doubt. He'll be at our research-and-development center tomorrow in Amiens. It's only about an hour-and-a-half drive. Take my Porsche. I know he'd love to have lunch with you, and it will give you a chance to talk to him about whatever's on your mind. You've already heard all of my ideas. Maybe you need some fresh ones."

Annick rocked her head back and forth as she contemplated her father's suggestion. "Okay," she finally said. "I'll give him a call in the morning."

"Good," he said as he took the last swallow of his drink and set the glass down on the bar. "Now, how about some dinner?"

She stood up, walked over to where he was standing and took his arm. "I'd be delighted."

Chapter Seventy

Annick had been in her final year of obtaining her baccalaureate degree and applying to medical school when her father bought his silver 911 turbo. The night he brought it home, she spent twenty minutes or so inspecting it and then began a two-day campaign of teasing him unmercifully about finally having the midlife crisis he so richly deserved. She was relentless but he withstood the heckling in good humor.

By eleven the next morning, she was out in front of her apartment looking over the Porsche convertible, which looked exactly the way it had the day he'd driven it home. It was about fifty-five degrees and overcast. She quickly dismissed the brief consideration she gave to dropping the top for her drive to Amiens. She took her seat, buckled up and pulled away. As she had hoped, the intolerable morning traffic had largely subsided and within a few minutes she was on N1 heading north and rapidly leaving Paris behind her.

Cruising at 130 kilometers an hour, she reached Beauvais in about forty minutes. The city, which was about halfway to Amiens, still harbored visible scars from two world wars. One of France's best known tapestry centers during the first half of the century, the city had become a quiet one over the years and was now considered to be off the beaten path of tourism.

Continuing north, Annick couldn't resist the temptation of putting the powerful sports car through its paces. Before she knew it, she had reached the outskirts of Amiens. She had received specific directions to the research-and-development facility from Philippe when she had spoken to him earlier that morning. Exiting N1, she entered the old brick city, which had also suffered major war damage. Besides boasting the largest cathedral in France, the city had an excellent medical school to which Annick had almost gone.

Following rue Victor-Hugo, Annick made her way to the opposite side of the city, where the research-and-development center was located. Set back off the road and well concealed by thick trees, the building was approached by a mile-long gravel road. Annick parked the Porsche in a small lot just to the east of the building. The structure was two stories, constructed in an international architectural style.

Annick crossed the parking lot, walked up a short flight of steps and entered the lobby through double glass doors. A woman with short black hair sitting behind an information desk greeted her immediately.

"My name is Annick Clement. I have an appointment with Mr. Descartes."

The woman pecked away at her keyboard for a few seconds, handed Annick a guest identification badge, the type that slipped over one's head like a necklace, and then pointed to a door behind the information desk.

"Mr. Descartes's office is on this floor. Just go through that door and follow the hall all the way to the end."

When she reached the door, a buzzer sounded and she pushed the handle forward. On either side of the hall there was a series of laboratories that were visible through large windows. From what Annick could discern as she walked slowly down the hall, they appeared immaculate and loaded with state-of-the-art equipment. Each of the technicians wore a dark blue lab coat with Luc Clement's corporate logo embossed over the breast pocket.

Before Annick reached his office, she saw Philippe walking down the hall, smiling broadly and waving at her. She stopped and returned his silly grin and waited for him. He hugged her and then placed his hands on her shoulders and kissed her twice on each cheek.

"How are you?" he asked. "I was so happy when you called and said you were coming up for lunch."

"It was Daddy's suggestion. I've never seen where you work and wanted to spend some time with you." She looked around and then raised her eyebrows. "You must really be on my father's good side for him to build you a place like this."

Philippe tapped his lips to conceal a yawn brought on by boredom, acting as if someone had just told him something he was already well aware of. Annick knew it was nothing more than his silly sense of humor.

"Oh, I don't know. I guess your father just recognizes true genius when he sees it," he said.

Annick shook her head. "Where's the ladies' room—I think I'm going to be sick."

"Not before lunch," he warned. "We have a great dining room and I've arranged for the chef to make you something special. Let's go," he said, pointing down the hall.

"How about the nickel tour? I'd love to see the place."

His shoulders sagged. "C'mon, Annick. It's a research lab. A lot less fancy and sophisticated than Dr. Aaron's. You've seen a dozen just like it. Anyway, I'm hungry, but if you really want to, we can take the tour after lunch."

"It's a deal," she said.

The dining room was everything Philippe promised. Beautifully decorated with modernistic tables and wood-paneled walls, it was clearly a nice perk for the executives. Philippe's private table sat under a large bay window that overlooked a meticulously landscaped courtyard with an opulent Roman fountain.

As soon as they were seated, a young man with a short white coat brought them each a glass of ice water.

"This is all very impressive, Philippe. After seeing this, I'm going to ask my father for a bigger town house."

"As long as he doesn't take it out of my budget, go for it."

"Hey, what's this I hear about you selling that beautiful airplane of yours?"

"I was getting tired of it. I'm looking for a higher performance one."

"Really? What do you have your eye on?"

"Nothing just yet, but I have my feelers out."

"I want the first ride."

"Was there ever a doubt?"

"What are you working on here?" she asked.

"We have two major areas of interest. One is the development of more efficient laparoscopic instruments and the other is advanced digital technology for complicated X-ray equipment."

"That's quite an ambitious undertaking."

"That's what I thought in the beginning but we've made incredible progress over the last several months. We're almost at a point where we can begin addressing marketing strategies."

"That's unbelievable."

"Well, we're still trying to work out some of the kinks, so I'm keeping my fingers crossed." The server returned with a ceramic basket filled with a variety of fresh croissants and rolls and carefully placed it down on the table. "What's going on with you?" he asked. "I spoke with your dad the other day. He mentioned you have a lot on your mind."

"That's a mild understatement."

"So, fill me in."

She looked at him skeptically. "Before I get too long-winded, how much has my father told you?"

Philippe tapped his chin as he thought, a signature habit that Annick could remember him doing since the first day she'd met him.

"I would say he's given me the basics."

"I don't know why I bother talking to him in confidence. You two babies tell each other everything when it comes to me."

He shrugged. "It stems from a deep mutual love we share for you."

"In that case, I forgive you both."

Annick spent the next few minutes bringing Philippe up to speed. She watched his eyes as he gathered in the information and processed it. He was an insightful problem solver and it was her profound hope he'd be able to shed some light on things for her.

"It sounds to me like everything is pretty much tied up in a neat bow," he said. "Their only problem is to find this fellow, Sim . . . what did you say his name was again?"

"Simione, Grady Simione."

"Then their only problem is to catch him, put him in jail and then throw the key away."

"That may be easier said than done. From what I've told you, what do you think the chances are that our intern, Kevin, was involved with Simione?"

Philippe took a final bite of his croissant and reflected for a moment. "It's hard for me to say, Annick. I've never met the man. But he certainly had access to the patients and could move around the hospital without drawing any attention to himself. Opportunity is probably the most important component of a crime. If it's true that he did have some kind of relationship with Simione and they did find all those boxes of kiddie porn in his basement, well, I guess I'd be concerned that he was involved."

"That's interesting what you said about opportunity. I hadn't thought about that."

"Well, it sounds like your friend's in big trouble. I don't blame him for hiring some big lawyer from Chicago." Philippe stopped speaking for a moment to allow the waiter to place their main courses in front of them.

"Poached salmon with dill sauce," she moaned in ecstasy. "My absolute favorite."

"I told you I had something special prepared for you." He took the first bite, set his fork down and said, "I guess I have the same concerns as your father."

"And what would those be?"

"You've already gone way beyond anything that any reasonable person would expect a physician to do. You're the one who led the FBI to this madman. If it weren't for you, the hospital would still be calling all of this nothing more than an extraordinary coincidence."

"What's your point?"

"My point is simply this. You're a pediatrics resident, not an FBI agent. It's time to back off."

She heard what Philippe was saying but her mind was already off in another direction. "What about the two women?"

"Which two?"

"The woman who pretended to be the aunt of the boy with botulism, and then the nurse who told me about Grady. What the hell happened to them? How come I can't find them?"

"Did you tell the FBI about them?"

"Of course," she answered.

"In the first place, I think they're in a better position to track them down than you are. And when they do, you'll see that they're real people and their involvement was legitimate."

"What do you mean?"

"That there's a logical explanation. People come and go. They change their names, they change their professions. Sometimes they're running from personal problems. There could be a million reasons to explain why you can't find them."

Annick's preoccupation with the events at Franklin Children's had no adverse effect on her appetite. The sauce that Philippe's chef had prepared was fabulous.

"Maybe you're right," she finally said.

"When are you going back to the States?"

"I'm supposed to wait for the FBI's permission but I think I may go back in the next day or two."

Philippe shook his head. "Your dad's not going to be very happy about that. I think you should stay in Paris until they catch that guy."

"C'mon, Philippe, that could be months . . . maybe years."

"Your personal safety comes first. If it means not returning to the States . . . well, then so be it."

"I don't think so," she answered emphatically. "I'm not going to let that sicko scare me into changing my life's plans."

"Well, I'm not claiming to be an expert on the subject but I would suspect you could receive the same quality education here in Paris that you can in America."

"Maybe, but that should be my choice . . . but I'll think about it," she said, more to appease him than anything else.

They spent the next hour and a half finishing their lunch and talking about other things besides Annick's problems. It crossed her mind that her father had called Philippe to brief him on what to say and even to encourage her to forget about Grady Simione and concentrate on her residency.

When they were finished, she personally thanked the chef and then Philippe escorted her back to the lobby, where they sat down on a soft leather couch.

"Hey, how about that tour you promised me?" she asked.

"You bet," he said. "Let's go."

"Mr. Descartes," a voice called from the information desk. "Yes."

"Your secretary just called. Your one-thirty appointment has been sitting in your office for a while and is starting to get a little antsy. He keeps asking when you'll be there."

Philippe slapped the side of his head with his palm. "I was having such a good time, I forgot. Can we do the tour next time?"

"Of course. Am I going to see you before I go back?"

"I'll drive down tomorrow night and have dinner with you and your father."

"Great," she said. "Thanks for lunch, and the conversation."

"I hope it helped."

"I always feel better after talking to you. When will you be in New York again?"

He shook his head. "Not for at least a couple of months, I'm afraid, but don't pout about it."

"I'll try not to," she said, placing her hand over her heart.

She gave him a hug and kissed him on the cheek. "God, you're even starting to kiss like an American," he complained.

She laughed out loud and then watched him disappear through the door. The trip back to Paris was uneventful. In spite of Philippe's advice, Annick had already decided to return to the United States in a couple of days. Of all the things Philippe had mentioned she was particularly intrigued by his comment regarding opportunity.

The sun had come out, taking the chill out of the air and prompting her to pull over and put the top down. Sitting in the car for a few moments, she marveled at the beauty of the French countryside. Once she had started out for Paris again, her mind kept returning to the same enigma—Kevin. A malcontent, he certainly spent a lot of time complaining about Dr. Howe and the way he was treated. He wasn't the most likeable person in the residency, but of more concern was the fact that he never demonstrated any real compassion for children, a distinct departure from other medical school graduates who decided to do their residency in pediatrics.

She passed a large diesel truck that was meandering along in the right lane. The driver, wearing a black beret, bounced up and down with a half-smoked cigarette hanging from the side of his mouth. The more she thought about it, the more she entertained the possibility that Kevin had come under the influence of Simione. Pushing the Porsche to 140 kilometers an hour, she even considered that Kevin had been duped into participating in such horrific acts as some bizarre way of getting even with the hospital.

Chapter Seventy-one

"Don't be mad at me, Daddy."

With disillusioned eyes, Luc Clement looked at his daughter.

"But Mr. Thorne recommended you stay in Paris for at least two weeks."

"Thorne's an old lady. I'm quite capable of looking out for myself. Anyway, if my guess is right, Grady Simione is long gone. The last place he's going to turn up is Long Island."

"And that conclusion is based on your extensive experience in the field of law enforcement?" Luc asked.

"Hardly."

"Then what?" he demanded.

"Instinct and common sense."

Luc threw his sport coat on the couch and walked across the spacious living room.

"Well, in that case, I guess I shouldn't have any concerns," he said sarcastically.

"I'll still be here to have dinner with you and Philippe tomorrow night."

"Actually, he called. He said he was sorry but he couldn't make it. He's going to South America in the morning. It was completely unexpected."

Annick crossed her arms. She tried not to act too disappointed to avoid stoking the fires of her father's suspicions that there was indeed something romantic between the two of them. "When will he be back?"

"He said a few days. You can see him then." Luc smiled. "Maybe that's a good reason for hanging around and not rushing back to New York."

"I'm afraid not, Daddy, but nice try."

"Well, unfortunately, Philippe will have the plane. So you'll have to fly commercial."

"I think I can survive that," she said.

"How was your lunch in Amiens today?"

"Incredible. That's some chef you hired up there."

"I'll take no credit for that. That's all of Philippe's doing. I just pay the bills. I have to twist his arm just to get a report out of him. Was talking to him helpful?"

"I guess that depends on how you view things. If you mean did he tell me everything you told him to, I guess he was helpful." Luc's eyes widened with his daughter's comment. Open-mouthed, he stepped forward and pointed his finger right at Annick. Before he could even utter a syllable, she jumped in. "Don't even bother trying to deny it. If you two had rehearsed that scene any more, you could have taken it to Broadway."

"You're an audacious brat, Annick. I can't believe a woman as fine as your mother gave birth to such an impertinent child."

Annick gazed over at the large oil painting of her mother in a beautiful black evening gown hanging over the fireplace. She tracked her father's eyes as they wound up in the same place.

"Are you taking me out to dinner tonight?" she asked.

"You bet. Where would you like to go?"

"How about Jules Verne?"

"An excellent choice," he said. "I'll make a reservation."

"Make it a late one. I've kind of got my heart set on a very long and very hot bath." As she walked out of the living room and headed for her bedroom, he blew her a kiss.

Chapter Seventy-two

The day Grady left the United States he was dressed as a priest with large oval eyeglasses and a curly black wig. He had no trouble boarding a Continental flight in Newark bound for London; the British customs official hardly even looked at his passport and processed him right through immigration.

Once in London, Grady found a hotel in the West End on Gloucester Street. It was moderately priced and somewhat off the beaten path of the dwindling number of tourists who came to London in the late fall. After several days of barely leaving his room, he was feeling more secure and ready to acquire the appropriate documents to start a new life. With more than sufficient money at his disposal, there was no question in his mind that he would make the necessary contacts to discreetly procure the documents he needed.

It was just after ten in the morning when he decided that not to see some of the more-well-known sights in London would definitely be a missed opportunity. He left his hotel, making the two-block walk to the nearest Underground station to catch a train to Green Park. He had already discovered that the tube, as the locals affectionately referred to it, was a much cleaner and efficient system of public transportation than the New York City subway.

Grady walked down the two flights of stairs, purchased a ticket and walked over to the platform to wait for the train. The area was packed, leading Grady to believe that the next train would be along at any time. He pulled a *London Times* from the pocket of his new wool jacket and began scanning the headlines. He detested crowds and resented the jostling and shoulder-to-shoulder bumping that was going on. A portly woman wearing a hideous scarf and carrying a bag of groceries looked over at him and smiled.

After five minutes, the train approached and the horde began their final jockeying for position. The harsh screeching of its brakes bellowed through the station. Just before the train came to a full stop, Grady got jostled by someone behind him. Turning his head, he scoffed at the elderly man with a bushy salt-and-pepper mustache holding an umbrella. The tiny needle that penetrated his thigh was so small that Grady never gave the barely perceivable pin prick a second thought. A moment later, the noisy doors slid open and the packed crowd, with Grady in the middle, moved onto the train.

It wasn't for another three hours, when he was standing outside Langan's Brasserie enjoying the lavish artistry of Green Park, that he was stricken with the first symptoms of the ricin. His first inclination was to dismiss them as food poisoning, but as he became more ill he decided to head back to the underground station. Crossing the park, he had to concentrate on maintaining his balance and staying on the path. Becoming more dizzy with each step, tiny rivulets of sweat began pouring down his forehead and neck.

With great difficulty, Grady found the park's exit. After a few moments, he started across the street, navigating his way by weaving between the slow-moving traffic. The cacophony of their horns was deafening. He wanted to cover his ears with his hands but he needed them to guide himself from one car to the next. In the next few seconds, his already blurred vison became even further impaired by star bursts of blinding light. Each step was a struggle and he soon found himself gasping for every breath he could manage.

He finally reached the opposite side of the street. Seeing the distorted outline of a light pole just a few steps ahead, he lunged forward for support but his grip was far too ineffective and he immediately spun around the pole like a child at play and crashed to the pavement. Keeping a cautious distance, several passersby began to congregate. While most of them stared or murmured in unison, one young man in a jogging outfit finally dashed off to find help. Before it could arrive, Grady Simione forced open his glassy eyes, clawed at the pavement with his trembling fingers, heaved a large and final breath and then fell silent.

The man, dressed in a black wool coat and a cap, emerged from the back of the crowd. With a strange look of gratification, he ambled across the street to hail a cab. The umbrella he carried earlier that day was distinctly absent. As he waited for a taxi, he found himself grinning. His only thought was to get home and remove the heavy makeup that had taken him so long to put on. Aging thirty years in one morning had not been an easy feat.

A black Daimler slowed to a stop in response to the man's raised hand. Opening the door quickly and climbing in, he wondered if the glue he had used to apply the thick salt-and-pepper mustache would be a chore to remove.

Chapter Seventy-three

THREE DAYS LATER

It was a few minutes before seven when Annick threw her plush down comforter back and swung her legs out of bed. It took her almost an hour to shower and get dressed. When she arrived at the breakfast table, she found her favorite morning meal of mixed berries, a croissant and a steaming café au lait sitting on the table. She assumed Sophie, the Clements' maid for twenty years, must have heard her showering and decided to prepare her breakfast. The *International Herald Tribune* was folded neatly on her chair. Annick sat down and was scanning the front page when Luc walked in.

"Are you packed?" he asked.

"Packed and ready to go," she said immediately.

"Make sure you call me as soon as you get to New York. I'm sorry I can't take you to the airport but the people I'm meeting with flew in from Munich last night just for this meeting."

"I'll be fine, Daddy."

They shared a pleasant breakfast without any further conversation relating to either Franklin Children's, Grady Simione or Annick's decision to return to the States. When they were finished, Luc escorted her to the limousine.

"Don't forget to call me as soon as you land," he told her through the open window.

"I won't," she promised and continued to wave even after the stretch Mercedes had pulled away from the curb.

The ride to the airport passed uneventfully. It was a dreary morning, which matched her mood regarding the prospect of leaving Paris and not seeing her father for several weeks. She knew her place was back in New York and that she had made the right decision but she was having a hard time shaking the funk her decision had caused.

Check-in and boarding proceeded uneventfully and the enormous 747's wheels lifted off the runway at Charles de Gaulle Airport right on schedule. The cloud cover was moderate but she still had a nice view of the city as the jumbo jet climbed and turned west. Before they were out over the Atlantic, she had already decided to call Thorne as soon as she landed to see if she could learn anything more about Kevin's arrest.

Besides reading several medical journals, she slept quite a bit. To her delight, the entire trip passed without any turbulence and touchdown at Kennedy was right on time. As soon as she cleared customs, she pulled out her cell phone. Punching in Thorne's number from memory, she waited impatiently for his secretary to answer.

"May I speak with Special Agent Thorne?" she asked.

"I'm sorry," came the response from a squeaky-voiced woman. "He's out of the office at the moment. May I take a message?" Annick's throat tightened as she suddenly found herself paralyzed with indecision. A few hours ago she was sure the right thing to do was to call Thorne, but all of a sudden she was second-guessing her decision and was consumed with an enormous wave of doubt. "Are you there, ma'am?" the secretary asked. "May I take a message, please?"

"Uh . . . perhaps it would be better if I called back." Before the woman could respond, Annick flipped the cell phone closed.

"There you are," came a voice from the back of the crowd of noisy people waiting to meet the dozens of international flights that were arriving. Annick looked up to see Mac maneuvering his way between a portly woman carrying a small pet cage and a man holding up a limousine sign over his head. Annick moved forward, put her carry-on down and hugged Mac as if he were going off to war.

"I'm so glad to see you," she whispered. After hanging on for several seconds, she finally took a step back. Mac reached down and slipped her carry-on over his shoulder. His smile was as jubilant as Annick had ever seen.

"Wow, it's nice to be so missed," he joked.

"You have no idea."

"So what was it like flying with the common folk?"

"It was fine," she said, unable to hold back an ample grin of her own.

"So, I assume you got your visa problem all straightened out?" he asked.

"Everything's fine, Mac."

He pulled the handle out of Annick's suitcase, turned the bag up on its wheels and pointed in the direction of the exit. "Your carriage awaits, mademoiselle."

"Let's go home," she said.

She locked arms with him and walked off with her head on his shoulder. They hadn't taken more than a dozen steps when Mac began telling her about all the interesting cases he'd seen since she was gone. His rambling made things easier for her, and by the time they reached his car she was more relaxed and willing to put her problems on the back burner at least until tomorrow, leaving her free to enjoy Mac tonight.

Chapter Seventy-four

Annick looked at Mac in amazement as he slept soundly on her couch. She was the one who had flown across the Atlantic seven hours earlier. The way he was sleeping, it appeared as if he were the one with jet lag. She threw a light wool comforter over him and then went into the kitchen. Sliding her Palm Pilot out of its cradle, she quickly located Kevin's phone number. She had asked Mac earlier about him, but he wasn't sure if Kevin was in jail or out on bond. Surprisingly, and to the best of Mac's recollection, the events of Kevin's arrest had not yet appeared in the media. They had talked about the problems at Franklin Children's for quite some time and Annick had been a little taken aback by Mac's unshakable position that Kevin was unquestionably mixed up with Grady Simione.

She picked up the phone and dialed Kevin's number. After one ring, the phone was automatically answered by a message machine. As soon as Annick heard the beep she began her message. "Hi, Kevin. It's Annick. I've been out of town. Mac mentioned you had taken a leave of absence. If you are picking up your messages, please give me a call when it's a good time for you at 555-7902. Thanks."

Annick hung the phone up and glanced out into the living

room at Mac. He hadn't stirred a bit. Her hand was barely off the receiver when the phone rang.

"Hello," she said, hoping the ring hadn't awakened Mac.

"Annick, it's Kevin. I'm sorry I didn't pick up the phone but I've been operating under the advice of my attorney. I suppose Mac told you everything."

"As much as he knows. I'm so sorry. I hope you're okay." Annick had mild reservations about treating him so decently. If he was involved in poisoning children, he wasn't worth even speaking to, but if he was innocent, the only way she'd get any information out of him was to treat him with kindness.

"I'm okay. I'm just afraid the newspapers or the TV stations are going to get ahold of this. I've been walking around in a fog for days. At first I was irate but now . . . well, I'm just trying to get from one day to the next."

"Is there anything I can do for you?"

"Yeah, find the guy who planted all those boxes of garbage in my basement."

"Do you mind if I ask you something?"

"Of course not."

"Do you know Grady Simione?" she asked.

"Only from the hospital. I mean, I know who he is but I've never had a real conversation with the guy. If you're just trying to be polite or beating around the bush, I can tell you that I know exactly what they're saying at the hospital. I'm not stupid."

"I'm sorry. I don't understand. What do you mean?"

"I've heard the rumors. They're saying Simione and I were great pals . . . that we were working together. Can you imagine, Annick? They think I hurt those children."

"Have you spoken to the FBI?"

"Are you kidding? They've been relentless. You even start to doubt yourself after a while."

"Were you actually arrested?" she asked.

"They took me out of the hospital in handcuffs. It was the most degrading moment of my life," he said in a cracked voice. "Thank God my family got me some hotshot attorney from Chicago."

"Does that mean you're out on bail?"

"Yes."

Annick had a million questions to ask him about Grady but didn't want to appear as if she didn't believe him when he told her he barely knew the guy. His words were sincere enough but Annick was unconvinced.

"How do you think all of that stuff got in your house?"

"I don't have the first damn clue. Never mind the porn, Annick. There was stuff in there about poisons and kids dying horrible deaths in all kinds of strange ways."

"Do you have any idea why someone would want to get you into such terrible trouble?"

"I don't know. I've thought about it for hours. My lawyer's asked me every question under the sun regarding anyone who would have a motive for screwing me. We've talked about everything from revenge to a sick joke."

"And?"

"I can't come up with anybody. The cops think I've been selling the stuff."

"You can't be serious," she said.

"Some of that smut turned up in one of the local junior highs."

"I just can't believe any of this, Kevin," she said, listening to him softly sobbing.

"My lawyer told me if I can't come up with some explanation for all this, I could go to jail for a very long time, especially if they try to tie me in with Grady."

Annick was hesitant to continue. It was obvious that Kevin was on the edge and she didn't want to push him over. Unfortunately for Kevin, she was well aware that people in desperate situations can be extremely convincing. After thinking it over for a couple of seconds, she wasn't ready to believe him.

"Look, Kevin. I don't know what to tell you. I wish I did. This is a terrible thing, but if you know in your heart you've done nothing wrong, well, then everything will be okay in the end."

There was silence and then he said in a dejected monotone, "That may be true in fairy tales and Hollywood, but not necessarily in the real world."

"Hang in there, Kevin."

"Please call me again. It's nice to hear from you guys. Say

hi to Mac for me. Tell him I know I wasn't the world's greatest intern but I really think the world of him."

"I'll tell him," she said and then hung up the phone.

Making her way back into the living room, she fell into one of her two matching club chairs. She tried to ignore the nagging anxiety gnawing away at her gut. Hundreds of facts swam around in her head begging for some order.

Getting up, she walked over to her stereo to lower the volume of the jazz CD Mac had selected. Thinking about her conversation with Kevin, she tried to recall every word. There was something about it—something he said that seemed out of place or inconsistent but she couldn't put her finger on it. She let her head fall back for a moment and closed her eyes.

"What's going on?" Mac said in a sleepy voice.

"Nothing. I was just watching you sleep."

"That's about as exciting as watching paint dry," he said.

"Unfortunately, it's all the excitement I can stand tonight."

His eyes were already at half-mast. He'd been working his tail off the last few days and he was obviously exhausted. Thirty seconds of silence was all he needed to fall back to sleep. Annick smiled, again put the comforter around his shoulders and walked into her room.

Sitting down on the corner of her bed, she stared blankly. Suddenly, her eyes widened and an unexpected wave of terror crested just under her breastbone. Standing up, she began pacing up and down. Enigmatic events of the last several weeks began aligning as if they had been scripted to do so. Feeling her breathing becoming too rapid, she steadied herself and concentrated on every breath.

With total resolve, she walked over to her phone and dialed Dr. Aaron's number in Paris. He picked up the phone on the first ring.

"Dr. Aaron. It's Annick calling. Did I wake you?"

"Annick, it's wonderful to hear your voice, and no, you didn't wake me. I'm a very early riser. I was just getting ready to leave for the institute. What's the problem?"

"I have a huge favor to ask of you."

There was a moment of silence before he answered. "I've known you and your father for a very long time. I think you know how I feel about the two of you. So what I'm trying to say is that there is no favor too big to ask me."

"Maybe you better wait until you hear what I have to say before you adopt that position," she suggested.

"I'm ready," he said. "Just let me get a pencil and some paper. From the tone of your voice, it sounds like I'm going to need them." Annick heard rustling in the background and could imagine him peering through those coke-bottle glasses and wearing his threadbare old sweater vest while he rummaged around for what he needed. "Okay, I'm ready. Go ahead."

For the next ten minutes, Annick spoke in great detail to him about certain technical information she needed. He remained basically quiet, asking her to slow down from time to time while he made detailed notes. She finished by emphasizing the highly sensitive and confidential nature of her requests.

"I don't suppose you want to tell me why you need all this information?" he asked.

"Would you be angry and hate me forever if I didn't say anything at this time?"

He groaned softly. "I suppose I can remain patient for a while." He then added as an afterthought, "You will eventually tell me, I hope."

"It's a promise," she assured him.

"Well, it may take me a few days to gather all this together. I'll start e-mailing and faxing you the information as soon as I can."

"I wish I knew how to thank you, Professor."

"I'll be going out on a limb here a little. I know you understand that. I'm confident you wouldn't ask me to do that unless you believed the information you're after is vital."

"If I didn't truly believe that, I wouldn't ask for your help."

"I'll get started today," he promised.

Annick thanked him again and mentioned she'd give him a call in about twenty-four hours. She still had dozens of things to sort out in her mind and the last thing she was interested in at the moment was sleep. From the credenza over her desk she grabbed a yellow legal pad and her favorite fountain pen, and then went back out into the living room. Mac had left just enough room at the end of the couch for her to sit. With her legs tucked in front of her, she started to compile notes at a feverish pace.

At two in the morning, consumed by exhaustion, her head fell to the side, landing on Mac's legs. It was exactly in that position that she remained in a deep sleep for the next six hours.

Chapter Seventy-five

Annick had just finished seeing two patients in the E.R. and was in the process of finishing up charting her findings when her pager went off. The code that appeared in the display was 717, indicating an outside call was holding. Reaching for the nearest phone, Annick dialed the operator, who answered on the second ring, and connected the call.

"Hello, this is Dr. Clement."

"This is Captain Bertain calling." The man spoke in French.

"Yes," she answered, pushing the phone a little tighter against her ear because of her difficulty hearing the caller's voice.

"I'm calling on behalf of your father. He would like you to meet him at the Euro-Aire terminal at Newark International at six-fifteen this evening."

"Where are you calling from?" she asked.

"At the moment we're at forty-three thousand feet over the North Atlantic."

"May I speak with my father, please?"

"I'm afraid he's in a meeting with the gentlemen he's traveling with but he said he'd try to call you before we land. If he's unable to, he will meet you at the terminal. Can I tell him you'll be there?"

"Absolutely," she said, feeling the excitement growing about seeing her father in just a few hours. She had a lot to talk to him about and had planned on calling him as soon as she was done with work. "Tell him I'll be there."

"He asked me to find out if you'll be bringing Mac," the pilot said.

Annick thought for a moment. "I'm afraid he's on call tonight."

"I'll convey your message, Doctor."

"Thank you," she said and hung up the phone. It had been a terrible morning and this was the first bit of uplifting news the day had to offer. It was approaching noon and she had promised Mac she'd meet him for lunch. After finishing her charting, she grabbed her stethoscope off the desk and hurried to the cafeteria. Unfortunately, their lunch together turned out to be even more abbreviated than she'd anticipated. They barely had time to enjoy their salads and have some innocuous nonmedical conversation when Mac got summoned to Dr. Howe's office. She told him about her father coming in and he told her how disappointed he was to be unable to join her to meet his flight. When he asked her how long he'd be in for, she had no idea. Annick spent the next few hours getting the rest of her work done so that she'd be able to get home and make the drive to Newark Airport and arrive before six.

Just before she left the hospital, she decided to call Rachel Warren at the CDC. It had been a long four days waiting for her call, but with the prospect of speaking with her father that evening, Annick was willing to appear a little anxious and give Dr. Warren a call. The residents' lounge was empty for the moment, providing Annick with the privacy she wanted.

"Dr. Warren, it's Annick Clement calling from New York."

"You must be psychic. I was just going to call you," she said. "We just finished working on that last botulism specimen you sent us. It took us a little longer than we expected because we had to purify the toxin."

"I appreciate your help," Annick said, feeling her anxiety heighten.

"The serotype is identical to the other ones you've sent us."

The information from Dr. Warren left Annick speechless. She swallowed hard and took a deep breath before asking Dr. Warren to repeat what she'd just said. "Our tests are quite conclusive. It's the same toxin that we isolated from Michael and Justin. I hope the information will be of some help."

"I wish I were able to find the words to tell you just how helpful you've been, Dr. Warren."

Annick sat on the couch with the phone loosely cradled in her hand. After a minute or so, the pulsating tone of the phone filled the room, which brought Annick back from her trancelike state. She slowly set the receiver down and closed her eyes. For the first time in weeks, things were crystal-clear.

She crossed the room quickly and slammed the door behind her. With the news she'd just received from the CDC, she really had a lot to talk to her father about. She recalled something Philippe had said at lunch in Amiens when he warned her against going off like a loose cannon if and when she finally got her ducks in a row. It was good advice, but Annick Clement was as sure about her facts as any reasonable person could be.

As she marched down the hall toward the elevator, there was one thing she knew for sure. There would be no whitewash of what really happened at Franklin Children's Hospital—not if she had anything to say about it.

Chapter Seventy-six

Arriving home at three-thirty, Annick took an hour to shower, put on her makeup and get dressed before leaving for the airport. With the afternoon traffic, the ride took her exactly an hour and a half, with the last ten miles on the New Jersey Turnpike being the slowest part of the trip.

It was already dark when she pulled into the brightly lit parking lot of Euro-Aire. The single-story building wasn't particularly large or architecturally impressive. As she stepped out of her car, she could see several private jets parked on the expansive tarmac protected by an eight-foot chain-link fence. It was a cool evening and she was happy she'd worn a leather coat.

"You're right on time," came a calm voice from behind her. Even though she recognized it, she was still a little startled. Turning around, she saw Philippe standing a few paces away. He was wearing a black cashmere topcoat and thin leather gloves.

"Philippe, I didn't expect to see you here. Where's my father?" she asked, looking past him toward the terminal.

"He's still on the plane. He's just making some phone calls . . . and waiting for you." Philippe's eyes were probing and the tone of his voice was devoid of its usual animation. He took a couple of steps forward and kissed her.

"The message I received didn't mention anything about you being here."

"It was a last-minute decision."

"I see."

"Your father suggested we join him on the plane."

Annick took a second look toward the tarmac. "Let's go. I can't wait to see him."

Philippe took Annick's arm in his hand and escorted her through the terminal, across the tarmac and up the short steps of the jet. As soon as Annick was aboard, she looked up and down the cabin. The door to the flight deck was open and both seats were empty. Annick moved forward a little to have another look around.

"Where's my father?"

He smiled and then shrugged. "Maybe he's in the bathroom."

Annick crossed her arms for a moment and then turned toward the exit, but Philippe moved quickly to his right, blocking her way.

"I don't know why you lied to me but my father's obviously not on board. Now if you'd please get out of my way, I'd like to get off the plane and go find him."

"Have a seat," he said evenly. "We have a lot to discuss, and don't worry about your father. If my geography's any good, he's about six thousand miles from here."

Annick's anger was rising. "If you don't get out of—"

"Sit down," he snapped, but then regained a civil tone. "This won't take that long."

Annick had a lot of questions and she was convinced Philippe had the answers. She glanced over at one of the captain's chairs, studied his determined expression and then sat down.

"What do you want to talk about?" she asked.

Philippe removed his coat, folded it neatly and then sat down across from her. With his long legs fully extended, he placed his coat on his lap. "I think you already know what I want to talk about," he said.

"Really?"

"Oh I think so. You've become quite interested in my affairs lately. I was kind of interested in knowing why."

"Because I suspect you're guilty of poisoning and murdering innocent children," she announced with total malice. "You're a despicable human being without a single thread of moral fiber."

Philippe's expression was unaffected by her accusation. He crossed his ankles and rubbed his wiry stubble.

"That's a hell of an allegation," he said to her.

"That doesn't make it any less true."

"I think you at least owe me an explanation," he said.

"Fine, how long have you been in financial trouble?"

"What makes you think I am?"

"Why did you sell your plane? You loved it more than life itself."

"As I told you in Amiens, I'm looking for a higher performance aircraft."

"Oh, I see. And what have you bought?"

"Nothing yet. I'm still looking. Buying an airplane isn't like picking up a set of new dishes at the flea market. It takes time."

"I would have guessed you would have kept your original one, located something new and then gotten rid of the old one."

"If you think that's smarter then I guess when you own a plane and decide to sell it, you can handle it that way."

"About six months ago, my father mentioned you borrowed some money from him last year."

"That's true. There was a unique investment opportunity in the Far East and he helped me take advantage of it."

She nodded as he spoke. "Since you never paid him back, I guess it didn't work out too well."

Philippe's cheeks turned a little red. "I guess there's no such thing as a sure thing, especially in high finance."

"Speaking of sure things, what happened to that Internet company you invested in a few years ago? It had something to do with a new information highway that was going to revolutionize wireless communication. I remember you talking my ear off about it. You already had your mansion in Monte Carlo picked out. But then I never heard another word about it. What happened?"

"I guess it never took off."

"How much did you lose on that one, Philippe?"

"If you must know, quite a bit of my own money and a tidy sum that I had borrowed."

"I guess things aren't going so well," she concluded.

"I'll tell you what. Instead of dwelling on the state of my finances, why don't you tell me what you think you know."

Sitting forward in her chair, she said, "You used me, you son of a bitch. Your whole little scheme was a setup and I was the unwitting dupe who made it all work. You played me like a concert Stradivarius, leading me right where you wanted me to go."

"Why don't you try being a little more specific?" he asked with his hands raised.

"I might be able to answer that if you tell me when you decided to get involved in the bio-defense industry."

"I didn't know I was," he answered.

"Is that so? Obviously you've forgotten about Prebiopar."

Philippe stroked his cashmere coat as he listened. "Prebiopar's a very small company in your father's industrial empire. I'm afraid it's dwarfed by dozens of much larger and profitable ones."

"So how come it's the only one you have a financial interest in?" Philippe had a gaunt neck and Annick could see him swallow hard.

"Now, how in the world would you know anything about that?" he asked.

"Because I've read every file, letter and memo to come out of Prebiopar for the last two and a half years."

"Yes, I thought you had. But if you must know, your father encourages his key executives to invest in his companies." He reached up and unbuttoned the top button of his dark blue dress shirt. "It sounds like you've been a very busy lady. This is all very interesting and probably makes for great theater, but how does it all tie in to what happened at your hospital?"

"You lied to me in Amiens about your research. You weren't working on developing new laparoscopic instruments or advanced digital technology. You've also been sending misleading reports to my father about your research and development program. He trusted you and had no reason to verify them. I'm sure at the right time you would have come up with some plausible reason to explain why they were so vague."

Philippe reached behind him to a small refrigerator and took out a large can of apple juice. Annick wasn't quite sure but she thought she detected a fine tremor in his hands.

"I guess you're going to tell me what I was really working on?" he asked.

She collected herself for a moment before answering. "You were working on devices and products that would save lives in the event of a major act of bioterrorism or warfare."

"For instance."

"Well, amongst other things, you perfected a filter system for skyscrapers that could prevent thousands from dying from any number of airborne biologic weapons released in their ventilation system. You also came up with a simple test to determine whether potable water supplies had been contaminated. And, it appears that you're well on your way to isolating cutting-edge vaccines that address a whole new area of immunology against bioweapons. There are many other projects but do I really need to continue?"

Philippe continued to sip on his juice and then set it down. "With all your training, what do you really understand about the risks of bioterrorism?"

"I'm not sure. Why don't you enlighten me?"

"Millions of innocent people could be wiped out in an afternoon by a single-engine plane making two passes over any large city. The average person has no idea. They're completely ignorant of the incalculable risks and dangers they face every day. They haven't prepared themselves because they're too ignorant to know any better."

"But that's where you and your company come in to save the day—and make millions in the process. What a noble man you are, Philippe. I read Prebiopar's memos and reports. They all pointed to the same incontrovertible problem. A little matter that became the thorn in your side. The very thing that stood in the way of you hitting the jackpot."

"And what might that be?"

"You said it yourself just a minute ago. In fact, let me paraphrase one of those highly confidential memos sent to you by your director of marketing. I read it so many times, I think I practically know it by heart. *All of Prebiopar's initiatives will continue to be a devastating financial failure unless there is a drastic awakening of society and key industrial leaders concerning the threat of a major biologic attack.* Is that about it?" Leaning farther forward, she raised her hand and pointed her finger directly at him. "Public awareness and fear about the risks of bioterrorism. That's what you needed."

"If what you say is correct and we're in agreement that people aren't convinced of the risks, then why would we organize such a complicated scheme to poison children in the United States?"

"Good question," she said without hesitating. "And that's exactly what I couldn't figure out, but finally it dawned on me. It was so simple, I don't know why it took me so long to see it."

"I'm waiting," he said.

"If the market wasn't there, then the obvious answer was to *create the market.*"

"I beg your pardon," Philippe said.

"What you needed was to get people's attention. A little preview of how devastating a bioterrorist attack could be. Once you filled the public with fear, the demand for your products takes off like a rocket. I guess it would be kind of like being in the bomb-shelter business in the 1950s when the threat of nuclear holocaust terrorized almost everyone in the United States."

"That's an interesting analogy."

Ignoring his comment she picked up right where she left off. "Prebiopar cranks up and starts selling the devices you've been busily perfecting. Profits go through the roof, my father's thrilled with what you've done and you become an instant multimillionaire and the mansion in Monaco becomes a reality." She shook her head in disgust. "It was all so easy . . . except for those poor kids. What's this really about, Philippe? It can't be just the money. Are you really that envious of my father?"

Philippe drummed his fingers on the armrest of his chair. "Well, now that you bring it up, it's not easy walking in his shadow. Especially when you have just as much intelligence and a lot more talent." Philippe picked up the empty juice can, squashed it in his hand and then tossed it in the direction of the flight deck.

"What about the children you poisoned and killed? Who speaks for them?"

He shrugged. "You sacrifice a few to save thousands. History's replete with example after example of the same thing."

"That's your answer? That's your justification for acting like a madman?"

"I'm afraid so," he answered in a nonchalant manner. "I'm not a monster and don't you dare paint me with that brush. You speak to me of a few children when we were trying to save millions."

"Save millions? Is that what you said? Are you talking about dollars or people?" she scoffed.

"It must be very easy for you to be so sanctimonious from the front seat of your BMW convertible. Just look at the publicity from Franklin Children's. It's been in the news all over the world. Our phones are starting to ring off the hook, for God's sake. People are finally waking up."

Annick couldn't believe the things coming out of Philippe's mouth. Of all the people she looked up to and admired, he was way up on her list. Could this really be the same caring and gentle man who was always there for her when she was growing up?

"If my father's not here then I assume it was you who arranged the little call earlier today asking me to meet him here."

Picking up a small cocktail napkin, he wiped his lips. "I really had no choice." He took a deep breath and then reached for the dimmer switch to turn the lights down a little. "Unfortunately, it appears that you've learned a lot more than I had hoped."

"What about Grady Simione? Where the hell did you find him?"

"It wasn't easy. I was looking for a special person with very specific talents. One of my more subtle inquiries turned up his name through someone who knew him in the military. Luck was a factor. I won't deny that. When he was offered enough money, Simione wasn't shy about talking about his accomplishments." Philippe stretched his arms over his head and then placed his hand over his mouth to smother a yawn. "As it turned out, he was the perfect choice."

"You're sick," she uttered in total contempt. "You make Grady Simione look like an Eagle Scout. How could I have been so stupid?"

"Don't be too hard on yourself."

"Tell me about Joelle Parsons. I assume you arranged for her."

"Of course. I had to make sure you were on the right track. Without Joelle you would have never known there was another case of botulism in the hospital."

"And the nurse, Danielle Sudor?"

"She led you right to Grady's front door, and I must say she was masterful."

"Not that it matters, but where do you find them?"

Philippe turned and looked out the small window. "With enough money, one can bring enormous resources to the table. These types of people are available if you know where to look. Both of them are highly experienced con artists. They picked up very generous paychecks for their efforts, didn't ask any questions and went quietly on their way."

"And how was all this supposed to end?" she asked.

"I'm surprised you haven't figured that out. With you spearheading the way, I knew the authorities would eventually get involved. Grady becomes their number-one suspect and a showdown is inevitable. I assumed the FBI would select his house as the safest place to make the arrest. I knew he'd never be taken alive and the FBI would be forced to kill him."

"Did you really believe all this would work?"

"Oh, but it did work," he insisted. "All except for Grady escaping. He only made it out by a couple of hours. If the FBI had killed him, it would have all been over. Nobody would have been looking for a conspiracy. Grady's dead and there would have been no reason to assume he wasn't working alone. The entire tragedy gets written off to the perverted act of a single lunatic." Philippe's demeanor remained calm and calculated. His explanations seemed logical and extremely well thought out. It almost sounded to Annick as if he were merely lamenting over a business deal that didn't quite work out. In what sounded like an afterthought to her, he added, "Probably the most important thing was that even though you were the key to the whole thing, you never would have been the wiser."

"Why me? I still don't get it," she asked. "You could have used anybody."

Philippe smiled. "Not really. You were already in place on an I.D. service of a busy children's hospital. That was key. To try and find someone in that position would have involved considerable risk. There was also something else."

"And what was that?"

"With you, there was an extra layer of insurance to address exactly what's happening here tonight."

"I don't understand."

"I never underestimated your intelligence, Annick. I knew I was taking a calculated risk to lead you just so far and then hope you'd back off. It may not seem like it, but I did consider the possibility that you'd connect me to the whole thing. If that was the case . . . well, I was kind of hoping you wouldn't get any crazy ideas about talking to the authorities."

Annick knew he was fishing a little, trying to see how sympathetic she'd be based on their close friendship. The thought of lying to him crossed her mind but she realized he knew her too well for that. Instead she opted not to say anything for the moment. He stood up and poured himself a glass of ice water and then sat down again.

"Well, I've answered all of your questions, now I have some of my own," he said. "How did I tip you off?"

Annick watched as a coy smile swept across his face. Crossing his legs, he remained silent but continued to stare at her. His question caught her off guard and she wasn't sure that sharing what she knew with him was the way to go. Not wanting to incite him she decided to tell him.

"At first, it was a lot of little things but I couldn't put them together. But then, when we had lunch in Amiens, I mentioned that one of my fellow residents was under suspicion for being involved with Grady."

"That would be Kevin," he said.

"I didn't think about it until later, but you distinctly made reference to his high-priced lawyer from Chicago." She stopped for a moment and looked at him. "I hadn't mentioned anything about that because I didn't learn about it myself until days later when I spoke to Kevin. You would have had no way of knowing anything about his attorney unless you were working with someone in New York who was keeping a careful eye on things. The same person I assume you paid to frame Kevin by planting all that filth in his basement."

He smiled and raised his glass in a mock salute. "That was an unfortunate slip on my part. I'm usually more careful than that. I guess it was pretty easy for you from that point on."

"What do you mean?" she asked.

"Oh, getting Professor Aaron to come up to Amiens on some wild pretext that he was completing some consulting work. If I weren't out of the city, I would have shot the old fool and pushed his car into a canal."

"That would have been right in character for you."

"Initially, I was a little unclear about his purpose, but later, when I realized he'd taken a specimen of our botulism culture . . . well, it didn't take a genius at that point to realize that you were behind it. I suppose by now you've learned it was the same serotype as the one Grady used at Franklin Children's."

She nodded her head slowly. "The CDC called me today with the results."

"I see."

Philippe looked around the cabin with a pained expression. Annick wondered if he'd have the sense to see the handwriting on the wall and give up.

"Now what?" she asked.

"Well, I'm guessing you haven't gone to the FBI with all this as yet. If I know you as well as I think I do, you probably planned on waiting until you discussed your revelations with dear old Daddy." Annick tried to remain expressionless, hoping that he wouldn't be able to read her face. After a few seconds, Philippe grinned. "Good, I thought so," he said.

Standing up slowly, he made his way to the front of the aircraft. Retracting the stairs, he closed the cabin door and sealed it with a large lever. He took a couple of steps toward the flight deck before stopping and turning around. "You know of course, this is nothing more than a minor setback. I wonder," he said, tapping his chin with his index finger. "How much do you think your father will pay to get you back in one piece? I'm thinking of beginning the bidding at twenty-five million dollars. What do you think?"

"From murderer to kidnapper? It's not as classy."

His face suddenly became red and his eyes narrowed. "Sit down and buckle up. We're going for a ride."

"Where are you taking me?" she demanded.

"To a lovely tropical island with very lax extradition treaties. Don't worry, though. As soon as your father ponies up the money, I'll send you home."

It was difficult for her to measure the amount of danger she was actually in. A lot of Philippe's behavior and implied threats could be nothing more than posturing and saber rattling, but she had no way of being sure and for all she knew she could be in grave peril. The realization frightened her but she understood the importance of maintaining her composure.

Philippe walked quickly to the flight deck, strapped himself in and reached for the radio. Every few seconds he glanced back at her. For a moment, she thought about trying to get to the cell phone in her purse. But the way he kept turning around, she didn't figure she had much of a chance of succeeding. As Philippe talked on the radio, her courage mounted. She started to move her hand toward her purse, but when she looked up, Philippe had already climbed out of the left seat and was heading toward her.

"The goddamn plane's been grounded for unauthorized use. It was on your father's orders."

"What did you expect?"

"I expected that he wouldn't find out I had taken it for another day or two." Philippe made a fist and pounded the headrest of the chair he'd been sitting in. "They won't fuel us or clear us to taxi."

"Why don't you just give up?" she said.

"Not a chance. Get up."

"Fuck you, Philippe. I'm not going anywhere," she shouted.

Without acknowledging her outburst, he reached down, removed a small semiautomatic from an ankle holster and leveled it at her head.

"Whether you live or die is a matter of complete indifference to me, you overindulged brat. I'm going to assume by now that you have some idea of what I'm capable of. Now, I'm going to tell you one more time—get up."

Annick locked eyes with him for several seconds before she slowly rose to her feet. His intensity had peaked but he was still clearly in control. Allowing her to step into the aisle, he moved in behind her and placed the muzzle of the gun squarely between her ribs. Using the weapon as a prod, he moved her toward the exit. When they reached the front of the plane, he turned the large handle that opened the cabin door and allowed the steps to unfold.

With the gun still pressed firmly against her, Annick stepped out into the cold night air and slowly descended the stairway.

Chapter Seventy-seven

"Just walk straight through the terminal and out into the parking lot," Philippe told Annick in a calm but deliberate voice.

Several large spotlights mounted on the roof of the terminal flooded the tarmac. Two corporate jets, smaller than Luc Clement's Gulfstream, flanked it on either side. A small refueling truck was parked off to the side, near the terminal. The roar of distant jet engines pierced the silence, leaving the smell of exhaust fumes hanging in the air.

Moving forward, Philippe walked shoulder to shoulder with Annick, making sure she remained well aware that the gun was still on her. She refused to look at him or utter a word. In spite of the pain, she tried to remain focused on her options for escape.

"You're hurting me," she told him after they had taken about twenty paces.

"Just behave yourself for another two minutes," he warned.

"You're out of your mind, Philippe. There's no place on this planet you'll be able to hide. My father will come after you with a vengeance."

"Why don't you let me worry about that? Just keep going."

A spotlight attached to the passenger-side window of the gas truck suddenly came on and was quickly turned in their direction. As an instinctive gesture to shield her eyes, Annick immediately raised her hand. Her vision was slightly impaired from the glare of the light but she had no trouble recognizing Gina Dandridge in her FBI windbreaker stepping out from behind the gas truck.

"Drop the gun," she screamed.

Philippe whirled around the back of Annick, placed her in a tight stranglehold and raised his gun to her temple. Keeping his head tucked in behind hers, he only peeked out for a second or two at a time.

For the first time since this entire ordeal began, Annick truly feared for her life. Closing her eyes, she began to pray.

"I said drop the gun," Gina shouted again.

"Back off," he yelled. "Lay your gun down."

Gina slowly took a step forward. Her own weapon, a Glock 18, was sighted just over Annick's right shoulder. "Let her go," Gina demanded.

Bobbing his head back and forth, Philippe screamed back, "I'll kill her. Do you hear me?"

"Let me go, Philippe," Annick begged. "For God's sake, please let me go." Annick went limp and let her head fall forward. At the exact moment, when Philippe was struggling to strengthen his grip, she slowly raised her right foot. When it was about eighteen inches off the ground, she snapped the heel of her boot down like a piston, striking Philippe squarely on the top of his foot. Two of the delicate bones of his forefoot cracked under the perfectly placed stomp, causing him to wail in agony and buckle under the pain. Feeling his grip falter, Annick spun away and rolled to the ground. She was still whirling when the single shot rang out with a crack and struck Philippe in his right chest, shattering the upper half of his lung.

Just as she opened her eyes, she felt Philippe's body fall across her legs and roll to a stop. His eyes, open for the moment, found hers. She could hear him gasping for air as he tried to turn the corners of his mouth up in a smile. His hand came forward in a feeble attempt to touch her. In the next moment, his hollow eyes rolled back and his head struck the tarmac with enough force to carve a two-inch gash across his forehead.

Holding the Glock with two hands and keeping it trained on Philippe, Gina moved in quickly. Shifting her eyes to the ground, she saw his gun and kicked it away. Never taking her eye off of the man she'd just shot, she helped Annick out from under his bloody body.

"Go inside and call for help," Gina told Annick. Instead, Annick approached him slowly, her face covered with his blood. "Don't get too close," she warned.

"Is he dead?" she asked Gina in a staccato voice, her body shaking.

"I don't think so. He's still breathing. Go call 911. Tell them we need both the police and an ambulance."

By this time, several employees and waiting passengers had rushed out of the terminal and had formed a small crowd. A young man in mechanic's overalls screamed that he'd already called the airport police and the paramedics. Almost before the words were out of his mouth, Annick heard the wail of a siren in the distance. The intensity of the siren increased over the next minute until she could see two vehicles with their flashing red and blue lights come into view. Another few seconds and they were on the scene. With her eyes still focused on Philippe, Gina spoke to the two officers who came flying out of their squad car.

Annick stood shivering, unsure if it was from the chilly night or the sheer shock of what she'd just been through. Even though she hadn't been more than a few feet from the action, it was as if she had been removed, similar to watching a movie on TV as she dozed off to sleep.

The commotion ended almost as quickly as it started. The paramedics started an IV on Philippe and inserted a tube in his windpipe to breathe for him. When they loaded him into the ambulance, an amorphous pool of blood stained the tarmac where he'd been shot. With their sirens blaring, the paramedics and the police disappeared into the night. An elderly woman wearing expensive jewelry smiled warmly and placed a blanket over Annick's shoulders.

"Let's go inside," Gina said. "It's a lot warmer in there."

Annick just stared at the FBI agent who had most likely just saved her life. A moment later she nodded and together they walked into the terminal and found a small table toward the back. A commercial-grade coffeemaker sat on a glass coffee table, filling the room with the aroma of hazelnut coffee. Gina walked over, poured them each a cup and sat down directly across from her.

"How the hell did you know I was here?" Annick asked.

"We've had an eye on you ever since you got back. I had the watch tonight."

Annick held the cup in both hands and took three quick sips. "Thorne?" she asked.

"You bet."

"He's worse than my father."

"Lucky for you, he is," Gina observed.

Even with the blanket over her shoulders, Annick continued to tremble. She took a few sips of the coffee, which definitely helped.

"Who was that guy?" Gina asked.

"He works for my father. He's been a friend for a long time."

"With friends like that, who—" Gina began before deciding not to complete her thought. "Can you think of a good reason why he was escorting you off your father's plane with a gun in your side?"

Annick drew a deep breath. "It's a long story."

Gina glanced down at her watch. "Well, Thorne should be here in a few minutes. I asked the airport police to call him. He lives in Islip, near the airport. I'm sure he'll be coming by helicopter. We might as well wait to talk until he gets here. I'm sure he's going to have a lot of questions for you."

Annick looked up, her eyes flooded with tears. "Thank you, Gina. Thank you for being there."

The FBI agent stood up, moved around to the other side of the table and put her arm around Annick. She looked the other way to conceal her own moist eyes. The two women remained just that way without saying a word for almost thirty minutes until Special Agent Quinton Thorne calmly walked through the door.

Epilogue

Mac stood in the middle of one of the Plaza Hotel's finest suites with his fingertips wedged in the front pockets of his blue jeans, awestruck by the lavish decor.

"Does your dad always stay in places like this?"

Annick looked around. "Hardly ever," she confessed. "Usually he likes a bigger suite."

Mac furrowed his brow at her curious sense of humor. "What does a place like this go for a night?"

"You're probably better off not knowing."

Before he could respond, Luc walked into the room. He was dressed casually in khaki pants and a light tan turtleneck sweater. He had arrived only a few hours earlier, leaving Paris immediately after Annick had phoned him. Their call had lasted almost half an hour, which brought Luc up to speed on the major events of the last twenty-four hours and what had led up to them.

"You don't look too worse for the wear," he said to his daughter, embracing her tightly and then turning to Mac. "It's nice to see you," he said, stepping back and shaking his hand. "Are you sure you're okay?" he asked Annick, reaching forward and holding both of her wrists.

"I'm fine, Daddy."

"Have you heard anything about Philippe?" he asked.

"I spoke with Quinton Thorne about an hour ago. He told me he was finally out of surgery. He lost an awful lot of blood but the surgeons are optimistic that he's going to make it."

"The whole thing's unbelievable," Luc said. "The man who committed those acts was not the Philippe Descartes I know. How could he have been capable of such things?"

"I really believe he was in desperate financial trouble. I also think as the years went by he was more and more tortured by his envy and jealousy of you. I guess eventually it became an obsession and he lost his sense of right and wrong."

"I still can't believe it," Luc said. "What about Grady Simione. What ever became of him?"

Annick walked over to the fireplace, admiring the ornate antique border that framed it so perfectly. "According to Thorne, he turned up in London, murdered. He was there on a phony passport so it took the British police a little while to match up his fingerprints with the FBI's and figure out who he was."

Luc shook his head and took a seat on an upholstered love seat. "I assume Philippe had a hand in that."

"It appears that way. He was in London on a forged passport himself. They found it in his apartment when they searched it this morning. I don't know who else would have used ricin to kill Simione except Philippe."

"I still don't understand how you figured out it was him. There had to be something more than just a slip of the tongue," Luc said.

Annick turned around. "There were a few things but that's really what got me thinking. There was no way he could have known the specifics about the lawyer that Kevin's parents hired unless someone was keeping him updated."

"I assume your friend's going to be okay."

"Kevin? I think so. It looks like the charges will be dropped. I spoke to him earlier today. He's understandably ecstatic."

"You said there was something else that made you suspicious of Philippe."

Annick crossed the room and sat down next to her father. Mac took a seat across from them on the couch.

"I saw Philippe in New York when he supposedly was in Venezuela. At first it didn't register, but later I remembered."

"When was that?" Luc asked.

"It was the first time I went out for dinner with Mac."

Luc stood up, walked over to the bar, filled a glass with ice and poured himself two shots of scotch.

"I was across the restaurant and Philippe had his back to me so I couldn't see his face. I only caught a glimpse of him but he looked so familiar. It just didn't compute because I never expected him to be there."

"Why would he be in the same restaurant as you?"

"I guess if you're the pawn in a multimillion-dollar game, the key player has a vested interest in keeping his eye on you."

Luc stirred his scotch with his finger, just as he always did when he was deep in thought. "But you just said you didn't realize it was him."

"I didn't, and I never gave it another thought until last week when Philippe and I had dinner in the same restaurant. He acted like he'd never been in the place. I stayed at the table to wait for change while he went to the bathroom. When he came out, I saw him from the exact angle wearing the same coat I had the first time, but it still didn't click. It was more like déjà vu. I didn't put it together until I got back from Paris."

"That's amazing," Luc said.

"The clincher was your research facility in Amiens. The day I had lunch with Philippe he intended to meet me at the information desk in the lobby but the security guard sent me back to his office. On my way, I got a look at some of the research labs. One of them was a rather sophisticated microbiology facility. Later, when I asked him what he was working on he told me that he was working on new technologies in laparoscopic instruments and digital X-ray."

"I'm not sure I understand," Luc said.

"Philippe would have absolutely no need for a microbiology lab if he was really doing research on surgical instruments and X-ray equipment. But, if he was working with botulism toxin, well, then a lab like that makes sense. I guess I should have realized sooner that's why Philippe didn't want to take me on a tour of the research facility." Annick shook her head and then added, "I was a little slow on the uptake but when I learned that the toxin he was producing in Amiens was identical to the one used by Grady Simione, there were no doubts left in my mind."

"I don't know why but I guess I pity him more than anything else," Luc admitted. "I don't think I've ever seen a more pathetic act of desperation and greed in my life. For all of his cleverness I'm not sure that Philippe really had a good understanding of human nature and what motivates people."

"What do you mean?" Annick asked her father.

"People still fly every day in spite of an occasional airline disaster but if there were fifty crashes a day, well, that might change their travel habits. In general, I don't think people worry about sharks until they're enjoying a swim in the ocean, look up and see a fin circling."

"So what are you trying to say?" Mac asked.

"It's quite simple. People ignore warnings and good advice every day of the week. They see horrible things on television, read about terrible events in the newspaper and then assume it would never happen to them. To get the public to take any kind of a real threat seriously, it would require an event of epic proportion that was so catastrophic and unspeakable that they would have no other choice but to sit up and take notice. I may be wrong but I doubt Philippe's attempt to terrorize people regarding the clear and present danger of bioterrorism would have worked."

"I'm not sure I agree with you," Annick said, "but I guess if in the next few months there isn't an increased demand for biodefense products, then your theory is right. But suppose we do see a surge in that industry. What about Prebiopar then?"

"Prebiopar no longer exists."

"Then how have we helped the problem?" she asked.

"I'm not sure we have, but I will be happy to turn over all the technology our facility in Amiens has developed to legitimate bio-defense companies."

"That's a wonderful gesture," Annick said.

"Hopefully, this whole mess is finally over," Luc said and then looked over at Mac, who continued to guard his silence. "Excuse me, Mac. I'm forgetting my manners. May I offer you a drink?"

"No, thank you. I'm fine," he answered.

"Annick mentioned to me you two have about ten days off over the Christmas holidays."

"Yes, we do. It took a bit of maneuvering and deal making but we managed to get the same time off," Mac said.

"I was hoping the two of you might consider spending part of that time with me in the south of France."

Annick looked at her father and suddenly smiled the brightest she had in many days. "Why the south of France?" she asked cautiously. "Do you know a nice hotel there or something?"

"Actually I've recently acquired . . . or should I say, re-acquired, a beautiful villa on a majestic mountain overlooking the Mediterranean."

Annick shook her finger at her father as if she were scolding a child. "And what made you do that?" she asked.

"I'm not sure . . . unless it was the fact that someone I love dearly was crestfallen when she learned I had sold it."

"I love you, Daddy," she screamed as she gave him a bear hug.

"What do you say, Mac?" he asked. "Can you make it?"

"I wouldn't miss it for anything."

"That's wonderful. Now, let's talk about where we're going for dinner tonight." Before he could elaborate, the phone rang. "Will you two excuse me for a moment? I'm expecting that call. I'll be right back." Luc started across the room, laughing as his eyes met Annick's.

"You're a lucky lady to have a father who loves you that much," Mac said.

"He's one in a million," she said, staring into the bedroom. "And so are you."

"Really?" he asked.

Annick walked over, put her head on his chest and then hugged Mac as if she never planned to stop. "Really," she said.